The Adventures
of
Alan Shaw

Craig Hallam

Embrace the Weird!

Inspired **Q**uill Publishing

Published by Inspired Quill: June 2014

First Edition

The Adventures of Alan Shaw © 2014 by Craig Hallam
Contact the author through their website:
http://craighallam.wordpress.com

Chief Editor: Peter Stewart
Typeset in Adobe Garamond Pro

Paperback ISBN: 978-1-908600-32-5
eBook ISBN: 978-1-908600-33-2
Print Edition
Printed in the United Kingdom
1 2 3 4 5 6 7 8 9 10

Inspired Quill Publishing, UK
Business Reg. No. 7592847
http://www.inspired-quill.com

Acknowledgements

It seems like a lifetime since Greaveburn was released and I stepped into the world of Author-dom.

I've met so many lovely people in the last two years who have embraced my writing and given me the will to keep doing what I love. To every one of you readers and reviewers, I send out a heartfelt thank you. The same goes to everyone who sent me pictures for the Reader's Gallery, or added their whereabouts to the world map; I loved seeing where you all hail from.

To my favourite Steampunks who have inspired me with their own ingenuity and creative visions at various conventions, signings and late-night pub meetings, a specific thank you. You're all incredibly creative people that I feel very lucky to be acquainted with.

Family and friends who put up with me in a constant state of daydreaming, I apologise and promise I *won't* use you into any future books. That's the greatest gift an author can bestow.

Embrace the weird, my friends.

The Adventures
of
Alan Shaw

Contents

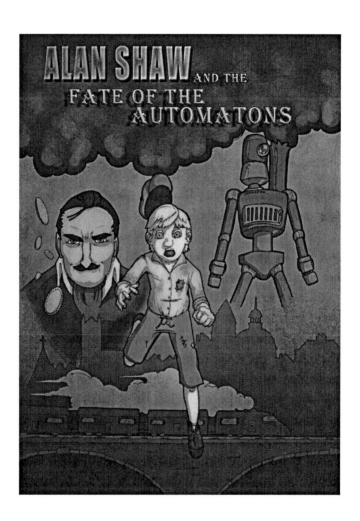

1

London, England, 1842

THE KEEN RASP of a policeman's whistle cut high above a chorus of leather soles on pavement.

With the wind and his own heartbeat thundering in his ears, the boy ignored the burning in his lungs and ploughed on, splashing through the alley's puddles of water and overflowing gutters. Rounding a stack of old crates at high speed he leapt clumsily, missing a slumbering drunk by inches and twisting as he landed. The ground came up hard. The hand he threw out to catch him slid in something that might have been rotten vegetable and what the boy hoped was water slapped him in the face. He rolled to the side and lay panting for a minute against a slimy wall, dazed by the cold and adrenaline. He shivered all over like an laudanum addict. Water seeped through the gaping seams of his shoes; rubbish bin hand-me-downs that he'd never known as new, and now his short trousers and thin cotton shirt were soaked too.

As a troupe of coppers ran by the end of the alley, the boy hustled himself further against the wall, hoping that the crates would shield him. The old drunk beside him muttered something and let out a ripping flatulence. Screwing up his face, the boy gave the old soak a harsh jab with his toe, but the drunk just rolled like a ship on the surf and settled back down again.

Allowing himself a smile, the boy hummed a few bars of *What Shall We Do With A Drunken Sailor* as the another police whistle rang out, much, much further away. But he wasn't daft. Wrapping his arms around his knees to fend off the cold, he sat to wait for a while longer.

The hand came down on his shoulder with such finality that it might have been Death himself who was taking hold of the boy's shirt. He screamed, thrashing on reflex, his elbows and knees all jagged edges until his whole body was a churning, spiked machine. The owner of the hand let out a yell and the boy dropped to the ground, but before he could muster his legs to scramble into a run, another set of arms wrapped about him. He was trapped; hugged close to the copper's wool uniform, his arms trussed at his sides. He wriggled and cursed with words he knew but wasn't sure the meaning of, but the copper's grasp was absolute.

"Give it up, son. You're nicked."

VOICES, CLATTERING HOOVES and a distant bell floated in through Inspector James Carpenter's window. A faint whiff of the Thames circled the room like a moist dog, thankfully diluted by distance. On the other side of the building where the monorail ran, a shuttle rattled by, making the police station shake from joist to foundation. Carpenter slammed one hand down on a pile of papers to stop them travelling, and pinched the bridge of his nose with the other until the shuttle faded away. Then he continued to read.

Line after line of cramped handwriting jostled under the Inspector's gaze. A constable's messy pen had left a trail of ink blobs across the report, and the spellings were creative, but Carpenter could make it out well enough to sign. Dabbing the nib of his fountain pen on the blotter produced a nectar-like ink drop. He scribbled, sighed, and shifted the paper to his out-tray.

Blinking once, twice, the Inspector allowed his report-induced blindness to adjust. Squinting through the glass partition which made up one wall of his office, Carpenter watched his police officers sashay back and forth or stand mumbling in groups. Papers changed hands here and there. *Probably checking each other's spelling*, he thought.

Simon finally came into focus. His back was to the window, and so also his father. The white label of his school blazer stuck up from his collar, still displaying the faded name his mother had inscribed there. One of the boy's hands propped his head, the other scratched at his hair and returned out of sight. Inspector Carpenter could tell the boy was reading. He was always reading. And Carpenter wouldn't have it any other way. Simon didn't even look up from his studies when Constable Jennings walked past, a very different kind of boy clamped under his hand like a fishing trophy.

The Inspector slid another report in front of him as the door rattled with Jennings' knock.

"Come in."

The constable leaned through the gap, helmet protruding first.

"We found the boy, sir."

"Give you much trouble, Constable?"

"Yes, sir. Plenty."

"Alright, bring him in."

Jennings disappeared. Carpenter took out his pen again, and dab-dabbed on the blotter.

From outside he could hear Jennings growling at his prisoner: "Don't make me carry you, lad. Get in there."

Carpenter kept his eyes fixed on the paperwork, skimming and signing, skimming and signing.

The boy came in at the end of Jennings' boot. The constable whipped off the boy's cap and handed it to him. The boy sneered, but didn't put the cap back on. Jennings went to say something, and thought better of it in front of his superior. Stood before the Inspector's desk, the boy kicked his heels against the meagre carpet. After a while he tried to whistle, but gave up.

"You assaulted three of my constables," Carpenter said.

"Wouldn't have done if they hadn't chased me."

"Just so you know, Sir," interrupted Jennings, "Reg will probably need some time off with his knee."

The boy gave a puckish smile.

Carpenter signed his name, let the ink dry a moment, and slid the paper aside. He finally looked up at the urchin. The boy was a puppet in badly made costume, every joint protruding from his bones as if added with afterthought. While he didn't flinch under Carpenter's gaze, pale hands wrung his cloth cap like a dish rag. Jennings was blocking the door, but the boy's eyes lingered at the open window.

He'd have to climb over the desk to get out, but Carpenter had no doubt he'd fly to it like a trapped pigeon if given the chance.

"Why'd you bring me here?" asked the boy. "Why not just take me to Bow Street?"

"Do you want everyone you know around Covent Garden to see you walking out of a police station, Scot-free? How'd that look?"

The boy looked at Constable Jennings to see if he was missing some joke. Apparently, he wasn't.

"So I'm not in trouble?"

"Not yet," said Jennings.

Inspector Carpenter slid a file across his desk, looking down to hide his smile. There were only three pages in the folder. He flicked through them while composing himself.

"What's your name, son?"

"Albert. But that's Prince to you," replied the boy, running his nose across a tattered sleeve.

Even Jennings smirked.

"I think your name's Alan," said Carpenter, not bothering to check the boy's reaction. "I think you're an orphan. You're about eleven years old, but you probably don't even know that for sure, and you ran away from St. Martin's workhouse just before it closed down. You've been living in and around Covent Garden since then, working odd jobs for food. You can stop me anytime, Alan."

The boy was silent.

Carpenter carried on before the shock waned: "Do you know what an Automaton is?"

The boy stayed quiet. His eyes had glazed over.

"Alan?"

"No."

"Have you ever seen this man?" Carpenter held a daguerreotype of a serious-looking individual. He could have been a second rate gentleman, scuffed at the edges, but Alan had seen eyes like that before. He was a villain. The kind that made his money at the expense of other people's injuries.

"No. Never."

"Alright, you can go," said Carpenter.

The boy's head swung between the policemen.

"I'm really not being done?"

"No. Thank you for your time."

Jennings propped open the door, and Alan wandered outside. The door clicked to the jamb.

"Sir?"

The Inspector was still watching Alan frozen beyond the door's glass. He passed his attention between the urchin and his son.

"Yes, Jennings?"

"Forgive me, sir, but I'm curious to know where you got all that information. I've seen that file, sir. List of contents and file reference, list of boy's names, and the picture. That's it."

"I made it up, Constable." Carpenter met Jennings' eye for the first time. "I knew his name, and where he's from. St Martin's was the nearest workhouse."

"St Martin's? So the lad already knows his way around the insides. That'd be useful for the kind of caper Rafferty's planning."

Carpenter nodded.

"You'll make Detective yet, Jennings. And when we squeezed Throaty for the list of children, he said to watch out for the Shaw boy. Throaty didn't like him. That's enough to make me think there's more to the lad than meets the eye."

"But if we can find him, Rafferty can find him too," said Jennings. He looked into the office where Alan stood as if unsure whether he could leave or not. "Poor little bugger, eh, Sir?"

"Poor little bugger indeed, Constable."

ALAN STOOD WITH his back to the office door. In and out, just like that. No trouble. No list of offences. Bloody hell, if they'd have picked five crimes at random, they'd have hit the mark somewhere.

He shook himself, straightened up, and puffed out his chest with a deep breath.

There was a boy at the desk beside him, about his age, maybe less judging by his size, dressed a little similar but minus the muck. There was a shield embroidered on his jacket. He had a book open on the desk in front of him. Alan leaned over. The page was full of words.

"Good book, eh?" he said.

The lad looked at him as if he were a rattlesnake.

"What's it about?" Alan asked, watching as the other boy looked between page and urchin a few times.

"Urm, biology," he said. "Science."

"Phew! Rather you than me." Alan doffed his cap. "See ya."

Striding away, Alan disappeared down the stairs to street level. The floorboards shook as the station door slammed.

Outside, breathing free man's fresh air, Alan tugged at his jacket. The air was sharp enough to shave with, had he been old enough to have growth, and a weak spring sun only warmed his wet clothes a little. A policeman came running along the pavement, excusing and apologising to the folk he jostled. Turning sharply, he almost skidded right past the station's steps and had to grab the stone banister to stop himself. He darted up, knocking Alan aside as if he weren't there.

"Oy!"

But the copper was gone, leaving only a swinging door.

Alan danced down the pavement. Jamming hands into bottomless pockets, he sauntered along the path, enjoying the feel of other people's expensive trousers against his elbows. The gentlemen and ladies avoided him mostly, weaving out of his way as if he were contagious. Someone suggested he walk in the road and Alan politely suggested that his backside and the gentleman's lips become acquainted. Somewhere beyond a horizon made of top hats and bonnets, Hackneys rattled along rutted cobbles. The scent of crushed horse manure was only a sniff away. Before Alan reached the end of King Street, he heard the familiar *flupflupflup* of running feet and ducked into the road just in time to avoid the coppers as they ran past, the one who'd grabbed Alan earlier at their head. There had to be twenty of them, he thought. One copper blew a whistle and, as they reached the junction, another group met them from the other direction.

At the end of the road, Alan could see what the commotion was all about. Another protest filled St James square. A mass of people, men mostly, some wearing postal uniforms, others dirty from the docks or the gas works. Some held banners scrawled with words Alan couldn't understand. There was chanting, but it made no more sense to him than the signs.

"Man over metal!"

"Oil and blood don't mix!"

He walked round instead of cutting through; no point pushing his luck with the police twice in one day. The coppers had formed a wall to one side; one of them was shouting at the protestors and not doing much good. The mob started to march in an increasing circle like the beginnings of a hurricane. Soon, someone would throw something and the whole thing would get out of hand. Alan was glad to be away from it.

Taking the most direct route to Covent Garden, Alan cut by Queens Theatre where another crowd was massing. This one was cleaner, quieter and Alan liked it even less than the last one. Summoned and banished by the whirring of pocketwatches, the whole upper class was as repetitive and lifeless as the wooden dancers on a Swiss clock. A gentleman snorted, a lady whinnied back. The men bowed to offered hands and the women pattered and faffed with their stoles. Stepping up beside one of the gentlemen, Alan thrust his thumbs into his waistband and waited.

"Geoffrey, you seem to have collected something on your boot," said one of the ladies, tittering.

Geoffrey looked down at his shoes, distraught, and

found Alan.

"Oh yes, Madam. So I have," he said. "Run along boy, there's nothing for you here."

Alan motioned to his ear, then his mouth, and made a sound he'd heard deaf-mutes make.

"Deaf, eh? Then there's no point engaging you, you little scoundrel. Be off with you."

The gentleman placed the tip of his cane in Alan's chest and shoved him. Alan tumbled back, only just remembering not to swear as he went down. Rolling from the curb, he fell into the road. His head jerked painfully as a hoof passed close enough to make a muddy stripe on his blonde hair, and he rolled back toward the pavement before the carriage wheels could claim any limbs. He lay in the gutter for a moment, panting, clutching at his head and looking for blood on his fingers. He turned over like a dog exposing his belly, and set glistening eyes first on the gentleman, then on his lady where they lingered.

"Oh, Geoffrey. There was no need for that at all," she said, and lifted her skirts so she could bend. "There now, let me help you."

"Oh really, Madame. Don't humour the thing. The doors are opening."

Alan recoiled from her hand as if it were a branding iron and scuttled along the gutter.

"See? He's healthy as a buck. Leave him."

Alan took one last look before disappearing around the corner. The woman had turned to scold Geoffrey, who was backing away. The other gentry were parting around them like a cock fight.

Around the corner, Alan smoothed his hair, straightened himself, and sauntered away trying to whistle. There was a reason he preferred solid work; begging just wasn't worth the effort.

ALAN HEARD THE honking before he saw the geese. A man wearing a long apron herded the fowl through Covent Market's crowd with a wooden staff, steering them toward a butcher's block nearby. Alan let them swarm around him rather than move, their swaying necks passing like reeds in a river.

Stalls made of barrels and planks ran in rows across the open square, all leading toward the arcade's columns where the official market could be found. Alan sailed past banks of flowers and fruit, bobbing in the crowd's flow like drift-wood. At a frame hanging with skinny rabbits he turned left, ducking under the makeshift counter, past the owner who was busy gutting another coney, and out the other side. Skirts and trouser legs extended to the sky; mottled with dirt and worn thin at the knee. But Alan was in a canoe now, and he carved through the textile river, waving to Indian braves and squaws who worked their fields far from London's drab and stench. He'd become quite good at mimicking a river's *swooshing* noises.

His adventure was cut short when a familiar voice hailed him.

"Master Shaw! Here, boy, here!"

Alan dug in his imaginary paddle, turning toward the voice. A grocer waved a rag above his head.

"I'm glad you're here, you can save my legs," said the

marketman.

"That I can, Mr. Barnsley. Of course, you understand that how easy your legs will feel depends on my wage."

The grocer bent over his stall to regard the boy with a squint. His apron had once been white and blue squares. Now it was one big stain from top to bottom, greens and browns ground in deeper than any dye could go. The same coloured his thick fingers, as if Barnsley had more than a fair affinity with his vegetables. He had a Yorkshire twang to his voice that Alan always found amusing.

"Oh, you want paying do you?"

"Only what I'm due for the work."

"Due? And what do you think you'll be due for carrying this sack of veg to Harker's?"

Alan ducked under the stall. The sack was almost as tall as him, hessian weave and full to brimming with potatoes, turnips and carrots. Hands on hips, he rounded the sack on all sides, then stood and rubbed his chin. Barnsley watched the boy, forcing back the curl of a smile when Alan looked up at him.

"Looks heavy," said Alan. "My pay is based on the sweat I shed while performing the task."

"By that stroke, I should call for an older boy. He'd find it less heavy and so charge me less. Thank you very much, Master Shaw. I'll be sure to bear your lesson in mind." Barnsley turned back to shouting the price of his wares.

Alan's stomach gurgled. He eyed the sack.

"I find older boys slower witted and greedy, mind you." Alan sighed as if the very thought of working with older boys was a bother.

"Oh? So you say?"

"Oh yes. Whereas you might pay less in coin, an older boy couldn't guarantee the safety of your delivery like I can. And if you're willing to barter, I'm sure we can agree what's fair for both of us."

"Barter, then," said Barnsley. He took a seat on a low stool, leaning forward to come eye to eye with Alan.

"As I said, the sack looks heavy—"

"Only if you can't carry it."

"—And it would take me away from other duties."

"Oh, God forbid."

"It's alright, I don't mind putting myself out for a regular customer."

"That's good of you, Master Shaw."

"Of course there's wear and tear on my shoes and coat where the sack will rub."

"Of course, of course," Barnsley nodded along. His large hand was now resting over his mouth as if in thought, but his eyes were watering.

"I'd say no less than a bob."

"A shilling, by God?" said Barnsley. "I dare say I'd rather risk my wares not making their destination than paying a whole shilling."

Alan shook his head. "That's your choice, Mr Barnsley. Can't say I didn't warn you though."

Barnsley walked to the sack, weighed it and set it back down. His back was to Alan, but the boy could see the Grocer's shoulders shaking.

"Well now," Barnsley's voice seemed to be under some strain. "I'll offer six pennies and want your word that this veg will reach Harker's without a single bruise or spilled carrot."

"You can have my word, Mr Barnsley, in return for eight pennies and the use of your barrow."

Barnsley span around, his hand extended. Alan darted back a step, his head flinching into his shoulders. Barnsley's smile faded. He knelt to the boy and took him gently by the shoulder.

"I wasn't going to strike you, lad. Only shaking on it."

Alan's face coloured. He held out his hand to the grocer who took it and couldn't help but notice the shaking in the boy's palm.

"It's a deal. You're a shrewd little business man, Master Shaw." Barnsley lifted the sack into the small barrow behind his stall and handed Alan eight pennies from the pouch on his belt. Alan checked the coins carefully before stowing them somewhere about his person. Then he was off under the stall, pushing the barrow ahead of him.

"Master Shaw!"

Alan turned, and caught the apple that Barnsley tossed to him.

SOMEWHERE BEYOND THE rooftops, Alan heard the *shak-kakak-kakak* of the speeding monorail shuttle. There wasn't a single street in the whole of the North Bank where they couldn't be heard now, either shooting overhead or in the distance. The noise faded as Alan steered his wheelbarrow into the alley beside the York Street pawn brokers. Steam ghosted from the alley's grates, tainted with a smell of cabbage and boiling fat that made Alan's stomach complain, but it'd be another day or so before he was proper hungry. Drawing up beside a cellar trapdoor, he opened one side and then the other. The faint rumble of Harker's tavern echoed up to him. Stowing the wheelbarrow under some old cargo netting and a barrel, he hoisted the sack down, step by step into the gloom.

Harker's was never in full light. A few lamps on distant tables gave a vague idea of where the walls might be, and only one showed how low the ceiling was. Dragging the sack between the small tables, some of them full despite it being barely midday, Alan rubbed shoulders with Pickpockets, Area Divers, Speelers and Cly Fakers, Maltoolers, Palmers and Dippers, Kidsman, Mutchers, Lurkers and Flimps. All of them were men, every one dirty and spending their only coins on the thin beer Callas brewed. The stink of stale ale had soaked into the floor along with blood and cat urine. The offender himself, Newton, came to make a nuisance of himself around Alan's feet as he made his way behind the bar and into the backroom.

"Get away, cat," said Alan, and slid the moggy sideways with his foot. Newton mewled and followed him, tail up like a flagpole. Setting the sack down, Alan stretched his back like an old man he'd once seen, with hands placed above his hips for a pivot. The back room had a long table to one side, and a few shelves to the other, and that was all. Under a trap door, steps led down again to the sub-cellar where the kegs were kept. Alan could hear Callas down there, swearing to himself in Spanish. Alan took the sack again, and quickly dragged it past the trapdoor before the bartender could come up and harass him. He went through the only other door to a kitchen where steam hung like a bottled storm. He slid the sack under a work surface made of a trestle and old planks.

"Sarah?" he called. No answer. "Sarah, are you in?"

From somewhere in the fog, a voice called back. Alan moved toward it.

"Where are you? I've brought some veg from Barnsley. You should open the window in here. I can't see a thing."

Out of the fog, arms grabbed around Alan's waist, hoisting him straight off the floor. He landed on the work surface's planks with a bump, squirming and thrashing to escape his captor.

Sarah's face descended out of the fog.

"Boo!"

She finally let go and Alan struggled himself to sitting.

"Bloody hell! You're funny in the head, you are," he said. "I thought you were one of the customers come back here to kill me. I could have hurt you!"

"You shouldn't curse," said Sarah. "And you wouldn't hurt me, Alan, you don't know how."

"Is that right?"

He leapt off the counter top and into her arms, tickling his fingers around her neck. She caught him but fought against his tickling as much as he had against her attack.

"What's going on in here? I know it isn't work, because it doesn't sound like work!"

Callas came into the kitchen like the murderer Alan had expected. He cursed in Spanish and hobbled into the steam pot belly-first to find the boy and barmaid.

"Oh god," whispered Sarah. They huddled on the floor beside the little oven, hidden from the Spaniard's wrath by the steam. "Quick, Alan, back to the bar."

She shoved Alan forward. He reached back for her hand and they sneaked across the kitchen, bent double behind the work surface. Sarah's hand was as clammy as his own, and he was sure that their hearts raced the same too.

"There had better be broth for our customers when I find you, Sarah. Or swear me down dead, you'll pay for it," yelled Callas.

He lumbered out of the kitchen and through to the bar. Every face turned to look at him. Sarah stood a little way off, handing a tankard to one of the customers. Alan was just coming down the tavern's steps. Newton sat at the end of the bar, playing along by licking himself.

"Is everything alright, Callas?" asked Sarah, her face pale with innocence.

Callas' eyes narrowed.

"If I ever find out how you do that, I swear I'll thrash you blue!"

The Spaniard lashed out at Newton, sending the cat flying with a yowl, and stormed into the back room to the sound of laughing customers.

ALAN SWERVED THROUGH the tables, balancing the old wooden platter so the empty tankards wouldn't slide off. He pretended that collecting and stacking the tankards took so much of his concentration that he didn't hear any of the conversations around him. In a night house like Harker's, it was best not to hear. Although a few Dollymops perched on knees here and there, it was still mostly men who hunkered over the little tables. So it was mostly men's voices that Alan was ignoring.

"Nah nah, we go in through the *up*stairs and work our way down. The guard's office is on the ground floor. By the time they find out we're there, we'll be gone—"

"—I tell you, he knows. Of course I was careful, but I swear he bloody knows—"

"—Jimmy says he can have us in the warehouse around midnight. All we have to do is get to Limehouse and get back again. Christ, we steal a carriage. It's not like we've never done it before is it?"

And so on, until Alan knew everything about every criminal activity planned around Covent Garden. And most of the men, plotters and thieves and murderers, just ruffled his hair as he swayed past with his tray. He finally slid the tray down on the bar and began to set the tankards aside. Sarah was ladling lumpy soup from pot to bowl.

"That'll be a shilling, my darling. Thank you. I put some carrots in it this time, just for you."

When the old soup buyer had shuffled away, Alan leaned in.

"Why do you talk to them like that? Like you like them. Like they're nice."

"The same reason you forget where your pay comes from, Alan. Because we have to."

"I can't wait to get out of here," he said, climbing onto a stool beside Sarah.

"Oh you're going somewhere are you?"

"America. All the way. Train to the coast and ship to New York."

"And what'll you do in New York?"

"Anything I like. In America you just have to walk in a straight line and throw your hat down. Where it lands, is yours. That's how it works over there. No one owns any of it until you walk up and say that you do." His eyes were fixed somewhere a thousand miles beyond the wall. Sarah smiled.

"You'll be a land baron, then?" she said. Another drunkard staggered over. Unable to speak, he just pointed at the pot. Her ladle dipped in and out again.

"Nah. I just want a place of my own. I'll catch rabbits and grow things. I'll wear bear skins and learn how to use a bow and arrow."

"All that on your own, eh? There you go, darlin'. Just a shilling because it's you. Thank you very much."

"I expect I'll make friends with cowboys and the Indians," said Alan.

"Oh, I expect so."

"You don't believe me do you?"

Sarah turned to him and cupped his face in her hand. She smelled like soup.

"Of course I do, Alan. You'll do whatever you want, and go wherever you want. You just have to want it *bad* enough."

"Have you never wanted to go anywhere?"

"Yeah, once. I wanted to go to Spain. But then I met *him*." She nodded toward Callas who was filling a tankard from one of the kegs. She giggled and set Alan laughing too.

"Are you the Shaw boy?"

Sarah yelped at the voice over her shoulder.

"By god, you scared me!"

Alan turned in his seat to see the stranger. He was tall;

taller than the average man. His brow sloped back like a gentle hill to well-oiled hair. Dressed in browns from head to foot with a black cravat, he could have stepped right out of the Police Inspector's daguerreotype. Alan's mouth filled with saliva. He gulped it down.

"Apologies, lass. It was your young friend I was after," said the man in a rich Irish accent.

"Alan? What could you possibly want him for?" laughed Sarah. But the stranger had turned serious.

"I reckon that's his business and mine. Why don't you go dish your soup along the bar there?"

Sarah did as she was told, not daring to look back. But Callas was on his way toward them. He leaned over the bar so his barrel chest was square with the stranger. "What business have you with the boy? He has work to do and gets paid by the tankard, not by the conversation."

The stranger looked to Alan.

"How many minders do you have in this place, boy?" Alan didn't answer. "Never mind. You just run on now Callas. Yes, I know who you are. Now unless you want someone to start asking why a Spaniard is running a tavern bearing another man's name, I suggest you go back to your kegs and bring me a pint of your horse water."

And the stranger actually made a shooing motion. And Callas actually went. Alan smirked despite himself. Callas shot him a look as he retreated.

"So, finally I reach the man I wanted. You are Alan Shaw, aren't you?"

Alan swallowed again.

"No need to be scared of me boy. I'm here to offer you a

job." He looked around the tavern. Alan couldn't help noticing how many men averted his gaze. "A quick job. A quick job with good pay."

"Where'd you get my name?"

"You're as shrewd as they say, then. A man by the name of Throaty, down by the docks."

Callas came back with a tankard and hovered for payment. The stranger dug in his pocket for a couple of coins and flicked them to the barman. "Good man, now be off with you."

Callas ebbed like the tide.

"Throaty Larson wouldn't send you to me. He doesn't like me," said Alan when his employer was out of earshot.

"That's right. He said you're too sharp. But that's not surprising from a man like Throaty. And lucky for you, sharp is exactly what I'm looking for."

"And who are you?"

The stranger's eyes twinkled.

"You don't last long around here without being sharp, do you? I wouldn't be surprised if you were a big man around here someday, Alan. You've got the mind for it, I can see."

"You didn't answer my question," said Alan. "I can't work for someone when I don't know who they are. That's how people end up washed in the Thames with holes in their pockets and another in their guts. Thank you, but I'm not interested in your work, sir. I don't think it will be for me."

The stranger laughed then took a sip of his pint.

"Alright. Let's stop this dancing. Do you know what an

Automaton is?"

Alan's brow creased. That was the second time someone had asked him that in the same day.

"I see by your face that you don't. That's fine, all will be explained. I have a vested interest in them, you see. But all you really need to know is the job. A delivery, in fact. You deliver things for people all the time don't you? That's good. This will be no different. I'll come back here tomorrow. You come with me and you'll get paid half the wage for hearing the rest. Decide to take the job, and you'll get the other half when it's done."

"Half pay even if I say no sounds like a fiddle to me."

"Aye, it would to me too. Let's call it payment for silence. You know how that works, don't you? Now do you want me to come back tomorrow? Or do I find another lad? Time is of the essence here, Alan. But you have first refusal because I like you."

"I won't be here tomorrow," said Alan. The stranger started to speak but was interrupted. "I work the gasworks boxing pit. If you turn up there, I'll think again about your offer."

"Little man, you've got yourself a deal."

With another sip of his pint, the stranger left; stools and tables scraping out of his way as he headed for the stairs.

2

THE SOUND OF meat pummelling meat rang out in the warehouse like the clapping of hands at a funeral. Cheers rose and fell from the crowd. Men with overalls and dirty faces had congregated from all over the gasworks. Betting slips were brandished like weapons in hands that often lacked fingers.

Two fighters circled each other in the dirt, stripped to the waist. With red hair weaving across his arms and chest, the larger man could only be Ramsey, small time bare-knuckle legend. He'd taken a few hits. One opened an old cut on his brow which looked worse than it was. A bruise was forming across his jaw. His opponent relied on speed, trying to finish the fight quick, but now his punches were getting slack. Ramsey swung forward like a derailed engine, connected with the smaller man's temple despite his block and followed it with a left hook. The ground hit the combatant almost as hard as Ramsey had. A mixture of cheers and disgusted yells erupted; betting slips flew like confetti, coming to rest on the loser's barely moving body. Ramsey turned away. A vendor patted him on the shoulder as he leant on a wood panel at the ring's edge. Someone handed him a smouldering pipe.

Alan came through the ring's gate, broom and bag in hand, a small team of men in his wake. He swept from the ring's centre to its edge in long strokes as the prone boxer was hoisted over the panels and out of the ring. At the edge, he bundled betting slips into the bag and turned to spread fresh dirt over a pool of blood that had formed under the loser's head. He bent down for a moment, wiped something on his trousers and then lifted it to the light.

"Hey there," said Ramsey. "What've you found, Mouse?"

Alan came over, lifting the little gold trophy.

"It's your tooth again, Mr. Ramsey."

Ramsey took it from Alan's palm with fingers as big as the boy's wrist.

"Blow me. The little bugger knocked my tooth out." Tucking the tooth under his lip, there was a wet crunch as it slid back into place.

"One day that thing won't go back in," said Alan.

"And on that day, it's yours. But until my gums shrink like the old man that I am…" From his trouser pocket Ramsey took a shilling and passed it down. Alan had to stretch to get it. "Good lad."

A hand came down on Alan's shoulder as he stepped out of the ring.

"Is that another one of your minders, Alan?"

"I don't have or need minders," said Alan, turning to the Irishman he couldn't help but think of as The Villain.

"Shall we go?"

"I'd like to see my payment before we leave, if you don't

mind." The stranger raised an eyebrow but slid a billfold from inside his waistcoat. He selected a few notes and extended them toward Alan's cartwheel eyes.

"Half of what you'll get, as agreed. For a night's work, my young friend, you could have that ship ticket and money to make something of yourself at the other end. What do you think?"

Alan slid the notes out of The Villain's fingers as if not wanting to wake a sleeping dragon.

"There's four pound here!"

"I suggest you take care of it, then. Let's go. I have a carriage waiting."

They came out of the warehouse on the riverside and turned along the bank. Coal barges slid through the water, their drivers stood, heron-like on the deck. One drew alongside Whitefriars as Alan walked by, the boatman tossing a rope to a boy on the dock who wrapped it twice around the mooring and tied it off. The gasworks' huge iron lung passed to their right, slowly rising as the giant breathed in. Railings and ladders linked the lung's scaffold, reminding Alan of bird skeletons dangling against an overcast sky. Pipes that Alan could fit inside came out at all angles and led away to bell-shaped tanks. Little men ran back and forth, carrying sacks of coal pills to keep the giant asleep. Walking around the works, they came to Temple Street where a Hackney waited for them. Looking around, The Villain opened the door and lifted Alan inside. Perching on the seat, he jabbed the ceiling with his cane. Alan fell back as the carriage lurched.

"Never been in a carriage before?" asked The Villain.

"Never had any need, sir."

"Oh, it's 'sir' now you've been paid is it?"

Alan tugged back the carriage's curtain to look outside. They turned into The Strand, slotting into the traffic like a cog tooth. Shop awnings of every colour went by at eye level. Narrow buildings of four storeys or more seemed a little shorter today. Each one had narrow windows, but every facade and roof was different. Some walls were plastered from pavement to tip with mouldering playbills. Hackney carriages, some even chugging with new steam engines, jostled like migrating buffalo, their driver's goggled and helmeted heads peeping above like birds. And down the centre of the road, dividing the traffic into lanes, great iron poles held the monorail aloft. Along many of London's major streets the monorail carried its steam-powered shuttles; sometimes riding above the rooftops, sometimes diving underground like giant worms. Alan shoved his head out of the window, trying to spin it full circle on his shoulders, just so that he could take it all in. The clop and creak of hooves and wheels and the occasional *put-put-put* of a steam engine made the carriage a ship. Alan felt the breeze of speed on his face, and tried to imagine that it didn't smell of the Thames, but was sea spray instead. Sailors heave-hoed on the rigging. A captain, one hand on the wheel, stood majestic at one end of the ship. Alan found a smile creeping across his face.

Where the traffic knotted at Charing Cross, they came to a complete stop. Alan peered through a gap in the buildings which gave a view of the river. As he watched, a locomotive left Charing Cross station (the line that would go all the way to the sea), taking the bridge which arched over the churning brown Thames like a great steel snake. Steam coughed from vents in its narrow face, making twin trails along the slender carriages. Sunlight skittered across the locomotive's panels in sheets of fire. Alan sighed as it accelerated and the passengers' tiny faces faded to dots.

The Villain leaned over and twitched the curtain closed.

"Before we reach our destination, I need you to understand that this job is a secret. No one can see you with me and no one can know. The delivery has to be…"

"A surprise?"

"Sharp lad. That's the word I was looking for exactly."

"Like a birthday present," said Alan, staring at the curtain as if he could still see through. "Someone once told me you get presents on your birthday."

"You've never had a birthday present, Alan?" The Villain seemed ready to make idle conversation, but his tone said otherwise.

"I don't know when it is."

Eventually the carriage swung right, swaying Alan in his seat again. The carriage juddered as the road became uneven, and steadied again.

"Nearly there," said The Villain as if he was able to navigate by the rumble of cobbles. They soon drew to a stop. The Villain leant over Alan to release the carriage's door latch. Alan had been in the proximity of many gentleman in his time. If only in their service or to be assaulted by one. But he knew the smell of shaving water, and The Villain didn't smell like that. He smelled of earth, or maybe hay as if he'd slept in a loft. Alan knew that smell well enough, too.

Instead of the door opening, The Villain opened the curtain. It seemed they wouldn't be getting out just yet.

"This is where you'll be delivering the package. I think you know your way around it already."

He pointed to an immense red brick building. Alan took it in from steps to roof, and tried to force the bile back into his stomach.

"The bloody workhouse?"

The Irishman nodded. "The bloody workhouse."

"I'M SORRY, INSPECTOR, I know you're very busy, but I just couldn't wait."

The little man dabbed his leaky brow with a handkerchief. He was pale, and behind his spectacles Carpenter could see that he hadn't slept. He was nervy at the best of times, but now he positively vibrated. Carpenter hacked at his typewriter and each keystrike made the little man twitch. Carpenter slid the shuttle aside with a final *shhping*. He tried to slide the apparatus aside, but decided he didn't want to score grooves into his desk. It could stay as it was.

"Not at all, Professor Normen. You have every right to pester me day and night until the unveiling."

"Three days, Inspector. Three short days."

"And I'm honoured that A division has been chosen to deal with the security. Let me fix you a drink. Do you have water in your scotch?"

"Oh no, no. I hardly think that will be necessary. Um, actually, yes please." Normen dabbed at his brow again. "With so little time, and the Unions threatening action, I wondered if you had anything? That's a most splendid carafe. Crystal is it?"

Carpenter weighed the thing in his hand as the scotch sloshed into a glass.

"A gift from Magistrate Fielding when I first set up A division." The professor took the glass from Carpenter, laying it in his lap.

"Ah, cut glass then."

"Probably," agreed Carpenter.

The little scientist smiled for the first time. He raised his glass to meet Carpenter's.

"Oh, I don't give the Magistrate his due. I do apologise."

"I think you're more polite about him than I could ever be."

The Professor giggled. Carpenter couldn't help but smile.

Outside the office, Carpenter caught a glimpse of Simon and his companion. The Professor followed his eye.

Simon was bowing to a girl two years his senior, offering some greeting that made her giggle.

"Your boy is growing to be quite the gentleman, Inspector."

"Despite me, I think. Helen seems to be reaching womanhood at an alarming rate."

"Yes. I often think I should turn my hand to halting the aging process rather than creating mechanical men. Every day she looks like her mother and every day it tugs my heart the more."

Carpenter took a long swig of his glass.

"I know what you mean."

The men watched their children for a moment as Simon offered his book to the girl and began to explain something which she found half as interesting as the boy's face. Both men looked to each other and realised they were smiling. Professor Normen broke eye contact first, turning back to the desk. He cleared his throat before speaking.

"And so, Inspector, to our update?"

Carpenter laid his glass aside and selected a roll of paper from inside the bureau. Opening it, he used his inkwell and scotch glass to weigh the map down.

"A Division's jurisdiction runs from Hyde Park to Covent Garden. A large area. Unfortunately, there's no telling whereabouts our villain is working from, or even if he resides in this area at all."

"I'm sorry, Inspector, but I fear we may have skipped a step. You have information on our villain?"

"I'm getting ahead of myself." Selecting a file from his desk, Carpenter opened it for the Professor to read. A single daguerreotype stared back at the Professor attached to a list of offences.

"Who is this man?"

"That, Professor, is *our* man. We've exhausted all means trying to find information and we eventually came up with this likeness. This villain, known as Rafferty, with a long list of alias Christian names, is an expert swindler. The gift of the gab seems to be his main weapon, and he's more than a dab hand at making things that explode. And generally arsonists make bad friends, so he's a loner."

"What does this mean for my Automatons, Inspector?"

Carpenter pointed to the map. "St Martin's workhouse.

Or it used to be."

"My Laboratory," said Normen, beaming. "And womb for my metal children. Oh, ha ha. I'm sorry. I should avoid abstraction. Writing has always been best left to other men."

"Not at all. My point is that St Martin's workhouse – now your laboratory – has all of your Automatons in one place. If that isn't Rafferty's target, then I might as well work the docks instead of policing."

Professor Normen jumped up.

"Then we just have to guard it until the procession!"

"Calm down, Professor. Take a seat. We've already drafted all of Division C to guarding your laboratory. They've been there all week in plain clothes."

"Oh. Awfully sorry. I've had very little sleep of late. I think I might be a tad on edge."

"A tad. Still, mad as he is, Rafferty is always one step away from any crime he performs. In all the history we have in this file, he's never been found at the scene of a crime. In truth, he's usually well away before the crime is even committed. And so our job's been to find his would-be accomplice. I hope this sets your mind at rest, Professor. Because I have a man shadowing that accomplice as we speak. What he knows, we'll know. And when we know all there is, Rafferty will see in the next century behind bars."

When Carpenter looked up, Normen's head was in his hands. "What have I done, Inspector? What have I done?"

Carpenter's brow knotted. "Professor?"

"Why does everyone seem so against my work? The public think I'm taking their jobs. There are anthropologists at the museum claiming that I'm removing the evolutionary imperative. Religious men claim I'm negating God. The Sociologists' views are so multitudinous that I can barely read an article before five more are written. And then there's this man. An insane man, clearly, who wishes to destroy my work entirely."

"And you're wondering if so many people can be wrong?" Carpenter filled the Professor's glass again, minus the water this time.

"Of course!" The Professor threw his arms up, spilling scotch on the carpet. "Oh dear, I'm so sorry."

"It's fine. The carpet was that colour already." Carpenter slid aside a pile of paperwork so he could perch on the desk. "Can I ask you a personal question, Professor?"

"Of course, my dear Inspector, I owe you much for the help you've already given me."

Carpenter raised his eyebrows. The Professor's glass was already three quarters empty, his cheeks were flushed, his eyes watery. Carpenter smiled, and nodded.

"What were your reasons for creating the Automatons?"

Professor Normen blinked as if stricken by a light.

"Reason? Well, there are many really. I saw the possibilities of Babbage's analytical engine, even if he has resigned himself to never actually producing the machine. Then of course, when I found how complex the punch-card programmes could become with the right encryption, there was no end to the possibilities. My own engineering expertise and Babbage's designs made my project obvious. To create a device which could perform simple tasks while following a set of predetermined instructions."

Carpenter brought his thoughts back from where they

had wandered to.

"And your mechanised men were the result. But that's not what I asked. What was your reason? Why bother to create something so complex? What's the ultimate purpose of your life's work?"

Normen's tongue searched the edge of his mouth. His eyes were somewhere else. Carpenter supposed that was the look he got when thinking. The Inspector decided to put Normen out of his misery.

"I think, Professor Normen, that your reasons for creating the Automatons are very much the same as my reasons for police work."

"Oh?" said Normen. "And what similarities have you drawn between your Law and my Science?"

Carpenter nodded toward the window where Simon and Helen were chatting. Simon laughed, covering his mouth. Just like his mother used to.

"Oh, I see. Very clever, Inspector. I see what you're getting at and of course you're right."

"Then I say tell all those busybodies and their professional jealousy to stick their noses where the Sun refuses to shine."

"I'll drink to that!" Raising his glass, the Professor found it empty. "Oh dear."

"TOMORROW, ALAN. DON'T forget," said The Villain.

"I won't."

The carriage rattled away, leaving Alan alone in a mass of people. A delivery in the dead of night to the old workhouse. Alan wondered if it was worth the eight pounds.

Eight pounds plus the shillings and pennies he had stored in the kitchen vent at Harker's. A ship, and a coastline; a new continent and a new life. That eight pounds could buy a lot more future than working the tavern for the rest of his days.

He walked along Haymarket for a while. The first fair weather of spring had brought masses of people into the streets and in every pocket the tiny chimes of midday rose like birdsong, prompting the Ladies and Gentlemen to produce their watches for winding. Alan took to the alleyways where the air was quieter, although rank with urine and garbage. Rounding a corner in the gloom, Alan didn't yelp as a hand wrapped around his mouth; he instantly put his energy into making thorns of his elbows and knees, and tried to get his teeth into his attacker's flesh. He fumbled at the coin pouch in his jacket, still fighting his assailant, certain that his new found wealth was already lost.

"Alan! Stop struggling will you?"

Alan fought harder. Most people who knew his name knew it for the wrong reason.

"Stop it, I said. Settle down lad, I'm not going to hurt you."

When no knife was produced or cuff around the ear felt, Alan thought the mugger might just be telling the truth. The hand over his mouth moved gingerly aside.

"Let go of me then, and I'll stop."

"Only if you give me your word not to run."

"Alright, just let me go."

Alan struggled free when the hands loosened and, without looking back, made a bolt for the end of the alley. But the mugger's hands were faster; Alan was yanked back by the collar of his shirt. The stranger spun him around so that the boy could see his face.

"Alan, for the love of God, it's me."

"Oh bloody hell," Alan said, when Constable Jenning's face came out of the shadows.

"Don't worry, you're not in trouble," the constable offered, and led Alan away down the alley.

"You keep saying that, and then you keep following me."

"It's for your own good."

Tucked behind a stack of boxes, Jennings lowered himself onto a barrel and gestured for Alan to do the same. The boy perched on the edge of a pile of shipping palettes.

"So what do you want? Or are you here to half arrest me again?"

"I'm here about—" Jennings paused as the Monorail rattled overhead, drowning him out. "—about that man. The man you were just talking to."

Alan looked down the alley in both directions and shrugged his ragged shoulders.

"I don't know what you're on about."

"Let's bypass the games, Alan. I need to know what Rafferty said to you. What does he want you to do?"

Alan sniffed, and avoided eye contact.

"Still don't know what you're on about."

"Alan—"

"Sorry, Copper. Can't help you." Alan hopped down from his seat and walked away, looking back before ducking out of sight. Jennings sighed to himself as the boy turned the corner, and then followed.

Covent market was starting to clear up. Carts were packed with collapsed stalls and any leftover produce. Barnsley had the smallest kind of cart; one he pushed himself like a large wheelbarrow.

"Good day, Master Shaw," he yelled, gesturing to his cart. "Not a turnip left! There are some hungry folk in London that are better fed today."

"You're a rich man, then Mr Barnsley?" asked Alan.

"Oh, about as rich as I'm going to get. How'd the boxing go today? Ramsey clean up as usual?"

"I didn't stay to the end, but I expect so. I had some business to sort elsewhere."

Barnsley's eyebrows lifted.

"Business you say? So you're a rich man yourself?"

"Richer than yesterday, but not as rich as tomorrow," said Alan, beaming. The more he thought of the money, the warmer he felt. He'd soon be talking to cowboys and teaching swearwords to the natives.

"And what manner of business makes a young man like you rich so quick? I hope you're not up to anything the law would want to know about." Barnsley's smile melted when he saw that Alan wasn't smiling at all. "Alan?"

"Nothing like that at all," said Alan. "I'm offended that you'd suggest it!"

He stormed away toward Harker's Tavern, not intending to look over his shoulder but unable to help it. Barnsley wasn't looking after him as he expected. He was talking to another man. Alan saw the flash of a badge, and the man turned just enough for Alan to make out his face. It was Jennings, talking to the grocer like old friends.

By the time Alan had rounded the arcade's corner, he was running at full speed through the remaining stalls. He leapt over a barrel as a fat little merchant rolled it by, threw aside a sacking curtain and headed for another alley. He found it blocked by a high wooden gate. Climbing over the wheel and into the bed of a cart by the alley's end, he swung himself from an overhanging awning so his feet cleared the gate's top. Landing in a puddle in the alleyway beyond, he stumbled away into the dark.

There was only one way he'd lose the Copper now. Above his head, twine hung across the alley like a web with white flies caught in it; clothing that swayed and bobbed in the breeze. At the end of the alley, Alan climbed a wooden ladder. The wood was part rotten, but Alan was light and eventually his foot met the roof's gutter.

Slopes of slate led away in every direction, perforated by chimneys and smokestacks. Alan ignored the urge to check behind him as he moved across the slick landscape. Confident as a mountain goat, he ran along gutters, picking up speed even as he vaulted over walls and trampled through the shacks and lean-tos of the roof-dwelling homeless. Keeping Covent Arcade's roof to his right, he skirted high above the square, making for a roof that would lead him down to Harker's. He darted past a small group of other boys sharing a chunk of bread by a chimney stack like sunken-eyed gargoyles. Some of them were from St. Martin's workhouse like Alan, and so technically friends, but he was moving too fast to stop for them. One called out to him but he ignored it. He *had* to lose that Copper.

Dragging breath into his aching lungs, Alan spotted a

larger gap in the roofs ahead where two ancient buildings leant away from each other. He narrowed his eyes against a sharp wind that dragged sore tears from the corner of his eye. Dropping his chin, he pushed his skinny muscles harder. To his left, a monorail track ran parallel to the buildings. As a shuttle hurtled by Alan imagined himself drawn into the speeding bullet's slipstream. Eyes intent on the gap ahead, he took a deep breath as if it would make him lighter. Heaving his legs like pistons, Alan's boots left the roof, kicking at thin air as his arms wheeled in mock flight. A score of pale faces pressed against the monorail shuttle's windows, their gasps almost audible as they witnessed the urchin's leap.

ALAN SLID THROUGH the high window of Harker's kitchen, dangling briefly before dropping to the work surface and down to the floor where he leant heavily against the wall.

"Alan, you're out of breath. Who you been running from?"

Alan jumped at Sarah's voice. She came toward him, wiping her hands on a rag.

"No one! Bloody hell, Sarah. Stop pestering me with questions. If I had a mother, she'd not bother me as much as you."

Sarah rocked on her heels as if Alan's tirade had been a wind.

"I didn't mean anything by it, love. Just a joke, that's all. What's got you all of a dither? Sorry, sorry, don't answer that."

Alan stormed out of the kitchen, but Sarah followed

him. He snatched two tankards from the bar by Callas, froth spilling down his hands, and stalked across the tavern.

"So he shouts at you, now does he?" spat Callas. "Needs a father's hand, he does."

"No Callas, he just needs a father."

Alan slid the tankards over the table, doffing his cap to the customers with no real feeling behind it. His cheeks were burning, his mouth full of spit. Everyone seemed to be at him. Policemen, grocers, even Sarah. The only one who wasn't pestering was a man he knew couldn't be trusted. His head rattled with voices and his chest felt heavy. But he knew all those things would be better when he was on another continent. When he was beyond their reach.

Ready to apologise to Sarah, he picked up the few empties he could carry and turned back toward the bar. His throat tightened. Alan rushed as if he hadn't seen the man in the corner. Was there no escaping him?

"Sarah, how long's he been here?" asked Alan jerking his head toward the corner table.

"Who?" asked Sarah.

"The bloody copper in the corner. How long's he been here?"

Sarah shot a look at Jennings who upturned his tankard and nodded to her.

"He's a copper? Oh, Alan, you *have* got yourself into something, haven't you?"

"No no, not yet, anyways. How long has he been here?"

"Since before you came back. And long enough that he wants a refill." She removed the wooden peg from a keg, letting the ale pour out. "I'd better obey the law."

"No," said Alan. "I'll take it. It's alright. I haven't done anything wrong. He can't do anything."

"Are you trying to convince me, or practice your speech for him?" asked Sarah.

"Both."

Sarah squeezed Alan's little hand in hers. He gave her a wink, but released a tear he didn't mean to.

The walk to Jennings' table seemed like miles. The ale's froth brimmed like the sea foam Alan was growing certain he'd never see.

"I'm getting tired of seeing your face, Copper."

"Really? I've become quite fond of yours. Could do with a wash, mind. Your vault over that gate was pretty impressive, Alan. Then running across the rooftops like a goblin." Jennings shook his head. "If I hadn't already known where you would go, you'd have lost me."

"That was the idea." Alan's voice was steady, his thumbs stuck into his trousers. But his eye was on the floor and Jennings could see that his face was wet. The Constable sipped at his ale.

"This tastes like piss, does your bartender know?"

"Yes."

"You spend a lot of time on the slates?"

Alan shrugged. "You can get all the way from here to West India Docks by rooftop if you know the way."

"And you think that's safe, do you?"

"I think a boy my size can get scragged walking the streets round here. People jumping you in alleyways. Happens all the time don't it?" Alan gave the copper a pointed look. "Leaping from rooftops is safer in most ways."

"Yes, a lad like you can get into a lot of trouble in London."

"Listen…Jennings. I haven't done nothing wrong. As it is, I think you're following me and that's a crime in itself. I'd like it very much if you'd leave me alone."

"I'm afraid it's only a crime if it isn't a policeman doing it. Sorry Alan, double standards. And I know you haven't done anything wrong. If anything, following you has convinced me you're a good lad. A lot of people speak highly of you. I reckon if you can stay out of trouble until you're grown, you could make something of yourself around here. Something good."

Alan ran his nose along his sleeve.

"I'm your friend, Alan. I know that might be hard for you to understand just yet, but I am. And the last thing I want is to see you come to some wrong at the hands of this criminal. Rafferty's a villain. A *real* villain." Alan winced at the word but wouldn't reply. "Let this be the last thing I say to you as your friend, then. When you make this choice, it puts me and you at opposite ends of the law. You realise that? Good. Then either way, I'll be seeing you."

Jennings set the tankard down, still half full, and left.

Alan watched him go, his eyes stinging with tears. He needed advice, or rather he needed more of it. A large part of his upbringing had told him not to trust coppers. Even ones that seemed ok like Jennings. They were often the worst sort. But what other adults could he trust? He looked back over his shoulder at Sarah, who was pretending not to pay attention. She was a nice woman, and he liked her just fine, but she wasn't his mum. They looked after each other for the most part, but Alan had been washed off people's hands before; he didn't want the same to happen with Sarah. Then there was Callas—No. Alan couldn't even bring himself to finish the thought off properly. And Mr Barnsley had already shown his distaste for any work slightly outside the technicalities of the law.

In a complete void of adult guidance, Alan decided to go to the next best thing.

3

ON THE CORNERS of Shoe Lane and Stonecutter street, where the square opened upon the stalls of Farringdon Market, a boy of Alan's age stood on the pavement by a stack of newspapers wrapped in twine. He was a little taller, perhaps, and wider at the shoulders like a clothes horse hanging with rags, but otherwise that boy and Alan could well have been the same urchin from cap to yawning shoes. The morning traffic clattered and bounced, occasionally kicking up a stone which the boy expertly avoided. He held one newspaper in his hand, waving it above his head, and yelled into the crowds of workers and toffs that strolled by. Occasionally one would stop and trade a coin for a newspaper, the boy would tip his hat and wait a polite second before hawking his wares again. As he spotted Alan walking his way along the pavement, he waved his hat.

"Well, well, well. As I live and breathe. Alan bloody Shaw."

"Alright, Dick. How's things?" Alan strode up, thumbs tucked into his waistband and elbows out, making himself swagger comically.

Dick slapped his belly, which was just a little wider than

Alan's own. Unlike Alan, who had been left on the orphanage steps with a name pinned to him, Dick had been named by the orphanage staff who took him from the asylum where his mother was deemed unfit to care for him. It had been Whitsunday, and so Richard Whitsun was given his name. But he preferred Dick.

"Can't grumble!" Dick turned away for a second, doffing his cap to a tall man in a long blue coat. "Good morning, sir. Newspaper is it?"

The man spoke in a rumbling whisper: "You got something else," he stated.

Alan looked away, making sure that he didn't make eye contact with the punter. He only got a general image of bristled jaw and deep-set eyes while Dick took a silent gulp, although never letting his smile slip. Alan could see that his friend's hands were shaking a little as he fumbled in a satchel beside his stack of papers. With one deft movement, he removed something from the bag, palmed it, and folded a newspaper in half with his other hand. At some point the two came together seamlessly, and the tall man strode away with the newspaper under his arm. Dick was left with a much-used envelope which disappeared into his jacket. The boy checked up and down the street, through the traffic and the people, and slowly came to relax. He turned a tired smile back to Alan, who was waiting patiently.

"You still working for the Them, then?" Alan asked. He stood with his arms crossed, and gave Dick Whitsun a square look.

The boy took another look around and stepped closer to Alan, removing his cap and lowering his voice. The casual onlooker might have thought them brothers. "Lads like you and me can do a lot worse than working with the Gentleman's Consortium, Al. I occasionally slip a little extra into the right gent's paper, collect the envelopes, and every other paper I sell, I keep the profit. You should try it." Dick ran his nose along a sleeve. "Might get you out of that shithole tavern."

"Harker's isn't so bad," Alan lied. Sometimes working Harker's Tavern was as bad as it could get for a boy in London. But a warm shelf to sleep on and regular soup also made it the best. Alan wasn't sure where Dick slept, but it was probably with a lot of other boys, crammed in like sardines for the warmth; perhaps on a roof, heating their hands over a smoky chimney top, or down by the river where the bridge's arches kept out the worst of the winter bite.

"That may be, but there ain't no—" and at this, Dick slowed his speech to emphasize each complicated syllable "-ca-reer pro-gre-shun. I might be starting out popping stuff into newspapers, but soon I'll be a Runner for the—" he looked around again "—GeeCee, and then I'll be one of the Boys. Better that than the workhouse."

"No arguments there," Alan said. "Still don't fancy being found feet-up in the Thames one day."

"Only if you mess 'em around, Al. And only a real no-noggin would do that."

"I suppose so."

Dick Whitsun went back to work for a second, yelling the day's headlines into the street. "Mechanical Men set to change the world! Day after tomorrow! Come on, Sirs and

Ladies, don't miss out!"

Alan looked down at the newspapers covered in complex squiggles. Occasionally he recognised a letter or two, the first of his name, for instance, but not enough to read what was written. The front of the newspaper bore an illustration of a mechanical man in size comparison with a human being. They would be huge, Alan thought. Eight feet of steel and whirring gears.

"Can you read that?" he asked Dick.

"Nah. They just tell us what to shout. This Automaton thing has everyone a bit scatty, though, right?"

Alan's jaw dropped open. "What did you just say?"

Dick stabbed a finger at the front page. "That's what they call these things. Some mad old bloke made a bloody factory out of our workhouse. It's where they build 'em. Day after tomorrow, they'll be walking around like regular folk."

Alan's mind started whirring, pieces of information falling like tumblers in a lock, and when he finally understood, his mouth ran dry.

"Alan? I said 'so what you down here for?' I thought you'd be swabbing some beer swill or picking teeth out of the mud at the gas works."

Alan swallowed hard before managing to say, "I've got a job on."

Dick's eyebrow arched. "So you say?"

Alan nodded. "Wanted to run it past you."

As they talked, Dick carried on working, yelling and then lowering his voice to talk to Alan like an expert ventriloquist.

"What kind of job we talking about?"

"A quick one, with good pay," were the words Alan used. But inside, he was thinking that Rafferty's secret package had something to do with the mechanical men at St. Martin's workhouse. And the coppers knew all about it. They'd said 'Automaton'. And Jennings said Rafferty was the villain. Bloody hell. Dick seemed to know exactly what he was thinking.

"Easy jobs don't exist, far as I know. 'specially not well-paid ones. If it's easy, it's cheap. If it's hard, it pays," Dick said, sage for an eleven year old.

A carriage rolled by, washing mud up onto the pavement. Alan helped his friend to drag the stack of papers back out of the way.

"This is enough coin to get me out of here, Dick." *Enough to be a long way away while the dust settles*, Alan added to himself.

"And the kind of job that'd mean you probably want to be far away when it's done?"

"Not really sure. I don't know too much. The boss is keeping it to himself."

"Good. Means if the Filth question you, you don't know anything." Dick beckoned to Alan so that both boys leant over the newspaper podium like old men in a pub, their faces close. "Listen, Al, if you want to know if it's a good idea, then I can't help you. All I know is lads like us got lucky when we got out of St. Martin's before they shut it down. Damned lucky. Christ knows where we'd have been sent otherwise. And we made that luck ourselves by escaping. Me, I keep on making my own luck, and I'd say you should do the same. You've done plenty that's dodgy before, just like the rest of us, and you will again. You want that money, you want out of London like you always said, then you take the job and make sure you get lucky."

Alan was silent for a moment. Dick reached over and patted him clumsily on the shoulder.

"Thanks, Dick." Alan nodded. "I reckon I know what I'll do."

"Good for you, pal. You come by and see me before you go swanning off with cowboys, right?"

Alan gave his friend a smile. Dick Whitsun always made him feel confident. It was his gift. He always had lads following him. That gift was what had made Alan one of the boys to crawl their way out of the workhouse. If Dick's advice had saved him then, maybe it would now, too.

"You bet," Alan said. And made to walk away.

"And Alan!" Alan turned back to catch Dick's impish wink. "Make sure you don't get yourself disappeared, eh?"

ALAN SHIVERED. IF there was one thing he'd buy before getting on that ship, it'd be a new coat. And some proper boots. He'd never had proper boots before, but once tonight was over and he was headed for the coast, he'd have a pair. That was if the shop owner didn't turn out to be Jennings in disguise. Then the train driver. Then the ship's First Mate. Alan wouldn't be surprised if the first Indian he met turned out to be Jennings in a bloody feather headdress.

The streetlamps were lit all along Haymarket and round onto Cockspur where he found the Gentleman's Club. The dull glow of the gas lamps allowed the night to pool in crevices and alleyways. Alan searched each shadow as he made his way along the street, always keeping arm's length away from any dark spots. When he was in America, living out on the open prairie, there'd be no alleyways; no hidey holes and dark corners for people to lurk in.

But first he'd have to do the job; deliver the package. He'd have to go back to the workhouse he swore he'd never see again, with a certain Villain behind him and a criminal record in front. But at least his talk with Dick had him as forewarned as he could be. Although at the back of his mind, Alan was worried about how easily his friend's conscience dealt with his criminal associations. Maybe Dick was just smarter, he supposed.

Rafferty had given him the address of the Gentleman's Club. If that was where people like Rafferty met, and if the rest were as bad as he expected, Alan would not be surprised if the police were watching it day and night. Another reason to be cautious. Alan walked up to the door and, checking over his shoulder, span the doorknob and slid through the smallest gap he could manage. There were sounds from the rooms upstairs; men's voices coupled with the rattle of glasses. Passing straight through the corridor, then the kitchen, Alan went to the back of the building like Rafferty had told him. Between the club's rear and the surrounding buildings was a small yard. Someone had put a tin roof over it, but it seemed only the servants would have reason to come out here. An old mangle, one of the big ones with rollers thick as Alan's leg, rusted in one corner. A bale of hay had been picked apart and strewn over the floor by some nesting birds. Everywhere was dark except where a hole in the corrugated roof let in moonlight. But Alan knew

Rafferty was there. There was the slosh of a bottle, and a loud glug as The Villain took some whiskey.

"You came," slurred Rafferty. "Sharp boy. The perfect boy for the job. And here he is."

Rafferty got up, a little unsteady, and made his way into the light. Alan made sure he stayed over by the door. Rafferty was clutching a satchel in his fist. He offered it to Alan, but yanked it back before the boy could take it.

"One last thing, Alan. One last thing," he said. "I always seem to be adding something, don't I? Just one more thing. This package, it's very fragile. I wouldn't shake it, and I definitely wouldn't drop it if I were you."

Alan took the satchel and slung it over his shoulder. It was heavier than it looked. He could feel something hard pressing into his side, and thought he heard the faint movement of fluid.

"If you'd just pay me the rest of my money, I'll be on my way to deliver it then," he said.

Rafferty slumped onto the bale of hay.

"Maybe I started celebrating a little too early," he said.

"I'd say," muttered Alan.

"Don't be cheeky!" Rafferty was across the intervening space and had Alan by the collar so fast that Alan didn't have time to flinch. "Don't you be cheeky or I swear to God!"

The Villain fumbled in his pocket, producing a small metal box which he thrust at Alan as if threatening with a knife. His thumb stroked a switch on the box's front.

"Or I swear to God, I'll show you."

Rafferty dropped Alan, who scuttled further toward the door. The Villain followed him, draining the last of his bottle and setting it down by the steps.

"Now run along, boy, and do your job. But don't forget I'll be watching you. I'll be following you all the way and making sure you do it. And if you don't, by God." He brandished the little box again. Alan was sure he didn't want to find out what that box was for. He climbed the steps to the kitchen, but froze when Rafferty called him back.

"Wait, wait. You forgot your money. You want to get paid don't you?"

Alan thought about it. He nodded.

Rafferty nodded back. "Go call me a carriage then, and wait. I'll be right out."

As Rafferty relieved himself in the yard Alan went back through to the street with his package. He shouted to a passing Hackney, the old horse-drawn kind, which drew alongside.

"You need a ride, boy, you better show me your money first," said the driver.

"Not me, my Boss. He'll be right out."

The driver nodded and fumbled in his jacket for a cigarette. Alan sauntered up and down the pavement, occasionally looking out across Trafalgar Square to where the Royal Academy blocked his view of the workhouse. But only temporarily.

Rafferty finally emerged from the Gentlemen's Club more composed. He checked the street either way before leaving the doorway and strode quickly over to Alan.

"Good lad, Alan. Good lad." He threw a pouch to the boy. "Now make sure you earn that. This'll be the last time you see me, but I'll be around. I'll be watching everywhere you go, and I know all your hidey holes. So make sure you do your job. Because if I have to come find you for my money, there'll be hell to pay."

Alan nodded; The Villain opened the carriage door before shooing Alan away.

With the satchel rubbing against his side, Alan set off across Trafalgar Square at a swift pace. Gods knew what was in that bag. *Don't shake it. Don't drop it.* Why would the villain want something so fragile delivered by a boy? Because it was a swindle, that's why. And it was far too late, with four pounds hidden away and four in his pocket, that any policeman would take Alan seriously. Even without the money, it would have been a hard sell. He was on his own. And if he didn't want to be on the business end of whatever Rafferty's little box did, he had to go through with it.

Watching out for Irish villains and policemen alike, Alan could see that the carriage had followed him, and was now parked on the opposite side of the square for a full view of his progress. His heart had been racing all along, but now it pounded hard enough that his hands shook with each pulse. Overlooking the square, the Royal Academy cast a deep shadow. Alan hurried down some steps to hug the Academy's wall, thankful of the darkness found there, and crossed to the corner. With barely a pause, he stepped out onto St Martin's Street. Then threw himself back into the shadows.

A policemen sauntered by, stopping at the edge of the square. In the dark, Alan stiffened until his whole body shook. His lungs quivered with the effort of holding his breath.

The policeman strode back the way he came, whistling tunelessly.

Alan released a shuddering breath. Not for the first time he wondered exactly what Rafferty was up to. Why were coppers guarding an old workhouse? Was this what Jennings meant? That they'd be waiting for him? He looked back. Beyond the fountains, the carriage had moved closer. Alan thought about the little box in Rafferty's pocket. What kind of weapon could fit into a little box? Could it get him from here? He had to think, and think fast. How was he going to get into the workhouse with coppers everywhere?

Alan felt a lump in his throat. His chest felt tight. Sweat went cold on his dirty shirt collar.

There was nothing for it. He'd have to get in the same way he'd once got out.

"METAL MEN WALKING the streets." The Constable jabbed his thumb toward the building beyond St Martin's main gate. "Are they cracked, or what?"

His colleague snorted. "It'll be fine until they break down. Or throw some gasket and run amok. Then we'll see what's what."

"Bloody hell. I bet we'll be called in to sort them out sooner rather than later."

Both men snapped to attention when a third walked out of the shadows.

"Lucky for you two, you'll not even be allowed on the streets again if you don't look lively," said Inspector Carpenter.

"Sorry, sir," said one constable. "Just idle chat. It won't

happen again."

"Idle is a word I already use for you boys from C Division. Make sure you prove me wrong tonight."

"Yes, sir."

"Of course, sir."

Carpenter moved off down the street to his next set of constables. Jennings was looking up and down the street like a tennis umpire.

"Doubt our villain will walk up and say hello, Jennings. Why don't you relax a little?"

"Sorry, sir. I just...I really want to catch this Rafferty character."

"So do I. But I'll settle for not having to disappoint her Majesty when she expects three hundred mechanical men on her doorstep the day after tomorrow. I'll be right back."

A police carriage waited across the road, the horse steaming in the cold. Carpenter peered inside. Simon lay across the seat, a long coat across him like the family cat. One of his books was on the floor, open where it had slipped from the boy's hand.

"I don't like doing it," Carpenter said.

"Simon understands, sir. And, if it means anything to you, so do the rest of us. I'm sure he'd rather be with his father than at home with some nursemaid."

"But not here, Jennings," said Carpenter. "Not right in the middle of it. I must be mad. Who knows what Rafferty's got up his sleeve?"

"You know if anything goes wrong the lads from A Division will be all over this carriage like a shot, sir. He's safer here surrounded by policemen than he would be at home."

"And what really bothers me," said Carpenter, "and this can go no further—"

"Of course, sir."

"—is that there's another lad out here somewhere, the same age as my boy, and God knows what trouble he's getting himself into."

Jennings turned to face his superior. He was shaking his head.

"I tried, sir. I really did. But he's a headstrong little sod. Pardon my language, sir. I—"

"I know Jennings. You've done a good job. In fact, I'll be requesting a promotion for you as soon as this is over."

"Sir?"

"You heard. Now all we can do is hope that Shaw boy hasn't got himself in so deep that we can't get him out."

THREE RATS CAPERED past Alan's foot. He kicked at them, but missed and almost tipped himself into the sewer. It stank as bad as he remembered. Things floated in the sludge that oozed past his feet, things he'd rather not think about. He moved slowly because the sewer's walkway was slick with rotting garbage. But there was a light a little way off, falling in stripes as if coming through…

The grate.

Jabbing his toes into the sewer wall's flaking masonry, Alan managed to raise himself high enough to see into the room beyond the grate. It was pitch black, which meant it was unlikely there would be anybody there. Lucky, because the grate gave an echoing whine when he lifted it aside. He didn't need any light. His memories of the workhouse's layout would be more useful than any lamp. Shoving the satchel in first, he dragged himself into the old boiler room where the ovens still skulked in the dark. Rats scuffled somewhere nearby and occasionally brushed Alan's feet with their coarse bodies. Lord knew how many made their nests in St. Martin's now. Alan felt for the wall and followed it to the corner, then along again. He tripped over a pipe, cursing but not falling, and when he eventually found the cellar stairs he had to use his hands to climb his way to the top.

He'd made it to the ground floor. Light came in through windows that ran the length of the room. The stairs were at the other end in a dark alcove. Alan was certain that Rafferty couldn't have seen him in the sewers, although the villain had insisted otherwise. Now he was surrounded by windows, the villain could be spying from anywhere. Rafferty had been very specific about where the package should be left, although Alan couldn't understand why it mattered in an empty workhouse. Still, the madman was rich, probably mad, and very drunk. Alan was certain he'd be hunted down if Rafferty got wind that his directions hadn't been followed to the letter.

Up the stairs and through another long room. The light was stronger here. Alan crossed to the windows and realised that he'd lost his bearings. The windows weren't bleeding light from the street as he'd thought, but from the central yard created by the workhouse's four wings. Light flickered around some sort of immense engine. It filled the yard, with only a small path left around the edge. Twin chimneys pumped smoke into the air. He could see steam escaping through valves all over the great machine, as if struggling to keep the power inside. Wires like some giant spider's silk ran along beams and up poles to a host of lamps wrapped in small cages. Hanging in bunches like grapes, those lamps were the source of the strange fluttering light; like no gaslight Alan had ever seen. It was fierce, and somehow cold. Steel walkways hung across the void, joining the great engine to the surrounding buildings. Alan watched as a man walked past, dressed in a white coat, carrying a clipboard. Ducking out of sight, the boy stepped away from the window, and wondered what to do. He wished that Dick was with him like the last time he crept through these rooms. Someone to tell him what he should do. But he brushed it aside. There'd be no Dick to tell him what to do in America, either. He'd be on his own, just like he was now. He had to carry it through. He had to finish it, or suffer the fate of that small metal box. He had to go now, or not at all.

Bounding up the stairs, arms pumping, the satchel bounced against his hip, and he burst into the room beyond—ready to be rid of the thing.

Alan knew the room. It had once been lined with looms, shuttles flying back and forth; women lined on either side, Alan and the other children huddled beneath the mechanism. It had been dull even in daylight, but now the room was brilliantly lit. Row upon row of glowing strips ran along the ceiling, screaming that cold light, forcing Alan to shade his eyes. When he could finally see, he caught his breath.

Formed in silent ranks, the Automatons waited for their christening. Each one was taller than any man Alan knew, a smoke stack rising over their left shoulder like the barrel of a slung rifle. They were shimmering brass from feet to pill-shaped head, with one glimmering glass eye offset on their faces. Their barrel-like bodies were squat, making the limbs look disproportionately longer. Alan found himself stood next to one without realising he'd moved. He reached a hand upward, stroking a plate on the Automaton's chest. It was engraved with a number and just below, a slot, wide as his palm but thinner.

"That's where the punch-card goes."

Alan span around, pressing his back against the Automaton which might as well have been a wall for all it moved. Professor Normen stood in a long leather apron, his shirt sleeves rolled above the elbow. He wore one pair of glasses over his eyes and another high on his head which appeared to have thicker lenses, and in one hand he held a sphere the size of a croquet ball. It was black and fibrous like charred wheat, with a red band around its centre. At the bottom of a nearby Automaton's body was a grate, similar to the one on the cooking range at Harker's. Opening it, Normen slid the sphere inside and closed it again. He patted the Automaton as he turned back to Alan.

"Now he just needs lighting. Wonderful stuff. Burns nice and slow. Very little stoking necessary." Making his way over to a table by the window, the Professor picked up a large ivory card. Holding it to the window, light speared through a pattern of little holes in its surface. "Each job has its own card. Each vocation, if you like. Miner, hauler, whatever."

Alan stuttered but couldn't make any words.

"I'll bet you're the boy that Inspector Carpenter told me

about. Alan, was it? A bright lad, he said. I insisted that I be here to meet you. Carpenter wasn't happy about it, but he also assured me that dog Rafferty would be long gone by the time you arrived, so I feel quite safe. Plus, lots more tinkering needs to be done before the procession."

Alan blinked up at the Automaton as if it might offer some sanity, then looked back to the Professor.

"Why don't we go downstairs and see the Inspector. I'm sure he'll be glad to know—"

The windows along room shook in their frames. Then came the sound; a crack so loud that it made Alan crumple to his knees, hands clasped over his ears.

"Oh dear!" he heard the Professor yell as the little man stumbled to the street-side windows. "Oh dear, oh dear."

"BLOODY HELL!"

From the street, Carpenter and Jennings watched the smoke column rise, under-lit with orange. The thunder of the explosion was coupled with another sound like a sudden summer rain storm; the sound of a lot of falling water. Simon's sleepy face was plastered against the carriage's window, he rubbed at his eyes and refocused on the inferno over the rooftops.

"Jennings, take some lads and find out what that is," yelled Carpenter.

Blowing his whistle, Jennings ran off toward the Thames where the billowing cloud of soot and smoke bloomed toward the low-hanging clouds. Carpenter leaned into the carriage where Simon was shuddering.

"Don't worry, son. Just an accident, I'm sure. Nothing

to worry about at all, we're safe."

"What about the people over there?" asked Simon, pointing to the smoke which was starting to roll in on itself. Carpenter didn't have an answer.

"Inspector, whatever has happened?"

"I'm afraid we don't know, Professor. It could just be a coincidence." Carpenter turned toward Professor Normen who stood in shirt sleeves and braces, one hand resting on Alan's shoulder.

"Ah, I believe you already know my young friend here."

CARPENTER AND PROFESSOR Normen stood beside the police carriage in tired debate. Jennings wiped the soot from his face as he approached.

"It's lucky no one was hurt. The explosion happened right out in the middle of the Thames. A few boats moored close by won't be much good other than as firewood, and Black Friars Bridge took a scorching, but nothing serious. Bloody lucky, really, sir."

Carpenter shook his head. Simon and Alan sat a little way off, side by side on the workhouse steps. Simon was showing the urchin one of his new penny dreadfuls, the type with only pictures and speech in little white circles. What did Simon call them? Graphical Adventures. Obscure things. They would never catch on. Simon was pointing to the page with Alan following along like teacher and avid pupil, both boys engrossed.

"Young Alan has made it quite clear," said the Professor. "It seems our urchin friend had a bout of good conscience. He stowed the device meant for my lab under the seat in

Rafferty's carriage, intending to escape to you gentlemen and ask for protection. However, the villain insisted that he would be followed until the task was done, and so the poor lad still had to break into my laboratory even though he no longer had the device."

"But Rafferty didn't wait around," said Carpenter, nodding. "The coward headed for the river, hoping to escape by sea. It'd be the last place anyone would look with carriages and trains being so much faster. The bomb had a timer, I suppose."

Normen shook his head. "I believe he intended to detonate the explosives with a small remote device. Alan says Rafferty had a box with a switch on it. It only looked like a box to the lad, but I think it's a fair assumption what it really was."

"Where'd a man like Rafferty get that kind of thing?" asked Jennings.

"It doesn't matter," said Carpenter. "The Automatons are safe, apparently. We've done our job. Get this thing under control, Jennings. I've got an arrest to make."

Striding toward the two boys, he removed the handcuffs from his belt. He could hear Simon explaining the Graphical Adventure book as he approached.

"And here Titus Gladstone is defeating the evil Mayan King with a right hook to the jaw. That's how heroes do it, you see? One punch. Pow!"

As the boys noticed Carpenter's shadow fall over them, they finally looked up. Alan's eyes had set hard and he raised his chin a little higher as Carpenter approached. As Alan stood on the steps with Carpenter on the pavement, they were almost eye to eye.

"I haven't done anything wrong, Chief. You know that," Alan said. But his voice still sounded a little wet.

"I'd say you've done plenty wrong. Breaking and entering. Aiding and abetting."

"I did the right thing, though!" Alan was almost whining, but stopped himself. He cleared his little throat to remove the lump.

"Yes, eventually. But you did it the wrong way, boy. You should have come to the police. And now you'll have to come with me."

"Father, you can't arrest Alan," said Simon, standing beside the urchin like his polar opposite. "Not—"

"Be quiet, Simon. Get in the carriage."

Inspector Carpenter slipped the handcuffs onto Alan, and realised that they wouldn't tighten enough for his small hands, so he held him by the arm instead. Professor Normen stood in Carpenter's way.

"I must insist, Inspector, that you let the boy go. No harm has been done and much more *could* have been if he hadn't been involved. As much as I'm grateful for what you've done, I simply won't allow it."

"I'm afraid the law is the law, Professor. At the very least this boy needs constant supervision. He's fraternised with a known criminal element. Who knows what trouble he could cause?"

"Then expect my complaint on your desk tomorrow morning."

Carpenter nodded. "I understand."

Both boys climbed into the carriage with Carpenter

behind. They jolted forward and, coming to the end of the street, circled around the square Alan had crept across not an hour before.

This was what people had always said. Never trust a copper. He'd heard it a hundred times and still hadn't listened. It was all he could do to not shout and scream and rant at the Inspector. He'd done nothing wrong. If anything, Rafferty had been blown up by his own damned device and Alan had saved the day. The other boy, Simon, just kept looking at him with eyes that wobbled like pork pie jelly. He wasn't a bad sort. Just a shame his father was a crooked old copper with manure for brains.

Eventually, the carriage pulled to the pavement and Carpenter opened the door. Alan hesitated before stepping down.

"This ain't the police station," he said. "What are you doing with me?"

The house was only a window and a door in width, but three storeys high and connected to its twins which stretched all the way down the street. Three steps led up to a door that had seen better days, but had once been painted deep red.

"Like I said to the Professor, Alan, you need constant supervision. There's no way I can let you go until we know what's become of Rafferty. So, you'll be staying with me and Simon until then."

"You can't do that," snapped the boy. "It's not fair."

"Oh Alan, it'll be fantastic," said Simon. "We're really going to keep him, Father?"

"He's not a puppy, Simon."

Simon laughed.

"Of course not, but he can really stay with us?"

"You can stay as long as you like, Alan. For all my joking, you've done a good job, albeit in a roundabout way. If you'll let us, myself and Simon would like to offer you a bed. And maybe a meal. Definitely a bath."

"So, Alan, what do you say?"

Alan looked to Simon's hand resting on his shoulder, then to the policeman and the house beyond.

"Woof?"

4

CARPENTER COULD HEAR the boys upstairs. There was some shouting, the occasional bang on the boards and a sloshing of water, but there was laughter in between so he knew that no one was being drowned. He sat by the fire, his nose pinched between thumb and finger, as if the pressure would squeeze some sense out of the last week. He almost leapt out of his skin when the front doorbell jangled on its hook. He got up, a little wobbly from the two glasses of scotch, and made for the hallway. There was no way of seeing who was beyond the door, something he always intended to fix, but his revolver hung on the rack next to it. Sliding the pistol from its holster, he braced his shoulder against the door and opened it a crack.

Professor Normen stood smiling like the idiot he wasn't.

"Awfully sorry to disturb you, Inspector, but I'm afraid Helen wouldn't rest until she'd met the hero of the hour." Helen stepped out from behind her father, lifting her skirts in a courtesy.

"We've met before," said Carpenter, shaking his head free of the whiskey cobwebs.

"Ah. Ahaha. I'm afraid I meant young Alan," said Normen.

"Oh, right. Yes. He's taking a much needed bath at the minute. But I doubt he'll be much longer."

Carpenter stepped aside and the Normens went through to the living room. He smiled to Helen as she passed him, uncocking the revolver behind his back and putting it away before following.

"I'll just go and see how the boys are doing. Help yourself, Professor."

Normen was already at the bureau, pouring himself a drink.

"Much obliged!"

Almost afraid of what he'd find, Carpenter made his way to the bathroom and knocked at the door.

"Hello? Who is it? Awfully sorry but we're a little busy at the moment."

There was laughter from inside and then:

"Boi moi loife, I've never 'ad a baath befow!"

Carpenter shook his head and ducked into the bathroom.

Alan and Simon were both stood in front of the mirror, Simon in a dressing gown, Alan in a towel. They carried on chattering, imitating each other's speech until Carpenter's head span.

"I swear, if you two carry on, I'll not know the difference between you," he said.

"Whoi eva not? This lad 'as blonde 'air while oi 'ave brawn," said Simon, laughing.

"I don't talk like that!" laughed Alan.

"Oi dant tawk loik tha'!"

"Alright, you two, enough. Both of you get dressed. We've got visitors downstairs."

"Visitors? Who would come at this hour?" asked Simon.

"Oh yes, Father, who ever would visit at such a monstrous hour?" chirped Alan.

Carpenter's jaw dropped. Father? He hadn't expected...but of course the boy was just imitating Simon. There was nothing meant by it. The boys were too busy laughing to even notice the faux pas. Carpenter cleared his throat and gave both boys a stern look. They tittered to silence after a few seconds.

"Professor Normen has come to visit. He's brought Helen, Simon."

"Oh no! Quick, Alan, we have to get ready." He pushed Alan toward the door, past his father and into the bedroom.

"I'll just wait downstairs then shall I?" said Carpenter.

PROFESSOR NORMEN SAT by the fire, across from Carpenter. Helen studied the single shelf of books in the house; three of them books of law, the rest were Simon's. She stood with her hands behind her back, rocking on the balls of her feet so that her skirts swayed back and forth, and hummed to herself. When she turned, her smile let Carpenter know that the boys had arrived.

Simon and Alan stood together, if only because Simon was shoving the urchin forward. Alan was wearing some of Simon's clothes, a little loose on him at the wrist and neck. Carpenter couldn't help thinking that with a few square meals, Alan would soon look healthier. And he was already much cleaner. His fingernails were too short and ragged, but the dirt had come out of his hair so that it almost glowed blonde; the only real difference between the boys.

Helen moved across the room, curtseying to the boys. Simon bowed and introduced his new friend who stepped forward and thrust his hand into Helen's shaking it wildly. Helen backed away as if struck. Carpenter held his breath. But Helen giggled and offered her hand again for a gentler shaking. Carpenter breathed out. There was still plenty of work to be done then.

"Father tells me that you saved his machines from being destroyed. He says you were very brave and very clever," said Helen.

Simon was nodding along, patting Alan on the shoulder.

"He's a hero!" he said.

"Well, I'm not sure about that. I think I was lucky, to be honest with you. And when it really counted the Chief was there. I'm just glad I didn't get blowed up."

Helen giggled again.

"Your accent is wonderful, Master Shaw," she said.

"You should hear Simon do it! Do it, Simon."

"Oi dant knaw what yaw talking abaht!"

The children laughed, and the fathers turned back to their own conversation.

ALAN STARED AT the dark ceiling. Simon was gently snoring beside him, his bottom stuck into Alan's side. Carpenter promised him his own bed if he decided to stay, even a small one. And he said there'd be clothes too once he'd fattened up so they wouldn't have to be bought twice. Alan had offered the four pound he still had in his jacket as rent.

Carpenter laughed and put it into a small ceramic money box that had once been Simon's. That was good, really, because Alan knew that he couldn't go back to Harker's to get the rest of his money, so he'd have to start saving for America all over again. Still, four pounds was a good start. If he worked hard maybe he could save the rest in a year. Carpenter must have things that needed doing around the house.

A thump from outside the window made Alan sit bolt upright. He turned his head to the square of moonlight beside the bed. His eyes expanded until they were like goose eggs. Outside, something slid across, blocking out the moon. Alan opened his mouth to wake Simon, but nothing would come out. Eyes fixed on the moonlight silhouette, he quested with his hand across the bed until he grasped Simon's pyjamas, and shook.

"What is it?"

Alan pressed a finger to his lips, then pointed at the floor where the silhouette was making industrious movements on the window ledge. Simon gasped.

"Oh my god. What is it?"

But Alan couldn't reply. The lump was blocking his throat so that he couldn't even gulp.

Both boys huddled together on the bed, shaking violently. There was a scraping, like a fork on a plate. Alan dared lean over to see the window. A thin knife blade was wiggling between the window's frame and sill, working its way toward the latch. Simon was clutching at him, trying to get him to draw back, but Alan was frozen. The knife finally found the latch, wiggled, wiggled, and slid it aside. Alan darted out of bed, grabbing the window frame, trying to yank it down, but whatever wanted to get in was stronger. The frame jerked out of his fingers, bumping as it shot up and the bogeyman squirmed through.

Simon finally found his voice and yelled.

The creature was upright, impossibly tall in the darkness, and had Alan suspended by the front of his pyjamas. The smell of old smoke and bilge water drifted from it. Simon stood on the bed, hitting the thing, trying to pry its powerful fingers from his friend. Alan started to struggle, kicking out as hard as he could.

"Stop squirming, you little brat. I'm only going to kill you," snarled Rafferty. His breath smelled like old bread. He lashed out at Simon, knocking him back onto the bed with a squeal. "Piss off, you. I've got business with your friend. So you're a copper's son, eh? Well, you had me alright, Alan. You had me fooled. But now I'm going to kill you so we're even."

The bedroom door burst open. Alan heard a shout and he was spun around to face the door. Rafferty's arm was across his chest, holding him close to the villain's damp clothing. He could smell charred wood on the wool, like a bonfire after the rain. So he'd been close to the explosion, but not close enough.

Carpenter levelled his revolver, backlit by the doorway, and shouted something again.

"I don't think so, Copper," slurred Rafferty. "Me and the boy here have business. So why don't you just run along so we can—"

There was a smash and Alan dropped to the floor. He

crawled, not thinking of direction, as Carpenter dove on the Villain. But Rafferty was already out cold. Through his ringing ears, Alan could hear crying that wasn't his own. Carpenter crossed the room as calm as could be, and sat on the bed holding Simon, the boy cupping a bleeding hand.

All around Rafferty's oozing head were shards of a ceramic pig and four glistening pound coins.

THE AUTOMATONS MARCHED from Trafalgar Square in three long rows, surrounded by cheering they couldn't appreciate. The sun seemed magnified on their brass skins, shifting over them in sheets of light. The sound of their feet on the old roads was the ticking of a clock carrying London into the future. People lined the streets, any plans for work forgotten for a day. Bunting caught on the breeze, banners flapped and hands waved as the Automatons chugged toward their baptism. Protestors with badly-spelled signs were lost among the celebrating hordes. From his carriage, Professor Normen waved to the crowd.

And on the front page of every newspaper was a daguerreotype of a shiny new Automaton, with a small blonde boy on its shoulders.

Extract from *The Morning Post,* Front Page,
April 24th, 1842.

Taking a circuitous route from their birthplace in the laboratory of Professor Lionel Normen, which was once known as the St. Martin's workhouse, a new fleet of mechanical men made their maiden march through the streets of London on their way to Buckingham Palace, in order to be christened by Her Majesty Queen Victoria. Named Automatons by their creator, the mechanical marvels are the first combination of analytic engines as designed by the reclusive Charles Babbage, and the new field of anthropo-engineering as championed by Professor Normen himself. Designed to perform manual labour such as dock work, mining, hauling and road maintenance, the eight feet tall Automatons have come under much opposition from the working classes, who feel that introducing the machines will deprive them of their livelihoods. However, the protesters were swallowed by the masses of cheering Londoners yesterday as three hundred Automatons marched into Buckingham Palace and performed the changing of the guard for the amusement of Her Majesty. What is perhaps most amazing about this historic event is how close to catastrophe it came. Inspector Carpenter, of the Metropolitan police force's A Division, described how a despicable plot to destroy the work of Professor Normen was narrowly averted with the assistance of a young street urchin from Covent Garden. It seems that the eleven year old boy, named Alan Shaw, once a denizen of St. Martin's workhouse himself, came upon vital information regarding the arsonist plot to use explosives in the destruction of the Automatons, and sought to assist Inspector Carpenter's A Division in apprehending the culprit, putting himself directly in harm's way in the process.

It seems that our fair city of London, the centre of a British Empire which continues to grow and prosper, would be far worse off today if it weren't for the actions of a peasant class boy from Covent Market and his unwavering bravery in the face of insurmountable danger. Not only did this small boy save many lives which might have been lost in an explosive blast, but also the future of our empire as the leading industrial power of the world.

Extract from *The Illustrated Times*, Page Four,
April 24th, 1842.

Last night, between the Waterloo and Black Friars bridges, an explosion on the river sent broiling smoke and a torrent of Thames water flooding both the north and south banks of the river. Damage to private and freight ships was widespread, but casualties were surprisingly low due to the river halting the conflagration's spread as the ship where it originated sank in swift order. The gas works, south bank timber yards and even Bridewell Hospital have all been rendered unusable, the latter being evacuated to several other hospitals nearby, as the stench of the Thames' water, which was sent sky high by the explosion only to rain down on the nearby streets, has made those areas inhospitable to any but the noseless. Inspector Carpenter of the police force's A Division has stated that the explosion was in fact linked to a supposed plot to destroy St. Martin's workhouse—

1

Norwegian Sea (Lat. 69.068563, Long.-1.494141),1846

CAPTAIN BREWER STEPPED out onto the deck, narrowing his eyes against the wind. A wave crashed against the SS *Precious'* side and she listed. Brewer wiped sea foam from his beard and turned up the collar of his jacket. Toward the aft, men dragged the trawl across the deck, feeding the net over the side where it spread out like a cauliflower head. Leant on the railing, observing the fishermen, was the young man Brewer was looking for. He didn't bother to shout over the sea's roar, instead making his way around the bridge, past the engine cylinders and the foot of the smokestack that chugged above.

Alan stared at a piece of paper, once folded in three, steadily reading the delicate handwriting with the determination of a weak reader. Brewer tried not to read it over the lad's shoulder, but he couldn't help noting the signature. Helen.

"How'd you get mail all the way out here, then?" he asked.

Alan jerked to attention, the letter disappearing from his

hand so fast that Captain Brewer wondered if he'd seen it at all; unlike a ratty copy of *Titus Gladstone Adventures* which was always on show, stuffed into the lad's back pocket.

"Ummm...I found it stowed in my duffle bag, sir. Must have been put there before we cast off," said Alan, adjusting his cap and tucked the scarf back into his coat.

Brewer stepped up to the railing next to him.

"A lady is it?"

"A friend, Captain."

Brewer set his jaw at the boy, and decided not to push it. He gestured to the men below, straining against the sea, the fish, the net, and anything else the universe threw at them. "Learning anything?" he asked.

"Yes, Captain. Learning every day."

Brewer looked out to the sea. "Me too, lad."

Alan could see the Captain was in one of his 'moods', as the crew called them. They hated it when Brewer was like this. Reflective. Quiet. As if he knew something they didn't. But one of the first things Alan had learnt on board the SS *Precious* was that seamen were superstitious at the best of times, and would attribute luck whether good or bad at the drop of a hat. Alan liked the Captain's moods. It was then that he was easiest to talk to. Most men had to be drunk to get that way. As far as he knew, Captain Brewer didn't drink at all.

"Something you need me to do, Captain?" asked Alan.

"Not right away, no. Stand a minute." He seemed to think for a while, eyeing the lad before him. Curls of blonde lifted around Alan's cap like yellow tongues. There was a faint shadow around his top lip and chin that might have been the beginnings of stubble in another year or so. Captain Brewer nodded toward the men hauling the net again. "Paying close attention?"

"Yes, sir. I'm hoping to help with the next haul if the Mate will let me."

"Maybe you should stick to other duties for now. We don't want you being dragged off to sea or end up in there," said the Captain, motioning to a pit of gasping fish that made up most of the aft section.

"Wouldn't be the first time I was somewhere I shouldn't be," said Alan, smiling.

"What makes a young man want to work a fishing vessel nowadays, Alan? There seems no sense in it. So many other things to do." Brewer spoke, but his eyes had turned where the ship's enormous paddle wheels churned the sea to a creamy froth. He jammed his hands deep into his pockets to stop his open coat from flapping since it had no buttons. Alan stood with his arms wrapped across his chest. His scarf flapped loose and he had to tame it.

"Wanted to see the world, Captain. And my father wouldn't let me join the regular navy."

Brewer nodded. "It's bloody dangerous on the sea as it is without picking fights. So how's your travelling of the world going?"

"Seeing mostly the wet parts so far," said Alan. Another wave cleared the railing. Alan spat the salt from his mouth and wiped it with the sleeve of his jacket.

Brewer laughed. "Maybe you should have joined a rail gang instead."

"Been in gangs, sir. Never was good for me."

"I'll bet you have. You've not always had good boots, have you lad?"

Alan looked down at his feet. His boots were up to his calf, with trousers tucked inside, and slick with seawater.

"It's a turn of phrase, lad. I mean you've seen the darker side of life."

Alan's eyebrows lifted.

"How can you tell?"

"You've something of the streets about you rather than the parlours. Accent, mostly. You talk well, but I can still hear it in you. And when you mention your father, you always sound like you're apologising."

Already pink with the wind, Alan turned a deeper red.

"Just an observation," said Brewer. "Sailors get to read people pretty well. Sometimes it's your only way of knowing someone out here. Russian, Swedish, French, all kinds of English. They're all gangs of a sort, just like in London. All talking different languages. And, as you know, it's best to know where a gang's coming from before you cross them."

"I thought you said you don't pick fights on the sea?" said Alan.

"You're a thrill seeker then, are you? All young men of your age are the same in some way. But no, we don't often. Not unless they try to take what's ours." Brewer fell silent. His mood had shifted. "I reckon King will want some potatoes peeling."

"On my way, sir."

Keeping one hand on the rail, Alan left Brewer alone to watch his men.

"I DON'T LIKE him," said King, wiping his hands on a rag. Three fish lay on the block in front of him, headless and gutted. As the ship rolled, a pan slid along the work surface into his hand.

"He's just a lad, what's not to like?" asked Resnick, the First Mate, in a warm Russian accent.

Alan sat across the kitchen on a little stool pretending not to listen. His fingers rolled a potato round and round, his keen little knife slicing off the skin before joining its naked brothers in the pile. The game was to see if he could peel it in one long strip. He was getting pretty good at it.

"Everything. Have you ever seen him eat soup?"

"I think you've been staring at fish heads too long," said Resnick. "Next chance we get, you're going ashore for a break."

"He looks at it. Really looks. Like he's looking at his Ma. He's odd," said the cook, eyeing Alan.

"The same could be said of a man who volunteers to wear a hat like that," the Russian smirked.

"There's nothing wrong with my hat."

"And there's nothing wrong with the boy. He just likes soup. A lot. Leave him be," said Resnick. "Alan? When you're done, Jones could use you."

Alan looked up from his latest potato and nodded. The Mate stepped out over the bulkhead, leaving them alone.

"How many spuds you done, boy?" asked King.

Alan checked the pile.

"About thirty. How many do you need?"

"About thirty. Piss off to the engine room out of my way."

Alan finished his potato. His eyes on the cook, he stabbed the little knife into it like an Aztec making sacrifice, and slammed potato and knife down next to the cook's fish. King sneered at him. Alan's eyes were slits but his mouth stretched into a smile. He doffed his cap before hopping over the bulkhead and bowing with a flourish.

King launched a fish head at him through the door, but missed.

2

JONES WAS JUST coming out of the engine room as Alan arrived, wiping his face with a rag which did nothing to get rid of the dirt. A dark-glassed visor hung around his neck, the same shape as the white circle around Jones' eyes. Heat and noise from the boiler belched into the corridor so that Alan leaned back from it. Jones stepped through the doorway, tugging on the waist of his overalls so the trouser cuffs cleared his feet. The shoulders hung half way down the little man's arms and he'd rolled the sleeves to clownish effect.

"You should get a belt," said Alan.

"I should get a new job, you mean. I'm thinking of working somewhere that needs a suit. Maybe The Strand. Do you think I'd make a good tailor?" said the engineer, leaning back through the door for his tool box and having to haul on the overalls' waist again.

"If they're your idea of a good fit, then no."

Jones laughed. "Cheeky! I'll send you back off to the kitchen if you prefer."

"I'll be good," said Alan, smiling.

"You don't know how!" Jones slipped his arm around

Alan's shoulder, steering him back the way he came. Their voices and footsteps echoed around them with a metallic tone as they moved down the narrow corridor. "Let's get up on deck. After that boiler, I could use the fresh air."

"After being up on deck, you'll be wishing you were back down here."

"Most likely," Jones chuckled.

Alan went up the ladder first.

"What needs fixing?" he said, bracing himself for the wind that would come when he opened the hatch. He yanked on the locking wheel. The wind caught the hatch as he expected but he managed to release it slowly and disappeared above. Jones' head followed, then his baggy shoulders and the rest of him.

"The trawl winch is sticking," the engineer shouted over the wind. "Why they don't tell me this before they cast it, I'll never know. It'd be a lot easier with the net slack."

"But then there'd be no fun in it, I suppose," said Alan, leading the way across the deck. They wove between other sailors at work; dragging tangled net, slackening rigging against the wind or weaving their way between tasks.

"Sometimes it'd be nice to have an easy job for a change," said Jones.

Setting his toolbox by the winch, he plucked a cord of the taut net like a cello and shook his head. Taking a screwdriver from his box, he started to remove the winch's housing.

"But if you didn't need me, I'd still be stuck in the kitchen."

"You've got an answer for everything, haven't you?"

Alan shrugged, miming that he didn't know what to say. Jones shook his head and handed Alan the metal plate. Alan peered around the little man who produced a pair of spectacles from a pocket with little shields around the lenses to stop the sea spray obscuring them too much. Around the drum, where the trawl had slid sideways into the mechanism, strands of frayed rope had collected like rolled wheat.

"Every bloody time," said Jones. "Here, take that and brace the drum from this side."

Alan took the metal pole, slotting it between housing and drum and heaved. The drum didn't move.

"That was pathetic. Come on lad, where's your cockney muscle?"

Alan set his jaw at the winch. Sliding his hand around and bracing the pole by his shoulder, he put his meagre weight behind his next push and the drum slid back a few inches.

"Good lad! Now keep it there."

Jones reached his hand into the mechanism, his little fingers prying at the collected rope. When that didn't work, he took a thin knife from his toolbox and began sawing at it. Alan was sweating. Something seemed to be tearing between his shoulder blades. Sweat and sea spray mingled on his skin like long-lost twins. Shadows started collecting around his vision.

"Bloody…hell—" he managed through gritted teeth.

"Just a bit more," said Jones, sawing faster. "We'll make a sailor of you yet, Shaw."

The cord came free with a *twang*, Jones yanked back his hand and Alan released the drum all at the same time. The pole clattered to the deck and so did Alan, sprawling himself out until his vision cleared. Jones demonstrated the winch's smooth running with a tug on the wheel.

"Perfect. Say, you alright lad?"

"Nothing a hot bath and a pork pie wouldn't fix," said Alan between panting.

"When we moor in London, I'll buy you one of each," said Jones, setting the winch's housing back in place.

BRACING HIMSELF IN the bridge's doorway, a seaman yelled across to where Brewer stood against the prow.

"Captain! I've got a distress signal!"

Brewer stomped across the deck, seamen stepping aside and then following in his wake until he had a school of sailors behind him. He stepped into the bridge where Resnick was leaning over the seaman's shoulder. The crew crowded beyond the door. A sphere coated in green material sat in a fat brass housing on the desk. Iron filings were released from a compartment in the housing, and sent crawling across the surface in bristling lines to the motion of the magnets inside. In two places, the filings coalesced into a solid shape, long and thin. A ship. The seaman clasped his hands around his ears, holding a pair of receivers like metal conches. Twisting a dial, he honed in on the radar's bearing. Brewer could hear a pulsing whine even from where he stood, then the mumble of intermittent speech.

"Resnick, what's going on?" asked the Captain.

The First Mate took one of the receivers from the seaman and pressed it to his own ear.

"Definitely a distress, Captain. Russian," he said,

thumbing toward the radar sphere.

"Sinking?"

"No, sir. They're under attack."

"By?"

"Doesn't say. But there's only one ship on the globe."

Brewer scratched his chin. "A submersible, maybe? Alright, Resnick. Get us there."

Resnick yanked a metal funnel from above his head and began to talk into it. Almost instantly, a dial above the steering wheel began to register extra pressure in the boilers. Captain Brewer left the bridge as the seaman rattled off a bearing to the First Mate. Resnick knocked the locking clamp from the ship's wheel and began to turn, easing the power lever forward. The *Precious* juddered against the acceleration and turned, with smoke from the stack streaming thin in the wind, carving its way across the waves.

Alan pushed his way to the front of the group as Brewer stepped out.

"Pirates," he said. The crew darted away without another word, spreading out across the deck. Alan was left alone before the Captain.

"Should I go help stoke the boiler, sir?"

"No. I want you with me."

The crew dragged long, steel crates onto the deck. The rifles inside, wrapped in oil cloth, were handed out to every man and a box of shells between two. They unwrapped their weapons like peeling bananas. Captain Brewer took two rifles.

"Do you know how to shoot, Alan?"

"No, sir. Not rifles at any rate. I can throw a stone

pretty well."

"Doubt that'll be of much use today." Brewer handed Alan the wrapped rifle and began to uncover his own.

"Slide back the bolt, check the barrel is empty," said Brewer demonstrating. Alan copied what he saw. "Take a shell and place it in sharp-end first with your thumb. Slide the bolt up and lock it." The rifle clack-clicked. "Got it? Good. Now, put the rifle into your shoulder. A little further over, brace it like this. That's right. Sight along the barrel. When you fire, it'll buck, so keep it held tight and widen your feet. Breathe out slowly. Squeeze, don't tug, the trigger. Got it?"

Alan lowered the rifle. His hands were shaking already. Brewer reached over and steadied him.

"It's only dangerous if you're on the receiving end, lad. If they fire back, just get down below the railing and stay there. No one expects you to get shot today."

Alan nodded because the tightening in his throat stopped him from talking.

From the bridge's roof, a sailor called out, pointing to the horizon. Smoke billowed there and Alan thought he could see the distressed ship, with something alongside he couldn't make out.

"What the hell is that?" said the Captain, as if reading his mind.

3

THE CREW BRACED their rifles on the port railing in two rows like medieval pike-men. No one spoke, each man steeling himself for the fight. But as they drew close to the Russian ship, mutters began to break out.

The Russian ship was twice the size of the *Precious*, a three-stack freighter with immense paddlewheels that towered above the little trawler. But it was the strange vessel attached to the Russian hull like a limpet that had the crew muttering. Its body was the length of *Precious*, perhaps, with a curved roof like an upturned boat, a dorsal fin at the furthest end stuck up from the water. But it appeared there was more of the ship under the water than above it. A row of small windows showed men moving inside, and twin domes at one end revealed a pair of men who wrestled with a complicated set of levers. But it was the tentacles that drew everyone's eyes. They extended out of the vessel's bow, and clamped onto the Russian freighter's paddlewheel and hull. The Russian crew could be seen above, prising at the tentacles, shooting them, running from place to place without purpose or hope as the paddlewheel was slowly crushed and wrenched from the ship's side.

"A squid," gasped Alan, his jaw slack.

"A bloody ship is what it is," Brewer answered. There was an insignia painted on the queer vessel; a red wolf, eating a small yellow sun. Brewer shook his head. "Although it's like no pirate vessel I've ever seen." He raised his voice. "Brace yourselves! It's just a ship, lads, and it'll sink like one."

The Russians crowded to their own railing, watching the little trawler approach. They were shouting, cheering.

"They're quick to cheer and quick to complain, Russians," said Brewer. "No offence Resnick."

"None taken, Captain." The First Mate loaded his rifle and braced it on the hand rail.

Alan wasn't listening. He was fascinated by the other vessel.

The *Precious* came about, bringing the rifles alongside the squid-ship. Inside, the pirate crew could be seen through the portholes, scuttling this way and that. The man in the nearest dome, face covered with some tubular breathing apparatus, looked their way and motioned to his partner.

Brewer yelled to open fire and the *Precious'* rifles released a volley. Alan fired, the first buck of his rifle knocking him backward. Sea water soaked into the seat of his trousers, straight through to the skin. He clambered up to the railing again to see the result of his shot. Bullets kissed the vessel's hull, making sparks but no damage. The squid lay unperturbed.

"The windows! Aim for the windows!" someone yelled and another volley loosed. This time Alan braced his shoulder, and managed to fire without falling. He thought he followed his bullet's path but it could have been anyone's. The squid's pilot flinched as bullets hit the dome around him, but they only left white scuffs across the reinforced surface. He made an obscene gesture and appeared to be laughing behind the mask.

Both pilots hauled on their controls, and the Squid-ship's tentacles shuddered, then began to rise. Like the fingers of a grasping hand, they released the Russian freighter, setting it rocking in the sea, and the Squid-ship slipped beneath the waves with a thrash of the mechanical appendages, the Red Wolf emblazoned on its side seeming to wink as Alan watched.

The Russian ship's crew began to cheer again as the Squid-ship slipped away, but Alan's stomach became full of lead when he saw the true damage that the pirate's submersible had done. On dragging itself close to the freighter's side, the odd vessel had bored into the hull, creating a hole big enough for men to pass through and steal the freighter's cargo. Lucky for the Russians the hole was above water level, and as Alan watched, a number of the crew appeared in the aperture and began to assess the damage.

Alan had just enough time to feel relief for the Russians before he saw an immense mechanical tentacle rise like a cobra from the sea beside the *Precious*. Water cascaded from the metal surface, causing a mist filled with rainbows as the sun hit it. Someone screamed. The crew scattered as the huge appendage whipped across the deck, wrapping itself around the trawler. From the sea rose three more, grabbing the ship from beneath and trying to peel it like an orange.

Sailors threw themselves at railings or grabbed for hatch covers as horizontal became vertical; the ship screeching a metallic lament as it heaved to the side. Pulled down into the sea, water began to lick the *Precious'* deck. The fish pit spilled its contents, freeing the captors back to their home in a silver avalanche.

Alan slid along the deck, the hungry sea reaching up to take him. Throwing his arms out, he caught the fore mast with his ribs, knocking the air out of his lungs. Men slid past, some managing to catch themselves, but others span into the sea with a brief yell. Screams and wails came from everywhere. Some of the crew had managed to steady themselves enough to fire at the tentacle. The sound of ricocheting bullets joined the human voices. Still the tentacles dragged at them. Alan swung his leg up onto the mast that was now almost horizontal. Safely held, he swung the rifle from his back and fired at the nearest tentacle. The gun clicked against an empty chamber.

Hearing a grunt, he turned to see King climbing up behind him. The cook had an axe in one hand, a knife tucked into his belt, his brow bunched into a hideous scowl. At first Alan thought the cook was coming for him.

"Out of the way, boy."

King shoved Alan aside, dragging himself hand-over-hand along the mast. Crawling up the slope, he moved, painfully slowly, toward the rising tentacle. At the top, the cook wrapped his legs around the mast and swung the axe as hard as he could to thud against a thick rubber joint where the tentacle's sections met. The tentacle shifted its grip as if unaware of its attacker, letting go of the doomed ship and leaving the cook with nothing to fight, with the axe still embedded in its side. The *Precious* righted a little but the sea wasn't going to let go so easily. Water flooded into hatches and portholes, pulling the *Precious* down. The tentacle swung again, cleaving across the deck, tearing the roof from the bridge and hatch lids from their holes. Someone yelled to abandon ship but it was cut short by a scream. The sailors with enough sense leapt into the sea before the tentacle struck again. Others weren't as lucky. Slamming against the broken vessel, another tentacle sent vibrations through the ship strong enough to make Alan's body feel numb where he clung to the mast. He heard a scream and looked up in time to see King tumbling into the sea. Alan watched the cook's slow-motion cartwheel with fascinated horror.

His mind was blank. Nothing much registered, be it the screams of drowning men or the yawning sound of tearing metal, until the sound of the cook's body slamming into the sea. Like a hypnotic, Alan blinked once, twice, and finally took in the carnage around him; the ship being shredded, the waving arms of men already in the sea, the screams of those who could still draw enough breath, a line of pale faces, high above, as the Russian freighter's crew saw their saviours torn to pieces and, like a thorn in a giant's foot, the little axe still stuck out of the tentacle's joint as it rose for another strike.

Alan could have whimpered, or cried, or screamed for his loved ones. But instead, he snarled. Down the mast's slope he slid, toward a box at its foot. Cracking the lid, he took out the buoyancy aid and slung the ring around his shoulders. Then he turned back, scurrying up the mast like a monkey where King had shuffled only moments before, headed for the tentacle, the axe.

Someone called his name above the din, but every strand of his being was focused on that axe. Near the mast's tip he swayed with the tortured ship's movements. This was just like home, just like running across rooftops slick with rainwater. And he'd run across that skyline a thousand times or more. Wrapping his wrist around a section of loose rigging, Alan rose to a crouch and shuffled around to face the tentacle's swaying mass, and threw himself forward.

Landing as if on a saddle, clinging to the tentacle's slick sides, Alan's flailing hand found a hold somewhere between metal and rubber. He dragged himself up, arms straining against his own weight. Far below, those of the *Precious'* crew still able were pointing and shouting. And on the seemingly forgotten Russian ship a crowd was forming to watch a boy attack the mechanical squid.

The axe was still there. Alan reached out for it. His fingers slid around the handle. The tentacle dropped away from him as it came down on the *Precious* again. Alan's thin body trailed behind, clinging to the rubber joint for dear life. Below, the little ship buckled, snapping almost in two. Fire burst from the cracked hull. The boilers exploded, punching a hole in the ship's side. Flame caressed the tentacle. Alan buried his face from the wave of heat as it engulfed him, fighting the urge to plunge into the cooling sea as his skin tried to crinkle, turning him to a roast turkey.

Alan screamed as he dragged himself up. He was crying now, although there seemed no use for it. He wiped his blurry eyes and saw that the *Precious* was lost. Standing on shaky legs, he steadied himself with the axe's handle. When the tentacle settled a little, he yanked on the axe, bringing it clear of the joint. Through the gash he could see the mechanism, a series of pistons and linkages ripe for the cutting. Raising the axe above his head, Alan screamed and swung it down as if executing a dragon.

The metal under his feet thrust up to meet him, sending the boy soaring through the air. His feet flew over in a cartwheel; head whipped aside with the force. There was a moment of silence as the wind tore at him, and he hit the sea like a rock.

4

CHOKING THE AIR into his lungs, a mouthful of water came with it. Alan dipped beneath the waves again but the buoyancy aid brought him back. He threw back his head, gasping, his arms clawing for air as another unrelenting wave hit him square in the face. He gargled, coughed, screamed and finally came to rest, sprawled like a dead seagull on the floating ring.

The Russian vessel was still there, the victorious squid coupled to its hull once more. But where the *Precious* had been was only a peppering of floating crewmen; some alive and clinging to wreckage; some not so lucky. Wiping the water from his face, Alan saw King float past, his face buried in the sea. Alan yelped and tried to scramble away but the buoyancy aid was stopping him. The cook's corpse floated closer. Alan scrambled at the sea like a dog, but couldn't escape. The dead cook was going to collide with him, drag him down, perhaps. That *would* be the man's way.

A hand came down on his collar, dragging Alan out of the water and up onto a section of broken mast. Resnick grabbed the quivering boy close to him, throwing off the buoyancy ring.

"It's alright, Alan. I've got you," rumbled the Russian.

"King…"

"I know. I know. Just catch your breath."

But Alan fought against the First Mate who eventually had to let go. Alan stared around, frantic, without really seeing.

"Alan, calm down. You're alright," said Resnick in his soft Russian accent.

"The Captain?"

Resnick shook his head. "I don't think so."

The tears came hard and fast. Alan's knees buckled to the temporary deck and Resnick had him in his arms again.

The body of the Squid-ship parted the waves, with that Red Wolf seeming to lick its lips with glee when it caught sight of Alan and Resnick huddled together. The uniformed men inside the submersible were clapping each other's shoulders and pointing at the destroyed crew. Alan scowled at them, his face streaked red with tears. He could see that they all wore a uniform. That same sun-eating wolf on their shoulder. He could have dived into the water, swam across, and torn the squid-ship open with his bare hands if only Resnick didn't have hold of him.

The water by the Squid-ship erupted in a geyser of boiling water.

Alan and Resnick threw themselves down as the torrent hit. Under the water, twin trails of streaming bubbles passed beneath them and blooms of red hit the squid's side. The vessel lifted out of the water, sending waves radiating as it came down again. The lights inside the vessel's portholes blinked a fiery red, making the squid look angry, panicked.

The pirates inside fought each other at the escape hatches.

Resnick was pointing.

"Look. There."

Sea water rolled as something huge passed, a narrow dorsal fin slicing a trail across the sea. Alan could make out a silver shape under the water, moving toward them at speed. Another stream of bubbles and the Squid-ship cracked open like a mussel shell. The tentacles still in view went slack and the squid-ship's carcass slid into the waves, spewing steam and oil.

Another submersible erupted from the sea like a basking whale, sea foam caressing its silver hide. Small flaps along its sides ejected excess water like briny fireworks, spraying Alan and Resnick where they cowered on their piece of wreckage. Men in blue uniforms crowded behind oval portholes. Larger windows at the front showed the vessel's bridge, manned by more uniforms.

A voice boomed out, crackling with static.

"This is Her Majesty's Submersible Class Vessel, *Encounter*. Are there any survivors of the merchant vessel?"

The crew of the Russian freighter cheered and wailed, clapping each other in embraces and pumping their fists in the air. Some ran to their rescue boats and began lowering them to the sea. Along the *Encounter's* spine, hatches lifted and crewmen began pouring out, running down to the sea's edge, unwinding mooring ropes from concealed compartments in the submersible's hull and tossing them out to sea.

Alan looked to Resnick, but the First Mate just stared at the empty patch of sea where his ship had once been, shaking his head.

The first Russian rescue boat drew alongside a few minutes later and they were hauled into it with the rest of the *Precious'* survivors. Only ten shivering men including Alan and Resnick were left. No Jones, no King, and no Captain Brewer.

As the Russians heave-ho'd the oars, bearing them toward the waiting *Encounter*, a thick-set Russian man lifted Alan into his arms. He threw a blanket around the lad and hugged him, babbling in a language Alan couldn't understand. Soon, there was a wall of smiling, chattering faces.

"I don't understand what you're saying," Alan said. The Russian laughed, although surely he didn't understand either.

"He said you're insane," said Resnick, managing a sombre smile. "But very brave."

Extract from *The Morning Post,* Page Five,
September 29th, 1846.

Reports of eruptions in the Norwegian Sea were denied yesterday by Admiral Tryon of Her Majesty's Royal Navy, who stated that the reports in yesterday's edition of The Morning Post *were much exaggerated. He went on to categorically rebuff 'the ridiculous superstitious ramblings of drunken foreign seamen' who had testified that a strange craft attacked their own freighter and sank an English fishing vessel using impossible machinery on September 21st, which were linked to a similar series of odd mid-sea thefts around the same area. Admiral Tryon also denied the involvement of a submersible class Royal Navy vessel as there were no such craft in the area at the time, and stated that the sinking of the fishing vessel was due to an ill-fated decision by its drunken Captain to trade with the much larger Russian ship, causing the former to be crushed and the latter to be dangerously damaged when the swell between the ships rose uncontrollably.*

Among the few survivors was one young London boy, who readers may recognise as the street urchin once made famous for thwarting a plot to destroy the St. Martin's workhouse. Alan Shaw, now aged sixteen years, was adopted by Inspector Carpenter of the police force's A Division after the event, but could not be found for comment.

1

London, England, 1851

A CARRIAGE BOUNCED along Hyde Park's tree-lined avenue, where the sun pierced the canopy like midday searchlights. Where the hackney's horses should have been, a small two-wheeled steam engine chugged with an urgent *puht-puht-puht-puht* like a mechanical wheelbarrow. At the other end of thick leather reins, the driver hauled the engine under control, tendons straining against the raw mechanical power. Eyes squinting behind his heavy goggles, his teeth gritted as the carriage drew up on the open lawn. Stomping a pedal by his foot released the engine's built up steam in a harsh gout. The carriage began to roll without the power and the driver eased on a second pedal. Brakes squeaked and the carriage slid to a stop. The driver sagged, lifting his goggles to wipe the sweat from underneath. Across his eyes was a stripe of untanned skin where his goggles had been; the tattoo of a London Cabbie.

Inspector James Carpenter stepped out of the carriage first, dressed in his best uniform. Then Simon in a brown suit and spectacles. Finally, the trio was complete when Alan stood beside them in dark blue, a lick taller than his father and equal of his brother.

"I wish you two would stop growing. You're starting to make me look bad," said Carpenter. "I swear you stored compost under your mattress as children."

"I wondered why there were laburnum under my pillow in the morning," said Simon.

"I had mushrooms," said Alan.

"That's because there wasn't mushroom to turn over, eh?"

Carpenter and Alan looked at Simon, who flushed.

"Sorry."

They laughed and Simon flushed a bit more.

"Alright boys, best behaviour. Simon, avoid telling jokes. Alan—" he paused, his brow softened to a pleading slope "—try not to break anything."

Carpenter set off across the park with his sons in tow. The lawn was full of gentlemen in tall hats and ladies pale beneath their parasols, all headed into the growing crowd.

The Crystal Palace sat on the lawn like an iceberg; glass walled from curved roof to lawn. The sun heliographed from the glass and steel, setting colours dancing across the grass and observers alike.

"Spectacular," said Simon.

Alan nodded: "Looks fragile though, doesn't it?"

"Let's hope we don't find out," said Carpenter, pointing at Alan with an accusatory finger.

As they approached, an usher began to address the crowd.

"Ladies and Gentlemen, I have the honour of welcoming such an esteemed audience." The usher clasped his hands together as if trying not to fidget. A red cord stretched across the Crystal Palace's door. A pair of scissors stuck out of the usher's pocket. "The Great Exhibition has been many years in the planning and, as you can see from this incredible facade, has already surpassed anything conceived by our age. What you are about to witness, Ladies and Gentlemen, is the largest collection of technological advancements and cultural achievements from around the world."

The crowd clapped with dull politeness.

"Bloody hell, I wish he'd just cut the ribbon already," muttered Alan.

Simon's mouth stretched in a smirk.

The usher continued as if he'd heard.

"But without further ado, let me say once more: Welcome, ladies and gentlemen, to the Great Exhibition!"

First holding up his scissors, the usher snipped the red cord with a flourish and pushed the great glass doors inward.

The crowd moved forward, everyone maintaining a delicate distance between their neighbour. No one pushing, and no one talking. So, when the first few people began to gasp, everyone behind heard it.

The main hall stretched straight up to a curved roof, the immense vault filled with refracted sunlight. Ranks of sculptures lined either side of the hall. Alan looked up as they walked under a marble stallion, hooves pawing the air. Soldiers in stone held out their spears, scholars their hands and busts of philosophers showed nothing but timeless patience to the milling crowds. Rounding a vase three times his height, Alan finally saw the most incredible addition.

Hung in the Crystal Palace's vault as if in mid-flight was a dirigible, its inflated sack of red material sat like a bloated dragon above the wooden gondola. Propellers turned lazily on either side of the barge-shaped hull, more for show than propulsion.

"Now *that's* impressive," Alan whispered, and then wondered why.

"It's incredible. Manned flight," said Simon.

"Do you think they'd let us take a look inside?"

"Shouldn't think so."

"One day soon, Gentlemen!" The approaching man had a stride like an Automaton. He clasped a pipe in one hand, the other held behind his back. With the pipe, he gestured to the dirigible. "These beauties will be carrying us all across the empire very soon if I'm any judge. A couple of years and they'll be common as carriages."

"And you are?" asked Alan.

"The man who'll be flying them. Apologies, young man, my name is Earnest Harrigan. Captain in her Majesty's fleet of the sea. Soon to be of the air."

"Nice to meet you," said Simon, offering his hand.

"Very nice to meet you, too," blustered the Captain, squeezing enthusiastically at Simon's metacarpals. "I'll leave you to appreciate the rest of the exhibit. But when these beauties finally go up, you be sure to ask for me."

"How could we possibly refuse?" said Simon, nudging Alan.

"You can't!" Harrigan strode away to pester someone else.

"What an arse," said Alan.

"He seemed alright to me," said Simon. "I wonder where father's got to."

They found him talking to Helen Normen and a tall stranger in pristine naval uniform. Helen had grown up considerably. In her bonnet with golden waves tamed beneath and a pale blue dress, she could have rubbed elbows with any royal ladies. Alan caught his breath when he saw her, and had it knocked out again when Simon elbowed him.

"Steady on," whispered Simon.

"Alan! Simon!" Lifting her skirts, but not high enough to cause a scene, Helen trotted toward them. Simon took her hand gently, but Helen had other ideas and grabbed both their hands, shaking them as if whipping a team of horses. Alan noticed the navy man raise an eyebrow.

Massaging his bruised hand he said: "I knew I'd rubbed off on you."

"And why shouldn't I greet my oldest friends with enthusiasm?" asked Helen.

"Maybe because your companion disapproves."

"I saw that too," said Simon.

"Companion? You mean husband, Alan." Helen leaned slightly forward at the waist, fists on hips, like she had when chastising him as a child. Only this time she was smiling. "I'm married. Not that you'd know, always being off on your travels and never writing. You can meet him now, though. Better late than never."

Helen bustled back to her naval officer with his permanently raised eyebrow and twitching little moustache.

"She looks beautiful," said Alan as they made their way

over.

"She looks married," said Simon.

"Apparently. So when were you going to tell me?"

"When you arrived back from Crete. Then at breakfast. Then before we got in the carriage. Then when we got *out* of the carriage. Then just now before she came over."

"You're a failure for not warning me," said Alan, clapping his brother's back.

"Yes, I know."

Their father turned to meet them. His eyes ran over Alan's face, checking if anything hostile was harboured there.

"Simon, Alan, this is Percy Harrigan," he said.

"Harrigan? Like the Captain?" asked Simon. "We just met him."

"Percy is a lieutenant," chirped Helen.

"Captain Harrigan is my father," added the officer.

The group fell silent. Carpenter looked to his boys for something to talk about. Alan was eyeing Percy over folded arms. Simon was looking from face to face for some conversational saviour. Helen decided to try.

"Alan was in the navy, too," she said.

Percy sniffed. "Civilian, I presume."

"Merchant," said Alan.

"A leaf floats but I wouldn't call it a Navy." Percy all but snorted.

Carpenter and Simon looked at each other like worried bookends with a violent tome between them. Carpenter stepped forward to make sure he could shield Percy if necessary.

"Percy, you're being rude," said Helen.

"Yes, Percy," said Alan. "Don't be rude. Especially when you don't know who you're talking to."

Percy sniffed again, as if something pungent were assaulting his senses.

"I know exactly who you are, Shaw. Where you're from, and how you live on the charity of others. How you followed my Helen like a puppy. Honestly, I can't think of a better thing for you to do than running off. You've saved my Helen the worst embarrassment of her life. I should probably thank you."

"Oh boys, don't fight over me," said Helen, laying a hand across her narrow bosom.

"I think you need to settle down, gentlemen," offered Carpenter.

"If you've got a point, you better get to it," said Alan, his fists balled inside his pockets, ready to draw and engage at the slightest excuse.

A lace glove slipped into Alan's arm. At the other end was a young woman dressed in deep red silk. Her skin was the colour of warm pine, with eyes large and dark. Her mouth made a delicate cupid's bow, adding to her doll-like appearance. A mass of mahogany tresses piled up, expertly tousled on top of her head.

"Am I interrupting?" she said in a rich Grecian accent.

"Actually, I think you're just in time to save us all," muttered Carpenter.

Alan turned to the girl who melted under his gaze.

"I'm glad you're here," he said, and extended a hand to Helen. "Helen, this is Adrienne. We met in Crete. Well, just outside, actually."

Adrienne giggled behind her hand. Helen barely concealed a sneer.

"She studies the sciences at the Heraklion Institute," Alan went on "Her family have donated some of the Greek artefacts for the exhibition. She gave me the pleasure of agreeing to meet me here before she has to run off on a research trip."

Helen eyed the girl's dress, how the skirts hugged her hips, the corset was obviously unnecessary in providing the pleasant curves, and there was much more shoulder on show than in Helen's own dress. She extended a hand but her face retracted.

"Charmed," she said. "The sciences are an interesting choice for a lady."

"Very pleased to meet you." Adrienne only managed to touch Helen's fingers before they were drawn back. "Um, I'm afraid I was never very interested in needlework and such."

Simon cut the yawning silence with a little too much enthusiasm.

"I've been trying to get into the Royal Institute, myself," he said, and realised that he was talking a little too loud to compensate. "Ahem, that is, there's so much competition. How did you find it, Adrienne?"

"Very hard. Bustles and Bunsen burners rarely mix."

Simon's generous laugh warmed the air which had grown chilly with verbal jousting. Adrienne laughed with him. Alan looked between them. He didn't even understand the joke.

"Percy, come on, you can get me some punch," said Helen, leading her husband away in a swirl of skirts.

Adrienne searched Alan's face.

"You're really glad I came?" she asked in her sweet accent, squeezing his arm.

But Alan didn't answer. His attention was already elsewhere.

THE EXHIBITS ON their wooden podiums were slices of worlds. The rugs of ancient Persia, tapestries and clothing from China, Native American carvings and weapons. Alan stood for a long while staring at those pieces of history, but he didn't see them. His mind, as always, was where these wonders came from. India, Japan, Africa. Parts of the British Empire and beyond that he'd never been. Simon was squinting into a glass case when Alan came over to him with Adrienne on his arm.

"Tell me this isn't proof of evolution," said Simon, gesturing to the case.

"What is it?" asked Alan. "It looks like a beaver half way through a duck lunch."

Adrienne tittered behind her hand.

"Exactly. It's a platypus. You can't tell me God got bored of making proper animals and decide to throw this together."

"I suppose not. Then again, God has ideas we humans can't possibly comprehend. Who are we to question?" said Alan.

"I didn't realise you were so God-fearing," said Adrienne.

"He's not, Miss. He just does it to annoy me."

"What other reason could there be?" Alan smirked. "Now come away from your specimens. The lower halls are filled with things much more interesting than your duck-creature."

At the entrance to the Technological Advancement area, a dirigible's propeller sat with the inner workings on show. Nearby, a stand held a trio of small logs like tightly bound wheat bales. Beneath, diagrams showed them being made from a process which compressed plant waste and laced it with small amounts of anthracite. According to the inscription, The Pressurized Combustion Alternative (or Jerry-Logs) devised by the eminent chemist, Hercule Gerrarde, would power the next generation of steam devices by burning hotter, cleaner and cheaper.

"Alchemy amazes me," said Adrienne. "There once were men in Greece who would spend their whole lives trying to turn lead into gold, or discovering the essence of life. All of the things they discovered. Think where we would be without it."

"I'd expect a woman of science such as yourself to find alchemy—how shall I say—quaint? Not quite up to our modern level of understanding." Simon huffed on his glasses and wiped them before taking a closer look at the exhibit.

"Lead to gold or blowing things up...seems like the same kind of madmen to me," said Alan.

"Well it's not," said Simon.

"I'll consider myself told."

"Actually, it seems somewhat more enticing than modern chemistry with its rules and methods," said Adrienne. "I think we have lost the sense of wonder that science one had. We have become perhaps too methodical, too objective. To experiment, after all, is to begin an adventure."

Simon was nodding along. "Very well said. Science has become rather devoid of love and intuition. That's where a lady such as yourself will always have an advantage over tweed-wearing old codgers—"

"You wear tweed all the time," interrupted Alan, but he was ignored.

"—If you don't mind, I would very much like to apply that argument in my Institute application next year. Bring back the adventure to science, I say. Excellent idea."

Adrienne bowed her head. "Be my guest."

A little way inside, people were taking turns in a large Faraday cage, squealing and laughing at the harmlessness of thousands of volts of electricity. Alan and Adrienne waited in line to try it, and Alan stole a kiss while a miniature lightning storm crackled around them.

But as they came to the next exhibit, Adrienne shrank behind Alan.

"Dear Lord," she said. "I don't think I'll ever get used to seeing those things."

The Automaton stood head and shoulders above them. Its head turned, scanning the crowd with its single eye. When it saw Alan, it nodded its head and mimed the doffing of an invisible cap. Alan nodded back.

"Do you know this one?" asked Adrienne.

"It was a little joke Professor Normen built in to the punch card programmes," said Simon. "Every Automaton recognises Alan. It's a kind of thank you."

"The old bugger had a strange sense of humour," said Alan.

But beside the functional Automaton was a new marvel; the Mark II. Smaller than its brother, the whole design was more compact. It now had twin roving glass discs rather than a single eye. Beneath, where a mouth might be, was a small slot. A foldable crank sat below the usual punch card input, and a paper label bearing the inscription 'Babbage Inside'. The plaque beneath it read:

> The new Automaton Mark II refines the earlier design to become stronger and more versatile. This model is powered by robust clockworks that require no steam to power. Each Mark II Automaton is now capable of winding its own mechanism for endless, uninterrupted service. The inclusion of a tickertape output combined with the latest Babbage technology allows the Mark II Automaton to relay messages and provide feedback on work it has performed.

"A clockwork heart?" said Adrienne. "Incredible."

"And they can talk," said Simon pointing to the mouth slot. "Albeit only on paper. There's something petrifying about that."

Alan just looked between the marvel and its older brother.

"I wonder what they'll say to each other," he said.

"The kind of philosophy best discussed over lunch," said Simon.

"Oh yes, Alan, I'm famished."

"Come on then. Plenty more to see this afternoon."

BENEATH THE DIRIGIBLE and between the rows of gesticulating marble, small tables had been set in place. Alan dragged over a couple of extra chairs so that everyone could sit together.

"I don't think they were happy about you stealing those chairs," said Simon, nodding toward a married couple at the table Alan took the chairs from.

"It's not my fault we're more popular than them. They've got a tongue in their heads."

Simon laughed but flushed. Adrienne tittered. Carpenter shook his head and said: "You can take the boy out of Covent Garden—"

"Who'd want to take the Garden out of me? It's part of my charm," said Alan, taking a bite from a small triangle of cucumber on pale bread. "Is meat not allowed at these things?"

The tea, brought by a host of imported French waiters with towel-hung arms, was strong and sweet and there was coffee for the others. Plates of sandwiches were nibbled rather than devoured until only one triangle was left. No one ate it. Above the diners, people still lined the balconies and walkways; mostly the lower classes who had come from all over the country with their day tickets, dressed in their least threadbare clothing with freshly washed necks and feet. Alan wondered if any of them could afford to eat today, and if they would have anything when they returned home.

He set his pathetic cucumber and bread triangle back on the table.

The polite murmur of afternoon conversation ruptured by a piercing scream. It cut across the Crystal Palace's vault and floated down like volcanic ash to the upturned faces below. Alan, who was swinging on his chair, nearly fell back.

Carpenter got up, dabbing his mouth with a napkin.

"No rest for the wicked—" There was a shattering of glass and accompanying screams from the crowd around him as men and women dove for cover. "Bloody hell!"

Alan was up, folding himself over Adrienne, shielding her with his back. Glass peppered his suit and hair. Looking across at Helen, he saw that Percy was in a similar pose, his jacket glistening. Their eyes met like crossed swords.

Alan searched around the room, looking up just in time to see a group of oddly dressed men running along the balcony above. Alan turned to Simon, a manic grin replacing his face.

"I'll flip you for it."

Simon checked his pockets. "I'm afraid I don't have a coin."

"Neither do I," Alan chuckled, and started to wade through the tables. But Adrienne grabbed his coat sleeve, halting him for a moment. Standing there, her skirts and bodice flaring around her body like the petals of an upturned rose, she managed to knock Alan dumb. All thoughts of thrills were lost as Adrienne placing her laced hand on his cheek.

"Please, Alan, don't go. It will be dangerous, I'm sure."

Taking the hand in both of his, Alan kissed her palm. Then he gave her a sly wink, and darted away, weaving through the crowded tables like a grass snake.

"No need to worry, Adrienne." Simon could barely keep the tiredness from his own voice. "He does ridiculous things all the time. He's quite good at it."

Alan swerved through the cowering gentlemen and ladies until he was lost in the crowd.

Carpenter's whistle rang out clear over the murmuring crowd and the scraping of chairs on stone. The Inspector began to yell to a couple of constables who ran in from the park. Alan barely heard any of it. He bolted along the hall, darting through the tables, his face turned up to the retreating criminals above. There were two elevators to the upper floors crafted from steel and glass, but both were on the upper level. Yanking on the call cord, one elevator began to crawl down toward him. He groaned.

Leaping across a gap under the elevator, Alan's fingers latched onto the counterweight as it hurtled upward, the *clack clack clack* of the mechanism counting off the wasted seconds. Every eye on the floor and along the balconies followed his rise as if watching a firework. Dragging himself up by the elbows, Alan dove off as the counterweight passed the first floor, and landed running. Finally, he could see the criminals properly. There were five of them, each dressed in brown overalls. Their hair and eyes were covered with tight leather caps and tinted goggles so they looked like sprinting toads. One carried a vase under his arm. Grecian, one of Adrienne's father's. One of the men saw Alan in pursuit and called out a warning to the rest.

"Oh no you don't," muttered Alan, doubling his speed. As he ran, he cast off his jacket, his waistcoat giving him more freedom of movement. A cowering lady was knocked aside with a squeal as he ran past. The jacket landed perfectly over her head and she screamed until someone uncovered her.

The criminals were by the balcony's railing, uncoupling a series of ropes which stretched out across the Crystal Palace's vault and up to a circle cut from the glass roof. Alan reached out his hand, grabbing for the nearest man as he closed in. His fingers managed to latch onto clothing as the criminal leapt off the balcony, swinging out over the hall behind his companions. The man jerked as the slack was taken up, dragging Alan out over the balcony. One hand on the struggling criminal, the other scraping fingertips to keep himself from tumbling, Alan was seriously debating letting the criminal go when the overalls tore, answering his dilemma, and the man began to fall. The distant floor of the Crystal Palace sprawled below, covered edge to edge with hundreds of upturned faces like baby birds waiting for the worm to drop.

Alan lurched.

Someone grabbed at his waistcoat and hauled, dragging him back to safety.

"Are you mad, boy?" he heard his saviour ask, but he was already running, tucking the scrap of brown material into his pocket.

He jogged away from the balcony's edge, skidded to a halt and reversed direction. His breath was hot in his throat and he panted there, only for a second, eyes fixed on the dirigible hanging in its vault directly over from where he now stood, feeling the burning in his thighs and calves. Exploding forward, Alan hurtled toward the balcony's edge, arms scissoring, eager to taste open air. Again, people scattered. Alan's foot hit the balcony railing and he shoved hard. Screams rang out below as his silhouetted form hurtled across open space, arms stretched out like a cat. Time ran liquid as the leap became a fall. All colour drained out of his face as the dirigible's balloon began to slip past. His arms wheeled, feet kicked as if he could swim the rest of the distance, hands grasping where there was nothing to latch onto. All nineteen years of his brief life began to replay in his mind.

Before he could finish a memory of the blistering winter when he'd taken a thrashing from three larger boys outside Harker's Tavern, his body slapped against the dirigible's balloon, hands scrambling for purchase on the netting that lashed it to the gondola. His shoulder wrenched, but numbed fingers managed to hold tight. He physically shook his head. With a brief glance at the distant ground, Alan began hauling himself up the netting.

The criminals climbed their ropes hand over hand, slowly ascending to a hole cut in the Crystal Place's roof. Alan spotted the one with the vase strung across his back. That was who he had to catch if he was to impress Hele-Adrienne.

Below, a horde of blue uniforms were ushering people out; some more clustered at the elevators. Alan thought he heard his father's voice above the crowd, probably yelling at him.

The dirigible's balloon shifted under his boots, giving him a comical, bouncing gait as he crossed the red material. Three tethers stopped the airship floating away. He moved from one to the other, prising at the knots with his fingers, making slow but steady progress. The first rope whipped away when released, almost taking his eye. The next one, he turned his face away. Checking his quarry above, they were also moving slowly. He had time. He could do this. The first and second knots undone, one end of the dirigible was starting to rise. As the balloon moved and the gas inside shifted to the highest point, Alan found the last rope slid away from him, slipping free of the dirigible all by itself. Finally free and with no other propulsion, the dirigible began to rise as a few constables and Inspector Carpenter made it to the upper floor railing. Carpenter yelled something. His face was bloated red, his neck pulsing. If Alan didn't make good, this was going to end in disaster. But he couldn't hear what his father said and so he just waved as he rose toward his quarry.

Moving so he was stood directly below the villain's escape hatch, Alan found he was catching them up as the dirigible built momentum. Reaching, he could almost grab the last man's boots as the villain crawled out onto the roof.

The dirigible hit the glass surface.

The glass was strong enough not to break, but the elastic material of the balloon bounced as it struck its upper limit. With the only outlet being the hole cut by the villains, Alan was propelled upward; thrown into the air like an acrobat with no net. His yell was cut short as he came back down again, slamming into the Crystal Palace's fragile roof, knocking the air out of him.

He froze.

Hands pressed against the glass pane, he watched as a crack formed underneath his body and snaked out across the fragile surface. He tried to hold his breath, willing himself to be lighter. But the dirigible's balloon pressing underneath gave the glass extra strength and Alan managed to roll aside before the pane could break properly.

His ribs hurt, his chest ached and one shoulder felt like it was made from a hot poker. He sat up to take stock and hold himself for a second.

The criminals were uncoupling themselves from their ropes when he stood up, his knees shaky. Sighting him again, they bolted for the edge of the roof.

This was it. He had them. There was nowhere left to go.

The thieves turned to run along the Palace's length. Alan tried to move faster but couldn't, his feet slipping on the curved glass surface where the toad-men's boots held fast.

Like perching ravens, five triangular frames coated with black material waited at the roof's edge. One by one, the thieves reached them and threw themselves forward without pausing; hurtling from the building like lemmings with the black frames in hand.

Alan gasped, and tried to stop, his bottom hitting the roof. Skidding along the smooth glass, he tried to spread himself out. His shoes hit thin air as he threw himself over onto his stomach and grasped at anything he could to slow his hurtling progress. Already bruised, his fingers complained as they gripped the steel frame of a glass pane and jerked Alan to a halt, everything from his chest down dangling over the lawn far below. This time he didn't look down. Gritting his teeth hard enough that they felt they might shatter, he hauled with everything he had left and finally scrambled back onto the roof and lay panting.

Wiping the sweat from his eyes, he watched the hang gliders curve away across London's rooftops.

2

THE CELL DOOR slid closed with a clank.

"Father, there's really no need for this," said Simon.

Carpenter ignored him.

Inside the cell, Alan slumped down onto the bunk and laid his head back against the wall.

"You're nineteen years old, Alan. A man, now. You need to grow up."

"I almost had them caught," said Alan. "I almost had them while your constables were falling over themselves."

"And you almost brought the Crystal Palace roof down on hundreds of people's heads. And you could have died in the process."

"I suppose you'd at least have had a spare cell, if I had." Alan kept his eyes on the ceiling and hands clasped across his stomach. Simon cleaned his spectacles feverishly with a handkerchief.

Inspector Carpenter pressed against the bars as if he were the one caged. Alan welcomed their protection but didn't show it.

"It took four hours to get the dirigible back down. It

wasn't a working model. They had to empty the balloon to lower it. There were foreign dignitaries from all over the world. Ambassadors and Princes."

"And what did they think?"

"I don't know. If they want your head, there's nothing I can do. Do you understand? Being the Inspector's son won't get you out of everything."

"It got me *in*to this cell alright."

"Gah!" Carpenter span away and stormed up the stairs to the station's ground floor. There was the distant sound of a slamming door.

Simon shook his head at his brother.

"I'll talk to him," he sighed.

"You might want to give him this," said Alan, waving the strip of cloth he'd torn from the toad-man's overalls.

"What is it?"

"One of their uniforms tore off."

"I'll make sure he gets it. Here, I got you something. Don't tell father, for the love God."

Simon handed a thin paper bag through the bars. Alan took no time peeking inside. It was the latest issue of *Titus Gladstone Adventures*, the cover displaying the eponymous hero, his dark hair long and shaggy, his shirt torn, rifle in hand. There was a beautiful young native American clinging to his arm, and a giant black bear raging on its hind legs before them.

Simon made to leave, but hovered by the door for a second. He took in his brother and the cell, something like an animal, something like a boy sent to bed without supper, with the Graphical Adventure in his hands.

"Turn to the back cover," Simon said.

Alan's raised eyebrow seemed to pull his face up with it, so that he regarded his brother.

Simon gave him a wink before stepping out.

Alan looked down at the Graphic Adventure in his hand and flipped it over. A smile smearing across his face like chocolate. On the back cover, as with every issue, was a leaflet the reader could tear away to display in a bedroom or save in a journal. This month's poster showed Titus, looking straight out of the page, pointing with a stern finger toward Alan's chest. It read:

Remember readers, when evil strikes…

…what would Titus Gladstone do?

WITH HIS HEAD laid toward the bars, Alan watched a rectangle of sunlight from the tiny window as it descended the wall, crossed his body and started to sweep over the floor. The sun went down somewhere beyond the window, pitching him into darkness, and woke him again when the rectangle of light reappeared the next morning.

The cell's bunk reminded him of beds gone by. Sleeping on shelves and in hay lofts, or under tables. What he would have given for a hammock as a boy. With plenty of time on his hands while waited for his sentence or release, he thought about Harker's Tavern, and his old friends. He should go back. See them. It had been a long time. Surely long enough that they couldn't be angry at him for disappearing. They'd be happy to see him. He wondered if Sarah was still there, and how she looked; if Callas had mellowed. He made a promise to go back while he was in London. But it wasn't the first time he'd made it.

As boots crunched on the jail's steps, Alan laid hands behind his head and closed his eyes.

"Good morning," said Simon. "Had a good sleep?"

"It's taking a while to get used to the bed not rocking under me, but I managed."

"Father spoke to the dignitaries."

Alan rolled over to finally face his brother: "And?"

"Adrienne's father supported you, and the other Mediterraneans followed suit. Some of them suggested you get a medal. One offered you a job."

Alan laughed, and swung his feet down off the bunk. "Which one?"

"Italian. He said he could use a young man of your calibre."

"And father said?"

"Something about the cost of the medication to keep you sane," Simon smirked. The iron key scraped in the cell's lock and the door slid open on its spring. "Come on, I want you to meet someone."

"What about breakfast? I'm starving."

"Afterward."

They climbed the steps to the station which had changed very little since Alan's first visit as a boy. A huge telegraph station with four operators took up one part of the room which had once been a number of desks, and an Automaton officer painted blue and with a faux-police helmet welded to its head stood idle in a corner for use in the event of rioting. Someone had hung a sign reading 'I'm only sleeping' around its neck.

Passing Carpenter's office, Alan caught a glimpse of his father through the office's horizontal blinds, but the Inspector didn't look up.

"How mad is he?"

"Worse now you've gotten away with it," Simon muttered.

They passed out of the station's rear door and across the yard to a ramshackle building at the furthest end. Simon opened the barn-style door and stepping into the gloom.

"Is he bringing me out here for torture?" asked Alan.

"Something like that."

The barn's insides were cleaner than Alan expected, but cluttered. Three rows of long benches took up the middle of the room. Stacks of shelves to the rear and by the door held jars and bottles of coloured fluid, some with bloated forms floating inside. Cabinets along one wall held all manner of dried specimens and powder boxes. Behind the nearest bench, eyes fixed to a large brass microscope, was a thin man in a white coat.

"Alan, this is Doctor Miles Schneider, the Police's scientific expert."

Dr Schneider's eyebrows lifted, dragging his eyes up with them. Trimmed short at the back and sides, a shock of blonde hair curled over the top of his head. Alan extended a hand.

"Alan Shaw," he said.

The doctor took his hand but instead of shaking it, turned it over to look at his palm.

"Shaw? That's not your name," said the Doctor in a

Germanic accent.

Alan looked to his brother, who was smiling.

"Yes it is."

"No no no. Look at your hair colouring, just like mine. The thickness of your fingers and squared tips. Brown eyes are an anomaly, I'll admit. Probably from your mother's side. But your shoulders and nose, my friend, state a Germanic ancestry much like my own. Your father's side, I presume?"

"I wouldn't know," said Alan, taking back his hand.

The Doctor's face fell.

"Ah, my apologies. Simon tells me that I sometimes take my work too far," he stuttered.

"And we're mostly grateful for it," said Simon. "Doctor Schneider works for the division as a consultant. He helps solve crimes with the application of advanced chemistry."

"So what does that have to do with me?" asked Alan.

"Ah yes, the clothing sample," said Schneider. "Interesting."

Shuffling under the bench, he brought up a long wooden box and snapped open the clasps. With a pair of tweezers, he lifted the cloth sample to the light.

"The brown material is unremarkable really. Nothing but common pollen spores, there. But the white cloth, now there lies the mystery."

"White? I didn't get any white," said Alan.

"On the contrary. When you tore the overalls, you snagged some of the clothing beneath," the Doctor patted the microscope beside him. "I found some interesting chemicals staining the cloth. Four separate ones, in fact, and managed to recreate them, with a little imagination."

He gestured to a set of vials in the box, containing what looked like sand, blood, tar and water.

Alan sniffed. He picked up one vial and shook it a little, then set it back down. He wiped his hand on his trousers, just to make sure.

"They're far more interesting chemically than they appear," assured Schneider.

"What are they used for, Doctor?" asked Simon.

Schneider sighed. Removing his glasses, he buffed them on the tail of his coat. His face had flushed a violent red.

"I have no idea."

ALAN AND SIMON wove their way along Haymarket at a leisurely pace. Here and there, the heads of Mk. I Automatons rose above the crowd, smoke coming in *chuffs* from their smokestacks. One carried a satchel, one stood in the road scraping manure off the cobbles. Steam-drawn carriages swerved around it at the last minute, but the mechanical man didn't seem to notice. Shop windows packed with ceramic jars displayed wares. A trio of children came out of a shop doorway brandishing long black strips of liquorice, already comparing the yellowing of their tongues. Taking a right, Alan and Simon soon emerged in Leicester square with its circle of cafe awnings like carnival bunting. Small tables with paired chairs behind silk ropes created an obstacle course for waiters in waistcoats and spats who darted back and forth. They eventually found a table straight across from the Alhambra. Simon ordered tea.

"I'll have a beer, anything is fine," said Alan handing the

waiter the menu without looking at it. "Thank you."

"Isn't it a little early?" asked Simon.

"I'm celebrating my release from prison, Simon."

The waiter shot Alan a pair of wide eyes, and darted away.

"You're incorrigible."

"If I knew what that meant, I'd probably agree with you."

Before they could get their drinks, a young man with an underdeveloped moustache approached their table. His pinstripe suit made him look even thinner than he was and his neck tie was so tight that his shirt bunched around a scrawny neck.

"Pardon me, Gentlemen. I'm sorry to interrupt your breakfast. Would you be the sons of Inspector Carpenter?"

The brothers looked at each other, silently deciding on the level of threat.

"Yes," said Simon, extending a hand. "Simon Carpenter. This is my brother—"

"Alan Shaw, yes," said the young man taking Simon's hand and then offering it afterward to Alan. "Earnest Sledge. Reporter for the Illustrated Times."

Alan took the hand and offered the young man a seat. By the time his narrow bottom hit the chair, a notepad had appeared in his hand. He drew it close to his chest as the waiter returned, leaning over him to reach the table.

"I'm sorry, sirs, I didn't realise there would be another gentleman joining you," said the waiter.

"Neither did we," said Alan. "Care to order yourself some breakfast, Mister Sledge?"

"Um, yes, thank you. Tea and some eggs on toast would be lovely."

"I'll have the same," said Simon.

"And one with bacon," offered Alan.

The waiter was gone again.

"So, Ernie, what have you come to pester us about?" asked Alan with a smile.

"I'm sure you know, Mister Sha—"

"Alan"

"—Alan. Your escapades at the Crystal Palace yesterday? I'm afraid I tried to get a quote from you then but your father said you were indisposed."

"That's a nice way of putting it," said Alan.

Simon sipped his tea, avoiding eye contact.

"We have a spectacular illustration of your leap to the dirigible. We're hoping to get it out on tomorrow's edition with your quote alongside? I'm afraid we've had to settle for a bare report for today."

"What do you want to know?"

"Anything you can tell me! Oh, thank you."

The waiter slid three plates onto the table and distributed them evenly.

"I think you'll know most of it already," said Alan, munching a piece of fried bacon. "They stole a Grecian vase, they were masked and they escaped on winged frames."

"Indeed. What was going through your mind at the time?"

"Very little, I expect," said Simon.

Alan feigned laughter, clutching at his chest, and sneered at his brother.

"I heard the screams, saw the men escaping and knew I had to stop them."

Earnest's eggs were going cold in front of him as he scribbled on his pad.

"And where were the police at this point?"

"Still outside."

"Would you say the constables were surplus to requirements?"

"Alan, don't answer that," said Simon.

"Of course, I apologise," said Earnest.

"I'd say I was in the right place at the right time. No one could've known what was going to happen. Now eat your eggs, Earnest. We can talk more after breakfast."

But before Earnest could set down his notepad, the familiar *flapflapflap* of police issue boots on pavement peaked Alan's ear. The constable rounded the corner, hopping on one foot and started to jog across the square. Alan called out to him before he could get out of earshot.

"Ho! Constable, what's the rush?"

"The museum, sir. Alarm's gone off," and then only an afterimage of blue uniform was left where he'd once stood.

"I suppose we're going, are we?" asked Simon.

Alan was already standing up, plucking the second piece of bacon from his plate.

"Ernie, you might want to tag along. There could be a story in it."

THEIR STEAM-CAB FLEW past the chapels of Broad Street and Bloomsbury, the steam-horse shuddering with pent up frustration. Veins stood out in the driver's neck as he struggled with the heavy leather reins. Cutting across the traffic, the carriage lifted off two wheels, honks and blue curses rising like war cries around it. Earnest sat in the corner of the carriage, arms pressed to opposing walls, feet spread wide. Alan was chuckling, giddy with speed. Simon patted Earnest's knee.

"We'll be there soon, Ernie. Don't worry. Alan has a knack for finding the most insane drivers, but we always get there safe."

"What's the point in being *able* to go fast if you're not going to do it?" said Alan.

Earnest's bottom slipped from the seat as the carriage slammed to a halt, excess steam released with the long hoot of a whistle. While Simon paid the driver, Alan walked over to Sergeant Jennings who was dishing out orders to a group of constables.

The British Museum's pantheon-style facade stood over them. It felt heavy to Alan, not only in stone but in crushing time as if every artefact in its walls weighed it down. It was surprising that the steps to the main entrance didn't buckle under the pressure.

"Morning, Sergeant."

"He let you out then, did he?" said Jennings. "I'm afraid you've missed it this time, Alan."

"Missed what?" That was Earnest.

Jennings looked at the thin little man, his eyes resting on the notebook.

"Earnest Sledge, Illustrated Times," said Alan. "They'll find out sooner or later."

"I suppose so," said Jennings. "We've had another robbery. More of your frog-eyed men. Chased them right through the museum and onto the roof."

"And they flew away," said Alan.

Jennings nodded.

"What did they take?" Earnest again.

"A Persian tablet. Clay with little markings in it. It was how they used to write. Imagine trying to take notes like that, eh, Mister Sledge?"

"What was on it?" said Earnest, missing anything but the facts.

Jennings rolled his eyes.

"No one knows. Dead language."

"Crikey."

"That's what I thought," said Jennings.

3

ACROSS THE SLATE landscape of London's rooftops, the wind drew a hundred smoke plumes into slivers. The gas works' giant lung, St Paul's and Westminster were hazy shapes in the distance. Alan stood by the roof's gutter, ignoring the drop to the street below, his scarf's tails whip-cracking behind him. Squinting, he brought the binoculars to his eyes again, sweeping the sky. He heard the roof's hatch rattle and squeak open behind him.

"Well, are you going to help me?"

Helen's beautiful head rose like a mole from the hatch. He reached down. With one hand holding her bonnet in place, the other holding Alan, Helen found her footing. Her dress fluttered out like a sail.

"Do you remember bringing me up here, not long after you came to stay?"

"I remember the telling off I got," said Alan, eyes still buried in tubes of wood and brass.

"I've never seen London in quite the same way since."

"The problem is, I can't see it any different." He swept across again, out toward the river.

"It's not your responsibility to find them, Alan. Let your

father handle it." When he didn't answer, she stepped closer to him. "Come inside. I'm cold."

"That's why I hate this place," he said. "Everyone's waiting for someone *else* to do something. So it never gets done."

Helen stepped closer, uncertain of the tiles under her boots. She wrapped her gloved fingers around the binoculars, pulling them from his eyes, but he didn't look at her.

"You don't hate London, it's your home."

Alan's face was grey with the cold.

"No, it's somewhere I come back to. Like a nightmare I keep having."

"What about me?"

He finally looked at her. The wind was making his eyes water.

"I think you might be the worst part."

Helen's face bunched.

"Sometimes, Alan, you're wonderful. And sometimes you're the coldest person I know."

She walked away, slipping on the slate and throwing his hand off when he caught her. Without another word, or meeting his eye, she was gone down the hatch and Alan was alone.

"I'VE GOT AN idea."

Inspector Carpenter didn't raise his eyes from his typewriter which *chuck*ed and *ping*ed like a little man-driven clock. He beckoned, and Alan stepped inside, closing the door. Stood in front of his father's desk still set his teeth on edge. The room hadn't changed in a decade. He wiped sweaty palms on his trousers. Carpenter carried on typing. Alan didn't bother trying to whistle.

"I'm listening," his father said.

"The things they fly on. They don't fly at all. Not like a dirigible flies. They glide."

"What's your point?" Carpenter mumbled, his attention clearly on the paperwork.

"Well, they had to get on the roof of the Crystal Palace and the Museum. So they'd have to set off from somewhere higher and float down."

Carpenter finally looked up. His surrogate son's hands were jammed firmly in pockets. A trick to stop him fidgeting under pressure. Carpenter nodded to the bookcase where the maps were. Alan obeyed, spreading a roll across the desk.

"Where do you think?" asked Alan.

Carpenter sat back in his chair, arms folded. Alan tried to ignore the tension in his father's minimal response: "You tell me."

"There aren't many places higher than the Crystal Palace or the museum and which are still close by. They want to be close for the approach and far away for the escape so they probably land on the ground afterward. That could be anywhere, really. But I spotted this."

Alan pointed to two points. The Foundling and St. George's hospitals. Carpenter *humph*ed, but nodded.

"Both hospitals. Both close to the robberies." Carpenter was nodding. "Both with towers or higher roofs. We should get some boys to take a look," he muttered, avoiding a direct compliment for his son.

"No need," said Alan, producing a box from his pocket

to show the samples inside. "I've already been."

ALAN SAT BY Schneider's work station with his feet up on a stool. As the Doctor rubbed his chin, scratched his head and sucked his teeth, Alan studied a piece of ivory paper. Soft handwriting crawled across its surface. A faint waft of flowers came from the envelope on his knee.

> *Dearest Alan,*
>
> *By the time you receive this letter, I will be gone. My father believes the vase to be lost forever, and has returned home. I am glad to hear that you didn't get into trouble for chasing those horrible thieves. You were very brave. But you must be careful. Please promise me that you won't pursue it further. I couldn't stand the thought of you getting hurt somehow.*
>
> *I wish we could continue our time together. It has been wonderful. But I must return to my studies. I may be travelling for some time before reaching home, going wherever my research takes me. If I can, I will send word, but there are too many unknowns at this stage.*
>
> *I'll never forget the stream where we met and the wonderful Spring we've had together.*
>
> *I'm sorry that this letter must be our goodbye. Please, don't be sad.*
>
> *Yours,*
> *Adrienne*

Alan folded the paper in half, turned down the corners once, twice, scoring the lines with his thumbnail. The paper plane looped once across the laboratory, thudding against the side of the rubbish bin under Schneider's desk. Alan didn't bother to pick it up.

"Bad news?" asked the Doctor.

"Not really."

"*Mmhm.* And where is your brother today?" asked Schneider as he scooped a small amount of dirt into two glass vials.

"Back at University. Knowledge doesn't learn itself, I guess."

"Indeed it does not," said Schneider, sifting the soil sample into a small dish and setting it on the heat. He added a few drops of some thin liquid before continuing. "My own studies have taken me across many countries. Many books. Many teachers. And what of yourself, Alan?"

Alan sighed. This was an old conversation, just in a different way. He'd heard it from his Father without end. "I learned my lessons on the streets," he said. "Then even more when father demanded I go to school with Simon. As I see it, just being able to read I'm ahead by a mile. Did you always want to be a chemist?"

Schneider turned the heat down on his Bunsen burner and lifted his goggles. His smile was distant as he spoke.

"Ah, excellently diverted, Mister Shaw. And no, until I was thirteen years old, I wanted to be a pirate," he laughed. "But chemistry is in my blood. Since my great grandfather's days. He was considered a leader in the circles of science. It seemed prudent that I follow him."

As if to make a demonstration, he lifted the little dish from the Bunsen burner with a pair of iron tongs, squinted at the remaining residue and made a note on the paper beside him. He set the equipment aside and brandished a sheet of tight scrawl toward Alan.

"Inspired deduction," he said.

"If you stare at something long enough, you can find a pattern to anything," said Alan.

"That's as may be, but this time you just happened to be right, my young friend. Look here. Samples taken from the roofs of both hospitals. Soil and grass mostly. From the criminal's boots, I expect. Certainly no other way for them to get up there."

"And?"

"Certain areas of London have certain types of earth, some with more iron content for instance, or where only specific plants grow. The soil we have here is of the common garden variety, I'm afraid. Nothing more telling. The grass, however." Schneider held up a small blade in tweezers.

"Is green," said Alan. "So, normal soil and normal grass. Brilliant."

Schneider ignored him.

"See the way the blade is shorn? Under the microscope, we can tell that it has been cut. This grass is from a lawn. How many lawns, do you suppose, are in the area of London, large enough to necessitate a driven lawn mower?"

"Not many," said Alan.

"Then maybe this grass isn't so normal."

CARPENTER BENT OVER the map on his desk, pins marking large lawns across the city. Alan sat across the room, one hand shielding his eyes.

"It was a good idea," said the Inspector. "It just doesn't help. Maybe this should be a lesson to you—"

"Don't."

"—that you should leave the police work to us, eh? Stop chasing villains across the city. You're no vigilante, Alan. You could be doing something better with yourself."

Alan's eyes finally came from behind his hand.

"Better, like what? I'm not Simon, Father. I can't be a scientist or a doctor or a solicitor. I'm not cut out for anything grand. I'm an urchin in fancy clothes and there's nothing more to it. If it wasn't for you, I'd be shovelling coal somewhere, covered in muck."

"There's plenty more to you," snapped Carpenter. Outside, heads turned toward the raised voice and thought better of it. "You're a smart lad."

Alan jerked open the door.

"Not smart enough."

The door slammed to the jamb.

4

THE FACT WAS that Alan had passed through most circles of London society at various stages of his life. As a boy, he scraped the underbelly with the other urchins, slaving in the petrifying dark of the workhouse, only to escape to the dangerous world of Harker's Tavern. Then the Carpenters made him a school boy, which came with dangers of its own for a child who was fundamentally different from the rest. But a keen right hook and knees like knives had gotten him through that, or rather, thrown out of that. Working on sea-vessels of all kinds meant the East India Docks were like home to him, and Simon's constant badgering made sure that the middle classes at least knew of his existence. His frequent appearance in newspapers took care of the rest. What that all amounted to was a reputation that preceded him, and a fair few people knew his face at second glance. And so, as he turned the corner of Lombard Street into Alsatia, Alan shrugged on a damp old coat, recently bought from a longshoreman for a pound with the cloth cap thrown in. Where he was going, he'd need the disguise.

The streets were never very busy around this part of

London. They were a little too narrow for much traffic, and the residents of the tumbledown houses were too poor to need carriages anyway. Everyone who came here walked quickly and confidently, their eyes never on the ground but careful not to meet another's gaze. The rumble of London seemed to ride over the rooftops of the streets rather than delve down into them, as if it the rest of the city were afraid to draw attention to itself.

Alan stalked along with his practiced gait that kept the long coat from flapping and revealing his good clothes beneath, managing to make him look tall and dangerous. Half way along the street, where there was an uncharacteristic gap between two houses, a small archway formed an alley. Alan stepped closer to the curb, careful not to pass the alleyway within grabbing distance, but when he reached the entrance, he swung around and stood stock still, staring into the dark.

It was a long minute or so before a voice came out of the accumulated gloom.

"What'll it be?"

"Information," Alan said, making sure his voice stayed low and even, his cap down over his eyes.

"You got the money for that, pal?"

"Money enough."

Out of the alley's shadow stepped a lithe young man, blowing smoke from his nose like a dragon. He crushed his cigarette with one hand and pocketed it before eyeing Alan. His face was a little too gaunt, decorated with tiny scars from years of cuts and scrapes, and his hair was slicked back with dirt, but he wasn't that much older than Alan, if he was at all. What aged him prematurely was the lay of his mouth, which had developed a pensive underbite as if he was constantly weighing up the world.

"That depends on what you want to know, cubby," grumbled the young thug.

"I was just wondering how you got to be so ugly—"

Before Alan finished his sentence, the youth slid a gruesome blade from his sleeve and extended it toward Alan as if he were about to carve up a Yule turkey. His face tightened into a jackal-like smile.

"You, my friend, are about to be cut up so small the worms won't have to chew."

Moving his hand as slowly as he possibly could, Alan tilted the brim of his cap so that the shadow fell back from his face. He grinned, but didn't put any feeling into it.

"Alright, Dick?"

The lithe young thug cursed something fierce. The tip of his knife dropped a little, but it didn't leave his hand. Out of a murderous glare emerged the familiar smile of Dick Whitsun.

"Alan Shaw, by God. You nearly got yourself perforated."

"Wouldn't be the first time," Alan said.

Dick leaned against the wall behind him, his knife stored back in its sleeve, and crossed his arms. As far as Alan could tell, that was Dick's idea of a companionable hug.

"But you always managed to talk your way out of it. I never found you that charming, myself."

"Careful Dick, words hurt more than knives sometimes."

"Not mine they don't."

Alan didn't doubt it for a second. He wouldn't wish Dick Whitsun on his worst enemy.

"You still working for the Gee Cee?" he asked, instead of thinking too long about his friend's schooling in violence.

Dick sniffed, and took a quick glance up and down the street without moving his eyes. "You here as my old mate Alan, or as the Inspector's son?"

"I would never dob you in, Dick."

"Damn right. I know too much about you." Dick gave a wink and the young men shared a brief laugh which led to an uncomfortable silence.

"The Gentlemen's Consortium has been kind to me, Alan. Very kind. It's looked after me, kept me warm of winters."

"Doesn't look like it to me," Alan said, but put a smile to it.

Dick scratched at his bristled chin, reading his hundreds of little scars like braille. "Nah, this was other folk. You should know Alan, old friend you may be, but the Gee Cee are my family. Good as it is to see you, old pal, I reckon you should say your piece and be off. This ain't no place for a copper's son."

Alan nodded, solemnly.

"You've heard about the exhibition thefts?"

Dick nodded.

"And you know I was there?"

Another nod.

"I'm looking for the people who did it. Quiet-like. No coppers."

The young thug sucked his teeth for a second, before answering.

"It was nothing to do with the Gee Cee. Organised they may be, and criminals to the core, but they're not stupid. There's no profit in stealing something you can't sell."

It was Alan's turn to nod. That made sense.

"Truth be told, Al, those crooks have put a lot of not very nice people in a not very nice mood. When someone does something this big without us giving the nod first, it gets people's backs up, you know? I reckon the Consortium might be behind you on this one."

"Oh Christ," said Alan. "That's the last place I want them."

Dick laughed. "Too right it is! I see all that caviar and wine hasn't dulled your brain at least."

Alan pinched the bridge of his nose.

"Sorry, Al. If I could help you, I would. But if the Consortium knew where your friends were, they'd have done them in already. You thought of trying Harker's, maybe? Place is full of idiots, but they're idiots with ears. Maybe someone knows something."

Alan nodded. Tugging his cap down over his eyes, he turned back the way he came, lifting a hand to Dick. The youth gave him a nod and slunk back into the murk of his alley.

ALAN STRETCHED HIS back against the plush upholstery of the Monorail shuttle's seat. The old coat lay across his lap with the cap on top. The glass panels of the shuttle's roof and sides had magnified the day's gentle heat to a swelter.

The faces of old friends transformed into swarthy thugs in his mind, and danced circles around the statuesque form of a certain Greek Goddess he'd known until yesterday; his father's reprimanding voice playing a polka-like *oompah oompah* accompaniment over the odd choreography. All of a sudden, he really fancied a neat Scotch.

The shuttle wasn't exactly steady as it hurtled over London, turning the slate roofs to swift blurs beyond the window. Occasionally, they were obscured by a cloud of steam from some chimney or other as if flying through the clouds. Alan swayed in his seat, often bumping the curved metal wall with his shoulder. To take his mind away from his swirling troubles, he watched the ticket girl sashay her way toward him in perfect time with the shuttle's movements despite the cumbersome ticket machine balanced on her hip. With her own feminine movements, her progress became a dance that sent the hem of her skirts swishing and exposing ankle boots underneath with a flurry of crinoline. Alan adjusted the collar of his shirt and wished that the shuttle's windows would open just a crack.

"Ticket, sir?" the girl asked in a cockney accent, much like his own had once been before it became diluted. Her cheeks were a rosy hue as if she'd pinched them before coming into the carriage, giving her face pleasant, youthful glow.

"Covent Garden, please." He reached into his waistcoat for his billfold.

The ticket girl hammered a few keys on her machine's main cylinder; with each tap, a ribbon of paper issued further and further from the side. She hefted the bulky mechanism, letting the leather pad sit better on her ample hip.

"One way, sir? Or will you be coming back?"

"I wish I knew," said Alan, under his breath. But the girl had better ears than he thought.

"If you don't mind me saying, sir, you don't sound very happy about where you're headed."

Alan handed over a few shillings.

"You could say that. Just a one way, please."

The ticket girl's eyebrows weakened. *So quick to sympathise*, Alan thought. She tapped a few more keys and tore off the ticket. When Alan reached out to take it, she didn't let go.

"You could always stay on the rail, sir. If it worries you so, there're plenty more places you could go, I'm sure. I'll be getting off at the end of the line, myself. My shift's over, you see." She finally let go of the ticket so that she could tease back a strand of hair which had fallen across her face from the mass of twirling gold piled on her head. "Maybe I could show you a nice place to lunch?"

Alan inclined his head, enjoying the girl's perfume as it drifted toward him. He allowed his mouth to creep up at the corners, and the cameo on the girl's bosom rose and fell as she forced a breath.

"That would be lovely," he said, and she showed him a row of dainty teeth. "But not today. I'll make sure I take this journey again when I have more time."

The ticket girl bobbed her head and pressed a few coins into Alan's hand before sashaying away again.

Alan tucked the ticket into his jacket pocket. London

seemed a little better when he next looked out of the window. He tossed the coins in his hand for a second, letting them jingle, and then checked the amount quickly before putting it away.

He stopped, and checked the coins again.

The damn girl had short changed him.

Pulling the moth-eaten cap down over his eyes, Alan shrugged on the longshoreman's coat. It still smelled of the sea. Alan wondered if he'd ever go back to the navy. His course was over now, and he was free to leave or return, but he couldn't decide. It was the exhibit that had done it. There were too many incredible places to see. He couldn't bear to die an old man with more regrets than memories. And no matter which way he looked at it, life on a ship had him staring at the sea more than anything interesting. His father was wrong and right at the same time. Alan knew it. He could do something. He was smart enough and fit enough, but it couldn't be a copper, or a doctor. And that had set Alan thinking. He'd failed to catch the criminals first time around, then missed them entirely, and finally the hospital rooftop samples had come up with nothing. Until this thing was solved, he was disgraced. But he was thinking too much like his Father. Too much like a copper. Now, he was thinking like a criminal. He knew more about those than he cared to admit.

The shuttle came to a stop with a squeal of brakes and a short jerk. Spurts of steam erupted from either side of the door as it popped free of the carriage wall and parted. Alan's boots made a hollow sound on the iron platform, nothing more than a grille suspended above the road below. He made quickly for the stairs and began shoving his way through the crowded square at Covent Garden Market.

The Market was just as he'd left it. Maybe the arcade's pillars were a little cracked, maybe there was more pigeon dung on the rooftops. The trader's faces were worn, darker somehow, but it was still fundamentally the same. Calls like foghorns lifted over the crowd's murmur, pitching strawberries and apples and potatoes. The occasional Automaton drifted through the throng like a battleship among rafts. And now, Alan was taller. He could see over the trestles and sacks. The crowd moved for him rather than battering him aside. He circled the arcade and past the end of Bow Street where a few constables were emerging from the police station. He turned his face away before they could spot him. If the coppers identified him here, his disguise would be useless. He took a left into an alleyway, catching a glimpse that no one was following before disappearing into the murk.

The entrance to Harker's had changed. A new trapdoor. The old one had probably rotted to mush. He lifted the rope handle and a familiar scent of stale beer and straw sent him back a decade. Making sure the longshoreman's coat covered the clean clothes underneath, he descended into the gloom.

Oh yes, it was just the same. The same shitty tables, the same crunch and squelch underfoot, the same bad lighting and hunched figures in the dark. Alan tugged his cap down until it touched his nose, and took a seat at the bar. He could hear clattering in the kitchen, pans being moved around. Leaning to see down the corridor, what could have been the same steam cloud still hung, blocking his view into the kitchen. There were voices back there. One rumble, he recognised as Callas. So the old bastard wasn't dead yet. And another, surely Sarah. He found himself smiling without cause. But the voices were strained. Callas' was raised, now shouting, now bellowing out through the door. As Alan sat at that old bar, he heard the crack like a whip and a yelp as if a dog were struck. Not a single head in Harker's turned around. Jerking up from his stool, Alan hopped the bar and was through to the kitchen before he knew it. The steam was disorienting, thick and tinged with the tangible scent of boiling vegetables. He let the boy inside his memory navigate the familiar room, but found himself hitting his head on overhanging pans where he hadn't before. Where the steam cleared, he almost fell over Sarah. She lay at Alan's feet, propping herself up with one hand, holding her face with the other. Callas was as immense as Alan remembered. The Spaniard looked up as Alan came out of the kitchen's murk.

"Who are you? You are not allowed behind the bar. Get out. This is none of your concern!" bellowed Callas.

Something churned in Alan. He could feel heat rising from his boots like a furnace to roast his face. He saw the blood on the Spaniard's knuckles, the spittle on his lip. He heard the whimpering of the woman at his feet. Alan snarled like a beast. Flinging of his cap, he launched himself over Sarah and into Callas' face. His fists were a barrage of jabs and hooks. Callas retreated, blocking the blows with his thick forearms. He was swearing in a mixture of his native language and English. Finally, Callas broke away, and swung a sledgehammer hand for Alan. The blow only glanced as

Alan swung himself away, stepping round just like a certain Scottish boxer had once taught him. Fist fights were common on merchant ships, and footwork on a rolling deck was much harder than on a stable floor. Alan was a weaving blur. Callas bided his time with the stranger, and finally struck out. Alan caught the fist in his chest, his heart seeming to stop dead for a moment as he fell back. Callas was on him, pressing him into the work surface, grasping at his throat. Alan's blows had become panicky, hitting at his opponent's face with no effect. Callas tightened his grip as if wringing a cloth. Spots of ink clustered in Alan's vision. The Spaniard was cursing, his spit peppering Alan's face as the young man began to lose consciousness.

Shtong.

And the hands were gone. Alan gasped for air, clutching at his own throat, and Callas was at his feet. Sarah stood beyond the unconscious bulk, her chest heaving. One side of her mouth was a bloated mess and one eye blinked away the blood from a split eyebrow. She was crying, holding a large pan. And, as Alan watched, she screamed and hit the unconscious Callas again.

Alan fell to her, taking her in his arms and pulling her away. She sobbed and sobbed into his coat, sometimes thanking him, sometimes making sounds without sense.

"I SHOULD HAVE YOU thrown in a cell for the rest of your shitting existence, Callas."

Alan rubbed at his neck where the Spaniard had tried to squeeze the life out of him. It hurt to swallow, and even more to talk. Where the glancing blow had hit his jaw, a bruise spread, making the gums inside feel raw. He dreaded the next time he had to eat. The Barman himself now sat with his back to the kitchen cupboards at the young man's feet. He spat blood on the floor and dabbed the lump on his head with a wet cloth.

"No, Alan, you can't." Sarah's speech was muffled. Her face had swollen even more in the last few minutes. If Alan hadn't seen her before, he would have never recognised her. He touched her face and she winced.

"He's an animal," he said.

She took his hand away.

"And what of me, then? They won't let a woman run the tavern on her own. What'll I do? You swan in after years, dead as far as I knew, and try to change everything. Will you stay around afterward?"

Alan turned away. He tried to spit but found that his mouth wasn't the right shape for it anymore.

"I didn't think so," she said.

Alan looked down at the Barman.

"If I hear you've touched her again, I swear I'll kill you myself," he said.

Callas said something in Spanish and chuckled to himself.

"I ought to knock some English into you, you—"

"Why did you come back, Alan? What do you want?" Sarah tugged at his arm so that he'd look at her.

"I came to see you," he said.

"So why now? What's changed that made you come home? You'd got away just like you wanted. Why would you want to see us again?"

"I thought you said I was dead as far as you knew."

"Don't be stupid. You've been in the papers enough. Once just after you disappeared, then when your boat sank, and just yesterday. Leaping from balconies to save some Greek's furniture. I've always known where you were, just like you always knew where I was. The only difference is that you could have come found me anytime you liked. I couldn't turn up at some rich man's house asking for a boy I once knew. Now, what do you want?"

Alan was shaking his head.

"What happened? I'm lost. I came here, saved you from this stinking waste pile—" he gestured to Callas "—and all of a sudden you hate me. I should've known better. It was fine while you were patting me on the head and humouring me. But when I got out you got left behind and you don't like it. Well, don't worry, I'll be out of your hair soon enough."

Alan couldn't tell if Sarah was crying or if her swollen eye was leaking. And he tried not to care either way. Sarah touched his shoulder, tugging him, and dragging him into an embrace.

"I've missed you. I'm glad you came back," she said.

He allowed himself a smile over her shoulder with the half of his face that could still move, and gave her a little squeeze.

HARKER'S WAS CLOSED. Or as closed as it got. It must have been dark outside because the customers had all left to go about their nightly misdemeanours. Sarah sat with Alan at the bar, pretending to wipe the sticky surface with the remnants of a rag. Callas stormed around behind them, collecting tankards, muttering, and occasionally rubbing his head.

"It's not so bad, really," said Sarah. "Yes, he's a bastard and he always will be, but he hits me much less now. I think he's getting too old for it."

"Doesn't look that way to me," said Alan.

"You can't always see what's going on from the outside. Especially not the distance you're looking in from."

"Was that another jab?"

"Only a little one."

Callas slammed the empty tankards down next to Alan then stormed off again. Alan raised an eyebrow at the barman. Picking up one of the tankards, he tipped out the dregs and plucked a cloth from the bar.

"Some things you never forget," said Sarah as her boy cleaned the mug.

Alan ignored her. "I need to know what you've heard in here, about robberies. Strange ones. Stealing old relics. A vase maybe, or something from the museum."

"You know how it works, Alan. I don't hear anything. Nothing at all. If this is police business, I'm not willing to get in trouble. You used to do the same."

"This isn't police work. It's just me. The vase belonged to a friend of mine."

Sarah's eyes went as wide as the bruising would allow.

"Alan Shaw, are you courting a girl?"

"No. Of course not."

Her finger prodded his ribs like a knife. Alan choked back a laugh.

"A pretty girl, then. She must be to have you running back home again. Fighting Spaniards. Rescuing dames."

"Will you stop poking me? It's not about the girl. Not anymore. I'm doing it for me. That robbery made me look stupid and I want to get whoever did it before the police do."

"Pride. That sounds more like the Alan I used to know."

"Can we stop talking about me, please?"

Sarah narrowed her eyes at him, but nodded.

"No one who comes in Harker's had anything to do with it. I'd know if they did. Don't look at me like that, Alan. I mean it. Looks like you got those bruises for nothing."

Alan leant over with his clean tankard, filled it and swilled his mouth with a gulp of ale before spitting it back into the waste barrel.

"Balls," spat Alan.

They both turned when they heard Callas laughing. He sat with his boots up on a stool, cleaning his own pile of tankards and chuckling to himself.

"What're you laughing at?" asked Alan.

"Stupid little boy. Always stupid little boy. Si quieres saber algo, no hablar con la mujer, niño estúpido. Me hablas."

"What's he talking about, now? Speak English, Callas, you bastard."

"Las ranas voló sobre el río." Callas laughed again.

"For Christ's sake. You want to go another round, you're on. Otherwise shut your pie hole," said Alan.

"He said 'the frogs flew over the river'," said Sarah.

Both men turned slowly toward the barmaid.

"What? You think I could work here all these years without learning *some* Spanish?"

5

DAWN WAS RISING over a chilly London when Alan finally left Harker's Tavern. Pigeons hooted a morning chorus somewhere above. Clothes lines spanning the void above his head rolled out white linen for the day's drying. The sound of moving crates and the first rumbles of the market echoed in the alleyways.

"You're going to have to let go of me, you know."

Sarah's face must have been agony but she buried it into his jacket all the same, arms wrapped around him like ivy.

She took his face in her hands. "You've grown up so much. Too much. You were always so good at looking after yourself—"

"Not good enough," he said, rubbing neck where Callas' fingerprints had swollen to bruises.

"—But I never thought I'd see you a gentleman like this."

"I'm wearing a soggy old long-coat and flat cap. It's hardly Lordly, is it?"

"You know what I mean. And now I'm losing you again. Off to make more stories for the papers. My little Alan."

"I'll come back to see you. No reason not to, now is

there?"

She prodded him in the chest. "No reason at all."

Alan hugged her again by Harker's trapdoor and made sure she could see him smile until he turned the corner. By the time he passed the pawnbroker on York Street, the cap was reset and his face firm. He'd learnt two things today, one expected, one not. The first was that there was nothing for him at Harker's. He'd known it as a boy but only in a sense of wanting to escape. The tavern was stagnant by its nature. Nothing would ever change there. A little part of him hated lying to Sarah, but he thought it was for the best. Rather have her keep on hoping than break her heart.

But the case was new. Daring robberies and Frog-men on some secret agenda. That was excitement itself. He could bury himself in it until the bruises faded and all thoughts of Harker's went with them.

Alan took the shortest route out of Covent Garden. The Strand traffic was still light at this time in the morning. In his youth, sweeping a track in the horse shit for Ladies to cross had brought good money. He wondered how the boys paid their way nowadays. There was no way they could remove the pools of motor oil or waft away the clotting stench of engine fumes. Even London's lush parks had begun to smell faintly of ozone. The Automatons took care of the dung cheaper and more effectively than the boys could and once the raised pavements and pedestrian bridges were built, there'd be no use for them at all. Still, at least the metal men could be reprogrammed and sent elsewhere. No such luck for the urchins.

Savoy Street led Alan down to the river. Along the bank,

the day's first train snorted steam from the undercarriage like a snake with metal scales, and began to build up speed with that unmistakable sound.

Shhhhhakuk-shhhhakuk-shhakuk-shakuk.

By the time it had crossed the rail bridge, it was nothing but a flash of sunlight on speeding steel.

It was easy to fool an untrained eye into believing that the Thames was like any other river. Wider than a comfortable swim, and running with a leisurely speed that all great rivers prided themselves on. But it couldn't fool Alan. He knew the surface's gentle undulation was nothing but a scab to hold the worst scents underneath. As the sun rose further and that churning slurry warmed, there would be the unmistakable stench of London.

On street level, Waterloo Bridge was an impressive causeway. Inspiring enough that London's suicides often chose it as their last place to visit. The deep arches had always put Alan in mind of a sea serpent's humps. But it was down below the arches that interested Alan today. Down there, the Thames' slurry coagulated into a crust that acted as London's lost and found. As he reached the top of some slimy stone steps, he caught the first calls of the Water Rats; whistles and hoots that wouldn't be lost in a jungle. With laces knotted, the boys hung shoes around their necks like leather scarves. So encrusted with dirt, they seemed like a part of the mud come to life. They scavenged in the solid sewage, sifting it through their fingers as barges and steamboats rattled by only inches away.

"Ho!"

At first they didn't hear him, or chose not to. It wasn't

profitable to stop and listen to some drunkard's abuse so early in the morning. But when Alan began to wave his cap, one of the boys waved back and slowly made his way over. Alan descended the final steps, coming around and perching himself on the stone embankment beneath Waterloo Bridge.

"Morning sir!" the boy shouted up. "Looking for anything specific, are we? Something lost over the side last night, perhaps. Very good rates for specific searches."

"It's your eyes, I'm after," said Alan.

"Sorry, sir. That's the one thing other than my hands that ain't for sale."

"Just a loan, then," Alan laughed and regretted it, rubbing his jaw. "Yesterday, and then the day before that. Something you can't help but notice. Five big birds. Black. You know what a triangle is?"

The boy's face contorted and he crossed his arms.

"Do I look thick to you?" he said. When Alan started to laugh, more Water Rats started to cluster around their friend to watch. Alan couldn't have described a single one of them under the grime.

"Course not. They were shaped like that, anyway," he said.

"Yeah, I saw them. We all did. Them's no birds, though. I've seen every bird on every rooftop in London. Not even the Tower ravens get that big."

"Did you see where they went?"

"Yep," said the Water Rat, smiling.

"And?"

"I think this is the bit where your hand goes in your pocket, sir."

IT HAD COST him a shilling to the Water Rat and two pennies to his friends who said they knew more. That was a shilling and tuppence he'd wasted, then. All the boys could tell him was what he could have guessed for himself. They saw the gliding frames pass over the river south of Waterloo bridge and disappear when the rooftops broke their view shortly after. Alan wasn't sure what more he'd expected. The river was hardly a vantage point. There was nothing for it. He had to cross the river himself and do the leg work.

He had always been a North London boy, even before his days with his Father and Simon. The gangs of the south side were a different ilk from those of the north. All men, most old deckhands or rivermen, and to Alan's younger self they were all united in only one way; their hatred of children. South Bank was a place to be avoided. And now that Alan looked back across to his own side of the Thames, he felt further away than on any ship.

Once away from the river, the streets were wider than North Bank, still reminiscent of the villages and the towns which Greater London had swallowed in its expansion. Between two larger buildings, in a space no larger than an alleyway, someone had hoisted a ramshackle roof in place. Four young girls sat under it in their bare feet, tiny fingers working feverishly at something in their laps. Alan moved over to see better. One of the girls glanced up at him. Somehow an old woman looked out from the place where a girl's face should have been.

"Darn your socks, sir?"

She held up a thick black work-sock as demonstration. Alan could see where the tips of her fingers were raw from passing the needle.

"Just curious," he said. "You got a mother?"

The girl looked back down the alley, into a dark space where Alan couldn't make out anything resembling a human shape.

"No sir, orphaned, I am. Looked after by a kindly old woman, given work and so fed. Maybe there's nothing else I can help you with?"

She stood up, taking one more glance down the alley. Lifting her arms wide, she started to turn on the spot like one of the moving mannequins in the Strand's shop windows. Her eyes were closed, screwed closed as if not wanting to see him looking at her. Alan knotted his eyebrows.

"What are you doing?"

The girl opened her eyes and where there had been tiredness, fear had taken over. An old woman shot out of the alleyway, emerging from the dark like an eel from its hole in an explosion of stained wool and rags. Alan stepped back, hands thrown up to ward off the ancient creature. Crooked hands grabbed at the girl, throwing her back. The crone croaked like a bullfrog.

"Be off with you, if you've no business. Go on, now."

Alan took a long step back into the comforting light of the street. The girl was crying but not on the outside. He could see it only in the waver of her eyes and deep swallows that held her tightened throat from squeaking. The other children didn't look up, but worked faster still. Something spurred him away and down the street as if a ghost had poked his ribs; something about tackling that crone just didn't seem worth it. And so he walked away at speed, trying not to look behind him until the crowds swallowed him up and he was safely on another street.

Steam carriages stung the streets with their rattling wheels. People became a throng as the work day began. Alan walked from street to street with no idea what he was looking for or who to ask for help. He walked until his feet pulsed in his boots and his stomach growled. Yesterday's breakfast seemed a long time ago. Stood beside the circular at St. George Circus, he finally raised hands to his face and let out a groan. Another dead end. What had he expected? That he'd see the Frog-men stepping out of a tavern together, one carrying a vase, another the clay tablet? They'd be laughing about their success and he'd apprehend them in the street? He groaned again, for good measure. He could have screamed there and then if only they wouldn't lock him in the nuthouse. Taking off the cap, he stuffed it into a pocket and opened the coat for some air.

"You look like hell, if you don't mind me saying, sir."

Alan looked at the paperboy sideways.

"Thank you very much," he growled.

"Just sayin'," said the boy. "Can I interest you in a newspaper, sir?"

Alan snatched the paper from his hand and fumbled more coins than were necessary into the proffered hand.

And there he was, staring at himself from the front cover. An older daguerreotype, but still recognisably him. The illustration of a man leaping across the Crystal Palace's vault between railing and dirigible. And the headline of

"Vigilante's bravery goes where the Law cannot." By Earnest Sledge.

Alan groaned for a third time. Surely that should be old news by now. But the sub-heading caught his eye.

Frog-man robbery foils police for a third time!

Oh god, there had been another. While Alan was being pummelled by an overweight Spaniard, the Frog-men had struck again. This time a Chinese painting. Not from the Crystal Palace, as Alan feared, but from the Chinese ambassadorial suite itself where Ambassador Li Hongzhang was staying to witness the Crystal Palace exhibit.

"A vase, a painting, and a clay tablet," said Alan. He threw up his arms, shook his head and finally turned to look at the overcast sky. "Are these people decorating their hideout?"

"Here, you're him aren't you?" said the paperboy. "Are you famous?"

Alan folded the paper into his jacket pocket and shook his head. "If I can't sort this lot out, I'll be the most famous idiot in London."

What would Titus Gladstone do? He'd have solved this thing by now, that's for sure. He'd have given the villain a solid right hook to the jaw, kissed the girl and made off on his steam-cycle to the next adventure. Not for the first time, Alan was getting the sinking feeling that life was very little like the Graphical Adventures would have him believe.

The sound of a carriage screeching to a stop made Alan jump and a blast of steam from behind nearly knocked him clean off his feet. His coat flapped to one side like a sail cut loose. The paperboy yelped as his papers tried to escape and he had to throw himself in top of the pile to save them.

Alan span around, and just managed to catch a flash of movement from the carriage's door before the leather cosh slammed into his head.

6

ALAN SLIPPED INTO consciousness like rising through dark water. The sound of something dragging on floorboards turned out to be the toes of his own boots. His shoulders whistled with pain as he dangled between two men by his arms; men with shoulders like sacks of rock. He tried to open his eyes and regretted it. Light pierced through high windows that passed to his left, setting his head spinning. Alan swung his head like a lead weight, groaning as the contents of his skull sloshed in their container.

A third man led the way. Alan scrunched his eyes and stretched them again, trying to gain some kind of focus. The leader was bald, shiny bald, and wide across the shoulders. A circlet of keys hung from his right hand. From collar to boots, he was dressed in white. Alan spotted a blemish on the back of the jacket, something for his damaged brain to focus on for a moment; a badly sown patch where the jacket had been torn.

Alan's eyes widened as he slurred his first words:

"Oh, shi—"

The third man turned just enough that Alan could see his face.

Nothing familiar. Then again, the last time they had met, the villain had his goggled cap on.

"Drop him there," the villain said.

Alan hit the floorboards with little ceremony, just a blast of pain in his head and hip. He could finally make out the room beyond his captor's boots. It was long. Not in feet and inches but surely miles. He couldn't see one end at all and the high windows seemed to stretch on forever. Joists arched overhead, supported by tall beams; just a dusty open space, like God's attic. And Alan wasn't the only captive. A swathe of grey and white rags all along the room turned out to be hundreds of rocking, wandering lunatics. Some gesticulated silently at the walls, other murmured and laughed. Some walked in tiny circles or hopped from foot to foot. Some could have been statues for all they moved. Everywhere there were eyes, just spots of colour with the whites showing all around. Alan spotted a man with a cage on his head, strapped beneath the chin with only his nose on show. And through all of them, like rocks among pebbles, orderlies roamed in their white uniforms, plucking and striking as they saw fit.

Keys jangled, a door creaked and Alan was jerked upward by one sprained arm. Hoisted across the orderly's shoulders, he hung there like a fox-fur stole. His head pounded again and his consciousness waned, chased away by the hot blood rushing to his head.

"ALAN…ALAN…"

Gentle fingers ran through Alan's hair, a comforting motion that made him think "mother" without a visual memory to accompany it. Something pounded an anvil in his head, each ring reverberating with a skull-cracking pressure, and the stroking did very little to soothe it. Still, he would have liked very much if it continued.

"Lay still. Rest. You've had a knock."

Alan tried to speak but his tongue had other ideas. The hand stroked and caressed, taking a strand of his hair and moving it aside, delicate fingers massaged his throbbing scalp. His head was cradled in the soft folds of a fragrant dress, the legs beneath supporting him. He considered his last memory, and this one, and couldn't imagine a way from one to the other. Then he stopped caring, as the gentle hands ran along his neck and into the collar of his shirt in long strokes.

Rising through the levels of his consciousness, he became more aware of the rest of his body. He was laid on his side, yes, and comforted, but a thick rope bound him to a vertical pipe at his back. So, no one had rescued him while he was unconscious after all.

"Are you hurt?" That soft familiarity came with images of wooden shutters thrown open to the sun, and the feel of tousled linen. Nothing like the hard wooden boards under him now. He tried for control of his eyelids, which fought back but eventually ground open. His eyes felt as if they were on elastic, bobbing around in their sockets to the pulse inside his head, but through the blurs and spots he could make out a sweet little face he knew, with hair like brown satin and cupid's-bow lips.

"Adrienne." He groaned, long and hard as his head flared to the sound of his own voice. When he spoke again, it was much quieter. "How did they-? You have to go. Have to—"

His stomach lurched. Alan was suddenly aware that he hadn't eaten in a day or more. At least it would have given him something to throw up.

"Don't fret. I'm quite safe, my sweet, sweet boy. I'm afraid the orderlies were rough on you. You have a concussion, I think," said the girl. "You really should rest—"

Struggling to correct the shadows in his vision, Alan looked her up and down, careful not to rouse the thorny dragon on his head. Her simple dress, pale blue, had an apron buttoned over her corset; a sight he allowed himself to linger on for a moment before taking in the long white coat she wore over everything else. Her apron was marked with a few stains here and there, and her hair was bundled up away from her face and neck so that thin curls surrounded her features. When the Frog-men took her, she must have been working in the laboratory, he thought. She was supposed to leave for her research trip two days ago. Had they held her in the asylum that long?

Like a snapping of fingers, Alan's mind finally caught up with the rest of the world. He groaned again. Fighting the hanging weight of his head, he sat up as far as his bonds would let him, moving away from Adrienne. She tried to help, but he jerked away from her.

"What have you done?" His voice came out in a rasp. He swallowed, winced. His mouth felt like someone had carpeted his tongue and added matching curtains around the back of his teeth. Adrienne shuffled closer, her skirts whispering on the boards. She raised a glass of water to

Alan's lips, tilting his chin with her other hand. Alan coughed on the first sip, and took another before mustering his indignation and turning away from the glass.

"Don't be silly, Alan. Drink."

But Alan's spite was sharper than his thirst. He jerked his chin away.

Adrienne laid the glass aside with a sigh.

"Don't be like that. I can't stand it. Will you at least let me explain?"

"You're going to jail, Adrienne," he said, but kept his eyes on the floor, just in case they betrayed him.

She gave a little giggle which, under the circumstances, chilled Alan's bones. And with the same sing-song innocence in which she'd once asked him to loosen her dress, a thousand miles away, on an island which had seemed the whole world for one fleeting season, she said:

"Whatever for?"

"For—" Alan finally scanned the room.

Small round windows near the floor let in a little light, but gas lamps did the main job of illuminating Bethlehem Asylum's domed loft space. Dusty crates were piled high at the extremities of the room, although the centre had been cleared. To Alan's left was the door, close enough to touch with an outstretched foot and far enough away that in his current state he didn't even think he could crawl there. The orderlies roamed the other end of the room, once again dressed in their frog-like uniforms. One of them stood by a complex apparatus containing four large glass canisters, checking a clip board through his goggles. Alan had seen the canisters' contents before. Red, black and clear liquids, as well as something like sand – the vials on Schneider's desk at the King Street Station. But here the canisters churned their contents, air bubbles rising like dark balloons or grains gliding over each other like a perpetual hour glass. A huge bellows to either side of the machine sucked and blarted air. Steam hissed from pipe joints, giving the loft's atmosphere the smell of ethanol that made Alan's temples feel sharp. Another of the orderlies hefted a thick rubber pipeline from the machine, carrying it across the room to a wooden vat braced with brass rings like a giant's beer keg. With a soft *shhhcuh* the pipe connected to a port in the vat's base and locked there.

"—whatever this is," Alan finished his paused sentence.

Adrienne laughed.

"I doubt it, darling." Her tone wasn't condescending. They could have been chatting over breakfast as far as Adrienne was concerned, not sat in a makeshift laboratory above hundreds of lunatics. "I'll soon be in a place well beyond their reach. Or perhaps I'll be everywhere at once. Some things remain to be seen."

"This is your research trip, I suppose? Playing hide-and-seek in asylums, building toys and stealing old junk," Alan slurred. That couldn't be good. Maybe his head was worse than he thought.

"Don't do that, Alan. This doesn't have to descend to cheap insults."

Damn, she had him there.

"Tell me, then, why I've been beaten half senseless," Alan said as he coughed his throat raw.

"Oh, Alan, I wanted nothing more than to keep you

away from this. That's why I told you I was going away."
She sat down beside him, resting her head on his shoulder.
He tried to move, but his bonds wouldn't budge. Adrienne
snuggled in a little more, releasing a waft of her perfume as
she rubbed her cheek on his shirt. She slid her hand onto his
and knotted the fingers. He had to fight not to squeeze back.
"Do you remember when we sat like this above the olive
garden? The sound of the sea and the moon bathing the
terrace as we watched the stars wheel overhead?"

"I remember that," said Alan. "With a girl I once knew."

Adrienne shoved herself away with a snort. Alan had
never seen her like that, arms folded, those tender lips
pursed like a sulking child.

"You're being difficult, Alan." Crossing the room, she
raised her voice so that it echoed from the loft's wooden
walls like a lecture hall. "I love my work, my research. But I
can love you both. If you could have ever loved me at all."
Her eyes glistened as she gave him a pitying smile. "Don't
look so shocked. Science has taught me to make conclusions
based on detailed observation, darling. And a woman knows
when she's being paraded like a trophy. You might as well
have held me over your head at the exhibition and ran a lap.
How that girl, Helen, looked at me. I could have withered
on the spot. You used me, Alan. And I thought I could
forgive you. But I see that you didn't even consider that you
might have done wrong. You just did it without thinking.
Especially about me. How can I have forgiven you for
something you're not sorry for?"

Alan stared at his knees and squeezed his eyes shut,
trying to force the painful light from his head. An hour ago,

maybe more, he'd been on the trail of thieves, searching for a vase that meant something to the father of a girl that he had decided never to see again. Only now that plan was foiled, and he had been forced once more to soak in her lines and her colours. Finding her like this, her perfect frame with its effortless grace, it confused him, made him want her again where he'd been working to forget her only hours before. But he had also found his villain, and wanted to scream at her. Not for her crimes, but for being more than just a girl; for being a genius, a thief, but most of all a complex woman who saw right through to his mercilessness; for being herself, and ruining what could have been a whole season of perfect memories for them both.

It could have been the concussion, this humming confusion of emotions, but Alan knew better. This was what he had wanted to avoid by simply losing touch and letting Adrienne fade into memory. If she weren't here, as a most vivid reminder of herself, being the very thing he couldn't stand to let go, he could have forgotten her. Especially with a different girl on his arm. That always made it easier. But now there was this crippling indecision which came with facing the end of a love affair bravely. Standing in front of each other and trying to forget all the little things that had once been. To Alan, it felt like grief for something fleeting and wonderful.

Adrienne broke the silence first.

"And now you can't forgive me for this, it seems. For hurting you, at least, I'm sorry. But not for stealing the artefacts. You must understand, no one would have loaned them to me if I'd explained my research."

On top of Alan's feelings for the sweet Grecian prodigy he'd loved all Spring, there were the thefts, the machines, and Adrienne's 'research'. And there, Alan found something that he could finally deal with. He grabbed at it and it dragged him to the surface.

"If even scientists think an idea is insane, it usually is," he said.

Adrienne's answer came too quickly to be spontaneous. She'd had this argument a million times in her head. Perhaps even with him. "Scientists never believe until they have solid evidence. And that requires no faith at all. Once I've proven what can be achieved, they can't deny that what I've done is best."

"Stop this, Adrienne. You can still go back—"

"Can I? To the Spring? To the stream and the terrace and the bed where you held me like a precious thing? Where you smelled my hair," she teased a strand which had fallen loose, "and told me the scent was finer than any flower. I don't think so. And I don't think you'd want to even if we could. We were over long before you chased my orderlies across London. Long before you saw my experiment. You were just too cruel to say it to me."

Alan let his head sag down to his chest.

"No, not that, I admit. But this can all stop and no one has to know who stole the artefacts. They can just—go back. Or be found."

Adrienne watched him as if she could hear the tick and clunk of his mind as sure as she understood the chemicals and contraptions arranged in the laboratory.

"You'd do that for me? Lie to your father. Defy the

law?"

"Yes. For you, and perhaps a little for me, too."

"Finally, you're being honest," she said with a smile. "Thank you. But I have to decline. Take back the vase, the tablet, the painting, if that's what you like. I've learnt everything I can from them. Keep my secret if it pleases you. But I'm not leaving here until what I've started is done. It's too much for my curiosity to bear. Too perfect a mystery."

"Adrienne—"

Adrienne sparked with temper, her face flared red as she cut off his argument.

"No. This is *my* adventure. I'm sorry that you got hurt. I am. But you shouldn't be so stubborn. This is the only chance I'll get to see my research through." She turned away, murmuring quickly to herself so that Alan couldn't get a word in to distract her. She talked as she move around the laboratory, to a work desk with a board above it, three pieces of paper pinned there; copies of the three artefacts' images, spread out and cross-matched. He could see, now, the dark circles under Adrienne's eyes like watermarked plaster. Had she slept at all since the first robbery at the Grand Exhibition?

Alan shifted his weight enough that he might strain to see behind him, the rope burning into his clothes as he twisted. He grimaced against the urge to vomit as the room pirouetted around his head. When his eyes opened, he could see the knot holding his bonds in place. His fingers began plucking at the ropes, teasing and testing for where they would give. Then he turned back and closed his eyes, the better to concentrate and not give himself away to Adrienne or the orderlies, the first ranting as the others worked on the apparatus around them.

"Three artefacts, all hiding pieces of an ancient puzzle. Or rather, an ancient solution long thought lost." Adrienne traced her fingers around the images with tenderness as she spoke. "Aristotle's vase with a constellation not recognised in the Earth's sky. A mistake? Of course not. A chemical diagram. Rudimentary but unmistakable. You'll just have to trust me, Alan, it's very clever. So clever that, in ancient times, it had to be broken apart—"

"Into three artefacts that you've had to collect, and all of them collected in London for the first time," said Alan with a measured dose of boredom. He stifled a yawn as his fingers fumbled behind him, seeming to make the knots worse rather than better.

Adrienne turned to him, that look of child-like surprise he'd seen before. But he couldn't think of that now. Too distracting. "Well guessed," she said. "A formula for the Universal Solvent."

"That sounds a lot like a fairy story, Adrienne," Alan said, after a few attempts to moisten his throat.

"Oh yes, a story that alchemists told for centuries, embellishing as they retold it, which became nothing but a story for the first chemists, and something of a myth in our own time. Such a myth that even you have heard of it, Alan. The transformation of lead to gold. Do you remember mocking it at the Exhibition? Mocking *me*? You were partly right, it is only a metaphor. But for something far more incredible." Adrienne was jigging with excitement. "It's *human* transformation for which the Universal Solvent was intended."

"Oh God, I had no idea," muttered Alan. She'd lost it,

somewhere along the line or maybe even before he'd met her. "I should have paid more attention."

Adrienne almost danced to the console beneath the churning canisters, flitting dial to dial, tapping their painted faces. She seemed not to notice the orderlies, who still bustled around. They kept checking something on the desk; a small book, perhaps Adrienne's notes. They looked to be relying on it a little too much for his liking. How much could they possibly understand of what they were doing? Or were they motivated by Adrienne's money; perhaps her looks?

He prayed for the sound of a police whistle, or for a rope-hungry rat to chew through his bonds. Neither came. And the blind tugging of the knot was getting harder as his hands became slippery with his own sweat.

I'm a sailor, God damn it. I can tie knots. Why can't I get the damn things open again, he thought.

Adrienne started talking, as if picking up half way through a train of thought. "—a solvent that strips away the unnecessary shell around the human soul. The lead, if you will, which shackles golden consciousness. But with the power of modern technology, I'm about to remove that intellectual essence from its fleshy confines. Set it free!"

She span around, her dress flaring out around her, like when they'd danced on the terrace under the stars and he'd spun her around and around until she collapsed into his arms and their laughter and kisses had mingled.

"You don't seem impressed," said Adrienne, panting a little, making pleasant motions under her corset.

"I'm finding it hard to be enthusiastic," Alan lied.

He could scream. Perhaps his brain was becoming less

swollen against the insides of his skull, but his head felt a little clearer, and with the clarity came dread. There was no kind of machine designed for what Adrienne was attempting, that was obvious even to Alan, but the fact showed even more disturbingly in the ill-fitting way that the components had been cobbled together for her purposes. He had no doubt that Adrienne was some kind of genius for putting together everything he saw, from the sticky-fingered orderlies to the artefacts to the formula for the machines. But there was a haste to the construction that made him skittish. He spotted slow drips between pipes, panels not quite flush, joints that rattled sporadically. There was a distinctly home-made feel all around him, and not in the way someone might take up building a pocket watch as a hobby. More like the way urchins played football in the street with a cabbage, making their own rules as they went along.

There seemed nothing for it. Nothing at all. As Adrienne tweaked the machines, either blissfully unaware or wilfully ignorant to the obvious danger, Alan began to resign himself to the fact that pieces of him would be found on the lawn of a lunatic asylum, burnt crispy by an explosion when Adrienne's experiment blew up in his face.

"Adrienne, is there any chance I can talk you out of this, maybe over dinner?"

But she wasn't listening at all now. He had to admit, that hurt a little. He would have liked to think that she'd pine for him just a little longer. But with her research reaching its final stages, he might as well have not existed.

7

WANDERING BACK AND forth, Adrienne was consumed by her experiment. She muttered to herself as she teased the contraptions toward some unknown end. The huge vat, the console with all its levers, switches and pressure gauges; no, Alan wasn't to blame for this one. Surely he couldn't be blamed for something he didn't even understand.

Giving up on the knot entirely, Alan started to work his arms up and down in an attempt to lift the rope currently wrapped around his chest to neck level. Bugger it. There was no time for subtlety and the orderlies and their alluring leader were busy tweaking their machines. As the rope shifted, Alan could feel the heat of the hemp through his clothes, burning with every movement. Sweat crept into his eyes, making them sting along with the ache of his bruised throat and ribs. The rope burns, combined with what was certainly warm blood running down his neck from where he'd been coshed made a striking variation of sensations.

Instead of his damned luck, which had already taken a beating today, Alan cursed the longshoreman's coat he still wore which seemed to have formed an intimate relationship with the rope.

Wriggle, wriggle. Inch by inch.

Forcing his chest and arms as far as they would go, trying to stretch the rope, Alan's head began to pound again until his consciousness wavered with the effort. There was a real risk of passing out, but the darkness subsided when he stopped exerting himself. He gave a jiggle, testing to see if he'd created any give.

If anything, the rope was tighter. And now the coat had slipped from his shoulders, jamming itself behind his back and hindering movement even more. Even if he didn't die, this was the last time Alan would ever use a disguise. It hadn't even worked well enough to fool a paper boy, and now it might be the nail in his coffin.

Exhausted and in pain everywhere from the waist up, Alan slumped to the side again, and let himself rest with a defeated groan.

Across the room, Adrienne yanked on a lever below the canisters.

Glot glot glot–

Sounding like a baroness chugging on a gin bottle, the canisters' contents began to empty. From the hollow vat came the sound of water, rising in pitch as the vat filled. When he turned back, Adrienne's face was right next to his own. Alan almost screamed.

"Not long now," she said, settling down beside him. "Once the solutions are mixed in the correct amounts, the solvent will be ready. An incredibly simple process."

"Too simple?" Alan said, as softly as he could. "Couldn't this all be too easy, Adrienne?"

"If only you knew how long I've researched the possibility of the solvent, you wouldn't ask that. I knew this would work long before I came here. Stealing the artefacts was just a formality. A checking of my sources, if you like. I've been using drawings of the vase in particular for years now."

"You went to a lot of trouble to check your facts. And gotten yourself into a lot of trouble, too."

"I'm not afraid of being caught, Alan. You had no clue where or who I was and the police are even further behind." She saw Alan's face droop and patted his shoulder. "Oh, but you were close, of course. You just couldn't put it all together."

"I know how you used the hospitals," Alan said a little too fast. "Using their roofs to send your Frog-men floating down to wherever they were stealing from. They could sneak in and out in their uniforms and no one would bother them."

Cupping his face, she kissed his cheek. "Better late than never, darling. I was wondering, when we stole the second artefact, why didn't you try to find out what they were? Find a connection? Do a little research of your own?"

"I…" Alan started, but couldn't finish. Why *hadn't* he thought of it? Because reading was Simon's thing, that's why. Leaping from rooftops was Alan's job. He didn't like this change in Adrienne's character. This little streak of arrogance. Alan wondered how he hadn't noticed this side of her before. Although it seemed like months, it was only two days since they'd last seen each other; walked arm in arm, been happy in each other's company. She can't have changed this much in two days. Simon had always told him that his infuriating sarcasm could drive people insane and now it seemed Alan had been just the thing to tip Adrienne over the edge. He should listen to his brother more. A dog who chases a stick too earnestly will drown when it lands in the sea. That's how Alan felt. He had chased this case across London, been beaten and bludgeoned, and now he felt like he was sinking. That, at least, was a sensation with little novelty to it.

"Even the newspapers did *some* research," Adrienne continued, legs tucked under her as if they were at a picnic in the park. "The vase from Aristotle's home in Greece, the tablet bearing the teachings of Rhazes. And the painting of Zhang Guo, of course. All ancient Alchemists. All with a piece of the puzzle. It was there for you to find if only you'd stopped to look for them. You could have even cheated and just read the newspapers."

Across the room, the sound of rushing fluids died away.

"I can't really believe it," she said, looking almost sad. "In that container is the Universal Solvent, a substance sought after for hundreds of years by men all over the world. And I've done it. In a loft in London's south side. And you're here to see it with me. Forget what I said earlier, Alan. I do forgive you. There's too much unknown about what will happen next for me to take that kind of weight with me."

Wrapping her arms around him, Adrienne cradled Alan's head against her bosom. He was too damn tired to fight her off again, and so let it happen and tried not to enjoy the feel of her against his skin. With a confidence that Alan had never seen in her before, she took his face in both hands and kissed him. He melted into the warm sensation despite himself. The fog in his head seemed a little thinner, the aching faded into an afterthought.

As she pulled away, Alan wished the ropes weren't holding him down for another reason entirely. The flushing of Adrienne's cheeks beneath her olive skin made her seem like a sculpture lit with some internal fire. Her eyes still heavy from the kiss, she said:

"Now, what do you say we change the world?" And with that, Adrienne was gone and there was only a beautiful, brilliant scientist stalking across the lab toward her instruments.

A rumble, which Alan felt rather than heard, brought him back to his senses. He spied the console's gauges where the orderlies were clustered. The needles were still rising, moving toward the red. His bottom vibrated like a carriage down a gravel track as the rumble grew, making his legs numb. Not certain why, he held his breath. The Frog-men worked, octopus-like, stepping over and under each other, arms almost knotting together. Whatever the plumbing problem was, it went back to sleep. Gauges slid down. Alan let out a sigh.

At the console, one of the orderlies span a large crank wheel. Like a leather spider, a harness descended from the ceiling to hang beside where Adrienne had pulled across a wheeled dressing screen, like they used in hospitals, blocking her from the orderlies' view. Although they couldn't see her, Alan still could.

Shrugging off her coat, she folded it across a nearby bench, kicking her shoes underneath. The apron was next.

Alan watched as she unbuttoned it, folded it neatly as if she wanted to wear it again tomorrow. Unable and unwilling to tear his eyes away, he watched as Adrienne untied the laces which ran down the front of her corset and peeled it off. Fighting against a primal part of his brain, Alan implored:

"Adrienne, stop this thing before it goes too far."

She just smiled at him, and turned slightly away as she slid down the sleeves of her dress. Alan swallowed, hard. Part of him was certain he should be looking away, another argued that the view was nothing new, that Adrienne could have stopped him seeing if she wanted to. Adrienne put the dress onto a hanger on the dressing screen, one arm laid across her breasts. Alan took in her profile, where her breasts and hips made casual curves like a Pre-Raphaelite muse, halted only by the folds of lace around her bloomers. Adrienne cast a look over her shoulder, and gave a little smile before turning her back on him entirely. Sliding off her bloomers, she laid them across the bench.

Alan's mind took him back to a certain Grecian stream where he'd once come across a young goddess bathing. The sight of the water cascading from her as she stood out of the water, splashed herself, letting the sun keep her warm as it rose toward noon. And how she'd sensed him there, covered herself as she did now with her arms, the look of innocent shock on her face. And how she'd slid back into the water to cover herself.

It was similar to how she eased that same alluring form into the hanging harness, a corset of sorts with high-legged pants built in, and a series of buckled straps. When she was ready, Adrienne gestured to an orderly and there was a clunk up by the loft's rafters. Cables, attaching the corset to a rig near the ceiling, snapped taught. Adrienne took to the air like a marionette, the harness bearing her across the room to dangle above the swirling vat of Universal Solvent. Lamps around the loft guttered as if the gas were being redirected elsewhere. The orderlies fought with the dials and switches but, all across the console, the gauges would go no lower than the burning orange section of their dials.

Alan finally realised what Adrienne had meant about not getting caught. She wasn't thinking of escape. Not in the traditional sense. She was going to dunk herself in solvent soup.

Adrienne's harness hoisted her up until her toes dangled over whatever liquid was now inside the vat. She really was going to do it. Until now, Alan had still been optimistic. Even just a little. The Adrienne he knew was many things, but adventurous wasn't one of them. She would turn around, realise the error of her ways. But he was apparently wrong for the hundredth time that day. Adrienne was hell-bent on seeing her experiment through.

Even if he had no intention of being with her, there was no way that Alan wanted the fluid in that container to touch Adrienne. He had to stop her. Get to the crank and raise the harness. Stop whatever that damn rumbling was, although he had no idea how. He tried to crawl his feet up under him, perhaps stand, only managing to rotate himself further round the water pipe and closer to the loft's wall. It was a change of scenery, at least.

Adrienne extended one delicate arm. One of the order-lies placed his hand on a large lever buried into the floor,

CRAIG HALLAM

and waited. Adrienne signalled to continue and the orderly squeezed the lever's brake handle before letting it go. The lever slammed forward and Alan whipped his head toward the vat just in time to see Adrienne disappear in an eruption of opaque green liquid. The harness's wires thrummed for a second, tight like a fisherman's line, then whipped back toward the ceiling.

The leather sash hung empty, dripping with the green fluid.

Adrienne was gone.

Alan darted his eyes around the room. The vat, the orderlies, the console, the door, and the damned pipe he was tied to. Frantic, he struggled against the ropes, not caring when his concussion fought back, little sounds of fear and anger and frustration in his throat like a trapped animal. Eventually his tightened throat let out a defeated bellow. The orderlies took little notice of him. They were too used to the screams of madmen.

"One of you had better cut me loose or there'll be hell to pay!" he screamed.

There was the other option, of course, that the orderlies would realise Alan had seen all their faces and decide he was too dangerous to keep breathing. But they weren't listening, and they weren't moving. One scribbled feverishly in Adrienne's notebook. Apparently there was more to see.

Above the formula, a mist was rising. Eddies formed. The hazy strands curled in on themselves, folding like ghastly dough.

"Oh my God." As Alan watched, the mist coalesced into a single cloud. A weak light ran around its insides, crackling with static. Rising clear of the vat, the mist drifted toward the ceiling. Alan and the orderlies followed its progress, the only sound was the scritch of pen on paper, until the cloud passed through the domed ceiling and out of sight.

Alan's face went taught, and he had to squeeze his eyes against it to stop himself from sobbing. Tears burnt. He fought against the lump in his throat, the stone in his chest, the cotton in his head. When he spoke, his voice was a rasp, and all he could think to say as he hung his aching head was, "She's gone."

The noise started under the floor, a rumble that set the water pipe at Alan's back vibrating. He snatched his eyes away from the ceiling, searching the room for the source. The Frog-men turned back to their contraptions, their goggles reflecting the console's dials in their lenses.

Tink

One of the gauges hit red.

8

ALAN KNEW NOTHING about the science of ancient civilisations, that was no secret. Neither were the holes in his knowledge regarding engineering and chemistry. But they had all become pretty important recently and so he regretted not reading more. Escapology was clearly a mystery as well. In the last few moments, as his day had gone from physical and emotional pain to potentially fatal, he became violently aware that he knew absolutely nothing that would have been of any use to him. In fact, sat strapped to a pipe in a Lunatic asylum's loft space with an exploding container of God-knows-what, he actually found it a little funny. It was hard not to smirk at the ridiculousness of it all.

Tink

Two out of four dials were now in the red.

Those gauges he understood. Never in his life had he come across one where the needle hitting the red area was a good thing. He guessed today wasn't going to be the exception. And he now knew enough about Alchemy, or this experiment at least, that he didn't want to be around when that green fluid exploded across the room. Whether consciousness had evaporated or not, Adrienne's body was gone. He was too fond of his fleshy bits to go the same way. He shoved her face to the back of his mind, out of the way, and focused on saving who he still could. Himself.

Tink

The console across the room began to rock where bolts held it to the ground. The orderlies looked at each other and started to back away. The one holding Adrienne's journal even stopped writing. The rumbling was rising, resting somewhere around the bowels now. Surely someone would hear it. But who was there to hear? Anyone within earshot was too busy arguing with the voices in their head.

Alan wondered how much of the formula had to touch you before you vaporised. Did you have to be immersed like Adrienne was, or would a drop be enough? He considered the loft's floor. The boards had warped and separated over the years until the vat's foundations rested on something resembling a huge sieve. When it burst, the Universal Solvent was going straight down to turn every lunatic, maniac and schizophrenic in the asylum into little clouds of floating crazy. Alan didn't want to think what would happen to London after that.

Tink

Four. That was four.

Every pair of eyes, goggled and not, jerked toward the vat. Alan could feel his bottom shifting across the floor to the vibration.

The orderlies moved as one, backing toward the door.

"Shouldn't one of you—" Alan was cut off by a piercing creak; a sound that reminded him of whale song, if the whale were in agony and trapped down a well. Formula started to come in little spits from the pipe connecting the canisters to the vat. On the console, one of the gauges exploded with a spear of steam, hit the opposite wall, and landed somewhere beyond the stacked crates.

The orderlies bolted, shoving and stepping over each other, fighting their way toward the door.

"Hey! Hey! Cut me loose."

The door slammed closed behind them and Alan heard a key clunk in the lock.

"Like that's going to help!"

The vat's barrel-like walls were straining at its brass rings like a fat man's braces. Droplets formed between the laths, dribbling down to the floor where they disappeared. Another gauge exploded, this time firing its glass face across the room to plink on the floor.

"Balls."

Fighting through the fiery cotton in his head, Alan tried to think.

The pipe at his back shook, rattling Alan with it. He looked up, looked down. The pipe was essentially held in place by where it entered the wall behind him and the floor below. He began to shuffle, hopping along the floor until he faced the opposite direction. Jerking his back, he forced his feet underneath him. The rope slid up the pipe until he was in a crouch. Now what?

The wall was close. Close enough. First one leg, then the other, Alan braced his feet against the old brickwork and started to push. The pipe creaked. It gave a little, taking the force but always returning to its original position when Alan rested. The pipe was old, its copper surface growing green patches all along its length. Using his boot heel, Alan slammed the pipe at its base, yelling in frustration.

"Break you damn thing! Break!"

Again and again, each time a *shtang* of struck metal. Taking stock of his progress, Alan saw that he'd made a dint. He braced the wall again. Shoving, jerking, throwing his back into it as flares went off in his vision. Christ, his head hurt.

From behind, the vat was in its death throes. Alan heard the crack of wood under pressure. Not long. With both feet against the wall, he squeezed his aching thighs. The pipe gave way, snapping at the top rather than the bottom where he'd hoped, hurtling Alan over backward. Where his boot had made a dint, the pipe bent, but didn't break, so that Alan was still tied, but now he laid along a downward slope with his feet higher than his head.

He cursed again as blood rushed toward his concussed head, making the world lose its colour. He fought to stay awake, knowing that a blackout now would be the end of him. Using his shoulders and feet, he started to squirm toward the pipe's broken end where it rested on the floor.

The rope slid off the end and Alan rolled over like a caterpillar. With the extra slack, the rope slid up and over his head. He stretched his fingers, grateful as the pins and needles showed that his hands would still work. Stumbling as he found his feet, there was no time to let the room stop spinning. Hoping that he wouldn't veer off course, Alan charged the loft's door, bouncing off when his shoulder proved too soft to break the old wood construction.

"Ow!"

He tried again, then kicked it, then shouldered it again. It wouldn't budge. He was trapped for good this time. Resting his burning head against the wood, he tried to ignore the sound of screaming machinery behind him.

From the other side of the door, someone knocked. A polite little rap. Alan stared at the wooden surface.

Another ratatat-tat.

There was no way. The concussion was finally getting the better of him, toying with his mind before his brain gave way completely. A mirage. A proverbial oasis in this dry madness he'd gotten himself into.

"Open up in the name of the law!"

Alan's eyes widened. Did hallucinations talk?

"Hello?"

"You in there, open up. This is the police. We demand you—"

"Jennings?" Alan screamed at the door. "Jennings, is that you? Jesus, man, break the door down. Break it down!"

A few seconds as the Sergeant barked orders, and the door spasmed. Alan moved away. They must have found something to ram it with. He looked at the hinges, the crack between the doors widening as they hit again.

"I might just get out of th—"

A lingering creak made Alan spin around in time to watch one of the vat's brass rings snap completely. The barrel-like container changed shape, the upper rim splaying outward. Formula sloshed over the edge like a bath overfilled.

That's all it was. A bath. A bath filled with green acid, but a bath all the same. Alan eyed the console, vat, empty canisters and the pipe at its base for the hundredth time. Taps, bath, boiler, plug hole. He had to take out the plug. Against his better judgement he ran toward the vat's base, carefully avoiding the waterfall of Formula down its sides, and to the pipe which was spraying more of the same. Alan shrugged off the longshoreman's coat and threw it over the leaks. Then he hugged the pipe. The pressure made it buck underneath him like fighting an anaconda, but he found purchase on the slick floorboards and heaved. The seal must have already been cracked, because it gave a little. The coat was already soaking. With his face pressed so close, he couldn't help but inhale fumes from the formula. Hoping that wouldn't be enough to turn his brains into mist, he hauled on the pipe again.

Somewhere behind him came the sound of splintering wood as the loft doors burst open, spewing blue uniforms. High-velocity splinters peppered Alan's body.

"Get out of the way!" he yelled, and gave the pipe one last pull.

He fell back, the pipe still clutched in his arms, and rolled away from the vat. Where the pressure released, the vat's outlet fired a stream of Formula across the room in a horizontal gush. Blue uniforms scattered to either side, some taking cover behind the door frame as the Formula shot out of the loft and down the corridor outside. There was the sound of liquid rushing down the staircase at the other end, all the way to the ground floor. At least it hadn't come crashing down on everyone below.

Gradually, the stream became a wilting thing that swiftly shortened to a dribble.

Alan lay on the floor, the pipe still held in a loving embrace, his eyes squeezed shut. As the sound of splashing boots approached, he looked up at Sergeant Jennings who was smiling despite everything.

"By God, Alan, you look terrible," said the Sergeant. "I see you've got yourself a new girl."

Alan looked at the pipe and tossed it aside.

"Very funny, Jennings. How the hell did you find me?"

Jennings whipped a handkerchief from his pocket as he knelt, doubled it, and applied it to Alan's head which had started to bleed all over again. Alan winced.

"A paper-boy reported you kidnapped. Said it was the fellow from the newspaper's front cover. He followed the carriage all the way to the Asylum. Looks like you owe that lad a hot meal."

"And the rest," muttered Alan.

"What've you got yourself into this time, then?"

Sitting up, Alan bought himself a little time to answer.

"Some lunatic from downstairs, probably. Gone in the head. Wanted to use Alchemy to melt himself," said Alan, breaking down his horrific afternoon as far as it would go and sprinkling it with half-truth.

Jennings turned to the vat, the dangling harness and the other contraptions in the room.

"Bloody hell. Looks like he managed it. Melting himself, eh? Mad."

Alan nodded, too tired to talk. He took the handker-chief from Jennings and reapplied it to his head. He looked around, half expecting to see Adrienne creeping out from some hidden trapdoor, then chastised himself for stupidity.

Jennings moved around the room, pointing to the equipment and constables in turns.

"No one touches that! God knows what it'll do. Someone call Schneider to come see to this lot."

"Jennings, what about the orderlies. The Frog-men," asked Alan.

"Looks like they let the lunatics out into the grounds then scarpered."

"They did something right, at least."

"Maybe so, but those lunatics are going to take hours to round up. They're everywhere. By then, those thieves will have a fair head-start. Probably never find them, now."

"Good."

"Sorry?"

"Oh, don't ask me, Jennings. I've had a crack on the head. Don't know what I'm saying."

9

A LOG POPPED in the fireplace, waking Alan from his doze. The book lay in his lap, at the page he'd randomly opened it to with no intention of reading. The Carpenter's living room was warm and comfortable enough that he could almost forget the various pains in his body. The door whispered on carpet and Helen burst in, skirts lifted to allow her to trot.

"Oh, my dear Alan. What did they do to you?"

She dropped onto the footstool beside him, skirts spreading around her feet, but the lace corset kept her back straight. Alan gave her a weak smile and began to melt against the chair's wings as Helen's hands lay across his cheeks and forehead.

"Rather what did he do to deserve it."

Alan leaned forward to see who else had entered.

"Oh lovely," he said. "You brought Percy with you. Sank anything recently, Percy?"

"Only your improbable reputation, Shaw," said Percy.

Alan leant back into Helen's fumbled attempts at nursing, shooting Percy a smile.

His father popped his head around the door, dressed in

his uniform.

"It's time, everyone."

Alan got up with a little unnecessary help from Helen and slid on his jacket. Everyone cleared out, with Alan bringing up the rear, plucking the Grecian vase from behind the living room door on his way out. It rattled with the clay tablet inside, and the scroll was jammed like a stopper into the top. A pair of carriages waited outside. Percy and Helen took the first and Alan climbed up beside his father in the second, sliding the vase between them.

With the hoot of a steam whistle, the carriage lurched forward and into the flow of traffic.

"How are you feeling?" asked Carpenter.

"Peachy," said Alan, his voice still a little croaky from his battered throat. He shifted the bandage around his forehead for comfort and tested the back for blood. "Stitches are holding just fine. Damn things hurt more going in than getting clubbed did."

"That's Police surgeons for you. It may not be pretty, and it hurts like hell, but they get the job done."

"I think he'd be better off working on blankets from now on."

The carriage swerved and they heard gravel under the wheels.

"Nearly there," said Carpenter, looking for something to say. "I don't suppose you can remember anything at all about the madman that caused all this?"

Alan looked out of the carriage window as if he'd never seen London it before.

"Not really. The whole thing's fuzzy with my head and all."

"Right, right," said the Inspector. "Only, we found a woman's clothes in the loft. Folded up, like. Odd that."

"Damned odd."

Carpenter narrowed his eyes at the back of Alan's head. In the end, he just nodded to the vase. "You could have left that with us, you know."

"And let it out of my sight again? Not a chance in hell." The carriage drew up sharp and Alan reached for the door.

"And it looks far more impressive when you step out of the carriage with it under your arm, right?" said his Father. Despite his attempts to maintain anger, suspicion, or even worry, Carpenter couldn't help but smile at this adopted son.

Alan looked at his father, innocence oozing from every pore in his bruised face.

"I hadn't thought of that."

He turned the carriage's latch and the door swung open to the flare of a hundred cameras.

Extract from *The Illustrated Times*, Page Three, 4ᵗʰ May, 1851.

A spate of recent thefts, including the removal of a Grecian vase from The Great Exhibition of The Works of Industry of All Nations in London's newest spectacle— The Crystal Palace, as well as a clay tablet of Persian origin from the British Museum and a painting from the Chinese ambassadorial suite, have all ended on a satis-

factory note today when an investigation by the Police Force's A Division led to the retrieval of all three artefacts. Closely involved was a young man of virtuous reputation and adopted son of the aforementioned police division's Inspector. Alan Shaw, the young adventurer who selflessly flung himself from a balcony in The Crystal Palace in pursuit of the thieves themselves, took it upon himself to further assist in retrieving the artefacts. When interviewed on his motivations for his involvement, Master Shaw stated that he simply "knew I had to stop them".

With the items now returned, Master Shaw has received a hailstorm of plaudits from European Ambassadors and representatives who witnessed his heroic act, and readers of the The Illustrated Times are already lobbying for a medal of bravery to be awarded him.

Extract from *The Morning Post*, Page Two,
4th May, 1851

...and what are the Police Force doing about the escape of almost fifty lunatics onto London's streets? Inspector Hector James of the South Bank Police Force stated this morning that "all that can be done, is being done". Meanwhile London, and the South Bank in particular, have been plunged into chaos. A stream of assaults of the most despicable nature, and obscure scenes from the darkest nightmares are a result of a mass-escape from Bethlehem Lunatic Asylum, reportedly caused by three orderlies who were involved in a recent spate of thefts

and who left the asylum gates wide open as they made their escape from the police. Thankfully, most of the lunatics had neither the mind nor the luck to make use of the blatant idiocy surrounding them, but some remain off the leash and on our streets. Who knows, in the days that come—

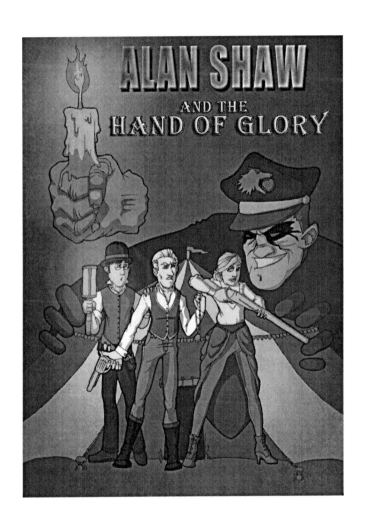

Brighton, England, 1853

WITH HIS HAT down over his eyes, his back to the old oak and his legs stretched out across the grass, Alan could have passed for a cowboy, if only his hat weren't a straw boater. He dozed, hands clasped over a copy of *Titus Gladstone Adventures* open on his stomach as the bright summer sunshine warmed the park's lawn. Around him, families picnicked under their parasols whilst ladies wantonly threw caution to the wind, daring to take off their ankle boots and expose an inch of lower leg. Children in little breeches and shirts ran circles across the grass, chasing and throwing balls just for the sake of it while their mothers yelled cautions from nearby. Men, similarly attired to Alan in their straw hats and shirt sleeves, light trousers and spats, puffed their cigars and read newspaper articles about a smoggy London which seemed a world away.

And to of all this, Alan was completely oblivious. Swaying in and out of slumber, the noises seemed distant. His mind wandered across vistas of sleepy images, never picking one particular subject, but rambling in a stream of semiconscious memories filled with smoking guns, dark taverns, tentacled mechanical beasts and death-defying leaps. Beneath the brim of his hat, a sleepy smirk teased across his lips. It wasn't until a pair of shadows fell across him that he snapped to attention, although without moving a muscle. One of his hands slid a little further across his belly, as if he were getting comfortable, and found a revolver where he'd nestled it under his armpit. He found the grip and slowly drew back the hammer so that it wouldn't click.

Then he waited.

"Miss Charlotte Ashdown, may I introduce my brother, Alan."

Alan tipped up the brim of his hat to regard Simon's shins, and followed the pinstripes all the way up to his brother's face. The revolver's hammer released as slowly and as silently as it had been cocked. Tiny circles of light sat over Simon's eyes where his spectacles reflected the midday sun. He was grinning, and it was pretty clear why. A young woman stood with her hand slid through Simon's crooked elbow, dressed in a pale skirt and frill-fronted blouse. Her face was heart-shaped, warm, surrounded by mousy-blonde hair that tussled up beneath her stylishly cocked hat. Alan couldn't help noticing her figure, which could only be described as well-made. If she had been a man, Alan would have said that she could handle herself pretty well by the set of her shoulders. Her hips were fuller and her bust more ample than Alan would have expected for his brother's taste.

Alan dragged himself up to standing, dusted his trousers, and when the young woman (for she certainly wasn't a girl) extended her hand, he took it. The grip was firmer than he expected.

"Charmed to meet you, Mister Carpenter." She had a forthright manner that Alan couldn't help but like, and seemed completely devoid of the snobbery that upper-class girls wore more thickly than make-up.

Alan took off his straw boater and skimmed it through the air, sending it scything across the sunlit park. When the breeze caught it, it took a long curve and lodged itself in a bush.

"No idea how you wear those things, Simon." He looked to the young woman, Charlotte. And drew a quick hand through his hair. "And it's Shaw, Madame, I never did take the name."

"Oh, no offense meant."

"None taken. We're brothers in every other way, aren't we Simon?"

"Only because we fed you and you kept coming back."

Alan gave a passable terrier impression. "So what's so fantastic about Brighton that I had to get up early this morning, dressed like a complete gooseberry – do you know he actually sent me a list of things I was allowed to wear, Charlotte? – and stand on King's Cross' crowded platform for an hour before being rocketed to the east coast?"

Charlotte gave a broad smile, which suited her.

Not a giggler, Alan thought. *Interesting.*

"Perhaps we should start by showing you, shouldn't we?" she said.

The young couple walked away across the lawn, Charlotte readjusting her lacy parasol so that it covered both her and Simon, Alan in their wake.

"Charming," he muttered with no real malice in it. "I'll just go and get sunstroke then shall I?"

Out of the park they waited beside the road for a space to safely cross between the humming *Obeissante* passenger carriages and other steam-cabs. There were so many styles and shapes, some with drivers raised up on high seats, some nothing more than an engine with wheels where the driver's seat seemed an afterthought; some with their motors shoved out front, others with big backsides like dung beetles; some chuffed faintly green Jerry Log smoke from stacks like riverboats, some excreted coal-based thunderclouds from exhausts at the rear. Everyone seemed to have their own idea of how the steam-cab should look.

Dodging across the traffic, the couple and Alan hopped up onto the wider walkway of Brighton's promenade. Houses with multiple storeys, painted in an array of pastel colours, faced out to sea, as if waiting for something to return from across the waves. The promenade itself was wide as any road, with flagstones which bounced back the sunlight in a harsh glare. A thick rail ran all the way along the pavement on its beachward side to stop idiots from falling onto the sand below, or rather to give people something to lean on in the sun. Alan breathed in, and had to admit that there was something vitalising about the air. This wasn't the harsh, briney onslaught Alan had fought against on ships. This was the sea playing nice, licking the coastline, tempting people to come bathe. And bathe they did. Wheeled wooden beach huts on ratchet chains delivered and received people from the sea so that no one would be seen strutting around in their bathing suits, and cause any undue commotion. Out among the breakers, Alan could make out the capped heads of men and women bobbing like Halloween apples; separated into their pens by buoy-mounted ropes so that no funny business could go on under the water.

Alan snorted. He thought back to a brief shore leave near Nice, where the girls liked to swim more than anything else in the world, glistening like pale salmon as they dived from the cliffs and into the warm Mediterranean Sea. But there hadn't been a whole lot of bathing suits to go around in Nice. Alan smiled. Those girls would have made Brighton's brightly coloured changing huts blush a uniform red, that's for sure.

The sand below was otherwise littered with canvas deck chairs, and smatterings of digging in the sand like crabs. Mothers wafting themselves with fans; fathers rolled up trouser cuffs and wriggled their toes in the golden grains of the beach.

All along the promenade, couples who looked just like Simon and Charlotte were everywhere, arm in arm, shaded beneath parasols. People's clothes were a lighter colour than were found in London. Maybe it was because there was no smog to stain the colours. Where London was grey and brown and black, Brighton was cream and yellow and green; leather elbow patches on tweed, and bow-ties. Everything looked and smelled and sounded fresh, as if God had baked that batch of the world just that morning. Even the few larking seagulls with their harsh brays were less of an annoyance than they should have been. Alan found himself smiling and nodding to strangers, passing pleasantries in the time it took to walk on by. But his smiles soon felt strained, fixed as a doll's. His jaw began to ache. It was tiring being so jaunty all the time. And the people's ignorance began to annoy him. They acted as if the whole world shared this very moment and place; that nothing could possibly be wrong elsewhere as long as Brighton had a summer day. But for Alan, it was different. No matter what he did to take his mind off of it, he was glaringly aware that somewhere, something bad was happening, just out of sight.

Alan walked a little quicker to catch up with Charlotte and Simon before the depression set in properly. They were talking about people he didn't know.

"Alan, you really should come to dinner. My friends would be thrilled to meet you. We've all heard so much," Charlotte said.

"Whatever Simon's said, it's all lies."

"Actually, I meant in the newspapers. You certainly have a knack for getting into scrapes."

"It's getting back out that's the trick."

That warm, broad smile again from Charlotte.

"Would you like to come? We country folk don't get much big city excitement. I'm sure you could tell us a tale or two. Perhaps about your latest voyage?"

"Actually, I'm done with ships for the moment and doubt I'll be going back. There might be a lot of sea, but it all looks the same. I've been travelling over land recently." Alan caught sight of his brother, who was managing to nod and plead at the same time without making a sound. "But it sounds thrilling."

"Maybe we can even find a lady to pair you up with,"

Simon suggested.

"Simon." Charlotte's reproachful tone sounded a little marital. Alan shuddered. "I'm sure he can find a woman all on his own."

Alan gave her a grateful smile. To his surprise, she winked.

THE JEWEL IN Brighton's sandy crown was the pier. Hundreds of wooden pillars rose from the sea, and then the beach, as it stretched out like a giant centipede crawling ashore, and the palladium roofs were the creature's crystal blue and steel carapace.

The trio turned to walk along the pier's length, the wind picking up slightly as they moved further from the land. They stopped to admire the palladium, but Alan found himself looking around at the people more than the buildings. People were always more interesting. When they had walked the pier's length, Charlotte made them stand at the furthest railing with Brighton behind them, so all that could be seen was waves on every side.

"It's just like being on a ship, I imagine," said Charlotte.

Simon caught Alan's gaze and made pleading gestures with his eyebrows.

"Yes, just like it," Alan agreed, and then added all the things in his head as to why it wasn't. Including the sturdiness of the ground, the lack of constant battering of spray and the absence of sweaty, grizzled men working their hands to paste.

Charlotte was still staring at the horizon when she said:

"Do you and your brother always speak in signals, Simon?"

The colour drained from Simon's face. Their little side-long glances and nods, devised long ago to counteract their father's meddling, had been spotted by Charlotte in a matter of minutes. Alan felt completely petrified for his brother, but couldn't help grinning. He had to press his lips together so tight that they quivered.

When Simon hadn't answered, Charlotte asked again.

"Simon?"

"Um, not often, no."

"So only in the presence of a lady when you don't want her to know what you're conspiring about."

Alan made a little sound in the back of his throat, a laugh cut short. Charlotte turned her eyes on him. She wasn't smiling, wasn't angry or annoyed or stern. Her face was comfortably blank. Simon was still dithering, not giving out complete sentences. He took of his hat, and dabbed at his brow with a handkerchief.

"And what exactly is it that you were saying to each other? Alan? What about you? Your brother seems to have been rendered incapable of speech."

Alan just shook his head. God knows what laughing in the face of a woman he'd just met could do to his brother's chances of romance, if they weren't destroyed already. And he had to admit that this unexpected turn of her mood had him on the defensive.

Something broke in Charlotte's face of which there hadn't been a sign of before. She started laughing, and not just laughing, but heaving in great gasping roars. The way the laughter shook her made pleasing motions with her curves. Alan felt a little pang of jealousy toward his brother, but squashed it.

Charlotte turned to Simon, tickling him in his ribs as if they were children.

"Oh, you London boys. You're so damned easy!"

Simon finally gave a nervous laugh. "I'll never learn."

"You got him, Charlotte. Good and proper," Alan laughed.

"I think I got you, too, Alan. I saw your face when you thought you were caught." She extended another tickling finger his way, but Alan threw up his hands in surrender. She smiled. "Dinner tonight might be even more fun than I hoped."

Alan made a mental note to never play poker with Charlotte.

When the cobwebs were firmly blown off by the brisk sea air, the couple and their spare wheel made their way back along the pier. Pasted to the lamp posts and benches, leaflets declared nightly entertainments for the visitors of Brighton in a shocking array of fonts and colours. The pavilion itself would host a burlesque troupe that very evening. Alan waggled his eyebrows. Simon blushed, and Charlotte rolled her eyes.

"Honestly, you men and your cheap titillation."

"Cheap? It's more than a shilling to get in," Alan said.

"And we have the meal later," Simon reminded him.

"That won't take all night. It'll still be the shy side of midnight once people have run off home." He seemed to be getting no joy. "Alright. What about this instead?"

He pointed to a sandwich board beside the bench, hand-painted and slightly peeling from long use. It read:

THE MASKELYNE FAMILY CIRCUS

introduces

The Wonders of the World

To

BRIGHTON BEACH

Including the awe-inspiring

CLOCKWORK CIRCUS

and the alluring acrobatics of

JESSAMINE

The board's image showed a troupe of brightly-dressed people performing acrobatic feats in a Big Top, and above, a girl swung from a trapeze. In smaller circles around the main picture were other attractions which Alan rattled off.

"Horacio, the World's Strongest Dwarf. The Alluring Snake-girl. Ki-Ki the Amazonian Bird Girl – better not leave those two together – Bertolli, the Man with Two Faces. Madame Arcane, Seer of the Future. That'd be good for you two, eh? See how it all pans out?" He waggled his eyebrows again and gestured to the final image for his final argument. "Now who doesn't want to see a bear on a bicycle? Simon, you're a biologist. Surely that fascinates you."

"Hardly—"

"Let's go see it! Look, Charlotte's smiling. She loves the idea."

The young woman heaved a sigh, threw up her arms and laughed. "Alright, alright, we'll go. It can't be so bad. But on one condition."

"Name it."

"Stop calling me Charlotte. My father calls me Charlotte. I'm Lottie to everyone else."

"Sold. Come on, Simon. I haven't been to a proper circus in ages. There'll be gypsies and everything."

"You're like a child," his brother said.

"What's your point?"

Simon looked to Lottie, and back to Alan. "Fine. We'll go. *After* dinner."

2

STOOD BACK FROM the beach, the Albion Hotel's giant white façade held a thousand windows which reflected the sunlight, making the building look as if it were glowing inwardly. Inside, the view was no less impressive where wide arches, roman pillars and spectacular chandeliers seemed to imbue the interior with its own impossible horizon. Once the stiff little concierge had insisted on taking Alan's bag to the elevator, and Alan had insisted otherwise with much less tact, they rode upward in the brass cage and onto an upper corridor carpeted with red like a dragon's gullet.

As it turned out, Simon and Alan had adjacent rooms; Charlotte was situated further around but on the same floor, facing the ocean. The boys converged in Alan's room which, somehow, had more liquor in it than Simon's. The room was big enough for the bed, a pair of chairs beside a small plaster fireplace, a little wardrobe, but little else other than pacing the carpet a little. Inspector Carpenter's boys sat at opposite ends of the mantelpiece.

Alan had broken off two chunks of ice from the hotel kitchen's clattering refrigeration cubicle and brought it up to pour their scotch over. They raised their glasses, but didn't name a toast.

"Separate rooms, eh? That's very gentlemanly of you."

"Grow up, Alan."

"It was a compliment!"

"Coming from you, I doubt it."

"You've always had more self-restraint than me, Simon. There's not a thing wrong with it. How come we're staying here, anyway? I thought Charlotte lived around these parts."

"Her parents have an estate outside Brighton. But it made more sense staying here rather than travelling back and forth every day."

Alan narrowed his eyes. "Really. I thought they were well off. They have a cab, surely?"

"Of course," Simon averted his eyes to the fire and sipped his drink. He heard Alan's barely concealed chuckle. "What?"

"Nothing," said Alan, but he was still smiling.

Simon sighed. There was something coming, he knew. "Come on. Out with it."

"You haven't met her parents yet, have you? Do they even know she's here with you?"

Simon looked at his brother for a moment of weighted silence.

Alan jabbed an accusing finger. "That's it! They don't know. You sly old—"

"It's not that." Simon's face screwed up, like a man walking in overly-tight shoes. "Lottie's father. He doesn't like me."

It was Alan's turn to screw up his face.

"You what? How can he not like you? You're you! Blimey, he should meet me!"

Simon sat forward in his chair, elbows on knees, and stared down at his scotch as if it were warming his hands. "I think he'd probably prefer you, actually."

"Well bugger him."

"Oh, what an image!" Simon smiled at his own innuendo, despite himself. "But I can't. He thinks that research biology isn't a man's occupation. A real man, I mean. And I have to get him on side—"

"What does Lottie say about all this? She's a woman with a brain, I can tell. I prefer mine without them if I can help it, but to each their own—"

"That's because you don't like them getting too close to you. Intelligent women ask questions."

"And want conversations," Alan faked a shudder.

Simon humoured him with a weak smile.

"She says to ignore him. It's our decision. She says she loves me, Alan." Simon avoided his brother's gaze. Alan's face had fallen at those heavy words. All of sudden, the room had become serious. "I'm thinking of asking her to marry me."

Alan realised he was spilling his drink only when he heard the sound of scotch hitting the carpet. He cursed, set his drink down and grabbed the handkerchief from Simon's top pocket so that he could mop up.

"Bloody hell, Simon. Why?"

"Don't you like her?"

Alan looked up from the floor where the worst of the spill had been corralled.

"She's fine. Nice, I mean. Attractive in a shapely kind of

way. It's just why would you do that to yourself? It's early, man. Enjoy it a while longer. Get down that corridor and woo her. Buy her flowers, eat food and drink wine if you like, take strolls and write bad poetry, but don't bloody run to the altar."

"When you find that person, Alan, you just know. You never want to leave them, spend a night apart, eat your meals with anyone else."

Alan peered at his brother through a cage made by his fingers. "Sounds like torture to me."

"You'll see when it happens to you," was all that Simon would say on the subject.

"I doubt it."

But Alan wasn't going to get the last word this time. Simon removed his glasses and stared right into him.

"Not if you keep treating women like they're disposable," he retorted.

Alan couldn't disguise his shock. He could feel his face burning. Not with anger, but embarrassment. He snarled to cover it up. "I only throw those back that aren't worth keeping," he shot back.

"And how would you know the difference?"

Simon had laid the last card. Alan had nothing.

They sat in silence for a while, sulking.

"Well this has got bloody serious, bloody quick," Alan mumbled, and drained his glass.

"That's because I was asking you a very serious question about a very serious decision, and I thought you might put some of your usual witticism aside for a minute, and just give me your God's honest opinion."

Alan looked into the fire for a moment, sipped at his drink, and thought.

"I'm being an arse, aren't I?" he finally said. "You know what I'm like, Simon. More than anyone else, you know. I don't mean harm. It's just the way my mind works."

"When it works at all," Simon huffed. Alan conceded defeat with a raised glass. Simon leant back in his chair and returned to his usual, calm tone. "It's a self defence mechanism, Alan. It's not really your fault. You're just squirting ink. But I'm your *brother*."

"I know." Alan said, somehow managing to add 'and I'm glad' without having to say it.

"Do we have to hug, now?"

"God, I hope not," said Alan, and reached for the scotch.

THE DINNER WAS far from thrilling. Alan sat tucked away at one end of the table, forking chicken and gravy into his mouth in a steady stream so that people wouldn't ask him to talk. His conversation with Simon had left him a little raw. His brother was always the youngest, the least experienced, the naïve one that needed Alan to show him how and tell him why. But that didn't seem to be the case anymore. Simon had overtaken in terms of Life, and Alan was left in the dust. And if Alan's role in the Carpenter family was no longer necessary, then he wasn't sure why he was there at all. When it came right down to it, Alan always knew that he was a cuckoo. He stuck out like a sore thumb in the Carpenter nest and, while he'd been schooled better than he could have ever been on the streets, there was still too much urchin in him to ever be like Simon. And people liked Simon. Sure, they liked Alan, too, but in more of a good-for-a-laugh kind of way, whereas Simon got respect and friendship and, right now, love of the proper kind.

Alan drained his glass, which had contained a healthy dose of scotch only a few minutes ago, and looked around for more.

Simon and Lottie sat together, their elbows lightly touching as if they couldn't live any other way. Alan found that he had to force his current mouthful to go down.

Dragging his thoughts back to the dinner table did very little to ease his mind. There were five other people, three women, two men, and Alan couldn't remember a single damned name. They all did something that involved owning something else, like that was a job. They dressed like they had money, but they were country rich, not city rich. At least they were a bit more easy-going than their London equivalents. There was a lot of laughter at the table, although Alan found himself merely smiling.

Scraping his fork along his plate, Alan realised that he was out of food. Damn. As if she had been waiting, one of the young women turned to him with a friendly smile and an inane question.

"So, Mister Shaw, what is it that you do?"

"At any given moment, I can be doing a variety of things. Could you narrow it down for me?"

The girl chuckled, even though it wasn't meant to be funny. Alan really wished someone would fill his glass again. Christ almighty, was there *no* proper liquor in this place?

"Well, if you weren't here in Brighton today, what

would you be doing in London?"

"Oh, there's trouble everywhere in London. I'm sure I could find some to get into."

Every time he spoke, Alan felt just a little more out of place. His accent really was grating when he compared it to the others. Simon never seemed to mind, he was used to his brother's Cheapside accent. But when Alan spoke, even though his accent had become watered down over the years, the others smiled at him as if they were letting a child take his time to speak.

The young woman took both of Alan's non-committal answers, and could do nothing with them. So she pretended to hear something interesting mentioned across the table and turned away.

Simon seemed to be enjoying himself. He drank the wine, ate his food (which was something stuffed with something else), and seemed perfectly comfortable that Lottie's father was paying for it all. It was the way of their world, but not Alan's. He ate when he could pay for it, and had been known to steal it when he couldn't, although that had admittedly happened far less since joining the Carpenter family. But at least he'd never owed anyone any favours; just court appearances.

Checking the carriage clock on the mantelpiece, which seemed to be running backward, Alan realised that it really wasn't too late to find something better to do. Did things not blow up in Brighton? Or get stolen? Or people get mugged and let out blood-curdling screams that could send him hurtling out of the room without having to suffer any elongated goodbyes. Where were all the psychopaths? It had something to do with the sun, he decided. Even the crazies were too busy playing croquet to plot anything diabolical.

Thankfully no one needed to get hurt in order for Alan to escape. The maid came in with her trolley, clearing the plates, and moving the evening along to its next phase. Now there was only dessert to make it through. A nice, short course.

Unless these lot were the cigar and sherry types.

3

THOSE LOT HAD been the cigar and sherry types. But luckily Simon and Lottie weren't. The couple had made their goodbyes with handshakes and hugs while Alan threw a polite wave from his spot in the doorway.

Alan pretty much ran down the hotel's steps and into the night air, and would have happily kept running all the way to the beach and swam to Belgium if he hadn't come here for the sake of his brother. Across the road, the odd Rapide or Rickett still chugged by, panting and puffing smoke to taint the evening air. Along the promenade's railing, the electric lamps had been lit, creating a string of pearls which curved with the coastline; the pier and the lit palladium hung like a glowing pendant casting its cold glow on the sea.

Brighton had a generator, it seemed, and each arc lamp along the coast had its own little relay to lasso the invisible power. But the soft glow of gas lamps could still be seen flickering against the inside of windows on the opposite side of the road. Even London only had electricity on certain main streets and squares, and only Buckingham Palace had it on the inside. It seemed Brighton hadn't entirely switched over to wireless, pipeless power either.

"What lovely people," said Simon, but the fact that he aimed it at Alan made it seem like an order.

"Very nice," said Alan.

Lottie tugged her coat against the brisk breeze that had rolled in after sunset. "I thought they were boring. Now where's this circus, Alan?"

Simon and Alan exchanged glances, but more carefully this time. Alan waved for a steam-cab which soon *phut-phut*ed at the curb as they clambered in.

A few miles down the beach, where Brighton's promenade gave way to countryside, a cluster of lights like mating glow worms drew the eye to a series of haphazard constructs on a grassy verge by the beach. Floating high above the cluster of peaked tents and curved caravan roofs, lit by a glittering anchor-wire, a zeppelin bore the name of "Cirque Du Maskelyne". A halo of lamps under-lit the massive balloon, while from the functional-looking gondola hung searchlights which sliced their beams back and forth through the night. The whole circus must have been drawing immense power from Brighton's generator. Alan wondered if that was technically theft since the power was probably going spare anyway.

The mouth-watering smell of cooking meat, coupled with the hubbub of laughter and joyous screams, swirled in the summer heat, rolling out of the circus to meet them as they passed under a wooden arch bearing the now familiar words "Cirque du Maskelyne", which had been hammered into the dirt as a makeshift entrance.

Tiny humming bulbs hung on insulated cables like

bunting across the circus' make-shift avenues. Others lined arches and rooftops of sideshows and penny games, or climbed the candy-stripe helter-skelter in a helix. The gypsy circus had managed to make day from night the way that Brighton or even London couldn't, albeit a daylight that flickered and pulsed. Smaller huts and stalls sold glistening foods, novelties and chances to be taken on foolish games. Alan steered Simon and Lottie away from them all, explaining carefully how the trick was done and how the odds were phenomenally stacked against them. He kept an eye out for the gypsies, although he knew there'd be very little trouble tonight. The Maskelyne family were onto a good thing so close to Brighton, and would never jeopardise that with rumours of pickpockets and cutpurses. They would come down very hard on any unsavoury types attempting illegal acts, he was sure. But they still weren't hard to spot, the gypsy men with their long black coats and boots, collars turned up and lank dark hair, wide-brimmed hats or hoods. They worked the games right enough, but their faces remained as shadows. If it had been anywhere but a circus, they would seem suspicious. But none of the holidaying visitors seemed to mind. They barely seemed to notice the gypsies at all, even as they handed over money or received food from them. Perhaps it was all the lights; another Brighton trick to make you feel more secure than you really were.

"Now you're talking," Alan shouted over to Lottie and Simon who had gone to a stall for a bag of boiled sweets. He pointed to a sign for the Big Top acrobat act. Simon passed him a long string of liquorice when they returned, and Alan bit off a piece. "This sounds amazing."

"It sounds ridiculous," Simon retorted, the white dusting from a bonbon spreading around his mouth. Lottie tutted, licked a spot on her handkerchief, and dabbed it away. Simon smiled at her as if she'd just given him water in the Sahara. Alan had that little pang of jealousy again.

"That's what I said. Amazing. Lottie? You're the tie-breaker. Don't let the fact that Simon dotes on you be a factor in your decision."

"I'd say it was the other way around," Lottie said. Simon gave a snide smile to his brother. "Let's go. I have to admit I'm intrigued."

"And the night is still young," Alan threw his arms wide, almost whipping someone with his liquorice lace. "Who knows what it could still hold?"

INSIDE THE BIG top, poles like shaved pine trees held the canvas roof, each of its stitched sections painted to the effect of dark wood. The floor of the ring was bare earth, swept to a finish so smooth that Alan could have easily been fooled into thinking that it was made of stone. There was the faint smell of lubricating oil and the tiered benches which the audience perched on gave off another pleasant scent. Children stood down by the ring's railing, a low circle of gold-painted wood, peering over or running marathons around it. But what made this big top different to any Alan had seen before were the cogs. Great things cut out of wood and painted gold, they were up by the ceiling, using the tents poles as their axles, teeth locking together in slow rotation above the audience's heads. And someone, somewhere, was beating out a ticking rhythm which Alan couldn't place inside the tent at all. The whole effect was that they were sat on the insides of an enormous pocket watch. Or perhaps they had been shrunk down to the appropriate size.

"And you said that this was going to be rubbish," Alan muttered to his brother. He stretched his legs out in front of him, getting comfortable, but really wanting to stop the children from continuously running past them.

Simon, with Lottie on his other side, gave a shrug. "I have to admit, they certainly have put a lot of work into this."

Lottie leaned over Simon's lap so that Alan could hear her as well.

"This looks incredible!"

"I wish Simon was as enthusiastic," mocked Alan.

"When they get started Simon will be enjoying it just like the rest of us," Lottie assured him.

The ticking sound, wherever it came from, slowed, slowed, and stopped with a *thunk,* something like a grandfather clock winding down. The audience sat in tense silence. Even the children stopped their snickering.

Where a pair of curtains hung at the back of the ring, there was movement. The squeaking of a winch pulled the curtains aside to reveal a round man in bright red stockings and bandmaster's jacket, complete with golden tassels and tall hat. Moving with the jerky, off-balance gait of an Automaton, he stepped out into the ring's centre, and raised a large steel cone to his mouth. Alan could see that, beneath his perfectly waxed moustache, the ringmaster's face was painted white, and two black lines ran down from the corners of his mouth to make him look like a puppet. The ringmaster's mouth snapped open and closed a few times like the little man on a Swiss clock announcing the hour, but never making a sound. And then he was moving backward, managing to make the exact reverse of his jerky entrance movements. The curtains closed.

Alan realised that he was grinning. Looking over to Simon and Lottie he saw that they were, too. The whole audience, in fact, were rapt.

Then the ticking started again, slowly building to a drumming two-tone beat that shook the benches beneath them. And then the show began.

4

IRST CAME THE tumblers, all dressed in baggy clothes buttoned with bright pom-poms and conical hats. Their faces were painted like the bandmaster's, lines leading down from the corner of their mouths, eyes wide and staring and rimmed with black. They capered and rolled, managing to look both jerky and agile at the same time. One stood at the side of the ring, clapping his hands like a clockwork monkey until the audience took up the beat. Another dropped on his back as if toppling by accident and bounded up again; another somersaulted overhead as if his legs were spring-loaded. Cartwheels came in never-ending circles and fake falls turned to effortless handstands. There was utter acrobatic carnage in the Big Top's ring, far too much to watch all at once, and the performer's impressions of machines just made it all the more amazing. Alan's attention was dragged this way and that, his head whipping around to see the end of some incredible feat only to be dragged away to the other side of the ring where something similarly fantastic was happening. And then the tumblers came together, piling high using each other's hands and legs as footholds until they were a swaying human pyramid. After much applause, each tumbler flipped or somersaulted to the ground. They bowed in unison and as the crowd clapped and cheered, the tumblers careened out of the ring.

Before the applause died away, the jugglers marched in, each movement in perfect unison. They split into two rows, facing each other, bowed in three jerky movements and all of a sudden the air was filled with projectiles. Balls of all sizes, clubs and swords meshing in the air like spinning atoms. As the crowd watched the air with slack jaws, a uniformity began to show in the performance; the jugglers' perfect timing creating something resembling the meshing of the churning cogs above. It could have been no less perfectly timed if the objects were painted on rotating discs and turned by cams and gears.

Another round of rousing applause as the jugglers marched back through the curtained archway.

And then, the final act. The lights on the ring floor winked out, plunging the Big Top into darkness. Gasps and whispers from the audience created a sound as if the wind were hushing through the tent.

Up where the great cogs turned, teeth knitting together, a single spotlight snapped on. There was the girl from the poster, Jessamine, in a shaft of light. She was perfectly still, only the gear's rotation moving her in and out of sight high above the ground. Her skin was painted the same eggshell colour as her leotard and tights, gems that sparkled like diamonds dappling her body, throwing off little fireworks of pale light. A short crinoline skirt made her look as if she were wearing an inverted rose blossom. Around her wrists, elbows, knees and feet, painted lines made it seem as if she were built with joints by some master artificer. On her cheeks, rosy circles had been daubed, her eyes wide and innocent. Her hair was tugged back into a tight bun that made her face seem even more doll-like.

As Alan took in every inch of her slender frame and its decorations, Jessamine fell forward, toppling headfirst from the gear's edge.

The audience gasped, a woman screamed. Alan jerked forward in his seat as the girl fell, his mouth open, ready to yell for what good it would do her. The spotlight followed her descent with morbid curiosity, lighting Jessamine's face and its look of perfect, innocent surprise as she hurtled toward the Big Top's hard ground.

The lights pulsed, shocking the eyes as a dark figure swung out from the tent's roof, arching its way through the air on whistling wires to snatch the girl from her deadly plummet. She curled in the dark figure's arms like a child as they came back on the return swing. Alan could finally see the figure, and realised that it was a man, his outfit not entirely black, but as detailed as the girl's in its own way. A few of the same gems decorated his legs and chest. He wore a black mask over his whole face, moulded into a sad smile. And then he was on the forward swing again, and he threw the girl into the air. She spread out like a bird, head tilted back to catch the wind on her face. And she was falling again. But the dark character was swinging in from another place this time, suspended by his feet from a trapeze. Jessamine seemed to be falling too fast, there was no way he could catch her. But then their hands locked and she was propelled through the air. At the end of the swing, she flipped, legs scissoring, and suddenly the Big top's ceiling was a mass of those dark figures, swinging back and forth, the cogs turning them in mesmeric circles. And against that swirling background, the girl looped and swooped and twirled and span. The audience began to clap and they didn't stop. Every time the girl was caught, they erupted louder, cheering and whooping. Screams from the women became playful rather than petrified, and the circus tent was filled with a tense, amazing energy.

But just as the audience were starting to become comfortable, chattering amongst themselves, pointing at the great feats of aerial agility and laughing, something seemed to go horribly wrong. The timings of the swings were off. All of the dark, saviour-like figures were swinging away from the centre of the tent, and the girl was in the air with no one on the return swing. She was falling. This time faster, spinning and twirling, she fell like a sparkling shard of glass. She reached out her hands and found no one there. Her fingers spasmed, pleading, arms pin-wheeling as she tried to grab at thin air. Her mouth dropped open, tilted toward the ground which was rushing toward her.

The tent was plunged into darkness once more. The drum slammed a final beat. Alan swore he felt the collision in the seat beneath him. He heard Lottie whisper: "Oh my God." Simon made an odd sound in his throat and both brothers began to scramble in the dark, ready to throw themselves into the ring and attend to the girl.

They reached the ring's edge before the lights snapped on again.

The floor was empty.

There was no indent in the ground. No crumpled girl in her tights and leotard.

A whistle rang out across the Big Top and people were gasping again. Alan drew his eyes away from the impossibly empty spot on the ground, up to where the cogs still turned.

And there she was.

Perched at the tip of the gear as if she'd never fallen at all, sparkling. She took a single bow, snapping at the waist, never breaking from her clockwork character, and the lights by the ceiling went out.

The audience erupted in a deafening racket of cheering and applause. Alan looked at this brother, and back at Lottie. Each one of them wore the same fixed, amazed, terrified grin. Alan tried to make a snappy comment, but his jaw wouldn't work.

"DEAR GOD IN Heaven. I think I've developed a heart condition," Simon chuckled.

Lottie was tittering to herself almost uncontrollably, with a faint tremor to her voice.

The cool evening air, blinking lights and round-about music from the circus seemed tinny and false compared to the Big Top's show. Alan had felt this way before, in the brief moments on waking from an intense dream where the two worlds co-exist, just for a moment, and nothing seemed certain any more. The crowd seemed to move in slow motion, flickering like characters on a zeotrope in the circus' stuttering lights. Letting his eyes wander, unfocussed, so that his brain could recover, his attention snapped toward a flash of red and gold in the crowd. The scent of the sea seemed to swell in his nostrils, Alan felt as if he were swaying on his feet, and then the sensation was gone as quickly as it had come. His head whipped around, searching for whatever it was that had sparked the odd reaction; a brief uprising of intense memory that teetered on the edge of his attention and then disappeared before he could register it fully. But the crowd had churned and swelled, and whatever it was that grabbed Alan's attention was gone.

"Alright," Simon interrupted. "We need to do something else. Quick. Before I start thinking about how they did that and my brain turns to mud." He looked over to Alan, but his brother was staring into the crowd, his eyes narrow and brow creased. "Alan? Are you alright?"

Alan took a minute to answer. He scanned the crowd, back and forth. When he eventually spoke, he seemed cautious.

"Yes. I thought I saw—" he shook his head "—never mind."

"Someone you know?" asked Lottie.

"Not quite. Something familiar. Just colours really. A shape—never mind."

"I think the show has turned your brain soft," said Simon, but the concern on his face was obvious.

"You're probably right." Alan seemed to shake himself, and smiled to placate Simon and Lottie's worried looks. "What shall we do now?"

Hooking his arms through theirs, he guided them away. As they walked, he took one more glance over his shoulder.

5

THEY WANDERED THROUGH the circus, flitting between the pools of light around each stall like the moths that clustered the bulbs above. Lottie and Simon forgot about Alan's sighting, dismissing it and getting back into the fun of the circus. But Alan couldn't. He was young, barely twenty one, but he'd been so many places already, met so many people. Sometimes his memories seemed a barrage of half-remembered faces and places, ports and bunks, nights in bars and wine houses that were even foggier than most. But somewhere in there was a memory that had made enough of an impression to stop him in his tracks.

He felt Lottie's hand on his forearm. She and Simon had stopped at a stall to watch people pitching stitched balls at coconuts, and Alan had almost sauntered right past.

"Alan, are you alright?"

"Yes, of course, just thinking."

"Try not to think too hard, eh? I'm sure it will come to you when you least expect it. These things always do."

Alan looked at the young woman. She was his age, and mature for her years – just like him, although in a different way. Alan had seen things that could make a heart quiver, survived things that had given him a very liberal view of his own mortality, far too young, but Lottie hadn't. Alan tried to read something in her eyes, those circles of dark grey edged with green. What had made her grow up so fast? Perhaps the over-bearing father that Simon had mentioned.

"Simon's on to a good thing with you," he said, instead of voicing his thoughts.

To his surprise, Lottie blushed. She looked over her shoulder, partly to hide the glow of her cheeks, partly to look at Simon who stood laughing with some strangers who had just missed the coconuts and were goading him to have a try. As they watched, he took up the challenge, removing his frock coat, laying it across the stall's counter, and then taking up the balls. He missed. Three times. Everyone laughed again, especially Simon.

"He's a good man," whispered Lottie.

"One of the best," Alan agreed.

"Do you think – no, never mind. I shouldn't be asking his brother."

"Yes." Their eyes met again. "He does. Very much."

Now it was Lottie's turn to study Alan. She obviously saw no deception there. She smiled that warm, broad smile.

Simon wandered over, shrugging on his jacket.

"What're you two whispering about?"

"How you throw like a sissy," Alan said.

"Hardy har."

"So, boys, what's next?"

"Lady and gentlemen, if I could, perhaps, make a suggestion?" They all turned around to see a stout little man with a walrus-like moustache who had joined the group unseen. Around the moustache was healthy stubble, as if he were trying to grow his beard in. Although short and wide, he certainly wasn't fat, but heavily built with forearms like hairy cannons.

Alan wondered how long he'd been stood there, right in his blind spot, and looked around to see where the little man could have come from so quickly and silently. They were out in the open, well away from any tents or stalls. That was annoying.

"Who the hell are you?"

"I, the hell, am Cicero." The little man bowed low. His accent was strong, European, and his general look of dark hair and eyes, coupled with a strong nose and chin, told Alan that he was of gypsy stock. That and the gold medallion that swung from his neck when he bowed. "I am the purveyor of this cirque's…darker attractions."

"Dare I ask?" said Simon.

"I do not know, sir. Are you brave enough to seek forbidden knowledge?"

"I get the feeling you're pitching more than you can sell, my friend." Alan managed to make 'friend' sound like 'little sod'.

"Do you know all that resides in Heaven and Earth, sir? Are you such a man? Come. Come with your friends. I will share with you gypsy secrets like nothing you have ever beheld."

Cicero walked off into the crowds without another word or backward glance. Alan looked to Simon, Simon to Lottie, and Lottie between them both.

"I'm game for a laugh," said Alan, and disappeared into

the crowd after the little gypsy.

Simon chewed his lip, but followed, whispering to Lottie.

"If the secret turns out to be how to rob three foolish English-folk, I'm going to be very disappointed."

Cicero led them across the circus, winding his way through the crowds of people as if he had some second sight, never bumping or having to struggle through sideways, but darting and gliding expertly. Alan was having no such luck. People flowed around him as if he were trapped in the middle of some elaborate dance where faces and skirts and dickie bows seemed to blur and phase together until the carnival kaleidoscope had Alan turning little circles rather than making any progress. He lost sight of the stout little gypsy several times, only to spot him again, ever further ahead, as the crowd naturally parted for Cicero but not Alan. Simon and Lottie strolled along behind, still arm in arm, as the trio were led past the blinking bunting lights, away from the flickering stalls and jostling people, and down an alleyway created by two tents.

Alan shot a look over his shoulder. Simon was looking more and more wary, Lottie wasn't far behind. But either Cicero's banter was compelling enough, or neither wanted to back away from a challenge in front of the other. In the back of his mind, Alan wished one of them would. Maybe it was the odd flash of memory playing on his mind, Cicero's cryptic babblings, or how they were being led into the bowels of the circus, but something felt off.

Rounding one of the tents, Cicero came to a tall, narrow tent, something like a cubicle, which appeared to be the entrance to a series of caravans, interconnected by canvas tunnels. The caravans were what Alan would expect. Curved roofs, huge wagon-style wheels, ornately painted and carved with leaves and curlicues. From the looks of them, they were still drawn by horses when in motion.

Cicero tugged the tent's entrance aside and gestured for them to enter without actually crossing the threshold himself.

"You're not going in?" asked Alan, one eyebrow arched.

"No, sir. I have seen this once before. And once is enough for any man. Good luck, my friends," and he waved them inside again.

Alan snorted, but stepped in, disappearing into the gloom. Simon and Lottie exchanged glances, spied Cicero's encouraging, gap-infested grin, and followed suit.

Inside the tent-cubicle, they climbed a few wooden steps into the first caravan. A faint orange glow lit the insides sparingly. The only sounds were the creak of the floorboards and the sputter and pop of hot candlewax as it hit the ground, collecting in amorphous mounds. Alan stepped forward to let Simon and Lottie in behind him, which meant stepping further into the dim caravan.

He almost fell over a boy.

Stood in the centre of the room, perfectly still, perfectly patient, the boy clutched a thin bamboo cane in his hands like the knight on a tomb lid, and stared at a spot somewhere a few inches behind Alan's head. His corneas were a milky white, heavy eyelids covering half of them. The boy smiled as the trio stood beside each other, exposing a row of tiny teeth which were well on their way to rotting, and turned away, tapping his cane on the ground. As he passed through a dusty lace curtain which covered a doorway to their right, the material whispered and floated back into place like a fog.

"I suppose we follow," said Alan.

Through the curtain, a short canvas tunnel took them across a makeshift bridge of wooden boards which led from one caravan to another. Then another curtain. The boy was waiting for them, cane in hand just like before. He stood at the back of the room, away from a wooden banister which penned off a section of the caravan's interior, a sign bearing the name "Bartoli" in fading gold curlicues hung from the ceiling. In the centre of the pen, under an old oil lamp, was a single chair. The man who sat there looked perfectly normal to Alan. He sat, legs crossed, dressed in a loose farmer's shirt and breeches. His hair was long, dark, hanging in curtains down to his chin. Not an unusual appearance for an Italian peasant. Spying Alan and Simon, he gave them a companionable nod, and aimed a bow of the head to Lottie, then proceeded to stuff and light a smoking pipe. It took him a while; long enough for Alan and his brother to exchange several glances, each becoming more frustrated. But, eventually, the pipe lit and Bartoli puffed a few clouds of smoke. He took a long draw, the bowl glowing amber, lighting his face with an evil brightness. Then he turned his head, and drew back his hair as if to tuck it behind an ear. Underneath, where his jawline, ear and cheek should have been, were features of another kind. Lottie gasped. Even Alan turned slightly away, although unable to tear his eyes from Bartoli's second face. Simon leant forward, fascinated.

Clustered together beside Bartoli's true face was a tiny upturned nose, the heavy hoods of two eyes which would never open, and a perfect row of prominent teeth. As they watched, Bartoli exhaled, and pipe smoke rolled out of the goblin face's nostrils.

Alan was ready to mutter something not altogether Christian, but Lottie beat him to it.

Bartoli turned back, replacing his hair, and drew on his pipe, the smoke coming back out in a long sigh as he looked at the floor. Apparently, he didn't want to meet their eyes a second time.

The boy's cane tap-tapped on the floor as he made his way to the next room, Alan, Simon and Lottie followed silently in his wake. Lottie mumbled something to Simon, who nodded back. Simon puffed out his cheeks and shook his head toward Alan. Alan agreed.

Inside the next caravan was another pen, this one lit with several gas lamps, the ceiling and walls hung with red fabric to create a warm, comfortable space. To the rear, a paper screen showed the glow of another lamp beyond it. The boy tapped his way to the back of the room and waited patiently. There was quiet for a moment, and then the whispering crackle of a gramophone came from somewhere unseen. Thin, reedy music filled the air that undulated and warbled an odd tune. Behind the screen, a silhouetted figure danced in the backlit space. It was obviously female, the well-proportioned body making pleasing movements like a wavering candle flame, arms above her head, hips serpentine. Alan smiled. It seemed he hadn't missed the burlesque after all. But his mouth snapped shut when the dancer's arm reached out from behind the screen, beckoning to him. It was slender, strong, but the skin didn't move as it should. From the tips of her fingers to the curve of her elbow the dancer's skin was covered in scaly plaques. One leg came next, toes daintily poised, and coated in the same way. The woman finally danced out into full view, dressed in the pale pink veils of a belly dancer, the colour of which only seemed to accent the soft grey of her skin. She was hairless, even without eyelashes, which made her pale blue eyes seem small and wily. Her attention was fixed on Alan and as she danced forward. With the music becoming an excited trill, her body stretched and bent like a willow branch. She lifted one leg, pirouetted, and brought the toes down on the pen's banister closest to Alan, her upper body folding over it as if making an offering to her Gods.

Between the differing reactions of his guts and his loins, Alan began to feel extremely uncomfortable.

The music finished its crescendo, and the woman made a show of walking back toward her screen, turning, and winking at Alan before exiting.

Tap tap tap came the boy's cane.

"You were right, Lottie. Alan *can* find his own women. I've no idea why I was so worried."

Alan gave his brother a jab with his elbow.

In the next caravans they saw a girl suspended in a gilt cage above the floor, dressed in a skirt of feathers, her body tiny and frail, and an avian face with a beak-like nose and sharp eyes; a midget who came out of his pen and lifted Lottie, seated on a chair, clear off the floor; a man who swallowed three straight-bladed swords without blinking and followed it by spitting fire into the air above his open-topped caravan. And then came the show which disconcerted Alan the most.

A powerful scent of acrid incense made his eyes water so that he had to dab at them with his sleeve. The floor was carpeted with mismatched rugs which puffed up dust as they crossed the caravan to a small table covered with black cloth which took centre stage. Behind a large chunk of rough-cut quartz sat an old woman, unmistakably gypsy with her long nose and eyes like oil puddles. She wore a headdress lined with tiny gold medallions, and a shawl over her shoulders that hid all of her body except for the one arm, wrinkled like a Hawthorne branch, which led to an outstretched palm. Alan made a show of patting his pockets. Simon rolled his eyes and pulled a few loose coins from his waistcoat. He dropped a shilling into the old woman's palm, bending forward and extending his arm as far as it would go so that he could maintain his distance.

Nothing happened.

Simon gave a huff and dropped another shilling, the same way.

The old woman's hand snapped closed like a bear trap, then extended out over the quartz crystal. The shillings were nowhere to be seen.

There was silence for a moment as the old woman's shaking hand hovered over the crystal. When she spoke, her voice was softer than Alan would have expected, almost weak rather than cracked and shrill. He was probably mixing up his imagery between witches and clairvoyants, although he could see little difference so far.

"You have already met the love of your life," said the old gypsy.

Lottie slid her hand through Simon's arm and gave him a squeeze. Simon squeezed back.

Alan made a faint gagging sound.

"You will marry soon."

Lottie's eyebrows shot up, and she searched Simon's face. He managed to pull a passable poker face.

"Your children will be healthy, wealthy, and long-lived."

Alan groaned. "If that's your three predictions, I could have—"

"You will lose someone you love. Sooner than you should," interrupted the old woman.

Alan shivered. The hairs on his neck did a Mexican wave.

Lottie and Simon exchanged glances, but in the glow of the other predictions, the last one seemed thin enough for them to ignore. The boy made his way out of the room with Simon and Lottie. Alan hung back. He eyed the old woman, trying to weigh her up.

"What a load of old tosh," he muttered, and made to leave. Before he could tug the doorway curtain aside, the old gypsy spoke again:

"Ask your question, you who are so sure of what is true."

He looked after Simon and Lottie who were walking on ahead, oblivious that he wasn't there, then back to the old woman. She still hadn't looked up from the crystal.

"Will I ever have—"

"Yes. Once, and only once," said the crone.

"I only need to find it once."

"You would think so."

"What does that mean?"

Beneath her hooked nose, the crone smiled.

"You should catch up with your brother."

Sliding a silver florin from his pocket, Alan flicked it with his thumbnail, and ducked through the curtain. Before hitting the table top, the coin blurred in the air, and disappeared.

6

WHEN ALAN GOT through to the final caravan, Simon and Lottie were waiting for him. The last room was longer than the others, and an open door to Alan's right lead out into the night. Sounds and smells of the more normal circus attractions floated in. The boy was nowhere to be seen.

"Where did you get to?" asked Simon.

"Got lost," Alan huffed.

Simon gave his brother a wary glance which read '*we'll talk about this later*'.

Around the final room, wooden cabinets lined the walls, and a few glass cases sat in the middle of the floor. Simon and Lottie moved from one cabinet to the next, opening their doors to show framed and bottled curiosities inside; pickled punks, obscure skulls, taxidermy freaks and creations, various mystical paraphernalia from the other side of the world, each with a neatly written paper tag attached. Simon read a few, but soon lost interest when he realised that the Latin used on the labels was bogus.

Alan made his way to the larger glass cases. In the first was a unicorn horn, over eight feet in length. He moved along with a snort. He'd seen Narwhal tusks in the wild around the Greenland coast the year before last and they were much more impressive there. The next case held the skeleton of a 'Rat King', several petrified vermin with their tales fused together. But the final display turned even his hardened stomach. On a wooden pedestal sat a human hand, clenched into a fist so that it could forever hold a dark tallow candle. The paper tag read:

"Hand of Glory – A hanged man's severed left hand, holding a candle made from his own fat and wicked with his hair. Deepens the slumber of those within a house so that burglars may enter unchallenged."

"I'm amazed they never caught on," Alan muttered, and gave a shudder.

A thud.

Through the canvas corridor, back the way they'd come, drifted the sounds of muffled argument. The old woman's voice he knew, the other was male, low and strained. But he couldn't make out the words. Simon and Lottie exchanged glances. The sounds stopped.

Through the doorway which led back to the clairvoyant stepped a man in uniform. His grey overalls, topped with a similarly coloured jacket, bore upon the right breast an embroidered red wolf eating a golden sun. It expanded in Alan's vision until it was all he could see.

Distant memories surfaced for the second time that night. The red wolf's victorious sneer towering over him. Sea spray stung his skin as the makeshift raft threatened to pitch him back into the icy sea. Distant screams merging with the roar of the waves – the roar of the huge red beast's glee at seeing its enemies defeated.

Alan shook his head, squeezing his eyes closed so that they could refocus on the present where the tip of an odd weapon wavered inches from his nose. It was vaguely gun-shaped, but the barrel was swollen like a wasp's belly to fill where the ammunition chamber should be, and a canister was screwed at an angle into the rear of the weapon, just above where the stranger gripped the wooden butt.

There was nothing for it. Alan raised his hands, slowly, while memories continued to coalesce. He narrowed his eyes at the man bearing the red wolf.

"I know you, now—"

The gun coughed a grey-green cloud. Alan took in the scent of ethanol and swamp gas, and his world went dark. The sound of his own body thudding on the caravan's wooden floor jarred his mind, then grew still.

7

ALAN SLAPPED SOMETHING away from his face, hearing it skitter across the floor. He sat bolt upright, almost head-butting Simon's concerned face, hanging over him. The room performed a neat little corkscrew. Clapping hands over his head, Alan quickly laid back down again, the swelling pain fading from blinding agony to mere dull torment.

"Why is it always my damned head?" he groaned.

His eyes opened just enough to take in his surroundings.

They were still in the caravan, although he was now laid on the floor between the display cases. Lottie went to retrieve the bottle of smelling salts that he had knocked from her hand. Simon sat beside him. Glass littered the floor over by the larger cases, and one now lay empty where a desiccated human hand had once been. There were sounds of weeping. Alan turned his head gingerly to find the source. By the caravan's entrance the old clairvoyant knelt on the ground, tears falling in crystalline droplets from her hung head, hugging the severed hand as if it were her child. And the young acrobat they'd all seen fall to her death not an hour before, Jessamine, sat with her arms wrapped over the

247

old woman's shoulders, still dressed in her sparkling tights and leotard.

"Alan?" Simon said, with a tone that suggested it was the third or fourth time. "Are you alright?"

"No."

Simon nodded to Lottie. "He'll be fine. I'd be more worried if he wasn't complaining."

"What happened after I went down?"

"Simon scared him away. He ran straight at him, grabbed his gun and gave him a fair fright, I think. Perhaps he wasn't expecting resistance."

"The world's gone mad," Alan muttered.

"I think you were very brave darling." Lottie aimed that at Simon, who blushed.

"I didn't think. I just did it."

"See? I keep telling you that not thinking is the way forward." Alan tried to get to his feet, but slumped back down. "Whatever you do, don't help me up." With an ungrateful groan, he let Simon and Lottie take a hand each and drag him to his feet. He swayed a little, and grabbed Simon's elbow to steady himself without anyone seeing. Simon let him.

"You seemed to know him, Alan. But from where?"

Alan tried to nod, but his headache flared. Instead, he muttered an affirmative through clamped teeth. "It was the uniform I recognised. The red wolf patch. Seen it before."

"Where?"

"Never mind," said Lottie. "Let's let the police worry about it. We all saw him, we can give a fair description—"

"No!" barked Jessamine with more fire than her petite body appeared able to contain. She fixed her eyes on each of them separately. "This is no concern of yours. Leave. No police."

"My brother has been assaulted, I'd say—"

Alan laid a hand on Simon's arm, silencing him.

"I think that's our cue to get off stage," Alan said. Simon took another glance at Jessamine, who was still scowling at them, but conceded with a huff.

Simon swung his arm around Alan's back and helped him to the door.

"Alright, Simon, I'm not an invalid."

"Shut up and let me help you."

"Fair enough."

They stepped down from the caravan and back into the circus night with the sounds of sobbing still filling the caravan behind them. As they made their way through the thinning crowds, Alan could feel Jessamine's gaze on the back of his neck by the prickling of the hairs, making sure they were gone. He took a glance backward and saw her in the caravan's doorway, arms folded and face stern.

"We should still contact the police," said Lottie. It was getting late, and the moon had already started its downward course.

"No point. They'll just deny anything happened," said Alan.

Lottie gave a nod. "I see. They'd never involve the authorities."

Simon gave Alan a firm look. "And you're going to leave

it, aren't you? Just walk away and admit that none of this is your business. Aren't you? Alan?"

"Yes, yes. Leave me alone. I've been bored, tricked, disgusted and gassed so far tonight, I don't need to be pestered as well."

8

A LITTLE WAY outside Brighton, along a track which led away from the main road and through a copse of trees to a manicured expanse beyond, Alan lay under another tree, boots crossed, dozing in the shade. His knotted hands made a decent pillow. Even under the tree, the day's midday heat was making him sweat, and he'd undone the top buttons of his shirt to let some air circulate.

He'd been to warmer countries, places where the geography was more striking than the gentle undulation of hills, fields and moors that England had to offer; places that thrilled the senses with exotic scents and sounds. But he had to admit that there was nothing quite like an English summer day with a perfect breeze carrying the not-quite-scent of fresh air to tickle his skin. It almost made the London winters worth braving and momentarily washed away the memories of curling up in Harker's Tavern, knees up to his chest and hands tucked under his armpits to protect against the gnawing frostbite.

He shivered despite the heat.

The rumble of hooves grew steadily closer. Alan creaked open an eye. A small group of riders came toward him, a dust cloud obscuring their mount's legs so that they could have been hovering. Lottie pulled up first, gently guiding her mount around. Her riding gear was something novel to behold for a city boy; a lady's top hat, white blouse with supportive corset around her waist, and long black boots that went up under a calf-length skirt. As her entourage rode up beside her, Alan noticed that the other women rode side-saddle where Lottie didn't. And then Simon pulled up the rear giving a valiant, though ungainly, attempt at staying upright on his mount.

"Having a nice time, Alan?" asked Lottie.

"Lovely, thank you." He kept his eyes shut, but spread a smile to soften his ignorance.

"Can we still not convince you to come riding with us?"

"Not likely."

"It's actually quite fun," Simon chuckled, swaying in his saddle. Lottie gave him a look that was half love, half pity, as if Simon were a child who was trying very hard but utterly useless.

"You won't catch me travelling on anything with a brain of its own."

"They're quite docile," offered Lottie.

"That's what they say about dogs, but every winter you hear of one who's hungry enough and has a mind to eat its owner."

Simon rolled his eyes. Lottie's friends grimaced, but she gave a weary smile. "Quite the image. We're stopping for lunch. I suppose you'll join in with that?"

"Absolutely!"

"I thought you might."

Lottie swung a leg over her saddle and dropped to the ground. With the billowing of her skirt, Alan could see that she was actually wearing a pair of flesh-tone trousers underneath. The skirt was a ruse, it seemed. Simon slid from his horse with a little more care, patted the beast's neck and made his way over to sit beside his brother. Removing his spectacles and bowler, he ran a handkerchief over his neck and face.

"How was it?"

Simon made sure the women were a safe distance away, laying out blankets and sharing out food from a large wicker hamper. "Bloody petrifying."

Alan laughed loud enough to scare a cluster of starlings from the branches above.

"What have you been doing?"

"Just relaxing. Thinking."

"I hope it wasn't about a certain circus thief."

"Of course not."

"Really?"

"Yes."

"Liar. Come on, you might as tell me."

"There's nothing we can do about it. They don't want our help, Simon. That's the end of it. That's what you told me."

Alan still lay in his prone position, a very careful not-smile on his face. Simon hooked the wire frames of his glasses back over his ears, and gave a sigh.

"Just tell me what you're up to."

Alan lifted himself up onto his elbow, grinning.

"I knew you'd come around."

ALAN STEPPED OUT of the Albion Hotel's doors, tugging his coat around him as the rising wind caught it, trying to expose the revolver dangling alongside his ribs. He stepped down to street level and turned right, toward the promenade. Glancing over his shoulder, he checked he wasn't being followed. The last thing he needed was for Simon to tail him and get himself into trouble. He'd promised he wouldn't get involved, and Alan had even convinced him that it was tactically sound for Simon to remain in reserve in case anything went wrong. But Alan knew his brother all too well, and with his heart firmly in the right place and a naive mind attached to it, Alan wouldn't put it past him to get in the way somehow.

Stepping up to the promenade's curb, Alan searched for the glow of a waiting hansom's lamp. The night was well on its way once more; the sounds of the distant carnival music drifted down the beach. Other than that and haunting whispers of wind, the promenade was silent.

After a while a hansom came chuffing along the promenade, its vacancy lamp glowing in the dark. Alan lifted a hand and the driver pulled in, nodding at the directions he was given, and Alan climbed inside. His bottom was on the seat and the carriage moving off again before he noticed the figure sat in the box's darker corner. Alan jerked back, giving himself as much distance as the confines of the carriage would allow, and yanked his revolver free.

"Woah woah woah! Steady on, Alan!"

Alan leant cautiously forward but not far enough that his revolver wasn't still prominent, letting his eyes adjust to the dark. The figure removed its hat, very slowly. Alan let out a sagging sigh, and uncocked his weapon.

"Bloody hell, Simon. You nearly got yourself perforated." Alan yanked aside the carriage's curtain, letting the false light of the promenade lamps fill the carriage. His brother sat in his frock coat and spats, a satchel on his lap and a look of relief behind his spectacles. He ran a hand through his hair, a calming gesture Alan was accustomed to. "You said you were staying behind."

"If you think I'm letting you go off on your own again, you're sorely mistaken. The last time you nearly got yourself killed. And who had to come back from University to monitor your concussion for three days? Me, that's who. I'm coming with you, and that's final."

Alan's one raised eyebrow was joined by the other. He sat back in his seat, holstering his revolver. He turned his smile toward the window.

"I see."

Simon's voice tensed at his brother's tone. "What do you see?"

"Lottie's rubbing off on you." Alan turned his smile back on Simon.

Simon went to say something but decided against it. He worked his jaw for a moment. "Maybe so."

"It's good. I like it," said Alan. "So what's our plan?"

Simon smiled and opened the satchel on his knee as the carriage hit a rut in the road, bouncing them along. "I've come prepared."

Alan watched as his brother set the contents of his satchel on the seat beside him. A small wooden box, a larger cardboard box labelled with paper that Alan couldn't read in the gloom, a knife with a flat ended blade like a machete in miniature, and something resembling a stick grenade made of metal. But it wasn't until Simon produced a handgun that Alan saw fit to comment.

"Where the hell did you get a gun from?"

"I can have a gun if I want. You don't have the monopoly on danger in our family, Alan. And if you think I'm travelling around England without a little something, you're mistaken."

"Let me see that."

Gripping the barrel, Simon snapped the weapon open as if breaking it in two halves, checked that it was empty, then handed it carefully to Alan. It was heavier than he expected. The barrel was stubby, but wide, like flare guns Alan had seen on ships. He snapped it open to see six empty chambers, twice the size of any bullet he'd ever seen. As if anticipating his question, Simon opened the cardboard box and handed a shell to his brother. It was blunt ended like a shotgun shell, although a little narrower.

"You carry some hefty ordinance, Simon. Have you ever used it?"

"Just once. In practice. I'm afraid I'm not a very good shot, so the shells give me more chance of hitting something."

"Shredding it more like." Alan handed back the weapon with a new appreciation for his brother, and watched as Simon loaded the chambers and checked the safety before setting it aside.

"Someone once told me that there's no point doing things by halves."

"Why do I get the sinking feeling that it was me?"

"Because it was. You might be glad of it later."

"Just make sure I'm well behind you if you use it, alright?"

Simon smirked, and shrugged off his coat which he folded neatly and placed inside the satchel. To Alan's surprise, he then removed his spectacles. Taking the wooden box, he placed them inside and removed something else before leaning way forward and fiddling with his eye. When Simon sat up he was blinking furiously until his eyes focussed in a way that Alan had never seen them do before.

"Lenses?"

"Sometimes glasses just get in the way. Especially when using microscopes. It's annoying. I can't wear them for more than a few hours at a time, mind."

"They must have cost you a fortune."

"Actually, I know a glass blower in Bloomsbury who makes parts for my scopes. We were discussing the benefits of ocular lenses and he said he'd wanted to try making some, so I volunteered to be his test subject."

Alan shook his head. "I'm getting the feeling that I don't know you at all."

"Maybe you should be around a bit more."

Simon's tone was light, and his attention firmly on his transformation, but Alan took the blow hard. He went quiet, and just watched as his brother turned from quiet biologist to crime fighting butterfly.

Simon continued unawares, rolling up his sleeves, emptying the box of shells into a pouch on a specimen collection belt which had been hidden under his coat, and slotting the knife in next to it. Then he checked his hand cannon once more and stowed it in the belt as well. With that done, still in his waistcoat, spats and bowler, Simon managed to look ready for action while still being undeniably a gentleman. Dressed in only his shirt, boots and jacket, Alan felt a tad underdressed for a night's adventure.

They sat in comfortable silence for a while before Simon spoke again:

"You haven't asked about Helen."

"I wondered how long it'd take you. Well done. Over twenty four hours is a record."

"I thought you'd want to know how she was. What she's up to."

Alan turned a forcefully blank face on his brother.

"How is she? What's she up to?"

"Sometimes you're insufferable."

"The suffering is entirely mine."

Simon huffed. "Oh Lord, listen to you. What did you ever do about it, Alan? What did you ever say? Even if Helen knew how you felt, would you resign her to a life of waiting around for you to come home? I doubt it."

Alan settled back, unperturbed by the well-worn conversation. Both brothers could almost answer before the other ended their sentence, it was so well practiced.

"Maybe I'd be around more if she gave me a reason to stay."

"Poppycock. You've wanted out of London since we first met. It was one of the first stories you ever told me, and the most frequent. Where you'd go, who you'd meet. And it was fine for a while. But it was a child's dream and, as you got older, it became a childish one."

"You wanted to be a soldier," Alan smirked.

"When I was ten years old, yes. I'm twenty one. *We* are twenty one years old, Alan. I have a job and a wonderful woman. You're still clinging on to childhood fancies and running around the world looking for God-knows-what it is you want."

"Did you bring Helen up just so that you could argue at me about staying in London?"

"Maybe."

"Well stop it. Or I might just clock you one and leave you in the carriage."

Simon grumbled, but before he did as he was told, there was just one more thing to say:

"She's pregnant."

Alan's jaw dropped.

9

"**W**HAT DID YOU go and tell me something like that for?" Alan asked as the carriage pulled up, half a mile from the circus' entrance.

"To make a point. Move on."

They climbed into the dark and Simon paid the driver by the weak light of the moon. The carriage pulled away. As the fog of exhaust dissipated, and the sweeping headlamps died away, it left them on a pitch black road north of Brighton where the glowing mass of the Cirque Du Maskelyne sat on the dunes which led down to the sea.

"Bloody hell, Simon. I've moved on. I moved on twenty women ago." To make his point quite literal, Alan moved on into the night, stepping from the road and crossing the surrounding fields at an oblique angle to come to the circus away from the entrance.

"I hope to God you're exaggerating," Simon said.

"Sorry to disappoint."

"I wouldn't even know what to do with twenty women."

"I didn't mean simultaneously, Simon."

"Still. Don't you get bored? Of going over the same old

thing, I mean?"

"You'd be amazed—" Alan grunted as he lurched in the dark, his foot disappearing into an unseen hole. "Balls. It's bloody dark out here. What kind of plan was this?"

"Your kind of plan. Here, hold on."

Simon reached into his satchel, accompanied by the sounds of Alan removing himself from the hole, and pulled out the contraption which could have been a stick grenade. Grasping the end, Simon rotated it to reveal three windows along the stick's length, and gave it a gentle shake. Light blossomed to life, reflected out into the night by a series of kaleidoscopic mirrors. Alan winced.

Simon gave a pleased little smirk. "Bright, aren't they?"

"You've got worms in a stick?"

"Arachnocampa Luminosa. We found their light doesn't disrupt the other insects as much as gaslight when we're studying nocturnal species."

"If this night gets any stranger, I swear I'll just go home and forget all about it."

"No you won't."

Alan smiled, the soft green light of the worms making him look manic.

"No, you're right. I'll be disappointed if it *doesn't*."

They set out across the dark, the glow worm torch saving them from spraining ankles or going sprawling in the field's ruts and runnels. Making swifter progress with a little light, they came to the edge of the circus where smaller tents and a few caravans made an encompassing wall. Checking in either direction, Alan slipped the knife from his brother's belt, and began sawing at a row of stitches between a tent's sown sections.

"Not exactly built for security are they?" said Simon, holding the torch high for Alan to see by.

"Who'd want to break into a circus?"

"Who indeed. Apart from us. What manner of military steals an occult artefact from a circus?"

"A barmy one, apparently. One that puts tentacles on its submersibles."

"We don't really know what we're getting into here, do we?"

"Not a clue." Alan's smile faded in the dark. "Listen, Simon, there's no shame in going back. Especially when you're going back to Lottie. Let me go on this goose chase alone. I'm actually pretty good at it. What I mean to say isn't that I don't want you here, but rather that you have nothing to prove. I know you're a good man and so does Lottie. I'd never forgive myself if something happened to you and, more importantly, neither would she."

Simon pushed by, shoving the torch into Alan's hand and ducking through the opening cut in the tent's side. "Oh stop your flapping and come on."

"So that's what it feels like to be sarcasmed at, is it?"

Simon's voice came slightly muffled from the other side of the canvas.

"It's about time you took a dose of your own medicine."

Inside the tent was crowded, although it was impossible to tell what with until Alan brought the torch in. The day's heat, trapped inside, had built to a stuporous cloud that made it hard to breathe, and warmed the stored hay bales so that the air smelled something like a rabbit hutch in summer. Alan handed the torch back to his brother and moved forward, squeezing his way between the stacked bales. Watching Simon try to pluck each strand of hay from his clothing afterward made Alan feel somehow much better about his own attire.

"Come on, Princess. No time for preening."

"Balls, Alan."

"I don't think I've ever heard you swear."

"You bring out the best in me. Let's get a move on, shall we?"

Ducking his head through the storage tent's door, Alan looked up and down the deserted part of the circus and waved his brother through.

Muttering between themselves, they picked their way across avenues with carriage wheels instead of shop fronts, and alleys with guide ropes that criss-crossed like fishing nets. The scent of animals was all around them, covering smells of buttered corn and toffee apples to only a whisper. The pulse and glow of lights played across the dark over the tents' roofs, the screams and laughter a memory until tomorrow night's opening. Horses huffed at them as they moved past an open area where the beasts were penned in.

"This place is huge," Alan whispered.

"They've certainly made a home for themselves. Take a left."

And finally things began to look familiar. Alan moved with more certainty as they crossed an alleyway, ducked between a carriage's wheels, and came out the other side just across from the curiosity caravan's exit; which was surrounded by six heavily-set gypsy men, all staring directly at them.

Alan's hand slid toward his revolver, but a hot breath on his neck, followed by a meaty hand on his shoulder told him not to bother. He didn't even need to look around, but could feel the gravity of the man's hefty mass at his back as an asteroid might feel the gravity of a planet. He moved lightly for a big man. Most of the others were carrying some sort of tool or bludgeoning weapon. The one directly ahead, a lithe man in shirt sleeves and braces with a face that could prise barnacles from a ship's hull, beat a steady rhythm on his palm with a gnarled billy-club. Alan had a strange feeling that when he stopped, the night would become just a little more interesting.

10

I N AN ACCENT thick with the mountain air of Hungary, or perhaps Romania, the brutish man at Alan's back suggested he step forward. The brothers did as they were told, Simon raising his hands, palm out.

"Put your bloody hands down. We're not in a hold-up," muttered Alan.

"Alan, I hate to push you, but what do we do?"

"You be quiet is what you do," snarled the sharp-featured gypsy. "Tobar, take their weapons."

"I get the feeling that I'm about to be shot with my own gun," said Alan. "That's embarrassing."

"You two, be quiet and quick march." The gypsy waved his billy club to the right, moving them away from the caravan of curiosities.

"We really are just trying to help," said Simon.

"You sneak, you break, you steal. Do not add lies to the list. Now move." Simon jerked as Sharp Face shoved him forward. Alan saw his brother's face cloud over.

"Some people have no manners," Simon muttered, and did exactly what Alan would never expect him to.

Spinning fast enough that his hat tried to stay in place

above him, Simon's arm came up in a curve that ended with an explosion of glass and glow worms as his torch shattered on the brutish Tobar's tree trunk neck, knocking the huge man to the ground with a surprised grunt and swift unconsciousness. Alan had time to register the stunned faces of the assembled gypsies, and even more so of his brother, before he grabbed Simon's shirt and hauled him into a run, making encouraging sounds without words. They hit a full sprint shortly after, Simon pressing his hat to his head with one hand, Alan shaking glass and glow worms out of the collar of his shirt, and laughing like a loon. The gypsy men's footfalls thumping like racehorses' hooves behind them.

Coming to a cul-de-sac in the circus' layout, Alan grabbed his brother's collar and dragged him aside into a tent, then shoved him to one side of the doorway as Alan darted to the other. The first gypsy to barge through the door caught a right hook on his chin which sent him sprawling back into the man behind him. And they were running again, out through the other side of the tent and into a slightly open space that looked vaguely familiar.

"This way!" whooped Simon, drunk on excitement and fear.

The sound of the gypsies grunting and arguing in some guttural European was growing louder. They couldn't run around like this all night. Alan corralled his brother again, shoving him toward a wide marquee. Inside, row upon row of low crates, filled with soil and sprouting plants gave them something to hide behind. Simon pressed his back to the wooden boxes, giggling slightly under his breath. He realised that he was still holding the handle of his broken torch and set it aside.

"Well, that was novel—"

Alan jabbed a finger to his lips as a herd of footfalls ran by the tent door.

Simon lowered his voice. "Do you think they saw us?"

Alan shook his head slowly, his attention strained toward listening. When he was certain they were alone, he gave a deep breath to settle his pulse.

"You clocked a man with a metal stick," he whispered.

"It seemed like a good idea at the time."

"I've had worse."

Simon pressed a hand to his chest and waited for his heart rate to slow down. "Phew. You do this all the time?"

"I try not to."

"At least I still have my gun."

"Don't rub it in. I really liked that revolver. I'd worn in the grip just right. I think we should go. They'll double back eventually."

Gathering themselves up and dusting off, they wove their way through the soil-filled crates. Simon bent over one, studying the leaves of the sprouting plants, like wide green snake tongues; then looked up at the ceiling with its hanging ropes so that the roof could be pulled aside to let sunlight in.

"Curious place for a root garden," he said, grabbing one of the plants by its leaves and hauling it up to take a closer look.

A piercing, ululating shriek split the air. Alan clapped his hands over his ears with no effect. The sound seemed to penetrate flesh and bone, reverberating in the cavities of the body and brain. Alan's eyesight pulsed in time with the shrill racket, and so he wasn't sure if the root in Simon's hand was really wriggling, or if it was an illusion that little underdeveloped limbs struggled like a baby held up by its hair. Alan yelled at his brother, who was trying desperately to cover both ears with one arm, but the root's screeching drowned him out. Alan made urgent gestures until Simon got the picture and shoved the struggling root back into the soil and covered it up. Somehow the silence left behind seemed even louder than the din before it. Simon's lips were moving, but all Alan heard was a high-pitched ringing like a tuning fork lodged in his brain. He shook his head partly to clear it, and partly to show that he didn't understand.

"—said, do you think they heard that?"

The sound of thudding boots from outside the tent answered the question better than the snide comment that Alan was working on. The sound of a revolver's hammer clicking back made Alan sag on the spot.

"How do you get into these things?" asked Simon, raising his hands again.

"Healthy curiosity and blasted luck."

"Turn around," said Sharp Face, stood in front of his gang with Alan's revolver. Tobar stood behind him, a rag clasped to his neck and a face like thunder. Another man that Alan vaguely recognised massaged his jaw. They were still captured, then. Only this time the gypsies were angry in a more personal way.

"I was going to let you go, but now I think I will just shoot you instead," said Sharp-Face.

"Don't put yourself out on our account," said Alan.

Simon nudged him. "Don't annoy him any more!"

"Why not? He's going to shoot us anyway."

"Yes, I am," said Sharp Face, and took aim at Alan first.

11

"**S**INCE WE'RE GOING to die, do you mind telling me what that plant is?" Simon asked Sharp Face.

"You're joking," Alan snapped.

Simon shrugged. "Professional curiosity."

Alan shook his head in disbelief.

"Be quiet, both of you!" demanded Sharp Face.

"Yes, be quiet."

The gypsies turned as one to follow the new voice. The group of men parted as a girl stepped through. It was the third time Alan had set eyes on her, and her outfit of head-to-toe sparkles was no less impressive. A short blue cape with fox-fur collar kept the night's chill from her shoulders. Alan took in Jessamine's face properly for the first time. Her nose was too strong for her face, her mouth a little too narrow, but all this was lost in the crystalline haze of her eyes. She'd taken down her hair and it lay over one shoulder in a single sweeping curl of ebony. She spoke again, with the firm confidence of a woman in charge. "Stop pointing that gun at them, Djordi. You can't shoot them just for being idiots."

The brute known as Tobar muttered something in his native tongue that Alan still managed to get the gist of. He disagreed, it seemed.

"Awfully sorry about that, Tobar. Slight misunderstanding wasn't it Simon?" Alan said as sweetly as he could.

Simon nodded along. "Most regrettable. Heat of the moment and all that."

"See? An apology," said Jessamine. "I think maybe you two gentlemen should come with me?"

"Couldn't agree more." Alan and Simon moved through the group of men, having to squeeze slightly to make it through. Simon tipped his hat to Tobar, who scowled like granite.

"Much obliged. Sorry again, old sport."

Alan thought about asking for his revolver back, but decided not to push his luck. And just like that, they were out into the night air, un-chased, with Jessamine leading the way.

"You gentlemen have managed to cause much trouble and see many things which have not been shared with anyone outside the Maskelyne family for a long century or more." Alan found the accent much more interesting now that it was coming out of Jessamine rather than any of the brutes.

"Your gardening project, you mean?"

Now that they were away from the gypsy men, Jessamine stepped between the brothers and linked her arms through theirs as they walked; a kind of familiarity that Alan had only been used to in peasant circles. "An old family secret. Mandrake root."

"Used for what?" Simon asked.

"I'll show you."

Without realising it, they had crossed some invisible boundary and were now back in the circus proper with its stalls and lights and busy paintwork, but no people. At this time of night, or rather morning, with all the punters at home, the circus took on an eerie effect; the lights beckoning, the scent of juicy food enticing and the hurdy gurdy playing its haunting round-about; like a trap left for children in a fairy tale. Jessamine led them between the stalls and drew a boatswain's whistle from her cape. Piping a high-pitched trio of notes, she waited patiently.

"And here we are," she said.

From out of the stalls on all sides came the gypsy workers in their wide-brimmed hats and scarves, their faces in shadow despite the circus' lights, and massed haphazardly in front of them.

Simon looked around, but found nothing resembling an answer. "I'm afraid I don't understand." Jessamine nodded to the nearest gypsy, who removed his hat, which appeared to have a fringe of hair attached to the rim, and tugged the scarf down from his face. Simon recoiled, but the girl held him firm. "Dear God!"

Alan muttered something even more blasphemous under his breath.

Where the gypsy should have had a face, there was nothing but the striated markings one would expect to find on a turnip or carrot. No mouth, no eyes, only a suggestion of a brow and chin.

"Quite the marvel, aren't they?"

"You have to be kidding me," said Alan.

"Only now you seem to think things strange?" Jessamine

rolled her eyes.

"A screeching plant I can handle. I can ignore it and pretend it didn't happen. A full-grown walking plant-man takes the biscuit."

"And steals the tin," Simon agreed.

"My family, large as it is, could never run this circus alone. And so we grow the ancient mandrake root and set them to work." The Root bowed its head and Jessamine gave it a pat before it returned its hat.

"How does no one notice?"

The acrobat led them away, piping another short call so that the Roots could return to their work.

"Who among you English would look a gypsy peasant in the eye? You were here last night. What faces did you see, other than those of the patrons? Describe them to me."

"Well—" Simon faltered. He set his mouth into a tight line.

"Precisely. Oh, wait here, please."

From out of the Big Top's entrance came a striking figure in black. Alan could see from the cut of his costume that the youth had powerful shoulders, a lithe frame, plenty to be jealous of. That was only heightened when the young man came toward Jessamine and hugged her right off of her feet. They shared a deep kiss for a moment before Jessamine demanded that she be put down.

"God's teeth, is everyone paired up in this town?" asked Alan.

"Almost everyone," Simon mocked. Alan shot him a scything glance.

"Luc, you should be gone already," Jessamine whispered.

"I'm not leaving you here alone." The youth had a soft French accent. So, not one of the gypsies, then. A performer they'd picked up along the way. "Not with those two. We don't even know them."

"Grandmamma says they're good men. She would know." Jessamine stroked the youth's chest as if yearning a favourite pillow. "She knew about you."

He couldn't help but smile. "A lucky guess."

"Please, Luc. Just do as she asks. Go with Cicero and the others. Keep them safe. I'll come to you when I can." She pushed at his chest, physically moving him along as if that were the only thing that could make him walk away. "Go."

Luc shot one last glance over at the brothers, but it wasn't the angry threat that Alan expected. Instead, his eyes pleaded silently for them to bring her back safe. Alan gave a barely noticeable nod, and the youth walked away into the night.

Linking arms once more, as if nothing had happened at all, Jessamine guided the brothers along a route they last took with Cicero the night before.

"Is there a reason you're showing us all this?" asked Alan. "Other than to make this night the strangest of my entire life. And believe me, I've had some corkers."

Jessamine smiled, and squeezed his arm.

"To prepare you, Mister Shaw. And to test you. If you can accept the truth of the Roots, what my Grandmamma will tell you next will come as little surprise."

"She knows your name, Alan."

"We know an awful lot, Mister Carpenter. And you're very lucky that we are willing to share it with you. But let us not get ahead of ourselves. Grandmamma would like to speak to you again."

12

ENTERING THROUGH THE curiosity caravan's exit, they saw that the Hand of Glory had been removed along with its broken glass case. It was the only blank space in the whole clustered caravan now, and stood out like a missing tooth. They were led back through the curtain and into the clairvoyant's caravan where the old woman sat waiting. Jessamine gestured for the brothers to drag over a pair of chairs and they all sat around the small table together. Where the shard of crystal had once been, the Hand of Glory now sat, its candle thankfully unlit.

"They came back, as you said Grandmamma." Jessamine's voice was softer than the stern confidence she had shown so far, and she laid a hand on the old psychic's shoulder.

"So I see," said the crone. "And what of Cicero?"

"He's taken all of the performers and camped them north of the circus in the sand dunes. Luc is there with him. They should be safe there. Only Cousin Djordi and a few others have stayed behind."

Patting Jessamine's hand, the old crone nodded in time. "Good, good. He will be back soon, my dove. Don't look so worried. Gentlemen, welcome back. I'm glad that you didn't disappoint me."

"Let's skip the part where you know all about us, and get to the what-in-hell's going on."

"Apologies," said Simon. "He gets cranky when he's confused. Which is a lot, as it happens."

"Jessamine has shown you the Roots?" said the crone. Jessamine nodded. "Good. Then your minds have been opened to the vast possibilities of the occult. The man who came here last night was but one in a larger group of devout men known as the Ordo Fenris."

"A cult," said Alan.

"An army, Mister Shaw. Older than you can imagine. Older than the Maskelyne family, perhaps. There is a belief, in the old Germanic myths that when the end of days arrives, the great wolf Fenris will swallow the sun and the earth will be pitched into darkness. This will be the first sign of the end. The Ordo believe that they are destined to unleash the great wolf."

"Why?" asked Simon.

The crone set her eyes on him, and her face seemed to lose its crazed edge. She sat a little straighter, the shadows pulling back from her face to reveal a very scared, tired old woman. "Who knows? All the information we have came from Jessamine's father, who often crossed them on his travels to collect interesting items for this circus. It was an obsession with him, and it pitted him against the Ordo many times. They have a hunger for occult artefacts which they believe will further their goal."

"And a flair for weird machinery," Alan said.

The clairvoyant nodded. "As you say. Most often Jessamine's father lost, but now and then he would come away with something the Ordo coveted."

"I get a feeling that this is where the hand comes in," Alan muttered.

"The hand once belonged to Elizabeth Clark—"

"The hand's label said that it was a hanged *man*," Simon interjected.

"The gender is irrelevant. Elizabeth Clarke was hanged for witchcraft in the seventeenth century and her left hand made into a Hand of Glory. You understand, a witch's hand would be expected to have more power than any mere murderer or thief. However, Elizabeth Clarke wasn't a witch. As with many of the stories about her, this is a lie. The truth is that she was an enemy of the Ordo Fenris, and a good woman whose knowledge of the occult was unsurpassed in England at the time. Upon her death, her hand was taken by superstitious dullards. But since she was innocent, the hand never worked its sleep magic and so it survives."

She gestured to the Hand where it sat on the table-lace, looking disturbingly innocent.

Alan shrugged. "This cult has taken a lot of trouble to come and steal a magic hand that doesn't work."

"The hand itself is unimportant."

"There are a lot of unimportant and irrelevant things in this story," said Alan.

The clairvoyant shot him a look before continuing. "Elizabeth Clark stole something from the Ordo Fenris; something that they have been searching for over two centuries to retrieve. The story goes that Clark took the item to her death, and even after she was hanged, she clutched it in her hand and wouldn't let go. That was her left hand. The Hand that holds the candle also has another secret nestled in its palm. Jessamine's father found it buried in the walls of an old inn in the English North, and it has been here ever since. The Ordo Fenris has finally caught up with it."

"I need a drink." Alan pinched his brow. "Submersibles with tentacles. Fine. I'll even stretch to plant-men if I see it with my own eyes. If you'd told me that this Ordo was a group of uniformed fanatics hell-bent on world domination, I'd be right along for the ride. But occult artefacts and age-old cults is where I draw the line."

"That's what you said when we saw the Roots outside," said Simon.

"Well, they keep lifting the bar on weirdness, so I have to keep re-evaluating."

"Re-evaluating?" Simon was grinning.

"Shut up."

Jessamine picked up the Hand and waved it at Alan, who found himself weaving to avoid it. "Whether you believe it or not, the Ordo Fenris will be coming back for it. And you're here, saying you want to help. So help."

"I may be labouring an old point, but why no police? We're clearly dealing with mad men here, and if they're really an army as you say, we're to be vastly outnumbered, outgunned, or out manoeuvred," Simon offered. "Probably all three."

Jessamine sighed heavily, leaning over the table, stabbing the wooden surface with her finger. "Do you think the

Brighton law enforcement want a gypsy host at their doorstep, Mister Carpenter? Of course not. They come with their families at night, play our games, applaud our tricks, pay their money. But in the daylight they find every excuse to run us out."

Simon had been swinging on the back legs of his chair to distance himself from Jessamine's tirade, but now he finally set all four feet back on the ground, gripping the table's edge as if he might fall off the world. Alan still had his face covered in one hand. The caravan grew silent until the creaking of its cooling timbers became a din. The Hand sat on the table between them, clutching at the heart of their problem. And the four at the table waited patiently for an answer to their predicament.

When Jessamine spoke, she was quieter, and Alan could tell that she held the pleading edge from her voice by sheer force of will. There was a tiredness to her, a resignation.

"Mad or not, magic or not, the Ordo Fenris will return tonight. They sent one man, and he failed. They will not make the same mistake again. Either help us or go home."

Alan stood up from the table, shaking his head, his chair scraping on wood. "These buggers are dangerous. They nearly drowned me once, and killed a lot of other men in the process, and now they're back with gas guns and magic hands and talismans."

Jessamine turned away from him, her mouth set in an ugly scowl.

"Just leave," she sneered. Alan slid his finger under her chin, but she jerked her face away. "Don't give me excuses or apologies—"

He cradled her jaw and pulled her eyes up to his as if he might kiss her.

"This is insane. You know that?"

Jessamine didn't answer. Behind her scowl, the glisten of restrained tears framed her eyes. Alan deflated. "Balls. I suppose I'll be needing my revolver back."

13

THE GYPSY MEN, led by Sharp-Face Djordi, had taken their positions back outside the curiosity caravan. Two stood in plain sight by the door, and Alan could see the rest tucked away in various shadows, including the hulking mass of Tobar who occasionally moved to rub at his injuries. Jessamine tugged her cape around her, nestling down into the fur collar. The cool night air was getting to her even inside the curiosity caravan where she and the brothers waited.

"I don't suppose your Grandmamma has seen how this all turns out?" Alan asked.

The girl smiled and fumbled in her cape for the severed hand which she cradled there. When she found it, she settled again.

"Didn't think so."

"Do you think they'll believe that the hand is still where it was before?" she asked.

"Let's hope they think you're stupid. Either way, that's where they'll start the search, just in case. All your boys need to do is put up a small fight, then—" Alan tensed in his crouched position, pricking his ears for a sound, and leant

281

out of the doorway. In the darkness outside, something moved that wasn't a gypsy. Alan watched as a stealthy figure crept up behind Tobar's undeniable form.

"Poor guy keeps being in the wrong place," he whispered, as Tobar gave a grunt and his shadow slumped to the floor. He turned to Simon. "They're here."

From out of the gloom, one man after another began to creep out, each wearing the grey Ordo Fenris uniform emblazoned with a star-swallowing red wolf. The first two soldiers crept up on the caravan's guards and took them down quietly, cracking them on the head with the butts of their guns, then beckoned to the darkness behind them. The troops came out in earnest, searching the night around them. There were more than Alan had anticipated. Maybe thirty. Too many. As the first soldier reached the caravan's steps, Alan waved to his companions.

"They're coming. Go, go."

All three of them stole across the caravan's creaking floor as quietly as they could, and through the curtain to the clairvoyant's room. Using the barrel of his revolver to part the curtain, Alan watched as the Ordo Fenris began to search for the Hand, knocking over cabinets and smashing cases. Glass fell in glittering avalanches, wood splintered, and the Ordo soldiers called to each other in a language which may have been German. But Alan kept his eyes trained on one particular box, and waited, hoping his breath wasn't loud enough to alert the soldiers to his presence.

With the search nearly over, the caravan's floor was littered in shards of glass and wood, tiny skulls, petrified insects and things which really should have remained in their jars. Alan held his breath as one of the soldiers moved to the back of the room and found the box which didn't belong there.

Producing two blobs of candle wax from his pocket, Alan jammed them into his ears. Simon and Jessamine followed suit just as the soldier raised his rifle and smashed the box's clasp open.

Soil spilled out onto his boots. And the mandrake root began to scream.

The soldiers dropped their weapons in favour of covering their ears, many of them falling to their knees or stumbling toward the caravan's exit, clambering over each other in an effort to escape. Most of them fell back again, unsure where to go, when they saw that the Root's scream had been the signal for Djordi's other men to attack. To add to the confusion, Alan swung out of the curtain and ripped off several shots which were barely audible over the Mandrake Root's shrieking. Two soldiers fell, one span as a bullet tore through his leg and went down, his screams unheard in the ululating racket. Simon was in Alan's wake, his own heavy ordinance raised and cocked. Alan threw up a hand to order his brother back, but the insatiable din of the Mandrake Root stopped his warning dead in the air. He threw himself aside as Simon planted a wide stance and raised his weapon. The shot was delayed as Simon mentally checked off instructions in his head.

Knees and elbows bent. Shoulders square. Neck relaxed. Gun held in both hands. Squeeze, don't tug. Watch for the kick.

The gun's roar couldn't be heard, but Alan felt it. Simon toppled back despite his preparation, the weapon's scattershot riding high from the recoil to tear a hole out of the caravan's wall three feet across, blowing wooden splinters into the air like dandelion seeds. A cabinet broke Simon's fall, toppling from its stand with the biologist in a heap. Peppered by scattershot and raining wood, assaulted by the Root's screams, the Ordo soldiers broke ranks and tried to retreat again. The few soldiers with their wits still intact returned fire as they were pinned between the brothers and the gypsies outside. Alan scuttled across the floor, firing wild shots, and managed to bustle his brother back through the curtained doorway. The curtain whipped into the air, perforated and torn by the bullets, as the brothers lurched aside.

Crouched in the corner of the room, arms wrapped over her head, Jessamine lay shaking, eyes wide, but still clutching the Hand as if it were her own. Alan made his way over to her, firing blindly through the doorway as he went, and laid a hand on her shoulder. The girl startled, and then threw herself around him just as the Root's screeching stopped. Alan tugged the useless wax from his ears.

"They figured that out fast," muttered Alan.

"So much for the element of surprise," Simon agreed. "It looks like these Ordo Fenris know more than we did coming in here."

From outside, someone barked an order. The same word, repeated. Alan could guess what it meant. Shielding Jessamine under one arm, Alan guided her, doubled over, to a safer spot in the clairvoyant's room as the Ordo fired again, this time without the Root's distraction. Their bullets tore through the table, the chandelier, shattering an oil lamp, and puncturing the back wall of the caravan where Alan and Jessamine had been moments before. Sprawled on the floor, trying desperately to pull his hat down over his ears, Simon let out a scream as a bullet scored a bloody line across his calf. His face burst out in an instant sweat in response to the searing heat in his leg. He clasped at it and rolled aside, while still managing to stay polite.

"Buggerbuggerbugger. That hurts!"

Trying to time his movements as the soldiers reloaded their weapons, Alan crawled forward, snatching the gun from his brother's unresisting hand, and fell against the door frame. He held a thumb up to Simon who nodded, but his gritted teeth and swimming eyes said otherwise. Blood oozed through the leg of his trousers.

Another volley of fire ripped through the curtain. Jessamine yelped and threw herself down as the caravan's wall took a beating. Alan felt the rounds thudding into the doorway behind him. Shoulders pulled up, forehead resting on his knees, he prayed that the wood was thick enough to take it. Then, a pause for reloading. Alan rolled out into the doorway. Laid on his back, legs apart, he hooked his boots onto the doorframe's outer edge to counter the recoil, sighted down his brother's weapon and squeezed the trigger; the end result looking like he was giving birth to bullets.

The caravan's outer wall, which the Ordo Fenris huddled behind, exploded in a cloud of dust, wood chippings, shredded grey uniform and blood. Panicked screams seemed to translate through any language. Alan heaved himself forward through the shredded curtain, taking up a spot in what was left of the curiosity caravan as the soldiers rallied in the night outside. Alan gave off another shot to make sure, but was badly braced for it, and nearly tore his shoulder out of its socket. Managing to keep his feet, he took up a defensive position by what remained of the caravan's doorway; Simon's weapon tucked under his burning arm, and reloaded his own revolver with one hand.

Simon crawled out of the other room, leaving a thin trail of blood.

"Get back there!" Alan gave a harsh whisper.

"Give me my gun, Alan." Simon dragged himself until he sat upright with his back to the opposite side of the doorway from his brother.

"No chance. You're lethal."

"Give me my gun and point me in the right direction."

Weapons in hand, Alan peered around the doorway. They'd managed to push the Ordo Fenris back, at least, and take out maybe six or seven with lucky shots and Simon's beast of a gun, but there were still a mass of grey uniforms outside. Alan spotted the gypsy men penned off to one side, unconscious or under guard. The rest of the soldiers kept their weapons trained on the caravan. Alan noticed a uniformity to the men aside from their dress sense; a certain proclivity toward blonde hair not unlike his own, but trimmed almost to the skin at the sides. And at the back of the troops, a single man stood with his hat tucked into the crook of his arm; a man with more stripes than the rest and the name Volkert embroidered on his breast above a row of medals like silver skulls. He was older, his blonde hair flecked with platinum and wrinkles streaked his face in a way that seemed to highlight the shadows around his eyes, the whites of which seemed all too visible in the dark. Something about the way the moonlight hit his uniform as he moved made it look as if his ribs rippled like piano keys underneath his jacket; an odd illusion that sent the hairs on the back of Alan's neck to attention.

Trying to suppress a shudder, Alan slid Simon's weapon over to him.

"I think we've got them right where we want them," Alan said, convincing no-one. "Just turn and fire. You can barely miss with that thing anyway."

"How many are there?" Simon managed, his face taking on a sickly pallor.

"One or two."

"Wonderful."

"We need to get that stopped or you'll be no use at all." Alan gestured to his brother's oozing leg and the spreading pool of blood under it.

"Mhmm." Unbuckling his belt, Simon slid off the pouches and paraphernalia and slipped the strip of leather around his calf.

"That's going to—"

Simon yanked on the belt. His head slammed back against the wall, eyes rolled. All of the colour drained out of his face, but he didn't make a sound. Alan felt a pang of brotherly pride. He knew how much the wound must hurt.

"Simon? *Simon.* For the love of God don't pass out."

Eyes screwed closed against the pain, Simon shook his head.

"You know when you said we should take the Hand and run with it, and I said it'd be no use and we should stay and fight?" Alan continued, giving his brother something to focus on other than the pain.

"Vaguely," Simon managed to growl.

"When will you learn not to listen to me?"

"I did. Five minutes ago. Five minutes too late." Despite the roaring agony in his leg, Simon's fingers wrapped around the handle of his gun, albeit with pale knuckles.

Alan leaned back around the caravan's doorway as the officer, Volkert, called to them.

"Well done, Gentlemen. Well done!" Alan had it right. They were definitely Germans. "You have taken us by surprise. No easy task, I assure you. But we will not underestimate you again."

"That's a shame, because we don't know what we're doing," Alan muttered.

The officer raised his voice again: "Our demands are simple. Give us the Hand and go free. You have one minute to decide." He pulled out a pocket watch and began to count out loud.

"Looks like we won't be getting any spare seconds, either. Feel free to jump in with ideas any time."

"I can't really think straight, I'm afraid." Simon grimaced. "I'm proving to be quite useless when it comes to pain. For the love of God, don't tell Lottie."

Alan took one more look out of the door, and found very little had changed. Except Herr Volkert was now staring at him, and smiling.

"Well, they've not got bored and wandered off, yet."

"Destroy the Hand. Burnt it. And destroy whatever it holds, too," offered Jessamine, who had been watching from the safety of the other doorway.

"I don't see how that's going to stop them coming in here and killing us," Alan retorted.

"It won't. But they won't get what they're after either."

"I was hoping for a plan with a little less death involved, to be honest," Simon offered.

"You asked, I gave," said the acrobat.

"Well think again," said Alan. The sound of Herr Volkert's counting was starting to get on his nerves. "You've got twenty-odd seconds to come up with something better."

Alan jerked back into the room as a gunshot boomed across the night; the throaty belch of a shotgun. But nothing hit the caravan. The Ordo soldiers began to shout and fire their weapons, but again nothing seemed aimed in the brothers' direction. Alan dared to take a look, and saw that the Ordo Fenris had made an outward facing circle and were shooting into the dark which lay between the surrounding tents and shacks. The shotgun roared again, and this time Alan caught a glimpse of the shooter by the muzzle's flare.

"You won't believe this," he said. "But I think we're being rescued."

14

ANOTHER ROAR OF the shotgun, and the flare came from somewhere different this time, again lighting up the figure Alan had seen before; Lottie, dressed in her riding gear, the shotgun tugged tight into her hip as she took chunks out of the panicking soldiers. And she was a damn fine shot. With each belch of light, two or three fell to buckshot, grabbing at themselves and wailing. Then she was gone, darting into the night, circling, coming at them from somewhere else. She was a one-woman taskforce.

"Simon, I may not have said this yet, but you and Lottie have my blessing."

Grinning, he stepped out of the doorway, brought his revolver to bear, and sent a few rounds whizzing into the confusion of the Ordo's defences. He sent a few choice shots toward the officer, but they must have run wide of their mark. There was only the *thock thock thock* of the shots hitting something solid and the officer remained unmoved. Alan reared back as the Ordo soldiers returned fire, swinging the muzzles of their rifles wildly to trade shots with both assailants. Simon taught them a lesson with his own weapon, which span him around on his bottom with the recoil. He winced, but was somehow laughing with it. Alan started to worry that the blood loss was making him giddy.

There was a scream – more of a frustrated roar, and the firing subsided. Most of the Ordo men lay on the ground now, groaning, bleeding, and wishing they'd stayed at home. That gave Alan a little smirk. But the struggling sounds weren't coming from them. A tight knot of the few remaining Ordo Fenris had arranged themselves around their officer.

A lead weight filled Alan's chest as Lottie was dragged out of the shadows by a pair of Ordo soldiers, one nursing a bleeding nose, the other limping. She'd put up a good fight.

"You continue to surprise," shouted Volkert. "How many little soldiers of your own do you have?"

Alan snarled, but didn't answer.

The numbers of Ordo soldiers had thinned, but not enough to provide a definitive victory. There was still no chance of Alan darting out into the open and ending the battle with a few choice bullets. And now they had Lottie hauled between them. Alan looked back over his shoulder to where his brother had drifted off into a pain-addled doze, the pool of blood once more spreading underneath him. Jessamine had scuttled forward and sat with him, but any medical knowledge she had ended at reapplying the tourniquet. Simon barely flinched this time. Alan looked down at his weapons, at the soldiers outside, at Lottie who stood between them, her chest puffed out and eyes searching for any opportunity to lash out again.

If she did, Alan wasn't sure that the officer wouldn't just shoot her to keep her quiet. There was a stolid mania to the way he smiled, the way he spoke, that set Alan's teeth on edge. He was obviously bonkers.

With Simon slipping out of consciousness and Lottie captured, Alan was at a loss for what to do. He had become quite fond of Lottie in the short time since they'd met, and even if he hadn't she was still Simon's future fiancé. The way she struggled against the soldiers even now made Alan like her all the more.

Simon muttered something. His voice was quiet, like a child fighting off sleep.

"Shush. Concentrate on not bleeding," Alan said, but Simon wasn't really listening.

"When evil strikes…" he murmured.

"I don't think Titus Gladstone can help us right now, Simon. Lay still."

But his brother smiled. "I always think, 'What would Alan Shaw do?'"

Simon finally gave in to injured sleep, leaving Alan to stare at him with a slack jaw.

Titus Gladstone wasn't there. If he was, he'd have a thought of a clever plan and they'd all be saved. But Alan *was* there and his brother was counting on him. Thinking had never been his strong suit – that had always been Simon's job.

There was nothing for it. Alan had to do something stupid if they were all going to live the night.

He shook himself and addressed the Ordo.

"Alright! Stop your counting!"

The officer snapped his pocket watch closed and stowed it away, his face slithering a smirk.

Alan heard Lottie snarl something which made the officer laugh. Lord knows what insult she'd thrown.

Crouching beside Jessamine, Alan slipped his arms around the petite acrobat. Taken by surprise, she tensed against the lingering kiss he planted against her lips. He pulled away slightly, setting her stock still with his eyes.

"I'm sorry," he said, and moved away as quickly as he'd come.

Jessamine looked around her as if waking from a dream, searching for an explanation. In her daze, she reaching into her cape for the Hand, and realised it was gone. She made a sound of protest without any words.

Over his shoulder, Alan gave her a weak smile before stepping out of the caravan's ruined door. Hefting the Hand, he thought about throwing it right at the officer's smug grin, but stepped out of the caravan instead. He stood atop the wooden steps and surveyed the carnage they'd wrought in the blood-soaked yard; the felled men, the soiled uniforms, the spent bullet casings and hastily applied field dressings. He caught Lottie's eye and gave her an impish shrug. He could feel the heat of her scowl like a branding iron.

"You're a very brave man," Volkert sneered. "You have made my night interesting, if nothing else." Wrinkles slid aside like ripples on a pond as the officer's mouth grinned, without making use of those too-bright eyes. "It has been a pleasure," he shouted.

"I have what you came for," Alan lifted the hand and waved it at the Ordo officer. He slid his other hand into his pocket. "Let the woman go and you can have it."

"I don't see how you could possibly stop me taking it." Volkert waved to what remained of his men, who drew into a tight group around Alan. Volkert held out a gloved hand. "Give me the artefact. I'd rather it not be damaged when you die."

Lottie roared, looking like she would tear the soldiers apart with her bare hands.

"Here, take it," said Alan and held the Hand out in front of him.

Volkert smiled, and stepped forward. The red Fenris wolf grinned at Alan from Volkert's uniform, licking the tiny sun with manic glee, just like the one he'd seen disappear beneath the waves years before. As Volkert came to receive the Hand of Glory, Alan remembered the faces of sailors he'd seen falling to their deaths as their ship was ripped out from underneath them; the screaming and flailing bodies thrashing the ocean to foam as a gigantic tentacle rose over his head. What the Ordo had been up to that day, he didn't care. The chances of meeting them twice were slim, and meeting them again even slimmer. All Alan cared about now was delivering a present to that red wolf; one that he'd kept safe for a very long time.

His right hook caught Volkert's chin hard enough to knock his hat askew. The Ordo leader's head snapped to the side, a trickle of dark blood instantly oozing from his lip. It ran over his chin and down his neck, gathering at the tight neckline of his uniform. The officer's smile never slipped. It just turned back to Alan, slowly, with purpose, like a salamander eyeing a roach. Volkert's eyes stared somewhere a few inches behind Alan's head, or perhaps into his soul.

His whole body began to shiver, a curious chittering like a legion of beetles rising from underneath his uniform.

Alan's smile slipped away as the officer began to take off one of his black leather gloves, finger by finger. Alan was dimly aware that, at the corner of his vision, the Ordo soldiers had all retreated a step.

And then he hit dirt.

His head rang like a struck bell, the side of his face burning. For a petrifying moment, he seemed unable to see from his left eye, and the oozing tears were like icicles being dragged down his boiling skin. With one hand pressed to his cheek, he looked up at the moonlit discs of Volkert's eyes, and felt the extent of his mortality for the second time at the hands of the Ordo Fenris. Letting out a shuddering sigh, he squeezed his eyes shut as images of Herr Volkert driving a gleaming boot down into his skull filled his mind.

A high-pitched whistle shattered the tense silence with three keen notes, drawing all heads toward its source, even Volkert.

Jessamine stood on the steps of the caravan, the whistle clasped daintily between her lips. Moonlight glistened from her diamond-studded leotard, making her incandescent against the night.

"Get out of my circus." Although her voice was barely above a whisper, everyone managed to hear it. "I want you gone."

"You've proven yourself to be quite the hindrance," said Volkert.

"I'll prove to be your undoing if you don't leave, right now," snarled Jessamine.

The Ordo's leader shook his head. "The audacity of you, child. You could no more end me than you could stop me from taking this from you." He beckoned impatiently to Alan who stopped nursing his swelling face just long enough to relinquish the Hand.

A particularly brave Ordo lieutenant dared to break the tableau by muttering his officer's name. Volkert snapped something in German and the lieutenant answered. The Ordo soldiers grew quiet, and began staring into the dark around them. Finally, Alan heard it too. People were coming. Lots of them.

The first Mandrake Root sauntered into view, still dressed in its gypsy garb. Others were close behind, and soon the whole yard was a mass of featureless faces in the gloom, more and more joining the mob until they were impossible to count. The Roots kept walking, their movement stoic and undeniable, pressing forward, forcing the soldiers back by their sheer numbers, with Jessamine stood over them like a Queen Ant, anger scarring her face.

The air filled with gun smoke and hot lead as the Ordo Fenris opened fire. Alan was jerked aside by his collar and into cover behind a wooden shack. He found himself hunched beside Lottie, who had slipped her captors in the confusion.

Bullets thudded impotently against the plant-men, who reacted with indifference.

Herr Volkert muttered an order and the soldiers began to retreat back into the darkness, back toward the sea, dragging their wounded comrades behind them. Volkert remained the longest; stood immovable as an obelisk as the confusion raged around him, his smile a violent slash across his face. As if dressing for dinner, he slid his glove back on, righted his hat, and tugged his uniform straight. Then, taking one last look at the approaching horde of Mandrake Roots, he nodded politely to Jessamine as if conceding a match point, and stepped back into the shadows.

15

"**Y**OU SELFISH PIG," Lottie spat.

Alan winced against his swollen lip and aching face as he spoke.

"Before you start, Lottie. He knew exactly what he was getting in to. I even tried to convince him not to come. Once I even forbid it. He came anyway."

"He's a very sweet, very thoughtful and utterly naive man, Alan. You have no right leading him astray like this. How do you think I worried when I went to his room tonight and found him gone, and then you—"

In pure self-defence, Alan tried to deflect some of her anger. He smiled with the side of his face that still could. "You worried all the way to the gun cabinet, did you?"

For all her self-assurance and capability, Lottie froze.

"You're an infuriating child, Alan Shaw."

"At least we agree on that, then. Simon's in the caravan. If your nursing is anything like your fighting, he'll need you."

"He's hurt?" But she was already barging past him, darting toward the caravan through the throng of Roots and hurling herself up the steps.

Alan stood for a moment, considering his next move, and decided he wouldn't be very welcome in what remained of the caravan right now. So he followed the Roots out through the circus.

Stumbling by the light of the moon, Alan used the Root's retreating sounds to guide him As the circus opened up to the beach's soft dunes, he hung back, staying in the shadows, and watched as the plant men pressed the Ordo Fenris back toward the sea. Herr Volkert led his cohort down to the waterline where a trio of narrow boats waited. The boat's engines sputtered and caught, filling the air with an incessant buzz, before sliding down into the waves and away.

Alan strode down the beach and fought his way through the silent Roots to the water's edge. He had to cup his hand to his mouth, and it hurt, but he shouted over the retreating boats' engines.

"Volkert!"

The officer turned only slightly.

Alan rubbed at his face which felt four times its usual size and full of venom.

"Be seeing you!"

Herr Volkert waved the severed hand jovially and disappeared into the darkness, his eyes seeming to linger a little longer than the rest of him, like sunspots burnt on the retinas.

As if recognising that something was over, the plant men began to file back toward the circus, leaving Alan alone.

The wind was picking up a little; sending the sand skidding across the beach in eddies. Sea foam lay like lace curtains at the waterline. Alan let the wind cool his face and tried not to moan as sea salt cleansed his injuries, listening to the thrum of the Ordo's boats die away, willing Volkert to feel his stare across the waves. Finally he shook his head, and was about to turn away, almost missing the lights. They pulsed once or twice, and lit sporadically, but soon enough there was a string of luminescent pearls out to sea, draped around a long form which laid low on the waves. With the help of the moon, and how the lights made silhouettes of the retreating boats, Alan could see that it was a ship of sorts, using its lights to guide the landing party home. It sprawled low over the waves like a swimming scarab, great appendages stretching out around it, touching the waves. He watched as the crew were raised into the ship's low-hanging undercarriage by a system of pulleys. But where Alan expected the rumble of engines, there was none. A faint hum, which could have been the wind or the ringing of his own damaged ear, was the only sound. The ship moved slowly at first in smooth, gliding movements, but it soon built up to incredible speed. The lights winked out, leaving only a scudding black shape which Alan quickly lost track of.

SOMEWHERE BETWEEN UNCONSCIOUSNESS and pain, Simon muttered Lottie's name, his speech a little slurry like a child prematurely woken. "What're you doing here?"

From his seat on the caravan steps, Alan said: "Saving our bacon, apparently."

Lottie ignored him. "When I came to your room and you weren't there, I knew you'd done something stupid. This was the stupidest thing I could think of. When I got here, I just followed the gunshots."

"I'm glad you're here. Lottie, I want to ask you something—"

"Just rest, Simon, dear. Please. Let's get a doctor to look at you and you can ask me anything you want."

Simon gave a drowsy nod. His hand found Lottie's and their fingers knotted together as he drifted into an exhausted slumber.

Alan scooched up on the step to make room for Jessamine.

"I don't think I've had a chance to say how much I admire your acrobatics," he said. "Best show I've seen for a long time."

Jessamine smiled and the severity of her features melted away again.

"You kissed me."

"Sorry about that. A bit of a distraction. Learnt it from a gentleman pickpocket from Haymarket."

"I suppose I'll forgive you. Although, you know that me and Luc—"

"Yes, yes. It was hard not to notice. I figured there wouldn't have been a repeat performance even without him. Not after I gave the Hand away."

Jessamine looked over her shoulder to where Lottie was kissing Simon's slumbering brow.

"The Ordo Fenris have caused so much damage. My father always said they were incredibly dangerous, but I didn't appreciate exactly how much until now."

Alan tried to stretch his injured face and nodded. "At least they didn't get what they came for."

Jessamine's brows knotted, as Alan tried his best to smile.

Reaching into his pocket, he held up a disc of elaborately carved silver. With teeth on its outer edge, engraved with runic characters and a sapphire at its centre, it could either have been part of an overly-elaborate machine, or a piece of jewellery. He weighed it for a second before handing it to Jessamine, who held it up, the moonlight streaming through the central gem in a way he'd never seen before, focusing the light onto her face rather than dispersing it to increase the sparkle.

"You opened the hand," she said.

"I learnt that from a pickpocket in Haymarket, too."

They both laughed, and Jessamine kissed him on his unaffected cheek.

"Alan? We need to see a Doctor," yelled Lottie, ruining the haze of victory.

"Come on then," Alan said. "Let's get our hero some medical attention."

16

BRIGHTON BASKED IN the sun, unaware of the previous
night's dark deeds. Sat on the promenade's railing,
feeling like he was held together with string and spit, Alan
rubbed at his ribs, his shoulders, and both wrists; aches and
pains that hadn't emerged until this morning. He'd spent
what was left of the night with ice wrapped in a towel
applied to his face, but the swelling hadn't gone down
much. A blossoming bruise covered his left eye. Herr
Volkert's glove might as well have had bricks in it for all the
damage it had done. He tried not to wonder what kind of
man he'd met last night. He would heal up, let it simmer,
and then decide how best to find the smug bastard and put
him out of action.

Jessamine looked odd without her skin-tight sparkles,
but not unappealing. A flowing white skirt and short boots,
deep red blouse and last night's cape loose over one
shoulder, made her stand out in the crowd; something Alan
always appreciated. Her earrings jangled like wind chimes.
What he didn't appreciate was the tall, handsome figure of
Luc by her side. A silent presence, but a striking one.

They had come down from the circus to breakfast with

him, and tell him that the circus' performers and workers were back in their tents. And also that they were leaving.

"We have been here too long. Grown stale. And we were too easy to find. The Cirque Du Maskelyne has been a travelling show since my ancestors first left Romania. We must go back to our roots. The world awaits."

"I couldn't agree more," Alan had said, and sipped his tea as carefully as he could.

They left the café and walked the promenade, stopping now and then to admire the sea or the tall buildings. Alan, once again, played third wheel. The Maskelyne circus already looked smaller. Even as they watched, canvas roofs lowered and caravans moved off toward the road. The great zeppelin above the circus winched up palettes of dismantled equipment covered with tarpaulins. As they watched, Jessamine just smiled and smiled. Eventually, they settled at a spot not far from the Albion Hotel, and waited for Lottie and Simon to arrive.

Simon was leaning on a thin cane, flinching with each limping step, but through it all he was grinning and his cheeks reacted well to the sea air. Alan knew it had more to do with the remarkable woman on his arm.

"You two finally got up then, did you?"

"How many times did you get shot last night, Alan?" asked Simon.

"Marvellous. That's all he'll be banging on about from now on."

"He's a hero," said Lottie, squeezing herself closer to Simon. "A stupid, ridiculous hero that had better not try anything like that ever again."

"I think you'll have trouble fitting all that on the medal," Alan snorted.

Lottie ignored him, and turned to Jessamine.

"And how is the circus? I hope there wasn't too much damage?"

"Nothing that we can't fix. And we have the time, now. We will be travelling for a while before we set down again."

"In your balloon?"

"Most of the equipment is flown, yes. The big top, the machines and the games. The animals and enough people to care for them will follow behind in the caravan. They don't take too well to flight. The Roots, of course, will be hidden in the airship. It's safer that way, and there's always plenty of sunlight for them above the clouds. Who knows where we might go?"

"It sounds lovely," said Lottie. "And what about you, Alan? You come here, make trouble, get Simon shot, and then what? Don't think we haven't noticed your duffle bag on the pavement."

Alan shrugged.

"I think I've caused enough trouble for one visit. I'll let Simon have time to heal up. Then I'll come back." He winked at his brother who waved a dismissive hand.

"Seriously, Alan." Lottie laid a hand on his arm. "There's no need to rush off. Stay a little longer, at least. I know that Simon would like to see you a little more. I've barely gotten to know you."

"I'd say you've learnt everything about me there is to learn. I'm not complicated," he said.

"Let him go, Lottie. He gets a kick out of the begging.

Go on you, be off with you," Simon said to Alan. "I'd ask you to write, but you'll only forget."

"See? He understands me. That's why we're brothers."

Lottie sighed.

Alan looked at the distance floating hulk of the Maskelyne Circus zeppelin, a ridiculous grin slathered across his lips.

"I was thinking of joining the circus," he said, smiling at Jessamine. "But maybe not. I have to find somewhere safe for this." He held up the talisman.

Simon plucked it out of his fingers. "It belongs in a museum. I know a man who runs the world exhibit in London. I'm sure he has a deep, dark box to put it in and forget about it. I'd like to see the Ordo Fenris find it there."

"Oh, right," said Alan, looking a little despondent.

"So you'd better stick around if you want to make sure it's safe," said Lottie. "And you can come back to London with us. In two days."

Alan looked around the small group of hideously grinning faces, and realised he was beaten.

"Alright, fine," he said. "But I'll be damned if I'm going to any more tea-parties."

Extract from *The Morning Post*, Page Four,
October 3rd, 1853.

...the night custodian of the British Museum, who reports being knocked unconscious by a cloud of chemical gas, woke last night to find the vaults of the museum left open and his attacker long gone. Due to the sheer volume of

artefacts stored for cataloguing and study in the Museum vaults, the custodian stated that it was almost impossible to say what had been taken at this time. However, the vault contains the rewards from many expeditions across the globe, some as famous as the obscure remains of giant lizards discovered by the Mantells and Richard Owen himself, and golden manillas recovered from African tribes of mysterious Benin...

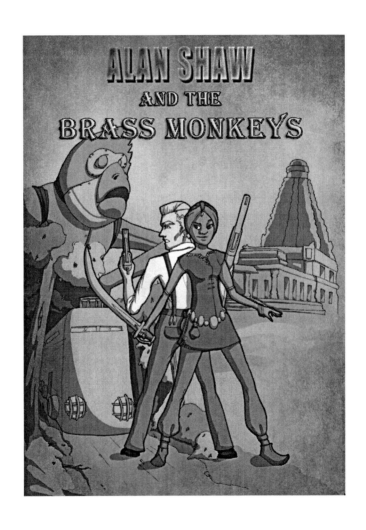

1

London, England, 1857

A DUFFLE BAG dropped to the pavement, followed shortly by Alan's feet. The carriage's chugging motor did little to drown out the noise of early morning London. Alan sniffed, taking in the oil and smoke; smells that were a constant backdrop in the capital. Each time he set foot on those flagstones, every beating, theft and indignity ever done to him as a boy came crashing down like a tidal wave over a rowboat. Every street he'd trod, every day he'd been hungry and had to steal or, worse, beg for a few morsels to stave off death. He loved to hate that damned city. But every time he got back something else warmed his core. The coiled spring of his spine released. He knew these streets. He could walk from Maida Vale to Limehouse with his eyes closed using just the scents and the feel of the pavement to guide him. He knew every Den and Free House, every restaurant; street merchant, pocket-picker, scoundrel and sham artist. Where the cabbies drank, where the scum floated, which urchins could be trusted and which couldn't. This was, as much as he hated to admit it, his city.

And he couldn't wait to get away again.

Nodding to the cabby, he shouldered his bag and took the first few steps to the house that he called home on the rare occasions he came back to London at all. Stood in front of that old red door he thought about just walking in, but something didn't feel right about it. He knocked instead. The sound of swift footsteps crossing the floorboards, the thuds close together despite a long stride, told Alan that it was his brother who would answer. Simon's face appeared around the door's edge. He was eating a crumpet and so didn't look up until the last minute. The crumpet hit the carpet with a squelch.

Simon swooped his arm around Alan's back, corralling him inside. Now inexplicably in the hallway as if there had been no intervening space, Alan swayed on the spot. His duffle bag and coat, a tan duster that rarely left his back, were stripped from him. Now removed from public view, Simon threw his arms around Alan in a bear hug.

"Bloody hell, Simon. Steady on, man."

Simon stepped back, straightening his waistcoat.

"Sorry, sorry. I had no idea you were coming back. What a surprise."

"I didn't know either. There was one train for Cairo, the other for London. For some stupid reason, I came back here. I've never been to Egypt."

"Just a lot of sand and pointy buildings from what I hear. Come in and have some tea." With that, Simon propelled his brother through to the parlour.

It was the same old room. Three high-backed leather armchairs sat around the fire. Alan chose the one that was traditionally his, but stood behind it rather than sitting. The entire place was still achingly bereft of any feminine touches. Although the dust and cobwebs were kept at bay by the part-time maid his father employed, cleanliness wasn't enough. The bay window had drapes which were for keeping out the darkness rather than decoration. There were few trinkets or mementoes. It gave the impression that this was a room to keep warm in before bed, rather than for living in. The same bookshelf still held the same books, although another oak unit had been added so that tomes now filled the entire rear wall, the newer case filled with the green leather spines of Simon's reference books.

"A scotch would go down better," Alan said.

"It's not after midday yet!"

"It is in France," Alan showed his pocket watch. "I'm still on their time."

"Have it your way." Simon decanted two fingers of whiskey and then himself a cup of amber tea while Alan lingered by the empty fireplace. "How was Paris?"

Alan chinked his glass against Simon's teacup.

"No ice?" he asked.

"Do I look like a barman to you?"

Alan looked his brother up and down. Waistcoat and sleeves, necktie, glasses.

"More like a waiter."

"You're hilarious," said Simon, without a twitch of humour.

"Paris was fantastic. It's London, but better. You'd love the bookshops and street musicians. I told you to meet me there. Two young Englishmen like us could tear a hole in that city."

"I'm sure you did just fine on your own. And I couldn't just leave, Alan. I'll never get a post in the Royal Institute laboratories if I'm gallivanting all the time."

"You know they have pavements that move?" continued Alan, ignoring his brother's feeble excuses. "The Champs Elysee is one long conveyor belt from the Grand Palace to the Arc du Triomphe. Rich folk just drift by, hopping on and off outside the boutiques like a fairground ride. And the girls, Simon. Dear God, the girls…"

Simon sipped his tea. "We have girls in London."

Alan looked around as if he might find one under the chair or behind the door.

"Not like those, we don't!"

Simon held up a hand. "Please, spare me the details."

"Fair enough. But you're missing out."

They sat for a while with their drinks. Simon's insides were warmed by his strong tea, Alan's by his scotch. Finally, Simon could put it off no longer.

"Thank you for your wedding present. Lottie and I weren't expecting anything."

"Nice to see her name's going first already," Alan grinned and pressed his thumb into the chair arm, grinding it there. Simon rolled his eyes. "They don't really sell gravy boats in Morocco, so I had to make do with what I could. You know that it's a fertility symbol?"

"Yes, even before we read the label. It has a certain something you can't ignore. Lottie keeps it in the cellar so it won't get broken."

Both brothers looked at each other over their drinks, lips

quivering, straining to see who would break first.

"It's supposed to be by your bed," managed Alan.

"Yes, that's what I told her. She suggested that I sleep in the cellar with it."

Alan's scotch spurted into the fireplace. Slapping a hand across his mouth to reduce the spray, he came up laughing. Simon's shoulders shook, one hand over his teacup to avoid spilling. As the laughter dribbled away, it left Simon seeming sullen. He set his teacup aside.

"I would have liked you to have come, you know. It's traditional that the best man attend."

"I know, Simon. And I *am* sorry. Really. And tell Lottie that too. You know how happy I am for you both. But I was at someone else's liberty at the time. I mentioned that I had a prior arrangement but they didn't seem inclined to negotiate." He shoved all thoughts of shackles out of his head.

"How can you be so flippant? We never know where you are, when you'll be coming home, who you're with. Don't think I haven't noticed that wound—"

Alan tugged down his shirt sleeve to hide the welt across his forearm.

"You're constantly putting yourself in harm's way."

"You'll find that harm puts itself in *my* way most of the time. You'd think it would learn its lesson. As for this scratch, it was an accident. A very cautious Parisian girl had a derringer stowed in her garter. As it turned out, it had a hair trigger."

Simon conceded defeat, and tried to change tactics.

"You've been gone seven months, a week and two days."

"You counted the days?" Alan wiped an imaginary tear from his eye.

"I've been acting as your damned postman for that long." Simon jerked his foot out, jostling Alan's chair and, trying to hide his smirk, he nodded toward the mantelpiece. Between the carriage clock and a silver framed photograph of Simon's mother was a wad of envelopes almost a foot thick.

"Anything important?"

"You're not going to let us talk about this, are you?" Simon waved at the stack of letters with a sigh. "I haven't opened them, of course. Some have a distinct scent of perfume on the envelopes. I don't think I could face their contents without vomiting. There is one, however…" Simon took the envelopes down a handful at a time, sifting through, passing them to Alan who marked the handwriting on each and either tossed them into the fireplace or laid them on the arm of his chair for later. "Here it is. Look at the post stamp."

Alan turned over the envelope to where a pair of stallions held a shield between their hooves. The ink was a little smudged, and the envelope dirty.

"Looks official."

"Looks like a court summons," said Simon, rifling through the rest of the mail.

"Bloody hope not." And with that, Alan slid his finger under the flap and tore the seal in half.

"What does it say?"

Alan's lips moved as he read. After a minute, he looked back inside the envelope and pulled out an elongated rectangle of thicker paper, perforated down the centre. He looked back at the letter again.

"Bugger me," he finally said.

"Well?" asked Simon.

"Take a look."

Simon read it aloud.

"Mister Shaw. Your reputation precedes you. Your heroism has come to the attention of the esteemed Lionel Sumner, Major in the First Regiment of His Royal Highness' Armed Forces. Bloody hell, Alan—"

"Keep reading."

"—Therefore, Major Sumner has requested your presence and assistance with a matter of national importance. Enclosed in this letter you will find a boarding ticket which will grant you passage to the port of Bombay where you will be met with transport to convey you to the presence of Major Sumner. We hope that this letter finds you well and able to serve your country in this most delicate matter. Yours sincerely. And a signature I can't read."

"Looks like I'm off to India!"

"Surely not. The letter gives no details at all of what this situation is or what you're expected to do. You can't just cross the world on the flimsy letter of some unknown soldier."

"I'm not. They gave me a ticket, too." Alan finally looked at the ticket itself, turning it over to read the information. Flipping open the cover of his tri-faced wristwatch he muttered, "Oh bugger."

"See? I knew something didn't smell right. Alan, where are you going?"

Alan darted for the hallway. Grabbing his duster from the hook and shouldering his bag, he made for the front door. Simon followed, yelling for attention like a school mistress after the bell had rung.

"Alan!"

"The ticket. It's dated for today!" Alan fumbled at the door with his hands full. "Are you going to help me with this?"

"You can't be serious. You only just got back. Father wants to see you. Can't you a least stay a few days? I'm sure we could get Helen and Percy to come to dinner at the very least."

Alan finally managed the doorknob, and froze on the threshold. His grin was a violent slash between his cheeks.

"Maybe next time," he said. "It was good to see you, Simon."

Alan extended a hand which his brother took only briefly. And he was gone, down the steps and across the road where he whistled a carriage. Before the noise of the street swallowed him completely, Simon heard him shout:

"Tell Father I'm sorry, and I'll be back as soon as I can!"

"When is soon? How can we contact you? Alan! God damn it!" Several people in the street span toward the curse, their eyes full of derision. On his doorstep, Simon flushed a deep red. "Awfully sorry. Slight misunderstanding." He turned back just in time to see Alan's carriage rattle off down the road. "Damn it, Alan."

2

"WHERE TO, SIR?" asked the driver, his voice muffled by his cloth mask.

"Hyde Park pylon," said Alan. "Quick as you like!"

The carriage's motor seemed to take that as a personal challenge and growled.

By the time they reached the end of the street, Alan had convinced himself that he didn't feel guilty for missing his father. The old man would understand. If truth be told, it was Carpenter's fault that Alan had developed such a reputation at all. It was his father who recommended that the Mayor publically commended Alan for his assistance in the Bethlehem Asylum robberies. The Londoners loved it, and him. Modesty only gets you so far and Alan was prepared to forego it entirely if necessary.

As the carriage bumped the curb onto Hyde Park, Alan could hear the mechanical drone that still made him tingle. A steel spire pierced the canopy of Hyde Park's trees, the sunlight strobing through its skeletal framework. It was identical in every way to its cousin on the banks of the Seine; taller perhaps, its feet narrower, but the same swarm of dirigibles circled its tip or swung from their mooring ropes nearer the ground. No two of the flying machines were the same. Alan could see the Italian Ambassador's ship, the galley shaped into a wooden ring with its balloon suspended through the centre, air wavering with the heat of the brazier below. Fish with eyes that showed men inside, wingless eagles, a host of shapes painted every colour from green and gold to cloudy blue circled overhead, either waiting to dock or pulling steamy streamers out across the London skyline.

Around the pylon, tiny forms threw silent semaphore messages across the air. A set of ropes slackened, dropped, and were drawn up into a dirigible's hull before it hummed a tight circle and flew out toward the river. Another, waiting patiently in line, dropped their own ropes and was guided down by the landing engineers.

Alan could have stood there all day and watched London's aerial hub as the airships rose and fell, but the boarding pass burnt hot in his hand. The only question now was which would be his bird? Carriages overtook him as he neared the pylon's ticket booth. Men and women in snappy grey and red uniforms hauled suitcases and chests onto carriage lids. Gentlemen took their first cigarette or pipe since their flights had begun and ladies fussed over whose baggage belonged to whom. The queue into the pylon, however, was thankfully short. Despite the French time still on his watch, Alan knew that the departure time of his dirigible was looming close. Luckily, the old woman in the ticket booth barely looked up at him and kept on waving as he moved through a clacking turnstile.

The elevator operator, however, was more attentive.

"Can I see your ticket, sir?" Alan handed over the slip.

"Right you are. You're on the third tier. Right up at the top. If you'd like to step in, sir? Ask the fella at the top and he'll see you right."

Alan thanked the operator as he stepped past and into the elevator's cage. He slid the folding shutters closed behind him and the operator did the same with an exterior set.

"Hold on, sir."

The elevator jerked once and then started to ascend, picking up speed until it was comfortably rocketing upward.

"Bloody hell, these things don't hang around," muttered Alan with one hand on his bag, the other on the wall. The elevator took a shuddering minute or more to reach the top of the pylon, slowing before it reached its destination but not enough to negate another jerk as the journey ended.

Trying to look official and polite as he braced against the wind, a young man drew open the elevator doors and gestured to Alan to step forward. As well as the same grey/red uniform and peaked cap as the other pylon employees, he wore a pair of ear muffs. His cheeks were a wind-battered pink.

"Might want to fasten your coat, sir. Very breezy up here," he yelled over the rush of wind. "Can I see your ticket?"

Alan handed it over and the young man tore the perforated strip, handing one half back.

"Docking number 3-2-7. Right around the other side, sir. Hold on, I'll take you around."

Stepping up to a small platform, the pylon engineer eased off a brake lever. Alan fought for balance as the floor began to rotate, sliding the whole third tier around the pylon at its core. What had been a view of London's misty suburbs changed to Buckingham Palace's roof, the river, and then the unmistakable tower of the Houses of Parliament in the distance.

"You could charge a fee just for this bit," said Alan.

"Don't think for a second they didn't consider it, sir," laughed the engineer "There's your transport, sir. I'll extend the gangway."

This time the usher wound a crank handle attached to the pylon itself. By Alan's feet, the gangway rose into place from beneath the tier, a section at a time, with safety railings swinging into place last.

"There we go, sir. Have a nice trip!"

"I'm sure I will," said Alan, adjusting the collar of his duster.

Dirigible balloons from the tier below extended in creaking walls on either side of the gangway, partially blocking Alan's view so that he could make out almost nothing at the furthest end. With one hand trailing the gangway's rail, he strode out across the air, knowing better than to look down. As the balloons gave way with the wind, Alan finally saw the ship that would carry him to India.

3

ALAN NEARLY DROPPED his bag. He looked back along the gangplank to where the usher was making encouraging gestures. Yes, this was his transport all right.

It was an airship, if only by association of its fellows. Its body was unimaginatively galleon-shaped to the point that Alan swore there were ancient barnacles scarring the wooden hull. At the prow, a pewter mermaid thrust her Pre-Raphaelite breasts into the air, her tail swept down to nurse a huge glass sphere, reinforced with steel bars, which was buried in the airship's prow as if it the boat had run aground on it. Twin propellers on each side of the hull looked reliable enough, although there were faded charcoal scars from some previous fire, and attached directly to the top of the hull was a domed balloon making the whole affair resemble a red-topped tortoise shell. It didn't look like one airship at all, but several welded together into a composite beast. Hand painted in gold-coloured filigree on the side of the ship was *La Custance*. The damned thing was French.

Alan groaned. If this was a joke, it wasn't a very good one.

With no one to meet him, Alan stepped over the airship's bulkhead and inside. As soon as he was in, the pylon's gangway retracted. This was it. He was in it for good or ill. With only stairs ahead of him and the door to a long drop behind, he climbed.

From the inside, the glass dome turned out to be the cockpit's window. It flooded the room with light and allowed the pilot to see both ahead and below. Alan noticed that one pane of glass had been replaced with a different colour to the rest, and wondered what there was at one thousand feet in the air to crash into and break a window on. An armchair, which could have been found in any parlour in the country, sat centre stage, its legs replaced with a complex mass of metal and pipes which fed across or into the floor. Consoles on either side held levers, switches, buttons and gauges which could have been vital to flight or all for show.

Alan spun around when he heard a grunt behind him.

A female bottom reversed toward him out of a floor-level vent. The woman's voice, echoing in the vent at first, became clearer as she climbed out, but Alan was none-the-wiser to its meaning. Dusting her knees, she finally stood up, muttering to herself in conversational French, the general tone sounding pretty unhappy. When she finally turned, it was obvious that she was expecting someone else but the shock only showed for a second. Plucking a rag from the wide tool belt at her waist, she began to wipe her hands, slick with oil all the way up past her wrists.

Her ripples of chestnut hair were held in place by a red bandana with a narrow-lensed set of welding goggles strapped on top. Climbing each ear lobe, four silver studs made it look as if her dainty ears were riveted to her head. A black bolero jacket hung open over a blouse and steel-ribbed corset. Alan had seen similar corsets before, but only ever used by dockworkers to help support their spine when heavy lifting. He had no idea they came small enough to fit this woman's narrow frame. Tucking her rag back into her belt, she rested one hand on either boyish hip, and spoke again.

"Oui?" she said, managing to make it sound like a question, boredom and an order all at the same time.

Alan responded with the only French he knew.

"Bonjour, Mademoiselle. Je m'appelle—"

The woman held up one soiled hand.

"Please, in English." Her voice sounded like whiskey, warm and smooth. "As much as I enjoy watching Englishmen stutter."

Alan slid the letter from his jacket and handed it over.

"I have an invitation—"

"We ain't no party ship, son!"

The owner of that voice stepped through from an adjoining room, ducking under the bulkhead in order to do so. His skin seemed dirty at first, but closer inspection told Alan that it was an ingrained tan. The man's hair was sun-bleached brown with a shock of grey combed in. He tugged at an old neckerchief, removing it from his collarless work shirt to wipe his brow. His waistcoat, with its herd of pockets, appeared to be well-tailored buckskin. As he stepped closer, it became evident that he towered over Alan.

"Let's take a look, Estelle." The man's drawl was part rumble, part slur, and marked him as transatlantic by birth. Probably somewhere in the mid-west from his ruddy skin. A thick moustache wobbled on his upper lip like a hastily-attached broom-head.

The French woman, Estelle, redirected the letter toward him. The man slid on a pair of wire-framed glasses which seemed comically small on someone of his immense size.

"What you have here, son, is a Letter of Marque."

"A job," said Alan. "I know."

"Do you now? Because it looks to me like you don't know much at all," said the American, replacing the glasses in his pocket. Estelle smirked as he continued. "A Letter of Marque is a contract. One that you signed by stepping on this ship. Never seen one that didn't lead to some sort of trouble. You ready for trouble, son?"

"Yes."

"I kinda wish you'd hesitated a little," said the American, but his face cracked into a broad smile. "But crazy ain't the same as insane. The name's Roy Ferris. Captain of the *Custance*."

"Capitaine? Ha!" laughed Estelle. And she poked Roy in the ribs as she continued: "Ceci est *mon* navire, Ferris. Vous n'etes rien, mais mon chauffeur!"

"If you're going to spout off, at least do it in English! Ignore her, son, she's just grouchy," said Roy, trying to waft Estelle away but looking more like he was deflecting a bullet. "Can't you go fix something, Sparky? There's always something broken round here."

Estelle threw her arms up and stormed out of the room, her sturdy boots bouncing on the floor. Alan followed her pleasant exit.

"That's a no-go, son. She's eaten boys like you before."

"I think I could handle it."

"Trust me, you couldn't." Roy laughed and offered a hand the size of a shovel's head. "Good to have you aboard."

The shake nearly took Alan's arm off.

4

ESTELLE WAS IN some other room, her flaming French curses punctuated with clatters and bangs.

"Don't mind her," said Roy for the third or fourth time, almost as if he was trying to convince himself more than Alan. He slouched in the pilot seat with his feet up on the nearest console – Alan's own legs wouldn't have been able to stretch so far – the bowl of his smoking pipe cupped in his hand. "She has a demon of a tongue but it's hard to get offended if you can't understand what she says."

"She's very…vocal," said Alan, making sure Estelle couldn't hear him and not knowing why.

"She's a pistol, that's for sure. Sparky! We ready for lift-off?"

From beyond the wall came a stream of French.

"Let's take that as a yes," muttered Roy and nudged Alan almost off his feet. "You ready to fly this tug, Son?"

"What about the rest of the crew?" asked Alan, looking around the cockpit as if they might have appeared without him knowing.

"The rest? We're it! Now go close the door, make sure it's tight, and we'll be making way."

Alan followed Ferris' instructions, closing the door, winding in the mooring ropes with a wheel which could have steered ships or lifted castle gates. With a shudder like a pigeon fluffing its feathers, the *Custance*'s propellers rose to an audible thrum of exertion. Alan made it back to the cockpit just in time to watch Roy guide the *Custance* away from Hyde Park pylon. The floor pitched as the pilot drew back on the lever in his left hand, pushed forward with the right. His feet shifted on the plates beneath his boots, adding and taking power with smooth, confident movements, despite the *Custance* giving the odd twang or rumble of complaint from its hidden workings.

Passing through a cluster of dirigible balloons waiting to dock, London came into view. The city stretched to hazy infinity in every direction, thousands of roofs in their rows like the grain in a mahogany tabletop. Chimneys and smokestacks seemed to be breeding these days, each one trailing dark clouds. The Thames, despite all its sludge and stench, still managed to give Alan a farewell wink of sunlight on water.

Roy caught Alan unawares with a nudge.

"Let me know when we pass over your house, we can always drop in for a drink," he said, and gave a gravelly chuckle.

"I'm not really from round here anymore," said Alan.

"That look you're wearing says otherwise. Never saw a man with a face like that who wasn't leaving home or thinking 'bout a lady."

Roy gave more power with both feet and the *Custance* rose until whiskers of cloud broke on the cockpit's globed window.

London fell away.

"YOU GOT A weapon, Alan?"

Roy sat with his head back, eyes closed, the smoke of his pipe rolling out of him like a locomotive. Alan had drawn up a stool to the pilot's side and was watching the unending landscape of cloud as it passed under the *Custance*'s hull. It was almost like being back on the water, only it was the wind that buffered the airship's hull rather than the ocean. If it turned out that there were no potatoes to peel, Alan could definitely get used to it.

"Of course," he said.

The pilot made a beckoning gesture and Alan went to retrieve his revolver from the bottom of his duffle bag.

"That it?" Roy said. He saw Alan's face collapse. "Not a bad a start, mind. Good weight. But you might be wanting something bigger. Come with me."

Roy hoisted himself out of the pilot seat.

"Are you sure we can leave?" asked Alan, eyeing the controls for any signs of drastic movement which might pitch them toward the ground.

"The locks are on. We'll fly in a straight line 'til the engines die or we hit something," said Roy.

Alan's face lost its colour.

"Don't *worry*, Alan. No mountains this high from here to Peru." Roy steered Alan away by his shoulder like a crane tossing a feather. "You haven't been on many airships, have you?"

"Honestly? My first time. I can never afford it. Trains

are cheaper."

"Cheaper, sure. But those land snakes ain't half as much fun."

They moved through another room lit by portholes, and up a set of creaking steps. The cockpit was actually in the lowest section of the airship's prow, the better to see both in front and underneath, and so as they climbed, they passed through what would have once been the ship's hold. Crates held tight to the walls with netting had things like 'Jerry-Logs', 'ammo' or 'canned goods' hastily stencilled on the sides.

"Best not get those mixed up, eh?" chuckled Roy, following Alan's eye around the room.

"You use Jerry-Logs?" asked Alan.

"Doesn't everyone? Don't look so surprised, son. We might seem a little thrown together from the outside, but thanks to some industrious borrowing of parts we're as up to date as it's possible to be. Anyways, coal just doesn't cut the mustard when it comes to flying. Too heavy, too quick to burn, too damn smoky. The sky'd be like ink if we all used it."

Another crate, hidden away at the back but larger than others caught Alan's eye. An insignia had been stencilled to its sides and lid, just like the others, but the wood was frayed as if someone had tried to scratch off the paint.

"What about that one?" asked Alan.

"Nothin'," said Roy. Alan couldn't help noticing that Roy's mouth was smiling, but his eyes weren't. "Spare parts. Probably best not to poke around down here, son. It's Estelle, you know. She can get territorial. Surprised if she ain't marked some of these things with her scent, if you know what I mean."

Alan took one last look into the dim hold before letting Roy draw him onward. For once the knotting in his stomach wasn't the familiar rumble of excitement.

Through the hold, they emerged into an undecorated corridor. The *Custance* was certainly a no-frills ship. Roy walked through the pools of light leaking from ineffective gas lamps. They passed a few closed doors, but one was open and Alan took a quick glance inside. It was well furnished with plush red and warm wood. A series of instruments, microscopes and many that were alien to him, were fixed to a long table against the wall. Books of the kind that made him think of Simon clustered every other surface. Roy leant past him, and closed the door.

"Not that way. Down here."

"Who's room was that?" asked Alan.

"Just another crew member. Former, you could say."

Alan furrowed his brow, but let the thought go. It probably wasn't best to pry too much at this point. And then they turned into another room, Roy gesturing for him to follow.

Bolted to the floor was a wide bed, a chair hooked securely to a desk at the other side of the room, and a few chests. It was no different from any other ship's bunk Alan had been in. Anything left out on a surface had a tendency to slide and so seamen, and apparently airmen, rarely had ornaments on show that hadn't been nailed there by the previous occupant.

"Over here," Roy said, ducking under the bed. There was a snap of metal clasps and the sound of rummaging.

Eventually he produced a long package and unwrapped it.

Alan took the rifle that was offered, gasping under the weight. His knees bent to take the strain.

"Don't worry, that one's mine," said Roy. Moving aside an oil cloth, he recovered another, smaller weapon from inside the trunk. "This one should suit you to the ground."

Alan hefted the smaller rifle to his shoulder. After a six-shooter, the long barrel with the ammunition cartridge huddled underneath felt unwieldy in his hands.

"Nice ain't she? Winchester Mare's Leg carbine. Short, easy to hide under your coat, there, and she'll punch a hole in a fuel can the size of your fist. Used to be mine when I was just a boy."

Alan's face soured.

Roy held up his hands in surrender. "Don't go pointing that thing at me, now. I meant no offence. It's a lighter model, is all. You ever shot one of these before?"

Alan let the tension in his face die away. There was no use getting offended and trying to punch a man twice his size, especially a man who could have thrown Alan out of a speeding airship without a parachute if he wanted to. And he was already starting to feel pretty relaxed around Roy and his runaway jaw, despite some niggling misgivings. The large man had a calmness about him that rubbed off. Except on Estelle, apparently.

"A rifle, a long time ago," he said.

"Good. Best to be honest. Now don't lift it to your shoulder. Brace your hip into it. That's right. Sight down this thing like a rifle, it'll tear your head off."

Alan did as he was told, picking an imaginary target somewhere beyond the room's porthole. The walnut grip on the barrel was well smoothed by use, and pleasantly warm. His palm shifted to find its spot.

"That's good," said Roy, letting Alan get a feel for the weapon as it moved in his hands. "The ammo cartridge snap-loads like any other rifle. It's lever action, but you should get used to it pretty quick."

Alan proved himself by cocking the lever. There was a satisfying clunk-click.

"Now you got a shell in the breach," continued Roy. "I reckon you know the rest."

Alan removed the ammunition cartridge, just for the fun of it, showing a row of bullet tips like metal pearls. Without any instruction, he slid the cartridge back on and reset the weapon, ready to fire.

"Quick learner, eh? Now that's yours. Take care of her."

Alan tried to give the gun back.

"I don't accept charity. I've got my revolver. It'll be fine."

Roy shook his head, serious again. His expressions seemed to swap between mirth and sternness based on the set of his moustache. His huge hand pressed the carbine to Alan's chest.

"Ain't no one ever given Roy Ferris back a gift, son. And ain't no one on my crew going into this thing without being properly armed."

Alan set the weapon's butt on his hip like he'd seen in old pictures as a boy.

Roy cracked a lopsided grin.

"We'll make a cowpoke of you by the time this thing's done."

5

A LAN SAT IN the pilot's seat with only the sound of the *Custance*'s engines for company. Roy had finally decided to sleep, two days into the journey, and so left Alan on watch. And by watch, he meant "don't touch anything". And that was fine by Alan. There was never much love lost between him and technology. Of course, he loved the speed of a locomotive, the powerful crash of a steam ship over the waves, the purr of a propeller. He could watch a series of complex gears knit together for hours, like pieces of the universe on show, spinning time into manageable chunks. But it was what the machines could *do* that he loved rather than having to work them himself. With that in mind, he stayed well away from the *Custance*'s controls. The only thing he'd ever learnt to drive was a motorised velocipede on the Italian coast. But that was all and that was fine.

Plucking an envelope from the stack he had brought from home, Alan tore open the end and slipped out the letter. The handwriting was familiar.

Dear Alan,

We all hope this letter finds you well. I am sorry that it has taken me so long to send word, but since Grand-mamma passed, the responsibility of running the circus has fallen to me. Of course the family help as much as I could ever hope, but the responsibility is a heavy one. And that is why I write to you now, with responsibility in mind.

We have heard tell of the Ordo Fenris once more. Herr Volkert has been spotted with a group of his men in a library in Alexandria. The Librarian himself was slain and so no one knows why they were there, but you can be certain that something was stolen—

Alan turned over the letter and saw that the date on the envelope was for months before. Damn.

—We have been informed of other sightings of the red wolf insignia across Europe especially. That the Ordo are allowing themselves to be seen is a great worry to me. Their focus seems to be on speed rather than secrecy now, a sure sign that they are nearing what they believe to be the completion of their work. I hope for all our sakes that these men are merely mad, but we have both seen what they are capable of first hand. Please, if you can, send word or visit us. We have returned to Hungary for a time and our posters will guide you from there.

As an aside, me and Luc are to be married! I hope you will come see us. Love to Simon and Lottie.

Jessamine Maskelyne

Alan turned the letter this way and that as if something

other information might fall from the page. That bastard Volkert was still on his grudge list. If only Alan could catch up with them, but everywhere he went, the Ordo Fenris was long gone. Simon would have told him to answer his damned mail, then. Alan smiled to himself and stowed the letter for later. One more package, one he'd been saving until last, sat in his lap. Its shape was familiar to him, and the anticipation of the contents was too. Breaking the adhesive seal on the package, he slid out the contents; the issues *of Titus Galdstone Adventures* he'd missed while he was away. Alan's thumb caressed the edge of the top issue's cover absently.

Titus Gladstone was in peril again, it seemed. The cover showed a hissing beast rearing over the hero, dripping with some vile green fluid, and all Titus had was his bare hands, and a damsel in scanty Peruvian outfit with strangely Caucasian complexion to protect. After all Alan had been through, all he'd seen, there was still something about Titus' Graphical Adventure books that he couldn't let go. In a childhood where his role model had been a Spanish barmen with heavy hands, Titus had shown Alan that men could be different, brave. Huddled under a lantern, Simon had taught Alan to read with those pages, and Alan's dream of leaving for America had changed to a simpler one. He wanted to be just like Titus Gladstone. To a certain extent, he had achieved his goal. Alan had a reputation for bravery and tenacity, a reputation which he enjoyed. He travelled the world just like Titus, had adventures just like Titus, and with each new adventure came another pretty face just like it did for Titus.

Forgetting entirely where he was for now, Alan swung his feet up so that he sat in the pilot's armchair sideways, his feet dangling over the arm, and shuffled himself comfortable.

Estelle stomped her way into the room, making Alan look up. Her thick leather tool belt swung across her hips like a gunslinger armed with wrenches and screwdrivers. It enhanced even further the only thing Alan could find attractive about her; the way she walked. London ladies, and even Parisians for that matter, in their long skirts seemed to drift along as if levitating rather than walking. Estelle's trousers and well-worn chaps made it very easy to see the pleasing motion of her legs and narrow hips. It was just a shame Alan couldn't get on with her. Or rather, she seemed uninterested in trying.

Ignoring Alan completely, Estelle dropped the object she was carrying beside a console to his right; a brass ring with a green glass dome in the centre, trailing wires from its underside. Alan recognised it as a telephonoscope like ones he'd seen on ships. In fact, exactly like he'd seen on ships. If he wasn't mistaken, this one had been ripped from some unsuspecting bridge pretty recently. Some of the screws were still in place with chunks of wood attached.

Estelle dropped to her knees by the console and unscrewed a panel to show a tangle of wires inside like ancient tree roots. With little ceremony, she pulled the cables free in clumps as if removing weeds from a garden. Alan found his knuckles turning pale on the chair's arms, waiting for something vital to be tugged free which would turn the airship into a falling coffin.

But nothing happened.

At the back of his mind, Alan swore to travel on the ground from now on.

Estelle tore the console's lid free, gauges and all, and tossed it aside to clatter on the ground. Pausing only to wipe the sweat from her lip with the back of her hand, she hoisted the telephonoscope globe into place and dove back underneath to begin reconnecting. With Estelle's legs still hanging out of the console like a metallic crocodile's lunch, the telephonoscope's globe pulsed once, twice, and then lit with a faint green glow. Lines slid across its surface in a shifting grid. One small dot in the globe's centre showed the *Custance*. A V shape of smaller dots entered the sphere, ahead of them as far as Alan could tell. Peering out of the cockpit's enormous window, he spotted a flock of geese in formation which soon passed underneath the *Custance* with honks of annoyance.

"I often amaze myself," said Estelle, wiping her hands on yet another rag. She seemed to have hundreds stowed away somewhere on her person. "Now maybe even Roy won't be able to crash."

"So you *can* speak English. And fluently?"

Estelle looked to Alan as if she weren't expecting him to be there.

"Oui," she said, more of a sigh with meaning than an answer.

"So why don't you?"

"Why don't you speak French?"

"I can't."

"Then which one of us is the ignorant one, Monsieur

Anglais?"

Estelle froze. As Alan watched, her face went slack. She pressed a hand against the *Custance*'s hull as if checking it for fever.

"What is it?" asked Alan, looking around for what Estelle had seen or heard. He couldn't find anything. Estelle held up a finger for silence. She went from standing to sprinting in a blink.

Alan darted after her, leaping over the bulkhead, and into the hold. Estelle had stopped dead.

From here, Alan could finally hear it, too. From somewhere beyond the *Custance*'s hull came a loud *SPRA-pa-pa-pa-pa-pa-pa.*

"Merde!" cursed Estelle. "Come!"

And she was off again; Alan tugged into her wake like a kite's tail.

Estelle yanked open the Engine Room door and the whine of struggling engines became ear-splitting. Through a wide observation window, smoke could be seen coughing from a starboard propeller. Charred feathers clung to the propeller's fuselage, and streaks of terminally accelerated goose blood stained the steel. Alan tried to curse but he couldn't think of anything to rival Estelle's stream of vulgarities.

"Not again," said Estelle, as she slipped a screwdriver from her belt like an assassin drawing a blade, jammed it into the engine's internal housing and popped the panel open. Smoke billowed into her face; she didn't seem to notice. "Damned birds should watch where they fly."

Grasping for a can of oil, Estelle dumped the thick

contents directly into the engine and tossed the empty receptacle aside. The smoke began to subside until Alan could see the mechanism working like the fretted pulse of a startled animal.

"Do something with this," snapped Estelle, gesturing to a winch wheel on the starboard side. Alan decided to just do as he was told for a change, pumping his arms on the crank until his breath burnt. Through the observation window, he saw two flexible wooden masts extending from the *Custance*'s hull. Shooting a look across to Estelle, he saw that she was doing the same to a wheel on the port side, lithe muscles standing out in her arms. Alan's winch stopped dead, almost jerking him off his feet.

"Done!" he informed her, although unsure of exactly what that was.

Hooking her fingers into a ring in the engine room's floor Estelle pulled, producing a long lever which had been hidden between the boards. Extending it to an upright position, she yanked to the left. Beyond the window, deep red fabric rolled out along the masts, billowing in the wind with a snap until they resembled the sails of a corsair ship.

"Sails on an airship?" asked Alan, when his breath was caught.

"Two either side, two above, one below," said Estelle almost to herself. "They will help carry us until I can fix the propeller." A glisten of proud sweat greased her brow. Her grin was infectious. Her breath made her reinforced corset rise and fall hypnotically.

Ah, so maybe she *could* be attractive, thought Alan. He stepped slightly closer to her as if to get a better look out the window.

"It's an incredible design," he said.

"If you don't remove that hand," said Estelle. "You'll be wiping your derrière with a hook."

CLOUDS WERE TORN to eddies on the cockpit window as the *Custance* lowered its altitude. The open plains of Southern France sped by below; cottages and patchwork farms clustered together, interspersed with rolling treetops. Ahead, Alan could see the Alps as a ragged purple shape breaking the horizon like a cresting leviathan. The clouds were low on the mountain's snow-capped peaks, and dense with the promise of more weather ahead.

In the pilot seat, Roy was smiling to himself.

"Mountains always remind me of home," he said. He took a pull from a bottle of cheap wine and sucked the excess from his moustache. Alan took the bottle when it was offered. "O'course you can see the Rockies from clear across Montana, not like these little fellas. But I still get those old butterflies anytime I see a decent range."

"I'm the same," said Alan with a gleam in his eye.

Roy chuckled. "Son, you want to watch that thing in your pants don't go off, you could kill someone."

Alan wiped the bottle's tip with his waistcoat, a habit he had caught from Simon, and took a long pull from the bottle. Roy raised an eyebrow.

"I was going to run away to America when I was a boy," said Alan.

"What stopped you?" Roy took the bottle back, shaking the contents which were noticeably lighter.

"I grew up, I think."

"Never had that problem, myself," said Roy. "When I was young I wanted to fly, I wanted to see the world, the whole package. Seems the only thing I never counted on was Estelle."

They cut their laughter short as Estelle came in behind them carrying a burnt chunk of the shredded engine. As she walked, her support corset adjusted for her gait, letting out little hisses. She snorted at the men's silence, which only made Roy chuckle more.

"The weather looks bad, Ferris," said Estelle in her husky accent. "We should wait it out. Land."

"Those clouds are just there for show," said Roy. "Go fix your engine. We'll be in the Mediterranean in no time."

"I hate to say it, Roy, but she's right. Maybe we should wait while the sky clears."

"Who's flying this thing, me or you two? I know what I'm doing. That weather'll be cleared to a drizzle by the time we get there."

6

THE *CUSTANCE* SHOOK like a crystal chandelier in an earthquake. Alan's body strained against his seat's harness as the airship was buffeted and rocked. Aside from the creaking of the hull and whistle of high winds through the cockpit's ill-fitting window, all he could hear was Estelle as she screamed at Roy in a stream of French so violent that Alan couldn't make out a single word, never mind understand them. The engineer strained against her own harness like a wild animal in a trap. Her boots kicked the floor and her hands were claws on the chair's arm.

Roy threw the ship to one side as a mountain loomed out of the blizzard's grey maelstrom. The *Custance* groaned with the effort. Alan could almost feel the jagged rocks graze the airship's hull. He gritted his teeth until his jaw ached and wished for solid ground, preferably with cobbles and gutters and horse manure and oil puddles.

"Couldn't we fly above the mountains, at least?" he yelled.

"No point, son. The winds will be twice as bad up there and the clouds're too low. We'll be flying even blinder than we are now."

Estelle changed gear and screamed in English.

"Ferris, if you crash my ship, I'll kill you!"

"Better hope I die when we hit the ground, then." Roy roared with laughter and yanked the controls to avoid another outcrop that grazed the *Custance*. Outside, the propellers whined as they churned the freezing air. The damaged engine was taking a beating, giving the occasional *scrackh* as the gears skipped a rotation.

The *Custance* groaned so deeply that Alan felt it in the seat of his chair. He grabbed for his harness with pale knuckles as the airship seemed to drop by twenty feet in one go, and bounce to a stop.

"Air pocket!" yelled Roy, like a tour guide with a death wish. "Ain't this the best bronco you ever rode, Alan? Yeeehaw!"

Alan didn't answer. His stomach rolled, the wine sloshing around inside him so he had to grit his teeth against the urge to get rid of it again. He remembered being shackled in a certain asylum's loft-space, and wondered if he'd felt more fear then or now. Another Alan restrained, another madman, and another suicidal machine that could be death of him. He had once heard that people learn from their mistakes, but he clearly wasn't people because despite the slick palms, aching body and certain death-by-ground, a part of him was really starting to enjoy himself.

The light in the cockpit began to lift from an oppressive grey hue to something Alan hoped was daylight. He strained to see around Estelle, who was still ranting, and caught sight of the ground through the snowstorm's swirling mass. Thankfully, it wasn't approaching dead ahead as he expected, but skipping along underneath like a child following a flying circus.

Roy whooped and laughed. Taking his hand from the controls to punch the air made the *Custance* list violently, and he grabbed the lever again.

"Woops! Sorry 'bout that."

The *Custance* punched its way out of the blizzard, the engines instantly picking up in the warmer air so that she almost danced. Light flooded the cockpit. The ground stabilised.

"Land! Land now!" Estelle screamed.

"Ok, ok. Keep your shirt on," said Roy.

Alan almost lost his stomach again as the *Custance* dipped toward a landing.

ESTELLE DANGLED FROM her harness, cracking ice from the starboard propeller with a hammer and chisel. Occasionally, she wound the crank on her belt which activated the pulley's ratchet device above, lifting or lowering her into place.

Alan and Roy stood below, dodging the ice which always seemed to fall where they stood, despite moving several times.

"Shouldn't we be helping?" asked Alan. He brushed frost from the shoulder of his duster. The weather on this side of the Alps was much fairer and a warm Mediterranean breeze meant the *Custance* would soon be thawed and flying again in no time.

"She wouldn't thank you for it, Alan. Estelle gets all maternal when it comes to her airship. She built the *Custance* from the ground up. Salvaged and stole parts from all kinds of old wrecks to make it fly."

Alan's eyebrows bunched in a 'you're fooling no one' kind of way.

"Don't pull that face near Estelle unless you want to wake up with a wrench where your teeth used to be. She knows more about mechanics than any engineer I ever met, bar her father. What do you think she was doing in the engine room, needlework?"

"Who's her father?" asked Alan, deciding that sexual liberation was a conversation he wanted to avoid with Roy.

Roy cocked an eyebrow, and paused for effect, "Only Etienne Budreau."

Alan's face could have been a wooden mask for all the movement it made.

"Of Budreau Aeronautics?" said Roy. "Damn, boy, he was the first man to design powered flight. The father of the airship. And not your German gas bubbles, neither. Proper power. Maybe if you get your head out from up girls' skirts, you'll learn something every once in a while."

Despite the jibe, Roy gave Alan a friendly nudge which made him smile rather than snarl.

"So why's she flying around on an old ragamuffin like the *Custance*?" Alan asked, to pass the time.

"Etienne died. Not in a flying accident as you'd expect. In his sleep as it should be. Estelle's brother Etienne – junior that is – took the whole family fortune, sold his father's last designs, and left Estelle with nothing but a boat ticket to New Orleans and her night clothes."

"So that's why she hates men," said Alan.

"Estelle don't hate men. If anything, she loves them a

little too much. It's *you* she don't like."

THE MEDITERRANEAN SEA was an immense turquoise gem that threw back broken reflections of the *Custance* as it passed overhead. Alan sat in the airship's open doorway, feet hanging over the speeding water and warm air in his face. Off the port side or speeding below, he had already spotted the coast of Italy and a cluster of Greek islands, places familiar although not from this angle. His thoughts stayed with them only as long as the *Custance*'s fleeting shadow caressed their hills and valleys.

Another coastline approached. Alan had left England over white cliffs, crossed the vast green spaces of France, and soared over the sprouting rocks of the Mediterranean islands, but this place was different again. It seemed dry despite the water lapping its crumbling shoreline, arid and of a uniform tan colour, as if God had forgotten to deliver the soil.

According to Roy, they'd rest in the shrublands for a few hours; let Estelle make her checks, fix any holes in the *Custance*'s hull big enough to let sand creep in, close the hatch for the last time, then head out across the Arabian desert. Two days. Two short days and Alan would be further from stinking London than he'd ever been before.

7

THE FLAT ROOFTOPS of Bombay spread out underneath the cockpit like mosaic tiles. Palm trees like upended mops leaned or stood to attention in clumps. The occasional temple roof, peaked like an orange juicer surrounded by garlic bulbs, rose above the other buildings.

As the *Custance* swung low over a vast marketplace, not a single face turned upward in awe, as Alan had expected. The people of Bombay were as used to flying machines as those in England, if not more. What the people did do, however, was cover their eyes or tug their collars over their mouths as the airship's propellers swung into landing positions, huffing up a cloud of sand. Alan jerked under his harness as the ship landed with an emphatic creak. It seemed that India hadn't made the leap to mooring pylons yet.

Roy tugged on the speaking tube above his head, calling for Estelle to cut the engines.

"Well, son, don't waste no time. I can tell you can't wait to get out there," said Roy. "Me and Estelle got a few things to sort here, but then we'll be right along. Don't go too far. And don't buy nothing with English money. Not here."

"I think I can contain myself," said Alan, taking his time

to remove the harness' clasps and retrieve his duster. Roy had informed him that they wouldn't be back to the *Custance* for a while, so he shouldered his duffle bag as well.

"Don't forget your gun, Alan." All of a sudden, Roy's moustache was tense as the whiskers of a spooked cat. "Now we're here, you don't go anywhere without it, y'hear?"

Alan nodded and slung the weapon in its protective holster under his coat. On reflex, he checked his sidearm was still on its shoulder holster, too.

"I feel like a pack horse," said Alan.

"At least you're the kind who can fight back when it's whipped," replied Roy as he disappeared into the hold.

The bulkhead's locking wheel popped as it spun and Alan inhaled the first Indian air of his life. It tasted like dung. Kicking a latch by his feet sent a ladder rattling to the ground, which he then slid down with his boots off the rungs. Accosted by a fly which seemed to want to live in his ear, Alan batted it away. His duster flapped, wrapping around him almost protectively. As the dust began to settle, the breeze kicked it up again, toying with the grains so that the ground was never still. Where London would have been filled with the rattle and chug of steam carriages, Bombay was a mass of lowing cattle, creaking wooden carts and raised voices. Around the marketplace, blank-faced buildings showed gaping holes where glass should have been, and beaded curtains where doors would have made more sense. Anyone could have walked in and out of any building there. The thought made Alan feel kind of ill. Even the loft spaces he'd slept in as a boy had doors.

The people were a throng. Where Covent Market had

always been busy, Bombay was bedlam. There was no front or back to the stalls, despite what the striped awnings might suggest. Sellers and customers could have been anyone. Money changed hands apparently at random. There were no signs, no pasted bills, no aprons or boots or pigeons.

Most people wore long robes to their feet, a single line of buttons down the front. But England was asserting itself in fashion as well as in Imperial bullets. Here and there, Alan spotted a waistcoat instead of a tunic, or a bowler hat rather than a turban. Or a suit the likes of which you might see on Oxford Street, only in orange or green stripes with bell-bottomed trousers ending at curled shoes.

Alan found himself feeling very, very far from home. To make sure no one noticed, he stuck out his chin, tugged his coat into submission and took a walk.

One old man among a host of others sat on the ground under a building's shadow, a rug in front of him with intricately carved boxes spread over it. Shifting the hang of his revolver, Alan crouched for a better look. The old man looked up at him with a sparsely toothed grin.

"English!" he said, as if making some great deduction.

Alan asked how much, but apparently the old man had exhausted his multilingualism.

Picking up a medium sized box, Alan dug in his duster for some coins. He produced a shilling and, based on the unveiled glee of the old man, decided it was more than enough. He went to stand up, but was dragged back down as the old man snatched back the box.

"Oy!"

But Alan stopped when the old man produced paper

and string, and began to bind the box tight. Alan nodded and forced a smile as his prize was handed back to him.

After wandering a little longer, Alan came back around to the rear of the *Custance*. The cargo hold had been opened up to the market place, the door now acting as a ramp. Estelle was wearing her bolero jacket with a neat little knapsack slung across her back. Her goggles were down against the billowing dust, and she'd found a revolver of her own, larger than Alan's, which she wore at the small of her back. She bartered with the market holders, seeming to make herself known through a mix of French and English which the merchants replied to in their own broken way. Roy was in the hold itself, sliding crates down to the crowd and letting them be taken away wherever Estelle gestured. Now and again, a crate went the other way, back into the hold.

With the major rush over, Roy spotted Alan and made his way over. Somehow, the American seemed to have generated a deeper tan already. He mopped his brow.

"Just because we're here on a job, doesn't mean we can't make a little something on the side, eh?" he said. "You'd be amazed what these folk'll buy given half the chance. Most of these crates are full of cloth, would you believe? But who am I to question? And the English don't mind the spices in return, so everyone's happy. What do you reckon, Alan? First impressions of India."

"Could use a spring clean. When are we heading for the rendezvous point?"

"Soon enough, soon enough. Hold that thought."

A man had placed himself at the edge of the crowd.

Although the merchants and market workers jostled and swarmed around him, Alan could pick him out like a sore thumb. His robes were a deep burgundy and a scarf wrapped the lower half of his face. On a wide belt, the stranger wore a sheathed blade. Alan got an impression of tense muscle beneath the dark cloth. Even when rescued from the streets, Alan had lost none of his childhood instincts. That man oozed villainy.

Roy made his way over to the stranger, holding out a hand, not in greeting, but directing the Indian to a quieter spot near the *Custance*'s rear doors.

Roy seemed to be doing all the talking. Nothing strange about that in Alan's experience. But the stranger never moved other than to give a terse gesture to a pair of workers who removed themselves from the crowd. Alan couldn't help but notice the looks they swapped as Roy pointed to a crate near the hold's entrance. The scarred stencils on its lid and sides told Alan which crate it was, but still not what was inside. Hauled down to the ground, the crate disappeared into the crowd. Alan realised that the dark-attired Indian had also gone, leaving Roy alone with a long box under his arm, the size that would carry a wine bottle. Jogging up the slope, the American went inside and reappeared a moment later without the box, rubbing his hands on the flanks of his trousers and his moustache set in a frown.

Alan made sure his attention was elsewhere when Roy came back.

OPEN TO THE street on all sides, the bar was more like a terrace with lots of small tables and stools clustered in a scatter pattern. The bar itself was just long enough that the *Custance*'s crew could stand by it shoulder-to-shoulder. Unlabelled and ingrained with dust, the stack of bottles could have contained beer, gin or engine grease.

"Ok, ok. I get where you're coming from, Alan," said Roy, sipping from his bottle. "Read it for yourself, if you like."

Alan held the American's letter of marque against his own.

"It's different," he said.

Roy gestured to the boy behind the bar for another round of drinks. Estelle's attention was elsewhere, with a small troop of British soldiers on the opposite side of the street. In their red tunics and pith helmets, they were a strange contrast to the busy figures around them.

"They usually are," said Roy. "Like snowflakes. No two the same. But nothing to hide, as you see. I just got a little more information than you did. Privateering's run on a need to know basis, and 'til now you didn't need to know. Hell, Major Sumner won't even know that you've taken the job until we walk up to him and say 'Hi'."

"But you knew what we were coming for all this time and didn't think to share it?"

"You never asked," said Roy.

Estelle came back to the group, taking a pull on her drink.

"Fine. Well I'm asking now," said Alan.

Roy sighed. "We're an escort—"

"For what?"

"—I'm telling you, aint I? We're escorting supplies to

the front line. The Indian revolution ain't just a story in the papers, Alan. It's going on right here."

Alan looked around. Everywhere were people going on with their lives, running back and forth, completely oblivious to the Privateers in their presence.

"Not *right* here," said Roy. "But not far away. People fighting for freedom against the British Empire. Your empire, in fact. And that's where we're headed, coz that's where Sumner is."

"And why, when there are so many soldiers here already, does the British army need our help to deliver their…boxes of tea?" Estelle purred.

"That's not all Englishmen think about," snapped Alan.

"No indeed, you often think about other things that are wet and warm…and which don't belong to you."

Roy's laughter propelled his beer right into the bartender's unsuspecting face.

"Oh Lord, son. I'm so sorry," he said, dabbing at the barman's shirt with his handkerchief and laughing all the time. "I'll pay for that."

"No no, sir. No trouble. No trouble," said the barman, trying to fight off Roy's politeness.

Alan ignored the engineer's jibe. "Exactly what I was thinking, Estelle. Why do soldiers want to employ Privateers for a job they can do themselves?"

"All I know is, there's been thefts from the convoys. There must be something funny about 'em or they wouldn't have sent for us," said Roy. "We're experts in 'different' aint we, Estelle?"

Estelle gave a knowing smile.

The first rumble came without sound, as a sensation that came up through Alan's boots until he felt it like a bass note in his heart. The barman dove for the stack of bottles as they tried to rattle themselves from the shelves, hugging them as if they were his long-lost mother. As the vibrations grew Alan became aware of a growing sound, the dull drone of an immense engine and crunch of hard ground under wheels. He and Estelle ran out into the street which the locals were clearing with all haste. The British soldiers had lined themselves neatly despite the growing noise, and the approaching dust cloud which blotted out the buildings all down the street.

Alan found his hand straying to his revolver as he and Estelle exchanged glances.

8

"**P**ROBABLY BEST TO leave that where it is, son," said Roy, putting his hand on Alan's shoulder.

With the dust cloud breaking on its prow like a battleship in the fog, the vast machine came barrelling toward them. Two stories tall and fashioned from a single piece of dark gun-metal, six steel-shod wheels churned the earth as the behemoth ground to a halt. Steam ejected from underneath the carriage as if the machine were gasping under its own weight.

Alan spat the sand from his mouth.

As it seemed to have been doing ever since they arrived, the dust settled again, and Alan could see that the immense vehicle's engine section was towing only a single carriage, fashioned in the same style as the engine. The only windows were tiny and high up. A pair of huge bulbs in steel cages were the only other facial feature of the snub-nosed beast.

A door-sized panel popped free of the vehicle's side and slid back along the chassis to reveal a soldier of the British Empire, a single sash of white across his red uniform. *An officer*, thought Alan, but of what sort he didn't know. Stepping down from the chassis, the officer produced a whip-crack salute, and was met with the same from the other soldiers who shouldered their rifles with clockwork precision and filed aboard the machine. Only then did the officer turn a quizzical eyebrow on the *Custance* Privateers.

Roy waved the seal on his Letter of Marque. Checking that the other soldiers were aboard, the officer visibly relaxed. Waving them over, he tucked his helmet under an arm and smoothed back his hair. As always, Roy advanced with hand outstretched. The officer shook it firmly, but wasn't ready for Roy's brute strength. Alan smirked as the soldier tried to hold back a grimace of shock.

"Blow me, good handshake," said the soldier. "Lieutenant Dawson of the 53rd Foot, at your service. I take it you're the lads who're here to solve our little problem then?"

Alan grinned, waiting for Estelle to go on one of her suffragette tirades.

"Oh, my apologies, Madame," said Dawson. "Just a turn of phrase, I assure you. We should probably get aboard. We can brief on the way."

Dawson offered a hand to Estelle, who took it in the most genteel manner, allowing the officer to help her onto the vehicle. With a husky *merci*, she gave the soldier a smile which made him flush a vibrant crimson.

Alan and Roy exchanged glances.

Roy shrugged. "No accountin' for taste, I suppose."

"Ahem, well, gentlemen," said Dawson, composing himself. "Welcome aboard The Camel."

"IT HAS TWO carriages, humps you see, and was designed for crossing deserts," said Dawson, setting his helmet down on the mahogany table top.

Alan had been in few places as plush as the Camel's upper gallery. He settled down into a deep leather chair, the wings so wide that he couldn't see Roy or Estelle who sat to his left. Trios of fizzing bulbs lined the gallery's ceiling in settings like daffodil trumpets. Light spilled through the narrow windows, refracted by many gilded mirrors hung to enhance the light. The only sign of an engine at work on the lower levels was the gentle tinkling of sherry glasses in their cabinet.

Dawson walked over to the window in order to peer out, the thud of his boots softened by a firm carpet decorated with amber curlicues. With warm sunlight on his face, Alan could get a better look at him. Surely no older than Alan himself, but already at officer's rank, Alan surmised that the Lieutenant was born that way. Boys with rich fathers didn't become privates or sergeants. Alan could feel his contempt for the man growing with every creak of the soldier's shiny boots.

"I hope you'll excuse me, Gentlemen and Lady. But I'm really not used to all this." Dawson waved an arm at the carafes of expensive liquor, the red curtains with their gold rope tie-backs, the cigar box and the dress mirror. "I probably shouldn't say so, and I never would to the men, but this is my first trip on the Camel. The last Lieutenant was discharged on ill health, poor man. Went quite queer." Dawson stretched his collar.

"I'm guessing that's why we're here," said Roy, throwing Dawson a lifeline.

"Precisely, Mister Ferris—"

"Just Roy is fine."

"—Thank you. Of course, refer to me as Dawson when the men aren't around."

"No first name?" said Alan.

"Yes, Mister Shaw, but it's Cuthbert, and I hate it."

"Dawson it is, then," said Roy. "Satisfied Alan?"

Alan didn't reply, but set his jaw forcibly toward the Lieutenant.

"Certainly," said Dawson, giving Alan a wary glance. Moving back toward the centre of the room, Dawson hooked his finger into a ring in the ceiling and drew down a map of India. Pointing out Bombay, he ran a finger across the continent as he spoke. "The supply convoys run from Bombay to the heart of India along the Aligarh Road. Weapons, food, and a hundred other supplies all bound for the front line in Delhi where the rebels still hold our forces at bay."

"That's where we're going?" asked Alan.

"Yes, Mister Shaw. Where the Aligarh Road meets the Grand Trunk Road here, that's where most of the thefts have occurred. That's where we're headed."

"No trains?" asked Alan.

"This road is over five hundred miles of uneven desert and hilly terrain which only rests for patches of dense jungle. It's almost impossible to lay any substantial track here."

"And you don't just fly it in on airships?"

Dawson hung his head and sighed, but maintained politeness.

"*No*, Mister Shaw. As I'm sure Roy and Miss Budreau can tell you, airships are fine for freight of lighter items of commerce. Not so when delivering tons of complex weaponry. A canon mount weighs anything in excess of seventy tons; a war wagon only fifty to sixty depending on the design. But I'm sure you can imagine the size of airship necessary to carry just one, never mind a fleet of them. And airships are very easy targets to shoot at."

"Alan, stop interrupting," said Roy.

"Thank you, Roy. As I was saying, between the Grand Trunk Junction and Delhi is where the rebels have been making their move. But that isn't unusual. Generally a small unit of foot troops would be able to successfully hold off any bandit activity. But what we have here, and why yourselves have been asked for assistance, is the nature of the thefts."

"C'est a ce moment que l'histoire devient differente."

"Exactly, Miss Budreau. I think you've hit the proverbial nail on the head. These robberies are very 'different'."

Alan audibly snarled. The toff could even speak French.

"The stories coming from my predecessor and his men are wild, gentlemen. Wild. Both he and his team of guards have been discharged to duties elsewhere, shall we say, which I'm afraid I can't disclose. I'm sure you understand, due to the mockery which would have been made of their reputation had this story leaked into the general army's ranks. It's blatant scaremongering and superstitious nonsense as far as I can see. However, Major Sumner has taken some stock of it and so we're here to investigate."

"Excuse me for saying, Dawson, but the Camel doesn't seem like an easy truck to burglarise. Hell, I was amazed when the damn thing managed to stop at all, never mind if the driver don't want it to," said Roy.

"Ah, a slight misunderstanding there. The regular convoys are run by Mancelle engines similar to those that Miss Budreau is no doubt familiar with. The Camel has been loaned to this operation by Major Sumner himself. Quite an irregular expense, which gives us an idea of what may be riding on our success. The fact that I've been removed from my position with the Old Five and Three Pennies to come meet you is another anomaly that I can't fathom."

"How long 'til we reach the Junction?" asked Roy.

"We should reach there day after tomorrow if we keep a fair pace."

"Looks like we've got at least that long to figure it out, then," said Alan.

9

ROY STOOD AT the circular rail which extended from the Camel's roof to form a steel crow's nest, braced against the wind that tugged his hair and clothes. The midday sun made flares on his the lenses of his goggles. They were a necessity if he didn't want to be blinded by speeding sand. The terrain whipped by on either side; dry, clumped with grasses and straggly trees. The few homesteads on the edge of Bombay had gradually petered out to an odd hut or two by the roadside. Occasionally, a shepherd would look up from his startled flock of goats to see the great machine thunder by. But the road itself was still busy. Traffic to and from Bombay was a constant stream of horse-drawn wagons and rusted, pock-marked trucks that made sensible little detours into the road's dirt shoulder to let the Camel hammer by.

The Camel's top hatch creaked open and Alan climbed the last few rungs to join Roy on the roof. Roy steadied Alan against the wind as the younger man swung the hatch closed. Alan covered his face with his sleeve as soon as possible, spitting out yet another mouthful of sand.

"Here," said Roy, raising his voice above the wind.

Reaching down into the neckline of his waistcoat, he handed Alan a pair of goggles. "I figured you'd need these. And don't open your mouth unless your back's turned. I ate a week's ration of bugs before I figured that out."

Alan slid the goggles over his head, adjusted the straps for comfort, and blinked a few times as his eyes adjusted to the tinted lenses.

"Seen anything?" yelled Alan over the roar of wind.

"Not yet. Just couldn't stand romping around that cabin any more. What's Estelle up to?"

"In the engine room, I think, telling the driver how to work his own machine."

Roy nodded. "She'll be right too, you mark my words."

They fell silent for a moment and watched what could be seen of the Indian countryside flash by. Up ahead, hills rose like fresh bread in a tin, the first lush greenery that Alan had seen here clustered around their feet.

"So what do you think of this whole thing?" asked Roy.

"Fishy."

"Good. That's what I figured, too. A whole lot of effort is going into finding out who these bandits are, and not much information coming our way."

"You think Dawson is hiding something?" asked Alan.

"Naw, he's too green. I reckon he's as suckered in as we are."

"But we're still here."

"Job's a job, Alan. In these strange and dangerous times, with Empires rising up everywhere you look, you take what you can get when you can get it. Everyone has their machines and they're just itching to throw them against each other. The Russians pushed in Crimea, the Brits pushed back. Next it'll be the East Asian Union pushing at India. You ever been to Japan, Alan? That's where the EAU are building their machines. I've been there. Automatons bigger'n houses that people drive from inside. Don't look at me like that, I ain't been drinking."

Alan forced his slackened jaw to close.

"Why would they want something like that?"

"Defence, they say. Mind you, with the funny chemicals they pump into the sea out there, you'd be amazed at what crawls back out. But you can be sure that ain't all they're for. They got submersibles like nothing you've ever seen. Imagine that behind the Chinese army. That's what this is about. And that's why the Brits are throwing everything at this revolution. It's a show. They're drawing a line across Asia with India as a buffer between them and the Chinese."

"Are you saying that the Brits are wrong for colonising India?"

"Ain't my place to say such a thing. But the Indians ain't necessarily wrong for wanting it back, neither."

THE CAMEL MADE its way into the Satpura hills, its engine labouring on the upward slopes, then racing down the other side. Estelle spent most of her time in the engine room, adjusting valves and checking gauges to make sure the behemoth ran as smoothly as possible. And when the water tanks dipped into the red, the Camel made its first stop.

Between the hilly ranges of Satpura and Vindhya, the Nerbudda river had carved a valley for itself and filled it with lush vegetation. The Camel stood idle by the road as the

British soldiers stripped to their shirts and began a bucket chain to refill the tanks from the river's flow. Alan rolled his sleeves and dug in with the rest, if only to highlight that Dawson hadn't, passing water back and forth in the baking sun, occasionally stopping to ladle some into his mouth. Sweat made half-moons under his arms and around his collar, his face slick with brine. Roy laid on the river bank with his hands behind his head and Estelle watched the young men work, smoking a thin cigarette.

Hearing the crunch of gravel, every head turned toward the Camel where a horse and rider rounded the great machine. The rider at the fore began steering her steed down the bank toward them. Her head and shoulders were draped in an orange wrap to form a loose-fitting hood with a coil of ebony hair tumbling out. A double breasted, military-style tunic in blue and gold and high-waisted harem trousers over Aladdin-toed boots made her seem both official and comfortable. In the sash around her waist, a long, cruelly curved sword seemed to growl.

Alan squinted against the sun. Yes, the woman was Indian. He could now make out the soft mocha of her skin and eyes like dark almonds; a small ring of gold in her delicate nose. She was pretty, although sternly so.

The British soldiers began to scurry past Alan, heading for the weapons they'd propped against nearby trees.

"Don't," the woman commanded in a clean voice.

The soldiers froze.

As if materialising out of the air, there were suddenly more riders, hemming the Camel and its crew within a circle of loaded rifles. The weapons looked old, but more well-used than ineffective. Out of the corner of his eye, Alan could see Roy moving almost imperceptibly. Estelle stood slightly in front of him, relaxed, as Roy's hand crept toward the revolver stowed at the small of her back.

The bandit woman took her eyes away for a second as she reached inside her wrap.

Faster than Alan had ever seen a man's hand move, Roy drew Estelle's pistol against the Indian woman and thumbed the hammer.

"I wouldn't do that, Darlin'."

A neighbouring click came from Dawson's own sidearm. Alan couldn't fathom how he'd managed to get to it. The Lieutenant shifted the sight between the other riders, attempting to cover them all single-handedly.

The bandit woman held up one open hand and drew the other slowly from her wrap. Between her tapered fingers was a folded letter with a familiar stamp. A Letter of Marque.

10

THE INDIAN RIDERS had led their beasts into the Camel's rear carriage. Tethered to overhead rings, the horses swayed against each other, their faces buried in nosebags full of grain. Alan made his way through the jostling animals, patting one that nickered as he passed. Eventually he found the bandit woman, tending to her mount. He leant against an upright post to admire her while she didn't know he was there. Which was a matter of seconds.

The woman spun around, catching Alan off guard.

Her sword appeared in her hand, the keen tip against Alan's throat. He pressed his back to the post, and tried not to swallow in case the movement of his Adam's apple made her kill him.

He was starting to wonder whether the beautiful bandit was worth the hassle he had previously been willing to expend. After failing to woo Estelle, or even get her to talk to him without spitting, Alan had found himself pining for English women with their fluttering eyelashes and tendency to swoon. But staring down a length of deadly steel into the bandit woman's eyes, Alan felt something else entirely. He could make out an early wrinkle beside her eye and mouth, but they were more like an artist's delicate brushstrokes than signs of advancing age. The Indian woman's eyes held a look of resignation tinged with resolve. She saw the world as it was. Dirty and cruel and hungry. The kind of look Alan had seen frequently beaten into young boys and girls on the streets of London. The kind of look he caught in the mirror.

"Why are you staring at me like that?" the woman demanded in perfect English with an intriguing hint of accent.

"Like what?"

"Like I should be in a cage."

Alan touched the tip of the sword, meaning to move it aside, but the blade might as well have extended all the way to the woman's shoulder for all it moved. He thought it better not to answer.

"You have a letter of Marque?" she snapped. Alan slid the paper from his trouser pocket. With a sigh, the woman removed her sword. "Then I suppose we will be working together. Better to not slit your throat. Just yet."

"I wasn't planning on it," said Alan, absent-mindedly touching his neck.

"Only Fate plans what happens to us, and she is cruel. Why are you here, boy?"

"Alan. My name's Alan."

"Rani Lakshmibai. If this conversation goes well, you can call me Rani. Now answer the question." She sheathed her sword in such a way that Alan knew it could easily be released again.

"Curiosity, I suppose," said Alan.

"I'm a novelty? Not a good start."

Alan crossed his arms; half in frustration, half in defence.

"I already feel as if there's going to be no winning with you," he said.

"Typical English boy, that you should see this as a competition." Rani shook her head. There was a jangle of earrings from inside her hood. A sliver of hair fell over her brow. With any other beautiful woman, Alan would have reached out to brush it back. But in this case there seemed a high chance of losing a finger in the process.

"I'm curious as to why you're working for the British Empire when there's a revolution going on."

"We have a common interest in this matter." Rani went back to brushing down her horse which gave her a gentle neigh of gratitude.

"The Empire is the lesser of two evils, then?" Alan moved around to stroke the horse's nose.

Rani let him.

"No. They are equal. But it is better to side with the devil you know. I want India returned to its people. But now is not the time. You British are too strong. Better to wait for you to get bored of your Indian toys and move on to something else."

"You know a lot about war for a—"

Her hand was on her sword again.

"I dare you to finish that sentence."

"—for someone so young," said Alan, implying with open hands that that was his intention all along.

Rani smiled, and shook her head, but the pretty expression was filled with derision.

"Flattery. Oh, English boy, you're so typical of your people. Even your compliments manage to patronise. I am much older on the inside. I worked in the Raja's palace from the age of four. I have been married, widowed, I have lost a son. I have lost my home. And it all comes from the Empire one way or another."

"I'm sorry," said Alan with enough solemnity that Rani traded it for a weak smile. He felt heavy, between his heart and his stomach, as if he had swallowed a lead weight.

"Thank you. But it's no matter now, and it's not for you to apologise for. There is no going back, only forward. Just because India has forsaken me, doesn't mean I will do the same to her. But what of you, Alan? With your good clothes, your light hair parted so carefully. Tell me something of this glorious England I hear so much about. The glorious England that is so small but can rule all of India."

Rani was smiling now, although thinly, like someone giving a cordial greeting at a funeral. Something had passed between them that Alan couldn't name, but he still felt the effect. Something inside him, something that had been firmly shut, creaked open; darkness spilled out of that crack and into the light.

"I'll tell you what England is really like," he said. He moved around the horse, stroking its flank so that she wouldn't see his face, but she followed him until they stared at each other over the beast's back. "The other side of the uniforms, the shiny boots, the gold thread and the tea parties, there's the real England."

Rani stopped her brushing. Her eyes fixed on Alan's. Her head tilted to one side as if she were inspecting something rare and mysterious. She listened to every strained word that Alan squeezed past his tightening throat.

"The real England," he continued, "where mother's milk isn't given on silver spoons and father's rank won't get you everywhere. *I* grew up in a London where orphans were mangled by the looms they slaved under and no one would stop the machines so they could be helped. Where I was beaten daily by a Spanish barman for scraps and straw to sleep on. Where the air tastes like soot and the river reeks like hot death. That's the England, the London, that I come from."

Rani had moved around to his side, her hand trailing on the horse's muscular form, and stepped closer to him now. Her well-worn hand rested companionably on his shoulder. She was nodding.

"It seems we have both been fuel for our country's machine."

Alan removed her hand.

"I'm sorry," he said. "Excuse me."

Rani watched as he disappeared into the carriage's gloom, and heard the door creak shut.

11

WHERE THE HILLS dipped to the lowlands, the Camel crested the peaks like a steel whale and dove down into the lush vegetation of the Indian jungle, spouting steam. Branches scratched at the Camel's sides, and grasses tugged at its wheels, but the Empire's juggernaut tore through. Alan stood on the crow's nest once more, watching sunlight flash between the tangled canopy above. The occasional grunt of some beast rose up to him, or the sound of thrashing water that he couldn't see. But the calls of the birds were what fascinated him. So many voices in chorus, just beyond his line of sight, twittering and cawing into a cacophony. He could see why the bandits would wait for the jungle before attacking. The foliage was so dense that anything larger than a horse would have real trouble navigating anywhere other than the road. The sounds of the bandit's approach would be dulled by such heavy cover. They could take their time, plan their attack, be everywhere.

It was only a matter of time before they reached the junction and the real action would begin. That was good. He could bury himself in that. Because since he'd spoken to the bandit woman, Rani, Alan felt just a little too exposed, like being caught in the all-together by a lover's husband.

The hatch creaked and slammed behind him. Expecting Roy, or even bloody Dawson, he didn't turn. But it was Rani who came to his side.

At the great machine's passage, a flock of bright birds burst across the jungle in a shower of colours. There were so many that Alan couldn't tell where one began and another ended.

"They certainly put pigeons to shame," he said. He daren't say anything else. Not this time. Lord knew what he'd give away if she gave him half the chance.

"So your defences are back up, now?" she asked.

What was it with this woman? Was she some kind of psychic?

"I'm sorry," he said, and found himself being honest again. "I don't know what happened."

"I think I do. It's terrible that you have seen those things. I am sorry for calling you a boy. I have my defences also." Alan looked down to where he held the rail, and Rani's perfectly formed hand had laid across his own. He could feel its warmth, as if her skin was made of fired clay. Drawn to look into her eyes, he regretted it. She was smiling. His mouth ran dry.

"Only a man of a certain maturity could express himself to a woman like that," she said. She looked away, back to the jungle. Alan caught himself longing for her hand to return when she removed it. "But if you tell anyone I said so, I'll have to kill you."

He coughed, licked his lips, and looked out at the tunnel of trees that hurtled by.

"Likewise," he said.

"I think we have a pact, then. Let no one else see the weakness that passed between us."

Rani made to leave as suddenly as she'd come, swinging open the hatch and climbing down. Before her head disappeared, Alan turned to her.

"If you ever need to be weak again—"

That smile of hers. His chest exploded.

Rani closed the hatch behind her.

OTHER THAN THE rumble of the engine below, and the distant sound of trees against the Camel's armoured sides, the gallery was silent. Roy and Estelle played cards at a small table. Alan sat alone, staring at the contents of his brandy glass until the refracted amber light burnt into his skull. There had been no sleep for him last night. He laid staring at the ceiling in his bunk; something resembling a train's stall with a bed crammed into the tiny space, listening to the guards pass every hour and trying to define whether they were British or Indian by the sound of their boots. Anything to distract him.

"What's eating you, son?" asked Roy.

"I have no idea," said Alan.

"Nerves is it?"

"Nerveux qu'il risqué de manquer d'eau de vie," said Estelle.

Sat reading a book in another part of the gallery, Dawson chuckled. Alan didn't rise to whatever jibe was delivered.

"No. Just—"

Alan slapped his jaw shut as Rani slid back the gallery's

door. He quickly set his glass aside and sat up from his slouch, but kept staring out of the window.

"There's something funny going on around here," Roy whispered to Estelle.

The engineer looked up from her cards, plucking a cigarette from her lips and blew smoke in a controlled slither. She looked around the room for the first time in hours, took in the other inhabitants. With a small grunt, she nodded in agreement, and turned back to her game. Dropping her concealed hand with a *fwip* of the cards, she sat back, and grinned. Roy leant over, looked at his own cards, then Estelle's, and threw his down.

"Damn it. I don't know how you do it, but I'm glad we ain't playing for money."

"Don't worry, Ferris, I wouldn't take your shirt. No one in this room needs to see such horror," said Estelle. Her laugh was cut short by a bellow from above. One of the soldiers on guard.

"They're here!" shouted Dawson, and dove up from his chair.

"It's about time," grunted Alan, tossing back his drink.

Dawson ran out of the room, pausing only to grab his helmet, closely followed by Rani. Men ran past the door on their way to whatever battle stations they were assigned. Half way out of the door, Alan was grabbed by Roy.

"Hold on, son. We don't all need to be in the same place. Let's think this one out."

Estelle checked the windows. "I don't see anything."

"The jungle's too thick," said Alan. "They could be anywhere."

"No. There's nothing to see," she replied.

Alan took a look for himself, but Estelle was right. There were no horses, no men, certainly no trucks.

"We're still rolling," said Alan. "There's no way that bandits are climbing aboard this hulk at such a speed."

"Listen," said Roy. Everyone's eyes were drawn upward. Aside from the startled yells of the soldiers, and distant crack of gunfire beyond the Camel's thick walls, there was another sound, one Alan couldn't place.

There it was again.

The *skrit skrit skrit* of metal scrabbling on metal.

A peal of gunfire. Someone yelled a curse. Dawson's voice rose above the others but they couldn't make out the words.

Skrit skrit skrit skrit skrit skrit

That sound was everywhere.

"What the hell is going on here?" muttered Roy. And his answer came swiftly after.

Estelle gasped, raised her revolver and fired off a round that ricocheted from the door's metal jamb as four small creatures swung or scrambled into the room. Before the Privateers could draw breath, little brass monkeys were everywhere; small, gold-coloured beasts running or swinging past the gallery's door, their metal feet going *Skrit skrit skrit* on the stairs as they headed downward. Others poured into the room, moving too fast for Alan to get any decent aim with his revolver. Estelle's bullets peppered the floor but they were a blur; dodging, leaping and running from walls to ceiling to floor as fast as Alan's heart could hammer.

"Christ alive, what was in that brandy?"

One of the little creatures landed on the table beside him. Rising up on its hind legs, it *screak*ed at him through metal jaws, grabbed a carafe from the table and bolted back toward the door.

"This is insane!"

Estelle pirouetted, a pistol in either hand, confident and swift in her aim. But every bullet slammed into the gallery's woodwork or made a dull *shpang* as they bounced off a monkey's brass hide. Alan was having no more luck. Snapping his revolver open, he tipped spent shells onto the carpet and hastily reloaded. His weapon cracked again, but it was a miss. He roared in frustration.

"We might as well be shooting fog!"

Roy reeled as a monkey landed on his back and fixed itself to his shirt, just out of reach of his massive hands. "Stay still you little—" They span together in the middle of the gallery, careening into a table, spraying playing cards into the air. A rush of wind whistled by his ear and the monkey careened across the room.

"Stop shooting at me!" Roy bellowed at Estelle's smoking barrel.

Estelle holstered her weapons and picked up a small table. She swung it at a monkey embracing an armful of bulbs it had unscrewed from one of the light fittings, but the tiny automaton hopped over her attack and out the door. The table shattered on the ground.

"*Ferme la port*! Close the door!"

Alan dove forward, slamming the door and pressing his back to it, gun outstretched in a double-handed grip. Most of the creatures had escaped already, but there was still one in the room. He could hear it scuttling under the chairs.

"Where are you, you little rat?" Roy lumbered forward, tossing furniture aside, but the monkey wasn't there. "Blast it!"

"Here!"

The monkey swung down onto Alan's head, ran across his shoulders and down his back. Finding no way out, the automaton seemed to freeze as if confused, just long enough for Alan to slam a well-placed boot down on it.

"Don't damage it!" yelled Estelle.

"Why the hell not?" asked Alan, but holstered his weapon. As his luck was going, he'd probably shoot himself in the foot, anyway. Reaching down, he took a firm hold of the miniature Automaton that tried to squirm out of his grasp.

"Hold it still." Estelle whipped a screwdriver from her belt and advanced toward Alan in a way that made him uncomfortable.

"I'm trying!"

Grabbing the monkey's chin, Estelle peered underneath, found what she was looking for, and inserted the screwdriver. The monkey went limp in Alan's hand.

"Bugger me," he said. "That sorted it."

The door burst open behind him, knocking him almost to the ground. He rolled, anticipating another attack, and trained his revolver on Rani, who stood panting in the doorway.

"Monkeys!" she said. "Little metal monkeys!"

Roy helped Alan to his feet.

"At least *everyone* was seeing them," he said.

12

THE PRIVATEERS AND Dawson sat around the gallery, some with head in hands, others staring at the ceiling.

"I'd offer everyone a drink, but it seems it's all been stolen," said Dawson "They took everything."

"Anything not nailed down," said Roy.

Dawson couldn't stop shaking his head.

"I never believed it. Who would? One of my men had his helmet snatched right from his head. The other went to reload his rifle only to find one of them had swiped his ammunition pouch. They were everywhere! But at least nothing important was lost."

"I guess with no real cargo, they just took anything they could get their grubby paws on. Not too smart are they?" said Alan.

Estelle had the captured machine on the table in front of her. She had managed to open a small panel in the monkey's body and was tinkering inside.

"They're just a logic engine on legs," she said. "The movement of the monkey primes the clockwork and the clockwork runs the monkey."

"So they could run forever?" said Roy.

"*Exactement*. And no need for a punch card. They have only one programme. Run, steal, return. An incredible design." Estelle was almost giggling with excitement.

"You could look like you were having a little less fun," Alan *tut*ted.

"This is what I feared," said Rani, who hadn't spoken for over an hour.

"You know who they belong to?" asked Dawson.

Rani nodded.

"His palace is in the hills somewhere east of Delhi, at the foot of the mountains. He has no people, but calls himself a Raja, ruling over the machines he makes. Fanciful things made of gears and metal. These are his devices, for certain."

Roy leant forward.

"Alright, I'll buy what you're sellin'. But what's the big picture? Someone like you're describin' always has somethin' else going on."

"Who knows? This could be for mischief alone," she answered.

"Or part of the revolution," offered Dawson.

"He's seeing how effective they are before he uses them on the army at Delhi," said Alan. "Sounds like a scientist's way of thinking to me. Testing, testing, then BOOM."

"What worries me is what other contraptions he's hidin'. If these monkeys're anything to go by, Dawson, you Brits should be pretty worried."

"So we go get this Raja, right?" said Alan.

The Lieutenant was pacing, hands clasped behind his back.

"No. We report to Major Sumner. We confirm the reports he already has, and we get further orders."

"Why? We should go find him ourselves, slap this Raja on the wrist and break his toys," said Alan. "Roy, come on. We were given a job to do, so let's go do it."

"Sorry, son. But Dawson's right. If we want payin', we do this Sumner's way. Whatever way that might be."

Alan scoffed, and turned his attention to Rani.

"Don't you want to see this thing through? If he's supporting the revolution, you can be sure he'll be planning on taking over when it's all done. Do you want a mad mechanic in charge of your country?"

"I'm sorry, Alan, but I also agree with Lieutenant Dawson," she said. "We don't know what we're getting into. This time, and only this time, maybe having the Empire behind us would be a good idea."

Alan threw his arms up. "Fine."

"I think you're outvoted by your friends, Mister Shaw," said Lieutenant Dawson. "You're free to leave, of course. But it's along a walk back to Bombay."

Alan gave Dawson a sarcastic smirk but otherwise remained beaten.

"Right, then, Dawson. Let's get this truck to Delhi," said Roy. "We'll see what Sumner has to say and then we'll see about sorting this Raja out proper."

THE CAMEL'S COURSE came to meet the Grand Trunk Road at a T-junction where everyone seemed to turn right, toward the east. Every cart and truck, even the people on foot, went east, and not one of them looked the other way.

Alan watched them disappear in the Camel's wake as the Privateers turned west toward Delhi, leaving the rest of the traffic as a dusty dream. And then there was only the jungle before them, the dust behind, and the creeping dread which Alan couldn't seem to shake.

Red sunset turned the river Jumna a vibrant orange. What had once been the city of Delhi, famed for its observatories and minarets, older than England's earliest memory, was a shambolic ruin. A cacophony of canon fire, followed by the whistle and slam of ballistic shells, demolished India's ancient capital. The few remaining buildings smattered the landscape like driftwood after a storm. Rising clouds of dust obscured whole districts. From the Camel's vantage point as it circumvented the city along a northern ridge, Alan could make out no signs of life at all. Delhi was target practice to the Empire's army.

Beside Alan, Rani muttered a prayer in her native language.

"I had no idea it had gone so far. I remember visiting Delhi when I was a girl. Such staggering heights and colours. People and smells. Do you think there are many people left?"

"If they were smart, most people would have left before the shelling started."

"Do you think so?"

Alan swallowed hard. If this had been his city, even the London he often despised with all the acrid memories stored there, he would still be devastated.

That empathy made him blurt out his thoughts:

"Probably not, no." Before he even finished, he regretted

letting the words escape.

"You should have lied," said Rani.

Instead, he slipped an arm around her shoulder, folding her into his chest, and let her weakness leak out onto his shirt.

From between the sobs, and muffled by his shirt, the bandit woman muttered something.

Alan pulled up her chin with his forefinger, wiping the tears from Rani's eyes with his thumb.

"What was that?" he said.

Rani's eyes were still flowing, but they had set hard, like bed-stones in a cold stream.

"I said that when this is over, I'll make sure the British pay for this."

13

FAR ENOUGH FROM the canon-mounts and their constant cracks of gunfire, the Camel had drawn up in the Imperial Army camp. Estelle and Dawson had gone on ahead with the rest of the British soldiers to find a tent they could commandeer in the army's canvas city. Rani had opened the Camel's rear doors and she and her men tended to their horses. Alan watched as Rani adjusted her horse's livery for the beast's comfort and stood for a while rubbing its neck as it grazed. She'd removed her boots and her toes curled in the cool grass. Her eyes were closed and face tilted up to the sun in what seemed to be complete bliss; that was, if Alan ignored the twitch of her shoulders every time a distant barrage went off. Her lips moved slightly as if she were talking to herself. Praying, perhaps. Alan wondered if she had any spare prayers for him.

Someone nearby was cooking the kind of thing that smelled like home, wherever people were from. Tearing his eyes away from Rani, Alan was amazed at how many women and children were in the camp. Families that followed their warrior husbands and fathers, even to the front line, in an effort to maintain some kind of normal life. If the Raja's machines struck here, it would be a massacre, and not just of men sworn to fight for their country, but their families, too.

Three rows of adapted Mk I Automatons marched past where Alan sat on the Camel's doorstep. The heavy *shank shank shank* of their footsteps came to an end on the bellowed word of a human sergeant and they turned about, shouldering their weapons like real soldiers would. Their breast plates were thicker than Alan was used to, riveted, and could probably take a grenade without much bother. The pill-shaped heads, once friendly-looking to Alan, were held in steel cages with reinforced glass to protect the delicate logic engines inside. One arm was now a short-barrelled shotgun loaded with devastating ordnance. The idea of those machines going up against humans made Alan shudder. It seemed so long since he'd seen Professor Normen's Mk Is march to Buckingham Palace, and here they were marching again. It felt like watching his oldest friends go to war.

"Company, Prime!" the Sergeant yelled from under his helmet and as one unit the Automatons opened their chests, releasing a chuff of embers and ash. A private wearing a full heatproof mask and thick gloves plucked Jerry Logs from his satchel as he went along the line, tossing one into each Automaton's furnace.

"At ease!"

The Automatons slammed their furnace doors closed. Marching away, the Sergeant left his machine-men stood as relaxed as their workings would allow. Unmoving, they stared out across the plains to the ruined city beyond without a single glimmer of understanding in their optical lenses. If the Raja was going to bring his mechanised animals against the British army, it would be one hell of a fight.

And across the plains Alan could see the source of Delhi's downfall; a line of artillery that dwarfed the men who worked on them. Seventy tons, Dawson had said. Seventy tons of gun-mount for each cannon to slam back into as the shells were propelled to decimate a city. And they never stopped. Like pistons in an engine. The constant crack and whistle of explosive death.

Alan almost jumped out of his skin when Roy spoke.

"Alan, I want you and Rani to stay here."

"Alright."

"Just like that? Everything's dandy?"

"You're right, Roy. I'm not thinking straight. This isn't what I'm normally like. There's something eating at me, as you put it. And seeing Delhi pulverised has just finished me off. I don't want anything to do with this army, and that goes for Sumner, too. I'll wait here. When you get back, we'll finish this job and I never want to be near the Empire again."

"I reckon I know what's going on with you, son."

Alan slumped down onto the lip of the Camel's door which brought him eye to eye with his American friend.

"I wish you'd tell me, because I don't have a clue."

"It's fair to say you've seen things that have changed how you think of your home country. I can relate to that. I've seen American men fight with themselves over some idiotic things in my time."

"I thought America was the land of hope."

"And my father would agree with you, but I don't. A country that treats other men like dogs just because they got different skin ain't a country I can be proud of. And you're seeing the same thing right here. It's cutting you up, and I ain't ashamed to say that I'm proud of you, son."

Alan looked up from his clasped hands.

Roy nodded. "That's right, you heard me. There's more to life than damned patriotism and blind faith."

"I don't think I could look at Sumner and not smack him square in the face," said Alan.

"And that's why you won't have to. We'll be back soon."

And Roy was gone.

Alan sat for a moment longer, wondering how a big brute of a man like Roy could see right through him, even to places that Alan couldn't see himself. He forced a smile, but it didn't feel right on his lips. With a sigh that shook his core, Alan climbed back into the Camel.

THE SUN PASSED through the heavy white material of the command tent, creating a uniform glow inside. Somehow, and for some reason, a whole oak desk had been brought into the field to hold Major Sumner's stationary and, at that very moment, his rather fine china tea set. An Indian servant, tall and lithe with a deep red turban which made him seem even taller, poured a brew from an exquisite teapot.

"I imagine you're all quite parched," Sumner said through a great white moustache, but he made no gesture toward his servant to pour more tea.

"We'd rather get on with business and be out of your hair, if it's all the same to you, Major," Roy replied. The

Custance Privateers, and Dawson, sat across the tent from Sumner like two armies eyeing each other over a battlefield. Roy had the sinking feeling that Alan had been right. They should have left Sumner out of it and gone straight for the Raja themselves.

The Major eyed him as he tried to decide if the American was forthright or rude. Deciding it was the former, he nodded and beckoned to his servant who brought over a large tin bowl of hot water. As Sumner continued to talk, the servant draped a white towel around the Major's neck, lathered a badger hair brush with shaving foam and began to coat Sumner's face with it.

"Quite so. Dawson, your report."

Dawson stepped forward, his helmet tucked neatly under his arm. He was sweating more than usual, and kept tugging at the collar of his uniform.

"It seems that my predecessor's reports were more accurate than we anticipated, Major Sumner, sir. We, that is myself and the Privateers led by Mister Ferris, were set upon by a horde of mechanised beasts, sir. Monkeys to be exact. Very fast, very cunning, and almost impossible to destroy or capture."

"Almost, you say." It seemed that Sumner was never a man to end a sentence with a question. He also wasn't the kind of man to let a meeting get in the way of his toilet regime. His servant had sharpened a razor and was slowly scraping it up the Major's throat.

Roy was suddenly very grateful that neither Alan or Rani were there. He wouldn't have been able to hold *both* of them back.

"Yes, sir. Miss Budreau, if you wouldn't mind?"

Estelle gave Dawson a smile that could melt belt buckles, and produced her mechanised simian. She laid it on the table with utmost care and didn't step back, as if ready to snatch it away again.

"Clever contraptions, sir," continued Dawson. "Incredibly clever."

Sumner didn't bother to look. The servant's razor kept on scraping, great blobs of shaving cream plopping into the water bowl.

"You have theories on their origin," he said with an even stiffer upper lip than usual, as the razor navigated around his carefully pruned moustache.

Dawson shot Roy a look. The American nodded.

"We believe there is a man masquerading as a Raja, sir. His headquarters are somewhere in the nearby foothills. We're anticipating that the monkeys may be the first wave of a larger mechanised force. Scouts, perhaps."

"Hmmmm. Quite likely."

The Indian assistant wiped the remaining cream from the Major's face and, turning to a lit brazier, opened the lid and produce a hot towel with a pair of silver tongs. The towel was unfolded and placed on the Major's face to steam as he sat with hands interlocked on his stomach.

The Privateers waited.

Even now, the Indian assistant didn't make eye contact with them, but stared at a point somewhere above Roy's head. Roy looked left and right to make sure that time hadn't just stopped flowing. Dawson was hastily wafting his collar, and Estelle's face was decorated in a disbelieving sneer directed at the Major.

Without any signal, the Indian assistant peeled the hot towel from the Major's face, dabbed it dry, and began to pack everything away. Sumner took a few deep breaths of fortifying air before hoisting his eyebrows at Dawson.

The Lieutenant took a gamble and continued:

"If I could utilise a small group of men, sir, I think it would be good sense to go against this Raja in a small, controlled confrontation where we could keep him from using his machines—"

"Out of the question, Dawson," said Sumner. "This is the very reason we invited Mister Ferris and his companions in the first place. What do you say, Ferris? Can you and your men see an end comes to this Raja and his machines? Quietly."

"We've had worse odds, I'll wager. A few things from yourselves will be all we need."

"See that they get them, Dawson. And stay behind a moment, will you?"

And that seemed to be the end of it. As the Privateers left the tent, leaving Dawson behind, Roy couldn't help shaking his head.

Estelle had scooped up the clockwork simian and was cradling it in her arms.

"The Major seems to understand our story a little more than we ourselves, *non*?"

"Damned right, Estelle. Let's get this thing over with and get out. I think we've got another Cape Town on our hands."

"Merde."

"You said it, girl. Well we haven't been caught out this time. At least we know why Sumner hired us rather than sorting this thing internally. Even he has superiors, and this monkey thing has made him look damn foolish. If he uses the army to end this, there will be reports, witnesses. But not with us. Let's get Alan, fix this thing, and get out of here."

They walked back toward the Camel using the sight of it poking above the tents' roofs as a guide. Roy was sucking at his teeth as if he had a piece of meat stuck in them. Estelle stared at him until he looked back. He smiled.

"Ok, fine," he said as if bending under pressure. "You know what I still don't get?"

"Why the Major involved the Bandit woman?"

"You noticed too, huh?"

"I notice everything," said Estelle with a shrug. "I am a woman. And we see what you men never can."

"Like what?"

"How she looks at him and him at her. How they avoid each other when we are all together, barely speaking, but they spend time alone. What do you always say about mixing business and pleasure?"

"I say you should never hump what you work with. My Daddy used to tell me that. Then again, he was a lumberjack working with woodchippers, so you can see his point." He nudged Estelle half off her feet and gave her a wink. "That's why me and you never get frisky, Sparky. We're all about the business."

Estelle slipped her free hand, the one not carrying her monkey machine, through Roy's arm and rested her head on his shoulder.

"Oh, *mon chere*, there are so many more reasons than that."

They both laughed, causing every other face in the camp to look up. It seemed laughter was an alien sound here. The Privateers sobered up pretty quick, their slight moment of levity killed by the camp's atmosphere.

"Let us just hope that whatever reason Sumner has for inviting the bandit woman does not upset Alan when he finds out," Estelle said.

"I never had you down as owning a caring streak. Especially not for the boy."

"I don't," she said adroitly. "Unless the man making googly eyes is supposed to be watching my back."

ROY'S FIST BANGED on Alan's cabin door, shaking the wall around it. Set out like the stalls of a train carriage, this meant that all the other doors along the corridor were banged on as well. Numerous heads poked out, some Indian bandits, some the Camel's crew.

"We're moving out. Grab what you need, folks. We're going light and fast."

Alan emerged from the door, stripped to the waist with a straight razor in his hand and shaving foam on one half his face. A towel dangled over his shoulder.

"You sure you're old enough to be using that thing?" asked Roy, gesturing to the razor.

Alan demonstrated by continuing his shave as they spoke, moving back into his cabin to use the wash basin.

"What did Sumner say?"

"Exactly what you wanted him to. Give the Raja a kicking. Or thereabouts."

Alan nodded approval, and quickly finished his shave as Roy leant in the doorway.

"I don't suppose you got chance to talk to Rani while we were away?"

Alan's answer came muffled through the towel.

"Should I have?"

"Thought you might, is all. Soldiers going into battle. Last night on earth. That kind of thing."

"It's not like that," said Alan, slipping on his shirt and duster without buttoning either. His revolver belt and carbine got slung over opposite shoulders. As an afterthought, he checked his duster pocket for the goggles Roy had given him, just in case. "What do you think?"

"I reckon that's all you'll be needing on this trip. Whatever's left you'll either come back for or can stay left. So you were saying about Rani, anyways—"

"No I wasn't. You were."

"Damn it, son, is this always how you play it, cuz I'm amazed you have any luck with women at all."

Alan punched Roy in the shoulder as he passed. Roy barely moved and Alan's knuckles stung. They moved out into the corridor and Alan buttoned his shirt as they walked.

"I get plenty of luck, thankyaverymuch."

"Seems you've had the biggest bit of luck on this trip that a man can have, and you're not doing anything with it. Seems a waste, is all I'm saying."

"I know you're a rambler, Roy, but I never had you as a bush beater as well. What're you getting at?"

With that, they reached the intersection of the corridor where stairs led down to the exit or up to the gallery. From their left came the waft of perfume so natural that Alan thought someone was delivering lilies. Both men followed the scent as it filled their lungs toward the approaching Rani. She wore the same outfit as when they'd first met; high-waisted harem trousers and double breasted tunic. But instead of her usual head wrap, she had woven a bandana of Estelle's into a small, feminine turban with her ebony plait still tumbling from behind it. A gold ring, almost too thin to see, decorated one nostril; probably the last item remaining of her old life. She managed to look incredibly dangerous and catch Alan's breath at the same time. Rani gave the men a nod as she made for the stairs, her eyes lingering on Alan for just a moment longer. As she descended, she began adjusting the lay of her rifle across her back and fiddling with a series of knives in her belt.

"You tell me you didn't see that, and I'll slap you square in the face," said Roy.

Alan thought it better not to say anything. But he was smiling.

"Yup. That's what I thought."

In Rani's wake came Estelle, who paused at the top of the stairs. Under the crook of her arm hung the mechanical monkey. Somewhere she'd found some black paint and painted certain panels on the body and highlights on the face, especially adding pupils to the little gold eyes. Estelle looked at Roy and the love-struck Alan for a moment before muttering: "Mon Dieu."

And she descended as well, fiddling with the inert monkey.

Outside, Rani had her bandits in two short but deadly-looking rows. The Camel's crew were nowhere to be seen.

Dawson stood close by, helmet under his arm as always.

"We ready to go, folks? Not much light left and there's all kinds of nasties in the jungle at night no matter what continent you're on."

"I'm afraid I have bad news," said Dawson. "I won't be coming along. Major Sumner gave strict instructions that the Imperial forces must all remain here to prepare the final assault on Delhi tomorrow morning."

"No problem, Dawson. Me and Estelle figured as much. Us and the bandit boys – sorry, Ma'am, no disrespect meant – will be fine."

"Be a shame to get those shiny buttons dirty anyway," said Alan, and snorted something about chicken excrement under his breath. To his surprise, Dawson didn't even make eye contact with him, never mind deliver a retort.

"We've provided the horses, packed with the gear you requested. I wish you the best of luck." And at that, Dawson went down the whole line, shaking the Privateers' hands with a grip both firm and earnest. He even waited patiently while Alan deliberated whether to shake or not, before finally giving up. "I am truly sorry," Dawson said.

And then he was gone.

"Estelle, your little friend ready?" asked Roy.

Estelle finished fixing a short cord to the monkey, attached at the other end to her belt.

"I have moved his programme along to a point where the creature would want to return home. All we must do is follow him."

"You got yourself a little pet there, Sparky?"

"With the proper programming, he could be quite useful."

"And he's a bit cute, too, right? That's why the new paint job?"

"Shut up, Ferris." Jamming a thin screwdriver into the monkey's side, she twisted and the little simian came to life as if touched by the hand of God. It leapt out of her arms, and made to escape across the grass, but yanked to a stop when the cord around its hindquarters pulled tight. Estelle reeled the thing in until it sat in her arms again.

"Learns fast, doesn't it?" said Roy.

"And now we know which way to go."

"Ok, Sparky, stop smirking."

Alan had watched all this, only getting the point right at the end.

"Hold on a minute," he said. "Did Dawson say *horses*?"

"Can't sneak up on someone in this heap." Roy banged his fist on the Camel's side. "We're going incommunicado."

"Incognito, *idiote*." Estelle made a sound not unhorse-like herself. Roy noticed that she was absent-mindedly stroking the jittering brass money in her arms. He suppressed a smile as he made toward his steed.

"I don't bloody think so," said Alan.

But Roy was already swinging a leg over his saddle, the beast straining a little under his weight.

"You never ridden a horse, son?"

"I spent the first eleven years of my life either under a machine or on a rooftop. The next few stuck in some god forsaken school or on a ship. Not much call for horses, Roy."

"It's easy! Just remember, the faster you go, the easier it is to stay on."

14

ALAN CURSED ROY in the foulest ways he knew. He gripped the reins as if they were lashing his soul to his body, his head down by the horse's neck, body folded over the saddle, and willed himself to be more adhesive. He could feel the horse's racing pulse next to his cheek, feel every snort and bunching of muscle. His thighs ached from gripping the horse's flanks as the beast bucked under him. Every gallop felt like riding thunder. If he were to vomit, it would have to be strained through his gritted teeth. He was managing not to scream and rant, but only because he didn't want to spook the horse into running even faster. With his eyes screwed shut, Alan missed the troupe's approach to the Raja's palace.

Roy, Estelle and Rani rode in line with Alan, exchanging practical advice on riding technique, feeble assurances, and gut-wrenching laughter between them. The bandits rode in single file behind. Only occasionally would Estelle draw to a stop, let the monkey run out its lead, and they would change direction based on this unusual compass.

In this way, stopping and starting, they came out of the Imperial camp and followed the road as it began to rise and the jungle enclosed them. They cut a line through the foothills which would save the horses until the ground turned from grass to thin shale as the mountains rose up from beneath the earth to meet them. The trail led gradually up until the treetops fell away to their right, and the mountainside stretched above and below. From here, they could see where other roads across the valley made crosshatch patterns on the opposing slopes, some nothing more than goat paths. When the trail thinned, they rode in single file, skirting the mountain's feet and still climbing. Coming around a tight bend, the jungle opened up beneath them and the Privateers caught their first sight of the Raja's palace as a cluster of rooftops peeking through the canopy.

"Would you look at that?" said Roy, over the sound of hooves on shale. "How does some mad mechanic get himself a place like that?"

The palace was more of a temple, extravagantly carved from the mountain's rock into a series of towers and tiers covered with weather-worn friezes. Crumbling around the edges, it appeared solid enough. As unofficial guide, Rani felt that some explanation was in order: "There are old Hindu temples scattered throughout the mountains all across India. Most of them have been forgotten or abandoned for centuries. Some more recently as the British have converted people to Christianity."

"Anyone can just walk in and make themselves at home?" asked Roy.

"That's right."

"Remind me to come back here when we have some free time, Estelle. I fancy myself one of those."

They carved their way across the mountain until the ridge brought them around to the temple's rear, on a level with the rooftops. The Privateers reined in their mounts, with Alan's stopping more from peer pressure than any control he exerted on it. Sliding from his saddle, Alan lowered himself all the way down to lay sprawled on the comforting stillness of the ground. His muscles felt like vibrating guitar strings beneath his shirt, quivering with spent adrenaline and petrified tension.

"I like levers. I like engines. I like wheels with suspension. But most of all I like things with *off* switches." Alan rattled off his personal mantra as Rani knelt beside him, patting his hand and trying to hide her grin.

"Was it really so bad?"

"I'm walking back if it takes me a week," Alan said.

Estelle reeled out the monkey on its leash. It reached the end of the line and started going crazy, clearly wanting to dive off the track, into the trees and to the temple beyond. She reeled him in one last time and, without ceremony, flicked open a little panel in its side and switched it off. Roy watched her, shaking his head and trying not to smirk as she curled the mechanical beast into a foetal position and stowed it carefully in her satchel.

Once Alan had composed himself, and after taking a long draught from Roy's hip flask, the Privateers belly-crawled to the edge of the road to take a closer look at the Raja's commandeered temple. Roy flicked out a telescope from his belt and took in the view, then handed it around.

"The ridge's brought us nice and close. No windows. No doors. No guards. Guess the Raja figured he wouldn't need 'em. We should be able to get in from one of the towers and make our way down fairly sneaky-like."

"That's a long jump," said Alan, pointing to the narrow chasm between the ridge and the nearest rooftop. Then he remembered himself. "But I bet Estelle's got a solution for that, right?"

The engineer gave a snort and went to draw a bag from her horse. She arrayed a series of parts on the trail and started slotting them together. By the time she was done, what looked like a large crossbow lay on a tripod at the ridge's edge. Taking a small pistol from her belt, she shot bolts through the tripod's feet and into the bedrock. It looked surprisingly sturdy when she was done. Then a coil of rope was fed through the machine and tied off to a thick grapple which slotted into the crossbow's snout.

"That doesn't look standard issue," Alan muttered.

Without waiting, Estelle braced the crossbow's stock with her boot and drew back the arm. She knelt down behind it, adjusting the aim, and let loose. The grapple disappeared with a *shpang,* followed by the soft whipping noise as the rope unfurled across the chasm. The steel hook hit the nearest tower's roof but, instead of hooking on, punched right through. Estelle raised an eyebrow at Roy, but he just shrugged, and started cranking off the slack on the rope. By the time they were done the rope was tight enough that it barely quivered when Roy plucked it. Taking a leather loop from Estelle's backpack, he attached it with a steel carabineer clip to the zip-line, and handed the bag around for everyone to take one.

"Ok, folks, you get the idea. Remember to let go before

you hit the wall, eh?"

Strapping his rifle square across his shoulders, Roy threw himself off the ridge, his body swinging back and forth across the chasm. In a matter of seconds he was across, his boots firm on the tower's parapet, and was waving them across.

Alan looked to Rani as Estelle threw herself after her partner.

"If it can take Roy's weight, I think we'll be ok," he said. He found that he was smiling, the idea of zipping across the chasm making him a little boy again. Rani seemed to take that as a sign. With her hands cupping his cheeks, Rani's lips touched Alan's, sending glorious tendrils of sensation through every inch of his skin as if she were somehow kissing him all over at once. And she was gone, over the ridge's lip, her plait trailing behind her. Alan looked over his shoulder, where the other bandits were eyeing him and murmuring in their native language. Alan gave them a shrug, a smile, and leapt after her.

Alan's boots kicked at thin air as the treetops whistled underneath him. The wind made rushing sounds in his ears, the speed drawing his face into a boyish grin. As the leather strap hummed above, he fought the urge to yell a 'yahoo' as he hurtled with giddy speed toward the temple's tower. As he came close to the parapet he shuffled his hand loose and dropped the few feet to the balcony.

He was still grinning when Roy yanked him aside just in time to avoid a bandit landing on his head.

"Should've mentioned you have to move pretty quick once you're down or you get a helluva headache."

Once everyone was across, they moved inside, leaving the rope where it was. Taking a spiral staircase downward, they found themselves in a store room stacked with crates. As Alan and Rani checked the corridor outside, Roy and Estelle began to dig around, lifting lids and scooping aside the woodchip packing inside.

"I don't like this, Sparky."

"Not all of this could have been stolen by monkeys," agreed Estelle. "Too big."

Roy moved around a stack of crates, checking the boxes for signs of where they might have come from. "I'll be damned. This look familiar to you?"

He pointed out a crate with an inked sign on the side, scraped off by a sharp tool.

"Mon Dieu. Some of these are our crates."

Roy grabbed her shoulder, propelling her away from prying ears.

"Quiet. No one knows that but us, right? God damn." He looked around at the crates, shaking his head.

"I know it is often bad to ask too many questions in our line of work, Ferris. But perhaps *some* would have been good in this case." Estelle looked at her partner and grabbed his hand. "This is very easy to make right, Ferris."

"Right, right," he replied, but Roy's mind was elsewhere.

Estelle carried on: "We came here to destroy this equipment, anyway. So we make sure we do it. Put things right. Then we leave. This is our first delivery, Ferris. Nothing we have brought has been used. These crates are still full."

"No harm done," said Roy, nodding. "Sure. You're right, Sparky. Let's nail this sonovabitch and forget it ever happened."

Roy began to split the group in two. Alan and Rani took half the men, Roy and Estelle took the rest, and they moved out into the corridor.

"You two find the Raj, me and Estelle will make sure his toys don't get too wound up," said Roy. Alan rolled his eyes, but Roy thought himself pretty funny. "Awww, come on, can't we have a sense of humour *and* be in danger at the same time?"

"The problem is, Roy, that we all have a sense of humour. You're just not funny, mate."

"And you're hilarious I suppose?"

"I'm a hoot, I am. Try not to die. You're piloting my ride home." And with a smirk, Alan led his group away.

The corridors were much like the temple's exterior. The floors were smooth, but the walls were a constant flow of carvings and alcoves. Alan and his team searched the upper floor, but found very little except storage rooms piled high with British Army crates.

"Most of these aren't even open," he said.

"Perhaps the Raj isn't stealing the crates for any purpose other than mischief," replied Rani, peering inside a box of metal rods.

"Seems like a waste to me."

"Or that the Raj is simply mischievous rather than malicious."

"You sound like my brother when you use big words."

"I didn't know you had a brother."

Alan smiled.

"Never mentioned him, that's why. Just don't tell him. He's a sensitive lad."

ROY DUCKED BACK into the passageway, his back to the wall.

"Ok, folks, this is the place. Open space, high roof. There's gadgets and gizmos everywhere, like a factory or something. Looks like maybe ten or twelve mechanics at the long tables to your right. Let's get in and sort this as quiet as can be. And make sure they don't turn those elephants on."

"Elephants?" said Estelle in a harsh whisper, but Roy was already gone, skulking across the factory floor with his rifle in hand. "Merde."

And there were elephants. Eight of them stood in what would have once been a place of worship. Lifesize, built from bronze and steel, incredibly detailed in their armour, and probably full of clockwork that would have Estelle salivating for weeks, Roy guessed. He could make out exhausts coiled in the decorative ears. So not just clockwork, then, but engines, too. It would take at least that much to propel the hulks forward.

When the whole group had crept out on the factory floor, Roy raised his rifle to his shoulder, sneaking up on the nearest workman as he tinkered at a long bench, and tapped him on the shoulder. The workman froze, instantly raising his hands, a little too quickly for Roy's liking, as if the man were expecting to be captured.

"Alright, son, put the screwdriver down, and tell your friends—"

But the other mechanics were already shouting. Estelle spotted a man in overalls and a small felt cap duck beneath a bench and come up holding what could only be a weapon of some kind; like a shotgun with three barrels aligned in a triangle. Estelle grabbed Roy's collar and hauled him aside, the mechanic that Roy had been holding dropped to the ground with his head covered as his colleague's weapon roared, the recoil making the muzzle buck upward.

"So much for quiet!" yelled Roy, as he threw a long trestle table over on its side and dived behind. Estelle huddled next to him, flinching as another weapon, a repeater, peppered the bench's oak surface. She muttered something in her native tongue, checked her revolvers were loaded, and stood up. Estelle returned fire, her special brand of heavy ordinance making thunder cracks. There were screams of fear and pain as a couple of mechanics were pinned down.

The bandits followed suit, popping up behind their own table, taking it in turns to fire and reload. The mechanics didn't return fire much. Apparently guns weren't their thing. But Roy soon heard a familiar sound that made his stomach churn; little metal feet scuttling toward them.

15

"**D**O YOU THINK they knew we were coming?" asked Rani.

"No, I'm sure they leave metal alligators lying around the corridors all the time."

A vicious chomp like the snap of a bear trap, and another bandit gave a petrifying scream. Alan threw himself forward, landing atop the metal alligator, almost sliding straight over the steel scales, and threw his arms around its jaws. The bandits were taking a beating. As well as the alligator that twisted and thrashed beneath him, there were golden parrots in the air which dove and rolled, taking chunks out of any exposed flesh with beaks like secateurs. Rani fired her rifle, knocking one of the parrots out of the air. Running over to it, she put a boot on its flapping body and emptied her weapon into its head, which shattered, spraying springs and tiny gears. She heard a warning shout, and span around just in time for the next bird to flash past, only scratching her arm. Making the full spin with her trousers flaring around her feet, she swung the rifle around by its barrel, and sent the parrot careening into a nearby room.

"Alan! We're losing!"

Rani's bandits were thinning out, most lay around grasping at oozing cloth where the parrots had gouged faces and abdomens with expert grace; others who had come foul of the alligator wailed against the loss of a limb. Blood slicked the temple's stone floor.

Alan grunted, feeling that he'd had to hold on to far too many bucking animals today. It just wasn't fair. With one arm still around the alligator's mouth, the hand reaching all the way around and grabbing onto his own shirt as an anchor, he managed to slide the carbine from his shoulder, unclip the leather strap from the barrel and stock, and started binding the alligator's jaws closed. With that done, and the strap tied tight, he threw himself to the side, rolling across the floor to come up against the wall, and drew his revolver. But the alligator wasn't in pursuit. It danced in circles, fighting against the leather strap.

"That worked!" said Rani, helping Alan to his quivering feet.

"Looks like the Raja made his designs a little too close to nature. Simon once told me that crocs and alligators can only put effort into biting down. If you can get their mouths closed—"

A whirring sound brought their attention toward the alligator. The gears at its jaw whirred again, and then reversed, shifting the torque in the opposite direction. The leather strap snapped like cotton.

"Oh shit."

Alan grabbed Rani's hand, and they ran.

ESTELLE HUDDLED UNDER the mechanised elephant, her feet kicking at the monkeys which were trying to drag her out. She saw Roy's boots dance past in little circles, heard his weapon firing, and then a grunt. The head of a brass monkey hit the ground and rolled toward her followed shortly by the body.

"Roy!"

The American's head ducked into view. Reaching out with one giant hand, he clasped Estelle's, and dragged her toward him, monkeys and all. Then he stomped his boot down on the metal simians, shattering them.

"That works better than bullets," he mumbled. Estelle yanked him aside by his shirt with one hand, reaching to her tool belt with the other, and hurled a wrench overhand which caught a mechanic on the temple. His weapon hit the ground, misfired, and hit another of the Raja's men in the calf, shattering the shin. The scream echoed back and forth around the hall.

"I think we're winning."

The bandits clustered together in smaller groups now, moving back to back around the factory floor to mop up the last of the mechanics. Whatever part of the monkeys' programme made them retreat after an attack, it seemed to have kicked in. They were retreating to the upper reaches of the hall's carved ceilings, to sit in their little alcoves and chitter.

"These little buggers were a lot more aggressive than the last lot," said Roy, wiping sweat and a little blood from his face. "Ouch."

"Reprogrammed," said Estelle. She kicked the steel foot

of an elephant, which gave a sound like a bell being struck. "We should thank our lucky stars that these weren't turned on."

"God only knows what else the Raja has up his sleeve."

ALAN SLAMMED THE door behind them and braced it with his shoulder. The alligator's gnashing teeth and sharp little claws made horrific rending sounds on the other side of the wood. Rani lifted an ornamental candle stick from a nearby wall and jammed it between the door's handles. It rattled, but held. They slid down the wall together, panting, applying pressure to a hundred little cuts and scrapes, and some not so little. It took them a fair while to notice the weighted silence in the room.

It was a bed chamber of sorts, although nothing like Alan had ever slept in. A wide balcony opened along one wall, letting the sunlight stream in, with an unencumbered view of the jungle outside. A low, wide bed sat in the centre of the room, its wooden frame surrounded by hanging drapes like spider webs, and covered in plump pillows which surely made it impossible to sleep in. The bed, large though it was, barely took up any space on the room's expansive tiled floor. Across from them, positioned to make the most of the sun, was a chaise lounge. A small family sat on, under or around it, their eyes trained on Alan and Rani with patient interest. The Raja sat centre, his wife's head resting on his shoulder, a young boy sat at their feet with some toy animal clutched in his pudgy fingers. But it was the older girl that Alan couldn't look away from. She was perhaps nine years old, long hair black as oil and eyes that seemed bottomless. She was smiling, and sat astride a tiger made of metal.

"You're having a laugh," said Alan. Thankfully, the beast seemed inert.

"Ah, I see you found me!" said the Raja. He was younger than Alan expected, perhaps mid-thirties, closer to Rani's age than his own. He was bald, possibly by choice as there was a dappling of stubble above the hairline. His face seemed well-built for smiling, which he did warmly and frequently. And he didn't seem too perturbed by the fact that two bleeding, panting Privateers had just barged into his bedroom. "I was expecting you, although not just yet. Where is Major Sumner?"

Alan and Rani exchanged glances.

"He sent us," said Rani.

"As I expected. Where are my manners? I am, of course, Raja Namish Bhat. This is my wife, Gunita. Deepa, would you get our guests some water?"

The little girl slid from the tiger's back and disappeared into an adjoining room, returning seconds later with a tin carafe and two china cups. Pouring one then the other, she passed them to Alan and Rani where they sat on the floor. Rani thanked her with a bowed head. Alan just kept on staring.

"And now, please excuse my family. I try to keep them away from current affairs as much as possible. It's so hard to maintain a supportive family environment with so much political upheaval. I'm sure you understand." Raj Namish made little shooing motions to his wife, who swept the boy up from the floor, nuzzling into his belly until he giggled, and they moved into the next room.

"You're pretty well spoken," said Alan. "I'd say your accent was proper English."

"Quite right, Mr—"

"Shaw."

The Raj's eyebrows slid upward.

"So you say? The infamous Alan Shaw, in my home! Well, this is an honour!"

Rani looked at Alan, a complete lack of understanding in her eyes. Namish continued:

"Miss Lakshmibai, oh yes, I know who you are, of course. I've taken great pains to find out more about you. I believe we have similar goals, in fact. But it appears you don't know as much about your companion as I do. This young man is quite famous among the British. He is an adventurer the likes of which you only find in story books. Quite impressive. Or insane?"

"It's been said." Alan polished off his water and set the cup aside.

The Raj laughed.

"Well, honoured adventurer, welcome to my home. You are quite correct about my accent. I was schooled in Britain for a time. I attended many lectures at the Royal Institution on Albemarle Street, in fact, before returning here to practice what I had learnt in my own way. I'm pleased to say that I witnessed the march of the first Automatons to Buckingham Palace and, of course, read of you in the newspapers. Professor Normen was a good man, although we disagreed on the methods of propulsion for our pets."

Raj Namish reached over the arm of the chaise, and

patted the tiger's head. Alan flinched. He really didn't want that thing to wind up.

"Now, enough of the introductions," said the Raj, clapping his hands together. "What is it that I can do for you today? Or, more importantly Miss Lakshmibai, what will it take for you and your esteemed friend to leave me and my family in peace?"

Rani's eyes narrowed. "Stop your attacks on the British Convoys."

"Why?"

It was such a simple question, and Rani couldn't think of an answer. The Raj filled in the silence. His voice was even, patient. He settled down in his chaise as if preparing himself for a lengthy debate among friends and sipped at a glass by his side.

"The British are on our continent, in our country, slaughtering and enslaving, taking and not paying, warping our religion and our culture. Of all people, Miss Lakshmibai, I thought you would agree."

"By attacking the British, you're prolonging the rebellion. It was a stupid idea, started by rash and thoughtless idiots."

"Perhaps. But we must work with what we have. If we wait, who will there be left to fight later?"

"No-one. Delhi is already lost. Ruined. Prolonging this thing is going to see us not just enslaved, but destroyed. You have to stop. Patience will free us. Patience and tolerance."

"You've fought against the British yourself at Jhansi. You escaped the siege at Gwalior and rode out against the British. I have heard the stories. You're a vibrant, powerful woman, Rani. Why are you here?"

It was Alan's turn to look at Rani, gobsmacked. She didn't catch his eye, but patted his hand.

"Jhansi fell. Gwalior fell. The British and their machines are too strong. I thought I saw a better way. A way where there might still be something left of India other than rubble and graves."

Namish spread his arms.

"*We* have machines."

"I think you're missing the point," said Alan.

"Not at all, Mister Shaw. I understand Miss Lakshmbai perfectly. However, I disagree. I was hoping that we could come to something of an accord. I've been very excited to meet you both and it has been a pleasure. However, if we disagree so earnestly, I'm afraid we must come to blows."

Alan dragged himself upward, although his legs and back protested against it. There was a stinging sensation across most of his skin from the various cuts and abrasions, but the clear water had done something to invigorate him. He stretched, bunching his shoulders and loosening them, dusted off his trousers, and then lent a hand to Rani. A gash in his thigh began to ooze again. Alan looked up at the Raja, and held up a hand for patience. Namish Bhat offered an open hand. Reaching up to the sleeve of his shirt, Alan yanked hard, tearing the stitching, and peeled the sleeve off. Wrapping it around his thigh, he took a handkerchief from his trousers, folded it in four and applied it to the cut, using his sleeve to hold it in place. He gave a little grunt as it tightened, but the pressure felt better rather than worse.

Again, he faced Raja Namish. He nodded.

"Alright."

The Raj gave that friendly grin.

"You certainly don't disappoint, Mister Shaw. Good luck."

Taking a gold key from around his neck, Namish reached across the chaise and popped it into the back of the metal tiger as it slumbered. With a few clacking turns, he primed the beast's clockwork and sat back. As an afterthought, he tucked his feet up underneath him.

The Tiger shuddered all over as if shaking off after a swim. A deep whirring came from somewhere inside, accompanied by an oscillating *snack-tack* sound as its metal innards came up to speed. If Alan hadn't known any better, he'd have sworn the beast *huffed* hot air as it swung up to a standing position. It didn't wait long. Bunching its pistons, the tiger's head came low to the ground. Barbed paws dug into the stone floor as the beast found purchase, and launched itself forward. Alan thumbed the hammer on his revolver, and heard Rani's sword slide from its sheath beside him.

16

THE RAJA'S MECHANICS were rounded up and all sat, back to back, in the centre of the factory floor, surrounded by the bits and pieces of their broken contraptions. Only the elephants still stood tall, their golden eyes fixed with disinterest on some imagined horizon. Roy struck a match on the nearest one's leg, dipped it into the bowl of his pipe, and puffed it to life. He let the smoke roll out over his moustache like a hairy dragon, and worked his jaw.

"Looks like we handled this pretty well, Sparky. Everything turned out the right way in the end. It's not often we get a solid win like this."

With her revolvers tucked back into her belt, Estelle made the rounds with her little satchel, the black monkey still nestled inside, picking up small parts from the floor or the few benches which still stood, examining them and either pocketing or discarding as she saw fit. She left the guarding and wound binding to the bandits. They better at it anyway.

"We have been lucky, Ferris."

"We'll be more careful in future about what we carry, that's all."

"Mhmm," the engineer agreed.

Roy was just about to suggest that a few of them peel off and try to find Alan when the room shook. It wasn't the kind of rumble that comes up through your boots, knocking you off balance and making the world vibrate. Not an earthquake. This came all at once; a vast rumble that shook the walls, floor and ceilings together; a thud that was felt in the chest as well as the ears. Dust and small pieces of masonry which had waited centuries to be free rained from above. Estelle steadied herself on a bench, and had just enough time to give Roy a worried look before another, louder slam turned the world into a maelstrom of exploding stone.

THE RUMBLE CAME as if from far away, but the concussive sound echoed along the valley outside and in through the Raja's bedroom window. All heads except that of the clockwork tiger snapped in that direction.

Namish's brow bunched and his jaw set.

"Your friends are making a mess of my home."

Alan decided to be honest. "We didn't bring any explosives."

The Raja's eyes widened and he darted for the window. Alan thought about drawing against him, but the thought was cut short as the tiger, which had prowled around in order to blindside the Privateers, decided to leap. Rani gave a warning shout without words, and tried to drag Alan aside, but he was too busy trying to push her out of the tiger's way and neither of them ended up moving. The metal beast caught both of them, sending them flying in opposite directions to skid along the floor. Rani came up against the wall with a bump, and was back on her feet in a flurry of material and sweet scent. Alan rolled aside by sheer intuition as the tiger's steel paw smashed into the ground where he had laid, its claws making marks like bullet holes in the stone. Alan rolled, trying to give himself enough time to stand and dodge, but the tiger was surprisingly agile for its weight. With the purr of spinning cams and compressed pistons, it was prowling toward him again, making Alan's only option to scuttle like a retreating crab until his head hit a stone pillar. The tiger had cornered him so quickly, so expertly. The Raja's analytic engine programmes really were something to behold. Either that, or Alan was just an idiot.

The beast drew closer, raising one giant paw for a killing swipe that would probably leave Alan in halves. He did what only an idiot would do, and threw himself at the indestructible animal.

"WHAT IN BLUE blazes is going on!?"

Roy yelled and no one answered. Somewhere in his mind, he realised that he was injured. One of his arms was numb, and his teeth hurt like hell. He spat the blood out of his mouth as he sat up. Where there had once been a factory was a wasteland of rubble with only the backs of the immense elephants still where they should be, cresting out of the rock as if they'd been fossilised. The sky was visible where a section of wall and ceiling had been only minutes before. Roy could smell gunpowder and things charring. He groaned, rolled over into his stomach, and pushed himself up with the arm that still worked. It wasn't that the other arm hurt, he just couldn't feel the damn thing. It would hurt later, and then he'd have to have it popped back into the socket. He hated that.

"Estelle!"

She could have been anywhere. A thick dust still hung in the air, and pieces of masonry that hadn't already fallen were taking turns to nose-dive. Roy's boots slid on the rattling ground. He climbed mounds digging here and there like a bird who knew the general theory behind finding worms but had no real skill. What was he doing? She could be anywhere. She was gone. His rump hit the floor, and he cradled his arm if only for something to do. There seemed to be no other survivors. The mechanics and their bandit guards had been right under the section of roof which collapsed. Another rumble shook the ground as the temple took another hit elsewhere.

"Sorry, Sparky. God knows how I'll keep the *Custance* running without you." Roy gave a sigh, and set his jaw.

He really wished he had his pipe.

At first the sound of falling rock was no different from any other until it was accompanied by a hollow voice, echoing and distant, as if coming from a deep well; a stream of aggravated French from beneath the earth.

Roy was up, sliding on the rubble, scrambling like one of those damned monkeys, one paw tucked up under him. Rounding a mound which had once been a mechanical elephant, he stopped to listen. But he didn't have to wait long. A gloved hand punched through the earth down near the ground, shoving rubble before it, and retracted again, leaving a hole.

"Sparky!" he slid down to the ground beside the hole and yelled inside. "You in there?"

"Ferris! Get me out of here, you big oaf!"

Roy started attacking the ground with his good hand while the sound of digging continued underneath. Soon enough, they'd shifted enough rock that Estelle could start to squirm through the hole. Roy helped as best he could. Estelle was painted head to foot in a uniform tan by the dust. She wiped it out of her eyes and spat mouthfuls of grit. Reaching around her waist, she uncoupled her corset and eased it off. Turning it around, she inspected the re-enforced steel struts that made the weight-bearing corset so useful. Two of them were crushed into uncomfortable shapes.

"Jeez-us, Estelle. That thing saved your damned life."

"Who is shooting at us, Ferris?" Estelle threw the corset aside to join the rest of the junk. Roy had to admit that underneath, the woman's shape was no less pleasant. "And stop staring at me like I am one of your beef steaks."

"I was thinking about a good bottle of wine, actually. Full-bodied red."

"Mon Dieu."

Roy gave his partner a nudge with his elbow and threw one arm around her.

"Just hacking on you, Sparky. I reckon it's that damned Sumner. Makes the best sense."

"We make certain that the Raja's machines cannot defend themselves. Sumner makes certain that we die in the rubble," said Estelle. Reaching around the big American's waist, she unbuckled his belt and reclasped it. Roy slid his afflicted arm through the loop and pulled it over his head.

Estelle looked at it with a perfectionist's dissatisfaction. "It will do until later."

"Thanks. Yeah, and he gets to bury Rani the Bandit Queen with us, dusts his hands, and goes back to his war. No one knows what's gone on except him and those who've got just as much face to lose if anyone finds out."

"Je vais le clouer au plafond par les testicules."

"That sounded nasty."

"It was."

THE TIGER'S PAW scythed through the air, whistling with speed, tearing through Alan's shirt and scoring bloody gouges across his back. But the slash was far from effective and Alan was moving too fast to present a solid target. He roared as if he were the predator, and his full mass barrelled into the tiger's weight-bearing paw, which slid on the smooth stone and pitched the tiger toward the ground. Alan squirmed away on his stomach, dragging his legs out from the tiger's undercarriage, leaving a bloody trail. Rani was by his side, her head suddenly under his shoulders and propelling him to his feet. Another rumble, this time a crash which seemed much closer than before, made them fall under each other's weight.

"Come on!" Alan yelled at himself. "Get up!"

And something about the yelling rallied his legs into shaky obedience. Rani grabbed his arm again and this time they got all the way upright. The second concussion had knocked the tiger clear over onto its side but its complex gyros and motors were already starting to right it. Alan growled under his breath and snatched a tall candle stand from where it had fallen on the floor.

"Alan, no. Let's leave. God knows when another shell will hit."

"Not a chance. This thing's got something nasty coming its way."

But the tiger had other ideas. In one synchronised burst of its inner workings, the tiger rolled, shoved and came into a crouch. Alan groaned. It was turning out to be a long day.

Behind the tiger, Raja Namish was scuttling back from the balcony, his head down, panting hard. God knows what he'd seen out the window, but it had him petrified. He ran across the room and through the door that his family had taken earlier. Gone.

"Coward," muttered Alan.

The tiger was looking shaky. Something about its fall or the constant rumble of the ground around it seemed to have affected its counterweights, and it wasn't moving with as much confidence as before.

"That's right. I guess you don't come across many cock-neys in the jungle, or you'd know better," said Alan.

He ran at the beast, the long candelabra extended like a spear, and jammed the trident end into a gap between the tiger's body plates before it had time to snap at him. As the animal thrust around, Alan braced the candelabra, keeping it at bay, forcing it to dance in circles.

Rani circled beyond its reach to the other side, trying to spot a way in.

"Now what?" she said. "You've got it, now what do you want to do with it?"

"Hadn't thought that far ahead."

She looked around the room, which seemed to be coming apart at the seams. When an idea struck her, she approached the tiger carefully, making sure that its attention was firmly on Alan. Then she dropped a powerful kick to the back of its metal skull. The tiger snapped around, but she was ready for the dodge and was well out of the way by the time the teeth clamped together.

"That's right, follow Rani," she said. She actually made cooing noises as she beckoned the ravenous machine toward her. Alan was nearly yanked off his feet as he struggled to keep his hold on the jutting candelabra. The tiger lunged and snapped, but never got far with Alan slowing it down. In that way, they got it out onto what remained of the balcony, and Alan manoeuvred around until the tiger was on the balcony's broken lip. One of the shell blasts had sent the balustrade tumbling into the jungle below. Rani made a quick feint, faking her motion so that the tiger snapped the wrong way, and darted to Alan's side.

"Easy as pie," she said. She was grinning but a nervous sweat also prickled her face. "Now push."

They heaved. The tiger fought back, but only until the first of its paws met thin air. Alan and Rani listened for the distant crash before carrying each other out through the bedroom.

"Where'd Namish go?" asked Alan.

"In there."

Rani pointed to a section of wall which had once been the neighbouring room that Namish's family had retired to; now a gaping hole which showed the sky and jungle beyond.

"Oh my god," Alan said. "Let's try and find the others

before Sumner flattens us."

As they reached the door, they heard a click which froze them solid. Unmistakeable. The hammer cock of a revolver.

"Please," said Namish, "don't move."

He was covered in dust, crusted brown in some places where blood soaked through from underneath. Alan felt the Raja's gun press into his back and he tensed. Managing to slowly push Rani away from him, he gave himself room for some movement without showing it.

"Put the gun down, Namish. This is stupid. We're leaving," Alan said.

"My family. They're gone."

"I'm sorry, Namish. I really am. But some of us still have the chance to get out of this alive."

Alan span, knocking the Raja's revolver aside with his left elbow, and bringing his own weapon between them with his right hand. The hammer pop-cracked and the muzzle flare lit up their faces in a freeze-frame flash. Alan saw the tears streaking tracks down Namish's dirty face; the slow-motion blink as the bullet hit him. The Raja's weapon hit the ground, and Alan noticed the little boy held in the crook of Namish's arm. The Raja's face creased into a mask of anguish, blood lining his lips.

"Make sure that my son is one of them," he said. Namish pushed the small boy into Alan's arms before every muscle in his face went slack. Alan watched as the light went out in the man's eyes and his body crumpled to the ground.

17

THE BOY WAILED in Alan's arms, looking down at his father without a shred of understanding, grabbing on to Alan's shirt as he screamed and screamed. Alan felt like joining in, but his body didn't seem to be working.

Something was tugging at him. At his sleeve.

"Alan, we must go." Rani came around, stepping over the body of Raja Namish Bhat, until her face blocked out all other sights. Her hands pressed against Alan's face. She tried to take the boy from him, but he wouldn't let go. He was screaming so loud. "Alan, please!"

"Alan!" It was Roy's voice that finally snapped him to attention. The Privateers, looking tattered and torn, burst in through the doors, now hanging off their hinges, with weapons raised. He caught Alan's face, the boy in his arms, the body of Raja Namish at his feet. Rani was crying, and begging him to move.

"Son, we're in some deep ca-ca," Roy said. "We gotta run. This place ain't gonna be worth a damn in a few minutes."

"Roy?" Alan managed.

The American stepped across the floor and took Alan by

the shoulders.

"Whatever just happened in here, it's for later. Right now we have to go."

Alan nodded, but slowly, as if agreeing with a dream. And still he wouldn't let go of the Raja's son. His legs worked well enough to run and, with Rani behind him, Roy and Estelle leading, they made their way through the collapsing temple as more thunderous rounds hit outside.

The tower they'd entered through was just a hole and the first few steps of a staircase. Most of the upper halls were either blocked off or their floors had caved into the floor below. In time, they found their way through the maze of falling masonry, across a mound which had once been an exterior wall, and escaped into the jungle.

ALAN SLOSHED WATER over his head and, when that wasn't enough, he dunked it straight into the river. The water was freezing cold, being mostly run-off from the mountain's icy slopes, but it made his heart race rather than falter. And once he was in, it really wasn't so bad. The cold certainly helped the pain in the gouges on his back. He had to admit, scars from a tiger's claws would look pretty impressive. Rock dust and other grime washed off of him, spreading out as the river took it into a comet tail of dirt. Near where his clothes were on the bank, washed and laid out to dry, Rani sat squeezing the water from her hair, her bare feet poking out from beneath the Banarasi sari that she'd been given by the villagers. Alan decided that it was a good thing he was bathed in ice cold water from the waist down.

Raja Namish's boy played just near the tree line. He was

young. That was good. Maybe if he didn't remember his family, he'd never feel grief as Alan felt the guilt. The building collapsing on Namish's wife and daughter – that was Sumner. But Namish's death was all Alan's fault.

It had been the longest day of Alan's life. He was down, beaten and bleeding, not thinking straight, he was protecting himself and Rani from what he thought to be a madman; Roy had said all these things and none of it made any difference. In the end, Alan made a rash decision and taken a man's life. That was a bad thing, and he felt it down in the pit of his stomach. It didn't help Alan's current malaise that on this trip he'd taken a philosophical beating as well, Rani being no small part of that. The way she made him feel was very different from anything else that had come before.

Helen Normen was a childish crush, no matter what spin Alan tried to put on it. His French girls and all the others were just playthings. But Rani was real. They didn't know a thing about each other, Raja Namish had proved that, but Alan understood the deep recesses of what drove her, and so what drove himself, too. Alan realised what deep and emotional material he was digging into here, and pulled back before it was too late. That was enough of that. Bottle it all back up again, and hope to God no one found a corkscrew.

"Shake yourself, Alan," he muttered.

When he felt physically clean, if not mentally, he waded back to dry land, making sure that Rani's eyes were averted before jogging the last few steps to his clothes.

He sat on the rocks beside Rani, and let the sun dry him. It didn't take long, and then he was sweating again. So much for making a good impression.

"So what happens next?" he asked, eventually.

"My psychic powers fail me, today." Alan smiled at her, but his heart wasn't in it. She squeezed his hand. "There is a woman in the village who has lost her son. She will gladly care for the boy. If he's lucky, he will only ever visit today in dreams."

"And you?"

"I've done my fighting, for now. The British will win no matter what. So I'll wait, and when it's time, I'll stand up with everyone else and start putting India together again."

Alan leant back on his elbows to take a better look. Her bare shoulders were something he could have stared at until his eyes failed him in old age; that swathe of ebony hair like a Saracen's black blade running down her spine.

"They'll build statues to you and your name will be on plaques all across India," he said.

Rani laughed. "Perhaps."

"But for now," he moved so that he could catch her eye. "For now, why not come away with me?"

"Away? From India? And what? Come back to England with you?"

"Not there. France."

"And what would an Indian woman and her English…friend do in France?"

"I don't know. I could be a private detective, maybe. I've learnt enough from my father and my reputation carries some weight, at least."

"I can't speak French."

"Estelle can teach us some. Enough to get by. We'll

learn the rest as we go."

Rani smiled and looked away down the river. Alan took her hand, drawing her eyes back to his.

"No, Alan. This is where we part ways." Alan's hand went slack, and Rani didn't fight to maintain the contact. "I could give you many reasons, if you'd like. But none that would satisfy you. And none that wouldn't taste bad in my mouth. You are wonderful. But my love has been given away, taken from me, returned. It's used and worn. I have lost too many things to fall in love the way I once would; the way a girl should fall in love."

Alan broke his eyes away, deciding to regard the mountains and treetops. His jaw bunched as if he were chewing. The silence rolled out until he felt that he could speak evenly.

"I understand."

"Oh, sweet boy. No you don't. At all." Rani swung her leg over Alan's lap until they sat facing each other. Pulling his chest close to her stomach, she kissed his forehead, his nose, and then his lips, lingering there as they breathed each other in. Rani broke away first, cradling Alan's head against her. Alan knew this didn't mean anything, this wasn't Rani changing her mind, just saying goodbye. But he tried not to think about it, and savoured the feel of her against his cheek.

"YOU READY TO push off, son?"

With his backpack on, Roy looked more like a hiker than a mercenary.

"I think so."

He looked back over Alan's shoulder to where Rani

stood by one of the village's little wooden huts. She still wore the sari, but her sword belt and boots made an odd combination.

"I guess she ain't coming."

Alan didn't answer, but threw his duffel bag into the back of the waiting truck.

"Yep, that's what I thought," Roy nodded.

Alan climbed up into the truck's bed and settled down across from Estelle, who was cleaning out her nails with a screwdriver, her eyes trained on him. His face was set firmly on where they were going to be rather than where they had been.

"Come on, Ferris. *Le Custance,* she misses us," she said.

Alan felt a little pang of gratitude toward her for trying to hurry the thing along. He gave the engineer a nod and was amazed when she returned it.

"Ok, ok." Roy climbed up into the vehicle, and it creaked around him. "Just trying to get my facts straight. Seems a shame is all—"

"Ferris." Estelle's tone was a warning, but he got the idea it would be the only one.

Some villagers waved them off, Rani stood with her arms firmly by her side. Roy watched her until she was out of sight, on Alan's behalf.

Roy talked the most, of course, about how they had lost out on this adventure; how Sumner had fleeced them. Estelle reminded him that it was better the Major think they were dead than coming to silence them. He agreed, Alan knew, but grudgingly. Alan spent most of the ride sleeping off the great weariness that had come over him. His mind was a grateful blank. No faces danced across his vision, no memories or regrets. He felt shut down, switched off, and couldn't bring himself to think of anything at all.

The cart rolled out of the jungle a day later and onto the Grand Trunk Road that had led them to Delhi. Alan still sat in the same spot, a copy of *Titus Gladstone Adventures* lay on his knee. He hadn't read it yet. He just kept looking at the cover. Another adventure. Thumbing the pages, he skipped right to the end. A full page picture of Titus against a vibrant sunset, this issue's villain lay trussed and unconscious at his feet, and Titus held a beautiful young woman who swooned against the power of his kiss.

Alan banged on the cart's side, and it drew to a halt. Estelle kicked Roy's boot, rousing him from a slumber.

"Huh? Hey. Where'd you think you're going?"

Alan jumped down off the cart and dragged his bag after him.

"I can't go back," he said.

"You going back to get her? Aw, Son, that's damned romantic of you-"

"I'm not going there, either." Alan shouldered his bag, heavy with the carbine inside, checked the set of his revolver in its holster, and lay his duster across his shoulders to shelter him from the sun. "You're going back to England. That's the last direction I want to take. I'm going that way."

Alan poked a thumb over his shoulder. East. The only direction he hadn't taken on the Grand Trunk Road.

"Wherever you're headed, it's a long walk in that direction," said Roy.

"I can't go back," Alan repeated.

"Let us drop you somewhere else then," said Roy.

Alan cut him off. "It's been a blast, Roy. Estelle. I hope I get to nearly die on the *Custance* again one day. But right now, I could really use the walk."

"Bu—"

Estelle laid a hand on Roy's arm, silencing him. She handed down a food package from the cart's stock, which Alan took it with a nod.

"*Bon chance, Monsieur Anglais. Au revoir.*"

Roy's big hand came down on Alan's shoulder, warm and friendly like a mother bear's claw.

"Alright, Alan. I get you. You gotta go your own way. I was kind of hoping you'd be part of the team, though."

"Maybe next time."

The cart turned right, back toward Bombay and the waiting *Custance*. Soon its dust cloud was a mere huff and then a sliver. He watched it for a minute, wondering if he'd done the right thing, until he looked down at the rolled Graphical Adventure in his hand. In one swift flick of the wrist, he tossed the book into the jungle's undergrowth where the wind could thumb the pages if it wanted to. Setting his boots firm on the road east, the sun began to set behind him, and Alan walked on into the dark.

Lightning Source UK Ltd.
Milton Keynes UK
UKOW04f1530220315

248275UK00002B/24/P